A Collection

of Hours

by

Blair MacInnes

POLLY PRESS
Morristown, NJ

Polly Press, LLC
Morristown, NJ

Cover illustration by Fran Wood
Back cover photo by Danielle MacInnes

Printed in the United States of America

Publisher's Cataloging-In-Publication Data
(Prepared by The Donohue Group, Inc.)

Names: MacInnes, Blair.
Title: A collection of hours / by Blair MacInnes.
Description: Morristown, NJ : Polly Press, [2016]
Identifiers: LCCN 2016960908 | ISBN 978-0-692-79834-8
Subjects: LCSH: Blair, Mary Anne Italia Mitchell, 1855---Fiction. | Trés riches heures du duc de Berry--Fiction. | Books of hours--Fiction. | Women art collectors--Fiction. | LCGFT: Historical fiction.
Classification: LCC PS3613.A35 C65 2016 | DDC 813/.6--dc23

*D*edication

Dedications come in many shapes and forms.

This book is dedicated to my mother, Mary Blair Farr Bartol. The main character, Mim, was my mother's Granny Blair, and Mildred was her mother. A Collection of Hours was Mom's story before it was mine.

This is a family story. Mildred is the grandmother I never knew and Mom became "Gigi" who (rightly) adored my sons, Ben, Tock and Alex and they her. They made her laugh; told tall tales and shared dirty jokes. As the wheels turned I became Polly to my Delicious Ones: Archie, Abby, Georgia, Gus, Oliver, Lila, Shep, Poppy and Sadie, all of whom are smart, funny and creative…in short, perfect.

The Delicious Ones did not appear by magic of course. Their mothers and my daughters-in-law- Beth, Danielle and Katie MacInnes, have dedicated themselves to our family with love, verve and have made our sons better than ever.

And then there is Gordon MacInnes, who has dedicated every day of his adult life to making the world a better place. He is irreplaceable in mine.

Preface

ETWEEN 1350 AND 1450, ARTISTS of the Middle Ages produced the most important and beautiful books in Christendom. Known as Books of Hours, they were crafted by monks living in secluded monasteries. Originally they were designed not as works of art, but as illustrated breviaries used to guide the monks through the eight daily liturgies of community prayer, each hour associated with an event in the life of the Virgin Mary.

In addition to prayers, the books often contained psalms, hymns, antiphons and responses, canticles and stories from both the Old and New Testaments. As time progressed, wealthy patrons commissioned Books of Hours and used them as private books of prayer and devotion. Some of the greatest artists of Europe enhanced the texts with magnificent illuminations and calligraphy.

These privately commissioned books represented a new approach to worship based on individual piety and a more personal relationship with God in general and the Virgin Mary in particular. Illustrators also depicted the full panoply of the life quotidian in the Middle Ages—saints and sinners, peasants and noblemen, kings, queens and the grotesque victims of famine, violence and pestilence. When used in churches, the pictures were essential tools for the majority of Christian worshippers, who were illiterate.

Typically the books were painted on vellum—calf or sheepskin soaked, shaved thin and then stretched. Scribes who used quill pens for their elaborate calligraphy copied the Latin texts. The manuscripts were painted in glorious colors, using lapis from Persia, indigo from Bengal and exquisite gold leaf for the final enhancements to the borders.

Arguably, the two most beautiful Books of Hours were by the Dutch brothers Herman, Paul and Johan Limbourg—The first, *Belles Heures* (1404) and the second, *Tres Riches Heures* (1409).

$\mathcal{P}$rologue

Chicago 1894

*T*HE PERSON SHE HAD BEEN had vanished and for the life of her, Mim had no idea where she had gone or how to get her back.

Normally Mim's internal and external lives were so well synchronized that friends, thinking they were delivering a compliment, said, "Mim, I wish my life ran as smoothly as yours does," or "Mim, you are a brick." Who in her right mind would choose to be a brick?

Mim had known for years that she was no beauty. A glance in the mirror confirmed that she looked every inch what she was—a respectable, wealthy, middle-aged Chicago matron.

At the moment, Mim had warm feelings for no one in her life other than her four children. She loved them beyond all measure, but she worried that her upcoming trip to New York City, for which she was now packing, would leave the household unsettled. Her usually fiery, dramatic twelve-year-old daughter, Italia, grew anxious and quiet when talk turned to trips, trains or absences of longer than a night. Ten-year-old Chauncey appeared indifferent to her imminent departure, other than wanting to be sure Mim remembered the present he wanted. Mildred, her "lucky child," now almost seven, was openly sad and Billy, nearly three, talked only of seeing the "too-too twain" at Chicago's Grand Central Station.

No, her children were not the cause of her current turmoil and irritability. Her pernicious streak of superstition fueled her fear that her trip's secret agenda might prompt God to punish her by harming them. Hence she hired an additional nanny in the belief that extra eyes might thwart the punitive impulses of the deity.

Her sister Hortense (Tennie), who was to accompany her to New York, had besieged her for days about the minutia of the trip. Only someone with as little to do as Tennie would have had time for the inane questions she pestered her with over the last week.

In their most recent conversation, the fourth of the afternoon, Mim had finally snapped.

"Tennie! I am beginning to wonder if I have made a mistake inviting you on this trip. If I were interested in taking a child to New York, I would have taken one of my own. It is inconsequential whether you wear white or black gloves with the floral. I have no idea how many days it will rain, and yes, if you run out of Avant, you will be able to buy some in New York."

After she apologized, Mim felt no better than she had before her spiteful tempest.

Mim knew precisely when her steady old self had disappeared. In fact, she remembered exactly where she was standing when she had opened the letter from Martin Gaylord.

Dear Mim:

I have returned from Paris and am now in New York City. I think I have found your Book of Hours.

It is sensational but the transaction may be complicated. I cannot obtain it for you in the normal way. You will need to come and see it for yourself.

I repeat. It is sensational.

Sincerely,
Martin Gaylord

Despite weeks of feigning ambivalence as to whether she should pursue this summons, Mim knew that she had to—no, she knew she wanted to—no, she knew she couldn't wait to go to New York.

❧

Mim was the owner of what many considered the best collection of Medieval and Renaissance art in the city of Chicago. With the addition of a "spectacular" Book of Hours it might well become the best in the country. Martin Gaylord, with whom she served on the Board of the Chicago Art Institute, had helped her build the Blair Collection. Though they had decidedly different artistic sensibilities, they had established a respectful rapport that more recently felt less respectable.

"But, really, Martin," Mim wrote back, "you have answered *none, not one* of my questions about what you have found. I feel like I am packing for a wild goose chase! An artistic safari with no guide!"

At the moment, Mim's husband, Chauncey Blair, was the one she cared least about leaving. He continued to call her collection "quite the daisy," an expression she detested for its hint of amateurishness and frivolity.

For days he had pestered her with the possibility that she might not be able to go. He seemed to almost enjoy taunting her with bulletins that the workers were planning to stage a strike against George Pullman's railroad and the train that would take her to New York.

"Mimsy, is there any reason you must get to New York this very week? I just spoke with Potter Palmer, and he agrees that there is a growing risk your departure may literally be derailed. You have waited so long for a Book of Hours, why not give me a little peace of mind and postpone your trip until this danger passes? Mr. Debs and his army of agitators are sure to be arrested soon and—"

"Chauncey, that is exactly the point. I waited so long for a Book of Hours. Martin tells me this one is spectacular and I must come as soon as I can to make a decision, and that is what I intend to do tomorrow—anarchists or no."

The Education of a Collector

Chicago 1868

*T*HROUGHOUT HER LIFE, MARY ANN Italia Mitchell Blair, or Mim, as she was known to family and close friends, surrounded herself with beautiful objects. This habit reflected more than a desire for accumulation. Each acquisition enriched her mind, and often her soul as well. She felt a genuine affection for every item in her vast and internationally recognized collection. Each of these friends offered a spiritual insight along with appreciation of its beauty.

In the presence of a landscape she felt the durability of the earth; in the presence of a portrait she felt a relationship with the person depicted; in the presence of a sculpture, she felt solidity, as if mitigating the fragility of the world; in the presence of a fifth-century Greek vase, she felt secure, for surely if an object had lasted more than a thousand years, it would survive her as well.

Mim's lifelong search for beauty was to give her abundant pleasure. She eventually realized she owed this all to her paternal grandmother.

Grandmother Mitchell was feared more than loved by most of her family. By the time she was 70 years old she had "mellowed," according to Mim's mother, but adults seemed to say that more as a matter of hope than fact. She had a steel-grey bun tightly drawn at the back of her head, though no number of hairpins could secure it adequately throughout the day. By teatime (the only time of the day when grandchildren over the age of ten had access to her), no more than half of her hair was under control.

And it was almost impossible not to look at the small, silver hairs growing out of her chin. Mim knew it was rude to stare. She tried to refrain from peeking, she really did. But she needed to check to be sure her latest count was accurate. Discretion required that she take her inventory in short bursts so as not to attract undue attention.

She had a strategy. She divided her grandmother's chin into quadrants, counted quickly, then multiplied by four. At last count there were sixteen. Things were getting worse. At Christmas time, there had been only twelve.

Mim was the family's official chin hair scorekeeper. In the nursery she could generate rolling-on-the-floor laughter when her cousins chanted "Little Pig, Little Pig, let me in," whereupon they would lower their voices, terrified that Grandmother was lurking, and say in hushed unison, "not by the 16 ugly hairs on Grandmother's chinny, chin, chin."

If you were over ten years old, your presence at Grandmother's tea was non-negotiable. She sent one of the servants through the house ringing what was called "The Grandmother Bell." The moment the bell tolled, all grandchildren knew they had five minutes, and only five minutes, to brush hair, straighten clothes, spit polish shoes and appear in the library. If you took six minutes, you were too late and the door would be closed. Later, Grandmother called to account any grandchild who had been locked out.

"Only unimportant people are late," Grandmother scolded. "And so, for today, you are decidedly unimportant."

Those in attendance would say, "Good afternoon, Grandmother," as the boys made a tidy bow and the girls bent in half-curtsey. If any grandchild mumbled the greeting, he or she was made to repeat it until the phrase was delivered forcefully and distinctly. The cousins learned quickly it was best to do it correctly the first time.

Before settling on the floor at Grandmother's feet, each grandchild was served a small cup of tea and exactly one cucumber sandwich, crusts removed. Grandmother's butler, Felix, entered the room carrying an enormous silver tea service on a gleaming rectangular tray. There were so many parts to the tea service that Mim wondered how anyone could remember which part was used for which function.

Grandmother respected her grandchildren enough to use her best china with them.

Mim loved Grandmother's china. Cream-colored, each plate, cup and saucer was decorated with an embossed pattern of flowers, so colorful and lush it was as if the imbiber were drinking in a summer garden.

Felix poured only a small amount of the deep amber liquid into each delicate cup, leaving plenty of room for the steaming hot water poured from another silver pot. For the younger children, there was more hot water than tea. The older they grew, the darker the tea.

An additional silver container, topped with an ivory-knobbed lid, held small white sugar cubes. From watching Grandmother and her older cousins, Mim learned to use the small tongs when taking a lump—and only one—of sugar. The tongs themselves were trickier than they appeared. Shaped like fish on the ends, if pressed too hard they could sail across the room, destination unknown.

Perfectly aligned lemons, sliced so thin they were translucent, adorned a small square plate. One used a miniature fork to gently but firmly pierce the lemon for deposit into the teacup. Mim's mother once told her that normally people offered hot milk with tea, but no such pitcher appeared on the tea tray at Grandmother Mitchell's. She was firm in her belief that milk did nothing but damage developing teeth. She had once read that eating lemons prevented scurvy among British seamen. Though none of her grandchildren appeared likely candidates for scurvy, or the British Navy, she believed, quoting Benjamin Franklin, "an ounce of prevention is worth a pound of cure."

Grandmother poured, then passed a teacup to each waiting hand. "Thank you, Grandmother," or "This looks lovely, Grandmother," were among the preferred responses.

Finally came Mim's favorite part of the tea ritual, selecting the small gold spoon used to stir the tea. Each spoon, no larger than a wishbone, was personalized. The child's first name was engraved in block letters on the front of the handle and, in slightly smaller letters, his or her birthdate was engraved on the back. Every Mitchell grandchild had a spoon, and all eleven were laid out for tea, whether or not all were in attendance. It was a reminder that, absent or present, you were a part of the family.

The spoon was diminutive in every way. The sipping indentation was more appropriate for feeding a doll than a real child. Mim loved to put a tiny drop of sweet tea on the spoon and pretend that she was a hummingbird.

The cucumber sandwiches were placed on the marble table to the left of the fireplace. They were cut into various shapes: hearts, circles, triangles, and long rectangles. Though slathered with butter, the sandwiches were neither tasty nor filling. However, there would be nothing else to eat until dinner at 6:30, so Mim unenthusiastically helped herself.

When formal tea was over, Grandmother would open whatever book or poem she had selected for the day. She waited for complete stillness, and only then did she begin to read. Grandmother was as autocratic in her selection of reading material as she was in all other matters requiring opinion. She favored British classics. American literature she disdained as "immature."

Each grandchild had his or her favorite. Mim reveled in stories of the deep past. Robin Hood topped her list. The way Grandmother read, the listener felt the sod of Sherwood Forest underfoot. As the despicable King John became greedier and Robin Hood's exploits grew more daring, Mim knew she had been there in another life, though unlike other girls, she had no interest in being Maid Marion. She would have been a scout and close confidante of the dashing Robin. She loved the episodes of the *Knights of the Round Table, The Sword in the Stone, The Epic of Gilgamesh*—anything that carried the mark of centuries.

Mim still smiled when she remembered the summer her cousin

Frances had boldly made a suggestion for an alternate teatime reading selection.

"I have an idea, Grandmother. No boys are visiting this week. May we read *Little Women*? It is new, I know, but Miss Kelsey read part of it to me and I would love to hear it to the end. It is a wonderful story about a family named March and their lives during the Civil War. There are four girls. Beth is my favorite. I think Mim would like it because it is history, and maybe even Tennie could understand it if we helped her with the difficult passages."

With a withering look, accompanied by a contemptuous tone, Grandmother snarled, "Firstly, my dear, your cousin's name is Hortense, not Tennie. And secondly, I know what *Little Women* is about, but unfortunately Mrs. Alcott is American."

It was stories of real life that Mim loved best. History for Mim began in Egypt. She intended to go there one day. She would see the ancient Sphinx, climb the pyramids, float up the Nile and, most thrilling of all, collect beautiful things. Someday she would have ancient scarabs made into jewelry and she would start a collection of the bronze figurines unearthed in pharaohs' tombs. Perhaps she would dig them up herself.

Mim liked the idea that when a pharaoh died, he was buried with his favorite and most beautiful things to enjoy in the afterlife. She was not the least bit afraid of death because she would simply arrange all her treasures when she got to heaven. She had already made a list of what she wanted her mother and father to put in her tomb—her first plum-colored satin hair ribbon, her monogrammed silver comb and brush set, the tiny floral porcelain jar with her first lost tooth and, most importantly, her diary.

Mim knew better than to tell her mother about her list, as she would instantly have scolded her for even thinking such ghoulish thoughts and demand that she tear it up.

No matter how she read and reread, viewing pieces of art was the only way Mim could remember ancient history. She could only remember the dates of the Punic Wars by first visualizing Grandmother's beautiful green patina bronze statue of a Roman gladiator poised to thrust his spear. Once she could see him in her mind, the dates came to her.

Grandmother had taught Mim how to recognize good art and, more to the point, what qualities made objects either beautiful, valuable, or both. She taught her the nomenclature of art so that her granddaughter would develop artistic fluency as well as a critical eye.

Even as a little girl Mim's taste in art was more traditional than her grandmother's.

"Mary," her grandmother once said, "you must be willing to consider that there has been some meritorious art produced since the fall of Rome." This was as close as Grandmother Mitchell ever came to teasing.

Grandmother had hundreds of art books. Many of them were so large that when Mim was small she could not lift them from the shelves by herself. Arranged with precision by century, then alphabetically by artist, they were treasures unto themselves.

No book escaped Mim's admiration. However, her favorite pages in Grandmother Mitchell's art library did not appear in a book. Her favorite treasures were sheltered in three red leather-bound folios and did not sit in the bookshelves but were laid in a stately row on top of the desk in the library. Each volume's title, etched in gold, shone. Inside, individually wrapped in tissue paper, were reproductions from important fourteenth- and fifteenth-century religious books known as Books of Hours. From the time she was seven years old, Mim had repeatedly asked to see what was inside those folios. The answer from Grandmother was either, "You must wait until you are old enough to understand the importance of what is in there," or just plain, "No."

Finally, when she was eleven, as a rite of passage, Grandmother had shown her the colorful plates and Mim had fallen in love for the first time. At the end of each visit she pestered Grandmother to show them to her again. Long before she valued their historical importance, she knew she loved the magnificent lapis blues and gold leaf, the intricately delicate filigree, and oh, the characters—kings, angels, the Virgin Mary and Christ himself. If she ever owned a book like that, it would be the first and maybe the only thing she would need in her tomb.

Mim's artistic training was rigorous and her teacher often fierce. Beginning soon after her eighth birthday, she spent hours studying the paintings and sculpture in books Grandmother selected, then spent more hours analyzing and, with her grandmother, debating the merits of each work. For a woman who normally brooked so little dissent in most things, Grandmother allowed Mim surprising latitude in forming and expressing her own opinions, even when they defied Grandmother's own stated view. The only standard she insisted upon was that her granddaughter's reasoning is well informed and the argument well articulated.

Every Thursday, at precisely four o'clock, they would meet. Mim would climb into the family carriage and be driven the three miles to Grandmother Mitchell's house on Dearborn Avenue. Though her mother told her again and again that there was no relationship between what she wore and how she performed on Grandmother's examinations, Mim was absolutely certain some clothes were luckier than others, so she always wore her starched white muslin pinafore with lace applique over her pale blue smock, set off by white cotton gloves, white stockings and ballet slippers.

Once in Grandmother's house, Felix welcomed her. She raced into the kitchen to receive a warm hug from Celeste, the cook, who tucked a ginger snap into her pocket to fortify her for her upcoming encounter. She gobbled it up en route to the morning room, both because she was hungry and because she was convinced ginger snaps were lucky cookies.

Felix made her feel very, very grown up when he formally ushered her in to see her Grandmother.

"Madam, Miss Mary Mitchell is here to see you."

Grandmother gave her something that passed for a smile and nodded a welcome as Mim took her usual place on the rose satin brocade settee next to Grandmother.

The rules never varied. Each week Grandmother quizzed her on ten works of art taken from the book Mim had studied that week. To keep her on her toes, Grandmother occasionally surprised her with a picture she had studied months before, to see if she had retained the information.

For each correct answer Mim received a point. Occasionally, for an answer that was technically incorrect but showed some knowledge or logical conclusion, she was awarded half a point. For each work of art, there were three possible points: the name of the work, the artist and the exact dates of his birth and death.

At the end of the month, Grandmother tallied Mim's score and gave her ten cents a point, a small fortune in Mim's world. More instantly gratifying to Mim, in any week that she had a total score over twenty (a most difficult feat), Grandmother allowed her to select a sour ball from the cut crystal jar she kept on her desk. The sour ball, if earned, was the only tangible trophy Mim could hope to take home.

She never saw whatever money she earned, at least not so she could spend it. When her grandmother arrived at a total, she went to her desk and wrote out something that she called "a cheque." It was a piece of paper with Mim's very own name on it. She would watch as Grandmother ceremoniously uncapped her dark blue fountain pen, grandly signed her name with a theatrical flourish, blotted the ink and then handed the paper to Mim's father, William, who always came to visit with his mother and pick up his daughter.

Mim knew that each of her brothers, John and Guy, and her sister Hortense, had bank accounts at the Illinois Trust and Savings Bank, where her father was the president. But Mim, and only Mim, had an additional account with printing at the top of each check that read: The Art Fund of Mary Ann Italia Mitchell. Mim sensed the account was a most valuable treasure, even if she did not fully understand how or when it was to be put to use.

Only later, after her grandmother's death in 1870, had her father told her, "You were her favorite, Mim. She was very impressed by your quick mind and excellent eye. Of course she would never have told you directly. The Mitchells detest giving compliments."

Even with five years of examination behind her, Mim always felt pressure build as soon as she entered the morning room.

Grandmother flipped to a plate in one of the art books Mim had studied the week before.

"Let us begin," said Grandmother. "Number 1."

"That is *The Bow of Penelope* by Matteo Di Giovanni, 1435-1495," Mim said confidently.

She had been enchanted by that painting the first time she saw it. She so loved the story of the steadfast Penelope, who rejected all suitors as she waited faithfully for her husband Odysseus to return after ten years of battle in Troy.

"Correct," Grandmother Mitchell acknowledged. "Number 2."

"Grandmother, I have known that one since I was eight. That is *The Pieta* by Michelangelo Buonarroti, 1475-1564," proclaimed Mim, proud of herself, even if her Grandmother showed no evidence of being impressed.

"The next one is harder," warned Grandmother. "If you have been paying attention, you should be able to make a reasonable guess from the style and the colors. I will give you half a point if you know the correct artist, but not the painting, and another half point if you can give me a date that is within 25 years of the correct one.

"One, two, three…" Grandmother intoned, a perfect imitation of a grandfather clock, although in this case it was a grandmother clock and a menacing one at that.

"Grandmother, that is not fair. That picture was not in this week's book. I know it wasn't."

"Four, Five, Six… "

Mim knew right away that she recognized neither the name of the work, nor the artist and his dates. But she was not willing to come up completely empty-handed without further thought. She still had a few more seconds to get at least some credit.

The colors in the landscape were dark, except for the brilliant orange-red sleeves of the ploughman. The setting sun was a focal point of the painting despite being in the distance. Something about the sun was important. Mim understood that the painter was telling a story, a story that was surfacing as vaguely familiar.

A ship was moored in a cove where…wait, what was that form in the water, near the sailing ship? Mim looked more closely, desperate for the picture to reveal the clues she needed.

"Ten, Eleven, Twelve…"

Grandmother counted, slowing down not at all when she saw her granddaughter struggling. Grandmother never, never, never let anyone, even her younger grandchildren win just because she or he was a child. And certainly she would not foster any laxity in her protégé.

Then Mim got it, or at least part of it. Maybe she could still salvage some credit. She now saw something near the ship that looked like human legs not quite submerged in the water. Combining the images of the legs and the prominent sun, she knew whoever had painted it had captured the myth of Icarus falling into the sea after coming too close to the sun. She knew this myth because Grandmother had read it to them last year. Mim had found it horrifying that the gods had inflicted such a harsh punishment on Icarus for boldness, which Mim thought was a good quality. But Grandmother had argued that he had been sufficiently warned and had simply gotten what was coming to him.

"Eighteen, Nineteen…"

"I have it," shouted Mim, making Grandmother wince. "I don't know who painted it, but I know it is a painting about Icarus, because I can see the sun and I can see his white legs poking out of the sea near the ship. His broken wings are already in the water, I suspect. And I am going to guess that it was painted in…in…in…1600."

"The painting, Mary, is by Dieter Brueghel the Elder, who was born in 1525 and died in 1569, so unfortunately you missed both the painter and the dates. But you are correct that it depicts the Fall of Icarus, and for that I am going to give you half a point."

Mim felt as though Grandmother had just given her the painting itself.

"Let's see, today we looked at ten paintings and you got six completely right, two partially correct, and two need more study. While that is not your best effort, it is safe to say none of your siblings or cousins would be able to come close to that achievement.

"Now, Mary, you may run along to the kitchen and tell Celeste I said to give you one more ginger snap. Only one, though, as I know she already gave you one when you came in. You might want to remember that ginger stays on your breath."

Years later, when Grandmother Mitchell died, Mim, alone of the cousins, truly missed her. So well did she know her grandmother's collection that her mother invited her to come along when the aunts and uncles were dividing up Grandmother's beautiful possessions. Her mother trusted Mim's eye and she had not been disappointed with the selections Mim had directed her to make.

Grandmother Mitchell felt strongly that all her grandchildren should appreciate art. Thus she concluded that the best way to encourage that impulse was to start gathering   beautiful items for each of them early on. It was part of the birthright of all Mitchell offspring.

Every Christmas and birthday she added to the collections held by Mim and her cousins. All Mitchell boy cousins got the same present—hand-painted, lead toy soldiers. This meant that on family holidays regiments of little enamel warriors gathered for fierce skirmishes in the nursery.

Grandmother had more flair choosing gifts for the girl cousins. The older girls got miniature china boxes, each painted in exquisite detail on a background of soft green or yellow. The smaller the box, the more intricate the pattern.

The younger girls received a glass paperweight instead of the enameled box. All her life Mim would be grateful because, for as much as she thought the boxes pretty, she thought the paperweights were dazzling. The first one, and Mim's sentimental favorite, was an autumn-apple red. It sat on her dressing table all her life. It held inside what she now knew were called milleflori canes. Bursts of color packed into a pattern. Inside each pea-sized red cane was white filigree cut into spirals, so that you could see through it. In the center of each was a miniscule dot of a deeper red. As a child she imagined them as goldfish eyes, though she really did not know if goldfish had red and white eyes.

The glass dome was flawless, so clear that, even years later, you could see a few stray air bubbles, as if part of the ocean had been captured inside. If you rotated the paperweight slowly from side to side, the illusion was of a swaying coral reef.

Someday she would give it to her first granddaughter, along with the rest of the collection…one piece at a time.

෯

Now, at the age of 37, Mim felt that all she collected these days were babies, servants and additional responsibility. But her art fund had grown, augmented by a large inheritance from her father. Her husband Chauncey was a successful banker, as was his father before him. Mim now knew what "cheques" were and had more than mastered how to use them.

A Rainy Day

Fall 1890

T HE PATTERN OF MIM AND Chauncey Blair's relationship was set in the earliest days of their marriage. Though they could not have stated it clearly to one another, or perhaps even to themselves, they fell into this pattern naturally, in that way couples have of institutionalizing the unexpressed. Instinctively, they focused on the major decisions in life. They were the easy ones. Mim and Chauncey handled them with little tension. But the details could be dangerous. Mim supposed that was why many people found the devil there.

Thus, after eight years of marriage, three small children, and without much ado, they decided to build a house at 4830 Drexel Boulevard. Mim knew the final product would be both beautiful and serviceable. But she dreaded the infinite number of decisions that would require negotiation. Fortunately, Chauncey had surprised her.

"I will handle the construction of the exterior, with your advice of course. You may exercise a free hand inside, with one exception," he said, smiling as he continued, "my smoking room. You have the best eye in the city of Chicago. You decorate to the Queen's taste, but I cannot spend my day worrying that I will come home to find you have decided buttercup yellow is the most suitable color for the only room in the house that is fully mine. You may suggest, you may advise, you may even purchase, but only on approval!"

Mim and Chauncey selected Drexel Boulevard on the South Side of Chicago at the suggestion of Martin Gaylord, who first brought the Drexel Boulevard property to their attention.

Martin Gaylord was one of the leading men of Chicago. Born into a profitable lumber and real estate family, he had been educated in Europe and had graduated from Harvard Law School. Though still in the family business, Gaylord was devoting more and more of his considerable energy to the cultural life of Chicago and to amassing what was becoming a renowned art collection. It was not uncommon, when someone who wanted to reinforce the validity of an artistic point to begin a sentence with, "Martin Gaylord says . . ."

Gaylord and his wife Catherine were social friends of the Blairs. Recently Mim's path had crossed Martin's with some frequency because they were both members of the acquisition committee at the Chicago Art Institute.

Chauncey had bumped into Martin at the Union League Club's Washington's Day breakfast and it was there that he had mentioned the property to Chauncey.

<hr />

Chauncey had been to every Washington's Day breakfast since 1887. Shortly after the Haymarket Riot, the celebration was established as an opportunity to ease class tensions, not by socializing with the staff of immigrants who stood uncomfortably around the room, but by talking about them amongst themselves.

It is not possible to overestimate the impact of the Haymarket Riot on the city's elite. It had shaken them to their core. It was urban violence complete with dynamite, the deaths of seven policemen and at least four civilians, plus countless injured.

Workers had rallied in support of an eight-hour workday near Haymarket Square on Des Plaines Street, peacefully at first. Someone,

someone who was never apprehended, threw a bomb into the midst of the throng and the police began firing. Eight union organizers were arrested. Though there was no evidence any of them had actually hurled the lethal dynamite, four men went to the gallows and the other four spent time in prison.

"Good riddance," was Chauncey's assessment of the outcome. "If I were in charge, I would have a special secret agent in every prominent home in the city, including ours."

Drexel was a boulevard in the Parisian sense. The street was lined with gaslights and oak trees, all standing at intervals mapped out with military precision, seeming to guard the privacy of those dwelling inside the mansions that lined the thoroughfare.

There were no street signs anywhere on these fashionable streets. This was not an accident of municipal inattention.

"If you don't know where you are, you don't belong here," was a statement of principle for residents of the neighborhood.

It was as prosperous a street as there was in Chicago. Rumor had it some seventy-six millionaires could be counted among their new neighbors. Mim and Chauncey felt certain their home would reassure all who cared that the Blairs would take their place among them.

In good weather Drexel Boulevard boasted an active outdoor life for the nannies who executed their daily perambulations with baby carriages and toddlers. Sunday afternoons brought out whole families—for entertainment, a little exercise after Sunday dinner and, not coincidently, to be seen. Children rolled hoops and played tag, often creating a moving obstacle course for those who strolled. Boys brought out their cloth balls and stick bats to practice baseball. Girls stopped to play hopscotch with friends en route. Best of all, on summer Sundays the Orange Man was sure to be there, offering ice-cold orange crush, the newest taste craze for young and old alike.

Chauncey moved at a banker's deliberate pace in the selection of an architect. He sought proposals from ten different firms, interviewed three and narrowed the choice to two, at which point he brought them to Mim, along with pages and pages of plans.

Despite her artistic eye, Mim had difficulty reading architectural drawings. It was not like reading the beauty of a painting or sculpture. Renderings unimplemented were cold and mathematical.

Both finalists were well respected. In the end, the Blairs selected Sheply, Rutan and Coolidge. (Charles Coolidge had taken the trouble to solicit Mim's views on what, after all, was to be her home).

"Chauncey, you know I am not a suffragist, but I resented the way Mr. Rutledge treated me as a frill. He never once looked at me, even when I was the questioner."

Once construction began, Chauncey reviewed progress on the house every day on his way home from the bank. He approved the use of both stone and brick to make the façade stand out. The three stories were perfectly proportioned and set off with two curving bay windows on each floor that beckoned morning sun into the front rooms.

The house was ready for occupancy in the fall of 1891. Everyone agreed it was a handsome home. Mim congratulated both Chauncey and Mr. Coolidge for the stately beauty of the exterior. When *City Life* magazine featured the Blair home in its 1892 winter edition, the editors had called it "fashionable," but also described the lines as "severe." Chauncey took umbrage at this characterization, as if the magazine had called one of his children "homely."

"That is the last time this magazine is coming into this house," he fumed, taking the offending weekly and throwing it in the trash. I may well sue them for defamation of character."

"Chauncey, you misunderstand. They love the house." Mim went over to the basket where Chauncey had tossed the magazine and retrieved the offending article. She read, "'…it was built on the rather severe lines of the Italian Renaissance period.' That is an accurate description of the style we chose. You know my passion for anything evocative of the Renaissance. What they wrote was the highest of compliments. Besides, I cannot imagine it is possible to succeed in a lawsuit defaming the character of a house."

In her first months at 4830 Drexel Boulevard, Mim spent hours going from room to room, somewhat astonished at all she had done. She felt proud of herself, but the joy of her daily inspection was rooted more deeply. Everywhere she looked, she saw something lovely, and her soul responded, as well as her eye. Slowly she was making friends with beauty: the gold-and-silver-threaded tapestries from France in the morning room contrasted perfectly with the rich, dark green Flemish tapestry in the library. The cherry red silk brocade on the walls in the reception room always drew comment.

Mim found decorating her new home both exhausting and exhilarating. Martin Gaylord brought many pieces from New York and Europe for her consideration, but, because she had learned so much in her years of grandparental training, unlike many of her American contemporaries, she had confidence in her own eye. She valued Martin's perspective, thought him right more often than not, but she was no milquetoast.

Mrs. Blair was indefatigable in her pursuit of beautiful things. She went to countless auctions, sitting quietly in the rear with her bidder's paddle at the ready, never succumbing to the novice collector's impulsivity.

Canton china was one of her first acquisitions. Originally used as ballast, the china was a rare combination in the art world—simultaneously practical and exquisite. The Chinese wove beauty into the most prosaic items. Plates, platters, soup spoons, pitchers and bowls with delicate filigree were designed to be useful as well as to delight the eye. Muted blues, vibrant blues, dark blues, and ink blues reminded her of the colors in her swirling paperweights, but the images were not abstract. Each piece showed Mim something of China—junks sailing on the river, pagodas, bridges arching gracefully over ponds, village houses, boulders and what looked to be weeping willows bending as if the wind moved over the plate itself.

Mim had once heard a friend say that if she had a valuable piece of art she would put it in her bathroom since she spent more time there each day than in the formal living room. That strategy made sense to her, so she displayed some of her most beloved pieces in the sitting room, her private sanctuary where she spent hours on her correspondence, needlepoint and conversation with her intimate friends.

True to his word, Chauncey gave Mim a free hand as she decorated the interior. And true to her word, Chauncey's smoking room was just what he wanted. Indian carved wood molding adorned the paneling, ancient Hindu images lurked.

"Eyes closed," Mim commanded as she led him into the smoking room for the first time.

"Quite the daisy," he said with a wide smile on his face.

"I detest that expression!" Mim said, annoyed at hearing such an understated comment where genuine admiration would have been appreciated. He had used the same phrase when he had seen his newborn daughter Italia for the first time. On the other hand, he adored Italia and spoiled her, so she supposed he meant to be complimentary.

Mim had battled Chauncey's detached banker approach to things and people since the early days of their marriage. However, this desire produced more frustration in Mim than change in Chauncey, so these days she was more inclined to let these moments pass. After all, she deduced, it was only a matter of style, not substance, and he had many qualities she could appreciate, if not love.

The entrance to Blair House bespoke grandeur, alerting the cognoscenti that the owner of the house was a devotee of things classical. Each of the three marble columns was a swirl of deep red, like the color of late summer cherries. But if the marble columns slowed the admiring eye, the staircase was eye-stopping—so much light, an unusual feature in the homes of the South Side. Even in the late afternoon of a grey Chicago March day, Mim could read or do needlework perched on the window seat on the first floor landing.

Some nights the light cast by the moon on the landing was almost as strong as daytime sun. One night she and Chauncey had not been able to restrain their passion and their bedroom seemed too far away. (Chauncey's erotic ardor was always enhanced by sexual pleasure taken in unconventional spots.) Mim was almost certain her daughter Italia, now six years old, had been conceived on that landing in the fertile shadow of the moon. Her four-year-old son, Chauncey Buckley Blair, had likely gotten his start in a more conventional spot—Mim's bedroom. She theorized that the atmospherics of a child's conception permeated the spirit of the resulting child. Italia was as flamboyant and daring as the circumstances of her conception, while CB had emerged with the temperament of a banker. She was not actually certain of the whereabouts of her younger daughter's conception, but given Mildred's easy disposition, it must have been in a place of idyllic tranquility.

Each of the fifteen mantels in the house boasted a different design and style of inlaid wood that in turn complemented the fifteen different shades of marble surrounding each fireplace.

When the carved mahogany pocket doors were fully open, a visitor could see straight through from the morning room into the gallery, creating an expansive feel to the house. Dozens of oversized porcelain urns potted with palms embellished room after room. But with doors closed, each room became a small museum.

Mim's penchant for decorative screens was apparent. She called them "moveable works of art." Her favorite was a triple panel of dark purple violets (her lucky flower) embroidered on ivory satin. She kept it in her bedroom and occasionally fantasized about isolating herself from all her responsibilities by pulling all three sides around her and enclosing herself completely in beauty.

"Mrs. Blair, Mr. Gaylord is here to see you," announced Robert, the Blairs' butler. "I suggested he remain in the reception room until you arrive, but he seems to be wandering through all the rooms on the first floor."

"Thank you, Robert. I shall be down in a minute," replied Mim, amused as she visualized Martin alone on her first floor, surveying walls and flat surfaces with an eye to additional adornments. The fact that this was neither a scheduled appointment nor a Thursday, her traditional calling day, must mean he had something to show her.

As it happened, today was the first day she planned to wear the new dress that had arrived last week, tailored by Chester Hibner, her personal dressmaker at Marshall Fields. It was a bittersweet chocolate-brown silk taffeta. The front panel, which extended the full length of the dress, was an even darker brown but in velvet. A thick brown-black lamb's wool choker collar adorned the sleeves and hem. The tightly-laced corset did its work. Her dress flattered her waist, even after three children.

The first time she met the tailor, Mim had little confidence that their would be a successful collaboration. But his European sensibility helped him to understand her figure, her taste and her style; consequently, Mim was always well turned out and some days she could even be called "chic."

Though her formal gowns came from Worth, the most famous couturier in Paris, Mim insisted that all her other dresses be tailored by Mr. Hibner. Four times a year they would meet to plan her wardrobe. They worked a season ahead, often sweltering through a Chicago heat wave to prepare clothes for a brisk Chicago autumn. Mr. Hibner was the only man, other than Chauncey, who had ever been in her dressing room.

As she prepared to greet Martin Gaylord, she took a quick look in the floor-to-ceiling mirror. She was not displeased, and mentally gave herself the only compliment that she felt truly applicable—"Not altogether bad today."

Martin Gaylord was a man of decided taste and opinions who, when advising on budding art collections, had to restrain himself so he could be helpful and not overbearing. The self–restraint seemed to work. Several of the most aggressive collectors in Chicago had chosen him to peruse and purchase innumerable paintings, sculptures and antiques, often in a frenzy of acquisitive competition.

The Philip Armours, the Potter Palmers and George and Hattie Pullman were among those who considered Martin Gaylord their artistic Delphic oracle. Martin was not so charitable.

As he saw it, the Armours bought indifferently as if simply covering the walls were the singular objective.

Cissie Palmer knew what she liked. Though she often bought indiscriminately, at least she had a point of view. She adored the new French school: Monet, Manet and Degas. Literally hundreds of their paintings hung in her galleries, creating a lovely if gauzy effect. Martin admired the work coming out of Paris, but if he were honest he often felt as if he had overeaten when leaving the Palmer galleries.

His most difficult clients were George and Hattie Pullman. Put simply, neither one had any taste. The railroad magnate himself was a bully more than a buyer. Martin rarely saw him, but his artistically insecure wife, Hattie, spent hundreds of thousands of dollars on pieces that had no coherence. She had a competitive streak, which invariably led her to ask, "What is Cissie Palmer buying these days?" or "Tell me again, Martin, what Mary Blair finds so interesting in the works of the Renaissance." The Pullmans were more trouble than they were worth, except that occasionally George, displeased with a purchase made by his wife, was cajoled into donating it to the art museum.

Unique amongst Gaylord's clients was Mary Mitchell Blair. She was vastly more discerning than any collector he had ever worked with, never betraying her artistic intelligence by responding to the impulse to buy for the sake of buying.

He believed Mim had a tendency towards rigidity, which limited her personal collection, currently a very good one. But with a little more imagination, it could be second only to the collection of the Potter Palmers, which by sheer volume overshadowed most collections in America or Europe.

Because he thought Mim had a natural eye, albeit one that needed educating, he enjoyed serving as her mentor. They had become friends.

Today he had brought her two paintings to consider. He knew she would like the Gainsborough. Painted in 1750, it was called *The Guardsman Seated in Landscape*. The landscape was lush and the foliage autumnal. The Guardsman was shown relaxing into a hillock, wearing a white satin jacket and a lavishly trimmed scarlet tunic. His green-blue breeches and white hose caught one's eye before it drifted to the peasant woman and children in the background. It was a restful and restrained painting; the depth of the color captured the English countryside. Martin visualized it in the smoking room, so Chauncey would have the final say.

It was not a risky choice, since it was by an established painter, but it was expensive. (Martin suspected Mim never directly lied to Chauncey about a purchase price. She simply rounded numbers to her advantage.)

"Mim, can't you get Martin to Jew down the price a little?" Chauncey would complain. "It seems that he accepts the first price he hears when he is selecting for us. You can be sure if it was Gaylord selecting for Gaylord, the price would be more favorable."

"Chauncey," Mim replied curtly, "Martin is consulting as a favor to us. He does not make a penny on anything we buy. Besides, Martin is so rich, he could spend until his last days and still leave a fortune."

"Well, you are certainly right on that point. There were few companies that did better after the Great Fire than before, but Gaylord Construction was one of them."

The second painting was by a young American painter whom Martin had come across in Paris, Childe Hassam. It was called *Rainy Day* and Gaylord thought it magnificent. If the Blairs did not buy it, he would, and donate it to the Art Institute. He often did this when buyers were not as astute as he.

Rainy Day featured unusual broad, broken brush strokes, and the depiction of the slick, wet sidewalks of Paris made you conscious of your footing just walking around the painting. The stone sidewalks dominated the foreground but did not interfere with the artist's intent to take you to the middle ground where one found the action of the painting.

Three figures came walking toward you in single file. Two were women, the shimmer of their black gowns hinting at elegance. Both held umbrellas in their right hands and slightly lifted their skirts to avoid the accumulating puddles. In the background was a church steeple, set against a lighter grey sky that promised clearing. It was an optimistic picture. Gaylord knew Mim would appreciate that right away. She admired light and balance.

Yes, thought Martin, Childe Hassam had talent. He was not yet sure if the young Bostonian had as much talent as his Parisian peers, the group that was making its mark creating works of impressions rather than defined images. Hassam was not an imitator of Monet and Manet, but one could tell he had absorbed much of their experimentation. Martin was curious to see if Mim had progressed in her willingness to trust her own eye and her natural instinct.

He enjoyed a little game with himself when he presented art to a potential buyer. He set the game up not because he cared financially one way or the other but because he liked to test his judgment of people and their tastes. Today he wagered with himself that Mim would purchase the Gainsborough and reject the Hassam.

"Good afternoon, Martin," said Mim, as she extended her hand for Gaylord to kiss. As well as she knew Martin and as often as she and Chauncey had dined with him and Catherine, men in their circle never ever took the liberty of even a chaste kiss on the cheek.

"Nice to see you, Mim. It is always nice to see you. I saw Chauncey at the Chicago Club this noon and he thought you might be home today. I am glad he was right.

"He, Marshall Field and George Pullman were playing poker at the Millionaire's Table—very serious. Tell me, Mim, does Chauncey play poker with George Pullman because he actually likes him or simply because he likes the Pullman account?"

"Martin, how you do love to create trouble! But I will tell you the truth, as both the daughter and the wife of bankers. In banking, there is no differentiation between personal and business relationships. They blend as naturally as the filigree on that tapestry over there. One cannot tell where the green ends and the blue begins," Mim said, pointing to one of the few things in the reception room that Martin had not seen.

"By the way, it is stunning, Mim. Sixteenth-century Flemish, I would guess."

"And you, of course, would be right. You do like it, don't you? That pleases me. It gives me confidence to know that I can buy something of beauty on my own," Mim teased.

"But, Martin, I think you are being a touch sanctimonious when it comes to George Pullman. He is as huffy and puffy as his trains, but he has a vision for railroads that has proved successful, and not just for him but for the benefit of the whole country. My father used to say that Chicago would still be a swamp without the railroads.

"So, what have you brought me today?" Mim inquired with a "let's get down to business" tone that replaced the jousting one she had been using.

"I have brought you two paintings. One to tempt and one to test."

"Martin, you know I loathe your tests. They put a knot in my stomach. I feel like a little girl facing Grandmother's quizzes."

"But she taught you well, Mim. You have more discernment than any collector in Chicago. I only bring you things that I know you will or should admire," Martin said, smiling.

Martin went to the corner and began unwrapping the Gainsborough. Mim made herself falsely busy by needlessly rearranging the Greek porcelain vases on the mantel because she never viewed a work until it was properly unveiled and placed.

"Meet the *Guardsman Seated in Landscape*," said Martin, stepping back to remove himself from the view.

"Oh, Martin, it is wonderful and so distinctively Gainsborough. Surely this is not the painting you think will test me. This is an easy decision. Not only do I love it, but I know that Chauncey will as well. Sold."

"Mim, don't you want to know the price?" asked Martin.

"Martin, I am not a shopper. I am a collector," Mim replied. "I like it. I am certain Chauncey will like it. I know the range in which a Gainsborough sells and I can afford it, so there is no point pretending to you, of all people, that I want to negotiate all day for a good deal. I trust you."

"Well, I appreciate that," Martin said with a slight bow.

"Before I show you the next one, Mim, let me give you a bit of provenance. The artist is named Childe Hassam. He is American, but I saw his work in Paris. In fact, Hassam won the Bronze Medal in Paris last year. For some reason, I thought of you when I saw it."

"I have heard of Hassam. I think I saw one in Cissy Palmer's gallery recently. I have to warn you, I did not like it. The images were too weak and the colors too strong for my taste. I am not inclined to the new French school," Mim said, preparing her defense, should she not be enamored. "But I shall honor you by trying to keep an open mind."

The preparations for this presentation seemed to take longer than those for the Gainsborough, as though Martin were a mother delicately primping a beloved daughter for an important piano recital.

"There," Martin said with a voice that was more a loving croon than his usual formal tone.

Mim had purchased a great many works with Martin's help, but today she sensed in him an unusual reverence. She said nothing at first. Nor did she make eye contact with him, because at this moment she did not need to see what his face was registering, she needed only to be closer to this painting.

It was decidedly French in inspiration, but instead of bold colors, this one was wet and grey. It gave her a slight shiver. Mim followed the angles of the natural light in the room as she paced in front of the painting. The only strong color was the buttery yellow of the street poster towards which the pedestrians were walking. Martin gave her time. He could see she was immersing herself in the painting.

"What is it called?" Mim asked.

"*A Rainy Day*," answered Martin.

"Tell me why you thought of me when you saw it?"

"Because of the woman in the forefront. She is elegantly dressed, as Childe Hassam's women typically are. But what I love is the energy of her stride. She moves purposefully, directly, knowing her destination. She does not fuss with the rain. She simply lifts her skirt, opens the umbrella and marches forward, just as you do," he answered, his gaze as direct as Mim's.

"I'll take it," she said softly.

A Glimpse of a Diva

Christmas 1892

*I*T WAS HARD TO FEEL worse and still be ambulatory. Mim had not told Chauncey yet, but she would have to soon. He would be pleased, though he was not the one who would be actively sick most mornings and remain tired for the next seven months. She had sailed through her three previous pregnancies, but she was now thirty-seven and her body told her, in not so subtle ways, that she was to find her delicate condition more delicate this time.

Mim thought she had been careful to avoid pregnancy since Mildred's birth three years ago. Two girls and a boy in the middle seemed a complete family, especially one in which the eldest daughter was as tyrannical as Italia.

Mim lamented to Nanny, "When Italia is happy, the rest of the household runs smoothly. When she's not, everyone suffers. And she is only eight!"

With panther black hair and dark grey eyes she was a dazzler, and

Italia carried herself as if she knew it, adding to her power, especially over her father.

Her brother Chauncey Buckley Blair, or CB as he was known within the family, was beguilingly different. He was quiet, but not shy. He knew to speak when spoken to. His complexion was paler than the swarthy Italia, so when he ran outside in the cold weather, his red cheeks complemented all his features. His nose was generously sprinkled with freckles, especially in the summer. While Italia held those around her in a forceful grip, CB's more affectionate nature allowed him to disarm rather than demand. He was not a "Mama's Boy," a taunt often hurled at him by Italia, but CB had captured his mother's heart while Italia held her father in thrall.

CB's imagination was his best friend. He had an unusual ability to concentrate and had loved the companionship of a book long before he learned to read. Where Italia intimidated playmates and had few friends, CB was a friend to all.

If there were a family popularity contest, the unanimous winner would be Mildred. When Italia was petulant, Mildred simply played around her until her older sister was on low simmer. When CB was absorbed, Mildred knew not to pester him with questions. She would just sidle up to him with her own project and play in parallel motion and quietude. She loved stories and both her parents allowed her more lap sitting and physical affection than they had allowed either of the older children. Mildred's eyes would fill with tears on the rare occasion she suffered a reprimand.

Mildred had auburn hair, which Nanny would brush twice a day. When it was "just so," Mildred was allowed to run in to see her mother, carrying whatever color satin bow complemented the day's outfit. When her underskirt was blue, her white pinafore starched to perfection, and the blue bow was in place, she reminded Mim of Alice in Wonderland.

Unlike anyone else in the family, Mildred had hazel eyes, set off by eyelashes that would have been considered long on an older woman. On Mildred they looked slightly abnormal, but it would be a pleasure watching her grow into them.

Mim had designated many features in her life as "lucky"—a dress, a cookie, a paperweight or a particular pattern at hopscotch. Her mother said such talk was sacrilegious.

"The good things in life are not a matter of luck. They are a matter of piety. Our gifts come from God. We earn them when we please Him."

Nowadays Mim kept superstitions to herself, but in her heart she knew Mildred was her lucky child.

⚬

Mim still physically shuddered when she remembered Christmas Eve. She feared it would be a mere morsel on the platter of life with Italia.

Christmas Eve was the one night of the year when the Blair children were welcome downstairs in the formal rooms at the annual Christmas party. It was a festival of cousins, aunts and uncles, close family friends and Chicago's business, political and philanthropic elite. All the guests dressed to the nines, women wearing elaborate gowns from Worth in Paris that featured the current fashion trends. Fingers, necks, ears, wrists, bosoms and hair were resplendent with jewels. Fresh violets were worn at the waist or shoulder or carried in bouquets, giving off a fraudulent hope of spring.

Men came in white tie and tails, black patent leather shoes, starched white front pieces that usually were studded with small diamonds, pearls, or onyx.

Italia had been excited for weeks about the upcoming festivities. To add to her exuberant anticipation, Mim had surprised Italia by ordering a miniature replica of her own black velvet gown—their first mother and daughter formal frocks. The only difference between mother and daughter would be that where Italia's dress had a Belgian lace collar, Mim's neckline was cut to show off the Blair family pearls, which would be looped many times around her neck, creating the effect of the world's most magnificent canine collar.

Mr. Hibner did Italia's first formal fitting at the same time as her mother's and the eight-year-old behaved like a seasoned model. He said he had never seen such a young child take so serious an attitude toward her ensemble. He usually had to deal with children squirming into and out of pins and tucks, but Italia had not moved a muscle.

"Mrs. Blair, your daughter, she is very beautiful. She never move, even when stick her."

On the evening of December 24, 1892, chaos reigned in the Blair nursery as Nanny, assisted by Alice, the upstairs maid, made sure Italia, CB and Mildred were bathed, brushed and buttoned. So when Italia announced that she was going to her mother's room to present herself, Nanny responded with relief at having one less child to manage, especially when that child was Italia.

Nanny had been in a tussle with Italia ever since her bath because the ten-year-old insisted that tonight she would wear her hair upswept, like her mother. Nanny was firm that she was too young to wear her hair that way, despite Italia's assertion that her mother had given permission.

"Nanny, I asked mother last week if I could wear it up and she said she would think about it. I am certain that she did think about it and decided that I could, but just forgot to tell you," declared Italia imperiously, as if she had been dealing with servants for years.

Truth be told, Italia was Nanny's least favorite Blair child, which reflected a unanimous sentiment below stairs.

"Miss Italia, I have never seen upswept hair on a girl under sixteen, at least not one from a refined home. You would look like a floozy from the Back-of-the-Yards slums. You would embarrass the entire Blair family. It is not something your mother would ever consider allowing. Besides, you and Mildred will be the prettiest little girls at the party. Enjoy it."

"Nanny, Mildred may be a little girl tonight, and she is pretty. I am not a little girl and tonight I want to be stunning. I will go check with Mother now. When you see me next, my hair will be up."

Nanny's logic and understanding of what was proper was no match for Italia's determination. She was a child on a mission, fueled by resentment that her mother would wear rows and rows of pearls while she wore lace. But she would have her own crown jewels, and crown jewels did not go into long hair with bows.

Italia knew exactly what she wanted: her mother's aigrettes, five white egret feathers splayed expansively over her hair and secured with a cluster of diamonds and seed pearls. Italia loved the way the aigrettes looked in her mother's hair, which to Italia was an undistinguished brown color, more squirrel than mink. She could only imagine how dazzling they would appear, set off by her black hair, which tonight would be piled atop her head.

She arrived in her mother's room, correctly suspecting that she would not be there. She would be downstairs reviewing last-minute details with the couple who held the keys to the success of the evening—Bertha, the cook, and her husband Robert, the butler. What she did not anticipate was that Margaret, her mother's personal maid, was still in the room, straightening and arranging it perfectly for Mim's return at the end of what would be a long evening.

"Miss Italia, you look lovely," said Margaret with a slight curtsey to her mistress' young daughter. Mim was not an employer who made friends with her servants, nor was she one to insist on rigid European conventions, like requiring servants to face the wall when members of the family or guests passed by. Still, her servants were expected to acknowledge social position, even with the children when they were not in the nursery.

"I just finished snapping your mother into her dress. You and your mother are beautiful twins tonight. But at the moment she is downstairs, if you are looking for her."

"I know that, Margaret. I just saw her and she told me to ask you to meet her in the morning room before the guests arrive, so you had best hurry."

"Yes, ma'am," said Margaret making a departing curtsey.

※

Italia loved the dressing rituals that occurred within these rooms. On special occasions, she was invited to watch her mother prepare for evenings of formal dinners and balls. She loved it because what she witnessed was nothing less than transformation. If a woman like her mother, who to her eye was the plainest, least glamorous woman she had ever seen, could be transformed from ordinary to special, she was certain much more could be done with someone whose fundamental beauty was as obvious as her own.

Italia had never seen her mother naked and hoped she never would. But she had seen her emerge from her bathroom, steaming under her mauve satin negligee, to seat herself at a marble-topped table with jars of creams and vials of oils standing as if at attention, awaiting their orders to beautify.

Margaret would first massage the amber-lavender oil into Mim's white legs and bathwater-puckered feet and then into her arms and shoulders, infusing Mim's essential fragrance into the room. Mim did not wear perfume. She let the rich body oil speak for itself. She was one of those women who had a distinctive and alluring smell, alerting people when she was entering a space and reminding people that she had been there when she departed. The oil was made especially for her in London.

When not pressed for time and in a patient mood, Mim would pour a drop of the oil on Italia's wrist for her to inhale. Italia would take a deep, appreciative whiff (much like her father did when swirling a brandy snifter under his nose), close her eyes, swoon slightly and pronounce it the most intoxicating aroma she had ever smelled.

The last item applied was the cold cream. Mim used different creams for different times of the day, a light cream for daytime and a more viscous one before bed. Both came from Marshall Fields and were prepared for Mim using precise amounts of almond oil, wax and rose water.

Once oiled and creamed, Mim would move to her green brocade dressing table where the final and most formal rituals were performed, and where Italia instinctively knew her place.

"Mother, you smell like the loveliest garden and you already look prettier. Everyone will want to be near you tonight," Italia once exclaimed.

"Prettier than what, Italia?" Mim asked her daughter, knowing, as soon as she heard the back-handed compliment that it was time to teach her daughter a small lesson in etiquette.

"Prettier than…well, just prettier than you were. Prettier than you usually are…Prettier than, well, just pretty, that's all," stammered Italia, sensing she had said something displeasing.

"Italia, you must learn to think before you speak. You should avoid making comparisons. They can be hurtful. My feelings might have been hurt when you implied that you usually don't see me as pretty, but that tonight I had made an improvement."

"But Mother, I have heard you say many times that you don't think you are pretty. I was just agreeing with you and telling the truth. You tell me all the time to tell the truth, and I did. You are not pretty when you are just you, but when Margaret works on you, you get prettier," Italia said with complete candor.

Mim pulled her beautiful but socially maladroit daughter closer to her and said, "I know I am not always pretty, Ity, but that does not mean I want to be reminded of it. When I have time, I will tell you the difference between white and black lies and under what circumstances you should employ them."

With a laugh she released Italia and said, "Keep going, Margaret, Italia thinks we still have more work to do."

The two women returned and the time-honored ritual began. In addition to the monogrammed silver comb, brush and hand mirror, Margaret had laid out hairpins, combs, crushed pearl powder, rouge, lip rouge and, most important to Italia, the jewels that had been selected for the gown of the evening. Mim did not wear much jewelry during the day. Even when she called on her friends or received visitors, she kept it to a minimum—some earrings, a locket, possibly a brooch. But when she dressed formally, she liked more sparkle and Chauncey had given her many treasures from which to choose.

After a robust brushing of Mim's hair, Margaret began the final ascent to full beauty. Her brown hair was pulled high off her neck and secured by the first of three diamond-encrusted combs. Margaret then parted Mim's hair down the middle, pulling out a few softening wisps for some gentle bangs. The other two combs secured the waves on either side of Mim's face and her remaining hair would be coiled and twisted into place, awaiting the placement of the aigrettes or any jeweled ornament selected for the evening.

Lastly, Margaret coiled the Blair pearls around Mim's neck and adjusted the drop pearl and diamond enhancers so they hung symmetrically from the necklace. Mim inserted the diamond and pearl earrings into her ears, pulled on her arm's length, white kid gloves, and the transformation was complete. Even Mim felt its power as she dismissed Margaret and headed back downstairs to greet her guests.

Italia wasted no time. She knew just where to begin and so seated herself facing the magic oils and creams. She planned to use them all and as much as she liked. Cupping her hand for the maximum amount, she poured from each vial, making a not so small puddle in the center of her right hand. If a few drops made her mother more appealing, a handful would make her own skin exquisite. In one movement she splashed the oil on her face as if she were rinsing off the soap when washing her face before bed.

"There," she said aloud as she moved her fists in sweeping circles on her cheeks, tilting her head back to keep the excess oil from her eyes.

"It feels so lovely, smells so lovely."

She reached for the hand mirror to check her progress, but the oil had made for a slippery grasp and the mirror fell onto the marble table-top. Happily, it did not break. Ity knew that a broken mirror would bring seven years of bad luck, and her mother would be more anxious about a broken mirror than angry about the invasion of her dressing table.

After making sure there was not even the smallest crack in the mirror, she applied the rose water, though she could not be sure her face was dry enough because there was so much oil on it. Nonetheless she proceeded with the creams. Though she rubbed hard, her face was not absorbing the globs of cream. Not wanting to look like a mime, she went into her mother's bathroom, took a hand towel, and removed some of the white lotion.

"That's better," she exhaled, relieved.

Italia heard Nanny ushering CB and Mildred down the stairs and knew she would soon be missed. Picking up the large, soft facial brush, she dipped it into the pearl powder and dabbed the luster gently on all parts of her face. She used a smaller brush to apply the rouge. Checking herself in the mirror, she had a moment of panic thinking that her cheeks were too red, making her look like a polished apple. But at least she knew that she would be noticed. At last she found the pencil-thin brush and the paper tube of lipstick. She outlined her lips almost perfectly and quickly moved to the finishing table.

Though she had practiced coiffeur for hours and hours in the privacy of her bedroom, tonight she had little time for perfection. She leaned over and dangled her head between her knees, grabbing her abundant black hair at its crown. She placed several day combs randomly in the mass, which certainly gave the effect of an upsweep, though one not particularly well executed.

What she needed now was the aigrette. If she guessed right, her mother would be wearing the white one to set off the black velvet of the dress, so she would be forced to wear the black one. Italia and her mother might not be identical twins tonight, but they could certainly be fraternal. Stepping into her mother's cavernous closet, she saw the feathers on the top shelf, on a hat mount, cushioned by tissue paper. Taking a shoetree from one of the shoes on the floor, she carefully climbed the lower three shelves, and, reaching up, she used the implement to flip the aigrette and hat stand onto the floor.

The aigrette must have been made for her to wear tonight because it went in perfectly, and more importantly, it would stay in place as her thick black hair welcomed it. A final look in the mirror and she knew that she had created a masterpiece. She was transformed. As she made her way downstairs and approached the landing, she could hear that the party had not waited for her. *Perfect*, she thought, *her entrance would be appreciated by a full house.*

⚶

Mim was especially pleased that Edith Rockefeller McCormick would be in attendance tonight. She always spiced up an evening. Edith's many eccentricities were off-putting to most of Chicago society except when they wanted to tap into her generous bank account. Edith appreciated art and dabbled in the occult, asserting to anyone within earshot that, of the many lives she had lived, she liked her current reincarnation almost as much as when she had been married to King Tut. Chauncey did not approve of Mim's devotion to Edith. He thought her dangerous, and Mim susceptible.

At the moment, Mim was doing what she was bred to do, circulating among her guests and effortlessly engaging each in a conversation she knew would interest them.

The only guests she had not yet approached were George and Hattie Pullman, who had just entered the room and were awkwardly standing alone. Mim liked neither of the Pullmans individually, and they were even less attractive as a couple.

George talked about himself, his workers' village, his business acumen, his favorite daughter, Florence, and his most recent acquisitions, then would end by telling you how glad he was to have caught up with you. When Hattie Pullman talked, she did so assuming the listener wanted to know as much as possible about her twin boys, who were regarded by all as hellions.

But Mim knew her duty.

"Good evening and Merry Christmas. How is the family?" After a ten-minute monologue from George and a briefer but equally boring one from Hattie, Mim saw Martin Gaylord out of the corner of her eye and motioned him over to join them and rescue her.

Knowing that Martin loathed George Pullman, and feeling slightly guilty for abandoning him, Mim nonetheless excused herself to "find Chauncey."

"Before you go," said Hattie, "you will get an invitation soon for a private tour of the workers' village that George has built."

"I call it Pullman's paradise," interrupted George. "There is nothing like it in the world. Pullman workers will be forever indebted to me but, more importantly, labor unrest in a Pullman plant will be unthinkable."

Chauncey signaled for the music to stop and the servants to discontinue food and beverage service. Then he and Mim took their places at the bottom of the grand staircase to extend Christmas greetings to their guests. It was at that moment that Italia, poised on the second floor landing where she could see but not be seen, stiffened her back, squared her shoulders, elevated her chin, and readied herself to make her way regally down the stairs to join them.

"Ladies and Gentlemen, family and friends. Mrs. Blair and I are so happy you are able to join us on this blessed evening. Each of you has enriched our lives this year." He paused to enhance the effect of his annual joke interweaving the festive and the financial.

"Some of you have enriched it more than others, and for that we are very, very grateful."

Mim cringed internally at Chauncey's little jest, certain that Chauncey had misconstrued polite laughter for true appreciation.

"Mrs. Blair and I wish each and every one of you a Merry Christmas. More importantly, we pray for a happy and commercially successful 1893. By the time we celebrate together next year, millions of people will have come to the grandest exposition in world history, and they will know that Chicago is no longer America's second city, but its first. The Exposition of

1893 will change forever the way the world thinks of our city."

Chauncey, please stop, Mim thought to herself. *This is a Christmas party, not a stockholders' meeting. Just wish everyone a Merry Christmas and be done with it. All I want to do is sit down or, more to the point, lie down in my own bed.*

Sensing that Chauncey had lost his audience, Mim noticed that others shared her restlessness. Several of the guests were whispering. Some were tittering. Mim forced her focus to remain on Chauncey and her smile, though tight, was securely in place. But the snickering grew into bolder laughter and finally into outright hilarity. Upon reflection, Mim was certain that she and Chauncey were the last to know.

After what felt like an eternity of dislocation, she sensed Chauncey was being upstaged by something that was directly behind them. She turned and saw a most incongruous tableau. There was her daughter, Italia Mary Ann Blair, aged eight, looking part strumpet, part clown, but vaguely dazzling.

Italia seemed not the least bit disconcerted that people were laughing at her so she continued, Cleopatra-like, down the stairs until she was at the bottom alongside her mother and father.

After a moment of frantic thought, but with no clear plan, Mim whispered to Chauncey, "Let me handle this."

Then, more slowly than she would have thought possible under the circumstances, and smiling directly into her daughter's painted face, she hissed to Italia, "Take my hand and we will walk upstairs as quietly as you came down them."

"But, Mother, I have spent a great deal of time getting ready for the party. It is Christmas Eve. I have many people I want to greet, and I have had nothing to eat since tea."

"Italia, we will now turn and go up the stairs. This is not a conversation. This is a command," said Mim, managing to smile and glower simultaneously.

The company was now fully engaged in the family drama playing out before their eyes. It took Chauncey a few agonizing moments to regain his demeanor, but he knew it was time to deflect attention from Mim and Italia.

He raised his voice and said, "Forgive me, folks, my beautiful and precocious daughter has stolen the show once again. Please, everyone, enjoy the rest of the evening and we wish you all a happy Christmas."

"Excuse me! Excuse me! I need to come through," came a voice from the reception room. Draped in her iconic lace gown, with her diamond and emerald tiara outshining any other jewels at the party, Edith Rockefeller McCormick made her way towards mother and daughter.

"Mim dear, let me handle this for you so you can see to your guests. I think Italia looks just beautiful tonight. And she has placed her aigrette in just the right place."

Turning to Italia, she continued, "I can never seem to get mine properly sited, but you have managed it on your first try. Well done, my dear." To Mim she whispered, "Maybe she and I can simply sit and chat a while."

"Edith, you cannot possibly handle this. You do not even have children! She has embarrassed us, and, worst of all, embarrassed herself. In addition, the aigrette is mine and looks preposterous, well-placed or not," Mim seethed.

"Mim, it is Christmas Eve, and Italia has shown flair beyond her years. I promise that she will not circulate among the guests, nor will she be allowed to open her party favor, but do allow me to talk to this fascinating young woman."

Gently, Edith removed the aigrette from Italia's upswept hair and handed it to Mim.

"Italia, say you are sorry to your mother whether you think it an accurate statement of your feelings or not. Then wish her a Merry Christmas. And follow me."

Speaking more to her feet than to her mother, Italia repeated the words as she had been instructed to do.

"No, Italia, try again. I am not that indulgent. You are to look at your mother, make your apologies and then kiss her good night. I will see to it that you find Nanny when we are finished talking."

Intelligent enough to know that Mrs. McCormick's intercession was as good a gift as she would get that night, she willed herself to authenticity.

"I am sorry, Mother. And please tell Father I am sorry. I thought you would want me to look pretty. Merry Christmas."

"Italia, this is not the end of this misadventure. Your father and I will discuss your punishment, but it can wait until after tomorrow. And when you say your prayers tonight, be sure to thank God that Mrs. McCormick was our guest this evening."

Mim walked off with as much composure as she could muster.

Italia and Mrs. McCormick sat side by side talking for a long time. It appeared to all who saw them an earnest *tête-à-tête* between equals.

Mim's prayer that night would be that this new baby would take after Mildred and not its eldest sister. She should never have indulged Chauncey's amorous impulses in the peony garden!

A Collection of Blairs

Winter 1892

*I*F MARY ANNE ITALIA MITCHELL Blair was born and raised to be a collector, her husband, Chauncey Justus Blair, was reared to be a banker from the moment the midwife declared his gender. Perhaps, if he had had an obvious natural talent for another vocation, there could have been some accommodation made, but since he did not, a banker he would be.

The same could not have been said for his father, Chauncey Buckley Blair. The third oldest of seven children, the senior Blair began his career working on his uncle's farm in upstate New York. Heading west in 1835, he reached Chicago in 1861, where he transformed himself into one of Chicago's leading bankers by the time he was fifty. In fact, Chauncey senior was legendary as the only Chicago banker who saw opportunity after the Great Fire in 1870, taking the controversial position that banks should extend or renegotiate loans for distressed customers rather than call them in. Bankers who followed his advice reaped the rewards of expansive growth in the next decade, and the Merchants Bank, commonly referred to as the "Blair Bank," quickly became the third largest bank in the city.

Shortly before his father's death in 1891, Chauncey Justus Blair became the president of the "Blair Bank." Chauncey Junior considered the old man infallible. At the time of his death, the Merchants Bank was fully capitalized and his estate was estimated to be worth five million dollars.

"Good afternoon, Mr. Blair," said Edward, the doorman, as the banker crossed the marble foyer of the Chicago Club on East Van Buren Street. It was another fair but frigid Chicago day and after the twenty-minute walk from his office on LaSalle Street, Chauncey was happy to be relieved of his top-coat, hat and gloves so he could absorb all the warmth the men's club offered. (Each member had recently been assessed another one hundred dollars to defray the cost of the installation of a new heating system, and as much as Chauncey had grumbled over the outlay, today he would admit that perhaps the new system had its merits.)

When his father had proposed Chauncey for membership in the Chicago Club, it had seemed to the junior Chauncey more of a rite of passage than a necessary prerequisite for a bank officer. Young Chauncey had no objection of course. He had loved the club ever since he was a youth. He always felt safe inside the building. As a boy, Chauncey had fantasized that someday he would learn the secret handshake, known only to members. Now he knew that there was a secret handshake all right, but it was a mental one, and more secret than Chauncey could possibly have understood as a boy. The secret was that inside these doors, privilege reigned in perpetuity.

To this day, what satisfied him most was the pervasive quiet of a men's club. Nods replaced verbal greetings. In the reading room, whispering was a practiced art.

Chauncey Senior had been a founding member of the Club in 1869 and he cherished its rich history. He relished telling his favorite story of the members' gentlemanly behavior during the Great Fire.

The Chicago Fire was actually two fires. The first was nearly extinguished, only to be reignited by the fierce Chicago winds. During its second manifestation, several club members had again sought refuge inside the building under the ludicrous assumption that the fire, knowing the status of the members, would simply pass over the building much like the plagues passed over the Jews in the land of Egypt. With flames licking the exterior walls, members evacuated again, but not before lining their pockets with cigars and loading their arms with bottles of whiskey. They then reassembled on red satin sofas on the lakefront for a somewhat delayed breakfast.

"Never lower your standards," Chauncey Senior would say in conclusion.

By 1891, the now 51-year-old Chauncey Junior belonged to many clubs, using each for a different purpose. He used the gym and the pool at the Chicago Athletic Club on Michigan Avenue for exercise and the Union League Club on Jackson Boulevard for purely business activities. Unlike the Chicago Club, where members were honor-bound not to discuss business, the Union League Club was unabashedly transactional. Some of the biggest deals in the country had been negotiated within its wood-paneled rooms.

Today, Chauncey was meeting his Uncle Lyman for lunch at the Chicago Club. Though the matter on his mind was business-related, no one seeing an uncle and his nephew dining would suspect they were witnessing a violation of club policy.

Chauncey stood at the entrance to the members' private dining room. (There was a less formal dining room on the fourth floor, which just this year had allowed women to enter for lunch on Thursdays, though they had to come in through a shabby side entrance otherwise used for deliveries.)

"Good afternoon, Arthur," said Chauncey. "I think I see Mr. Lyman Blair over there in the corner at his usual table."

"Indeed you do, sir. I will be happy to seat you," replied the maître d', who was considered "new" despite his ten-year tenure.

"No need, thank you, Arthur," Chauncey said, already en route.

On Saturdays a free buffet was served; as a result the dining room was more crowded than it would have been on a weekday. Chauncey

Senior had always been derisive about the Club's "free buffet."

"It is not free. All it means is that you will not get the bill today."

Lyman Blair had both loved and admired his older brother Chauncey Buckley. He was also grateful because his shares in the Merchant Bank had contributed considerably to his net worth. Lyman was currently the second largest shareholder.

Senior Chauncey had made it very clear to his son that he would be wise to keep Lyman apprised of business issues and to seek his counsel when needed.

Chauncey was certain his father's peers considered his ascension to the presidency of the bank an example of the apple having fallen a goodly distance from the tree. He felt the pressure continually.

He had lamented to Mim just this morning, "What I need more than anything else is for America's expansion to continue. Father was wise and resourceful. He used those qualities to enormous shareholder and personal benefit. He made us all very rich. But he was also lucky to be born when he was. America was growing so fast that a man with his wits about him and a capacity for hard work had a huge advantage. But the American Midas Touch cannot continue forever."

Mim was moved by such vulnerability in her husband. Some instinct led her to want to enfold him in a tender embrace. But such mid-morning foolishness would feel awkward to both of them. So she settled for a peck on his cheek and a few encouraging words.

"Chauncey, you can make your own good fortune, especially now. With all the opportunities coming with the Exposition, every banker, and hopefully all of Chicago, will be enriched," Mim said.

"Mim, I am certain the fair will be a success. We have sold five million dollars' worth of bonds and I see no reason why the next lot of five million will not go quickly as well. But to my mind the Exposition is masking some ominous weakness in business fundamentals.

"I am talking to Lyman today about an important matter that will soon come before the board. He will be a valuable vote should I need it, so I am laying the groundwork."

"You are making me nervous, Chauncey. I will spend the entire day seeing calamity around every corner," said Mim, as she watched Chauncey prepare to leave, adding, "But I will send you off with a piece of positive news I have been saving for just such a moment. Martin is getting me $3000 for the Chinese porcelain vases in the dining room. I paid only $750 when I purchased them four years ago."

"Congratulations, Mimsy. With that rate of return, I should make you my chief investment strategist."

Chauncey gave her a somewhat lingering kiss as he left the morning room. "You're quite the daisy, you are."

"Stop, Chauncey. You know how I hate that expression. It trivializes everything it touches and when it touches me, I cringe."

"See you for dinner, darling. If you sell any art today, make sure we make another twenty percent. And don't buy short."

❦

Despite the fact that it was a Saturday, Lyman, like Chauncey, was dressed in business attire. Though Lyman had retired more than ten years ago, his sartorial formality was a matter of habit.

Chauncey saw that his Uncle Lyman had spotted him and was rising to his feet.

"Uncle Lyman, sit yourself back down. Getting up looks like an awful struggle for you, and one you should not have to wage for me," said Chauncey with authentic affection and concern in his voice.

"That is kind of you, my boy, but if I start surrendering to the small skirmishes of old age, I will never win the battle," Lyman replied, and continued with his successful rise to his full height.

"That is a battle none of us is destined to win, Uncle Lyman," Chauncey said.

"Just another of the many reasons I miss your father. As long as a man has an older brother or sister, he doesn't feel so vulnerable. Now that I am the oldest Blair, my survival is very important to a lot of people."

"And I am one of them," said Chauncey warmly.

❦

Chauncey had a romantic feeling about the preceding generation. His father and uncle, and hundreds of men like them, had been admirably opportunistic, filled with entrepreneurial drive. They had come to this city when it was a swamp, where scavenger pigs were the earliest garbage collectors. By the time these gentlemen aged and died, Chicago had a symphony, an art institute, and a new university. In the 1830s, Chicago's growth was financed by capital from the east. Now Chicago banks financed projects all over the world.

By the 1870s, more than ten lumber ships an hour pulled into Chicago's port. Construction never ceased, and when the prairies bled into the forest, Chicago simply switched from horizontal to vertical growth. There were now more skyscrapers in Chicago than anywhere in the world. Engineers had built a water sewage system, which meant that when you turned on the tap, you no longer needed to fear that fish would accompany you into the bathtub.

That master of retail, Marshall Field, made a success of his mission to "give a woman what she wants," and what she wanted, by the millions, was to shop in one place for anything under the sun. To cater to his customers' convenience, and not coincidentally to his bottom line, he purchased cable cars that deposited eager shoppers within two feet of his front door.

But there was a darker side to Chicago by 1892. The Second City was often referred to as "the liquid city"—a saloon for every two hundred people. Rich and poor alike breathed the odor of the stockyards, especially on windy summer days.

It was a city of extreme contrasts, with newly dreamed cultural aspirations and low levels of depravity sometimes vying for the same urban space. The least well-kept secret in Chicago was the pervasiveness of prurience. In the Levee district, prostitutes plied their trade in rooms both elegant and filthy, some wood-paneled and others roach-infested, some carpeted with imported Belgian rugs, and some with holes in the floor. Patrons were lucky not to leave with splinters or syphilis. The rationale that prostitutes made the city safer for upstanding women by allowing men an outlet for their carnal desires was considered flimsy by many, especially those belonging to the growing temperance movement.

Chicago policemen, from patrolmen to captains, were paid handsomely to ignore what lay directly in front of them. One madam, Mary Hastings, was reported to have four upscale houses of ill-repute throughout the city; she paid up to $400 a week to officials to look the other way.

"So, Chauncey, how are Mim and the children? Three now, right?" asked Lyman. "Soon to be four, I am told. But let us order drinks and then get some food," Chauncey suggested, snapping his fingers for attention.

"Yes sir, Mr. Blair. What is your pleasure this afternoon?"

"I will have a sherry—very dry. Lyman, something to warm you?"

"Something a little stronger for me. Willard, can you bring me a whiskey?"

After the drinks came, Chauncey asked, "Will you be at the board meeting next Tuesday, Uncle Lyman?"

"Well, my boy, if it is the third Tuesday of the month, there is nowhere else I would consider being. I have not missed a directors' meeting in over 30 years. I am still the second largest shareholder now that your father's shares are yours. I am not casual about protecting that much money."

"Good. I wanted to talk to you about a matter I will bring before the directors. I want to be assured of your support, but I also need your honest assessment."

Chauncey awaited some comment from his uncle. Instead what he got was a stare and the sound of a delicate sip, so he proceeded, feigning more confidence than he felt. "An emissary from Jay Gould came to see me a few weeks ago and brought with him a proposal we must consider."

"Go on. I am intrigued. Gould has never come to Chicago for financing whether it be for his railroads or for the commodities he transports on them. I am told he controls forty percent of the gold in this country and it all travels on his rail lines."

"Well, it appears Mr. Gould wants to diversify his banking choices, and make our Merchant Bank part of the Gould network. He is planning to add another five thousand miles of track between here and Oregon over the next two years and he thinks a well-capitalized bank like ours would offer not only good rates but, perhaps more importantly, less scrutiny than prevails with his New York bankers. His reputation in the east has been besmirched beyond mere blemish. There is plenty of talk about his proclivity to bribe congressmen, local officials and even judges."

Lyman Blair had not moved a muscle since his nephew began speaking. "Is there more?" he asked.

"Not a great deal more, only that in addition to the financing for the additional track, Mr. Gould's representative talked at some length about the coupling of railroads and telegraph opportunities. Where the new rails go, the telegraph will follow, so we would have a chance to add that utility to our financial priorities."

Lyman thought that his nephew had paused, but in fact he had stopped. Sensing that he was expected to respond, Lyman said, "And now, before I opine, give me your thinking on this matter, because at the end of the day, your shares control the board. Only if I think you are making a colossal mistake will I publically argue against you. But it would be nice to be in agreement. So let's hear."

"Uncle Lyman, I will be blunt. I have been the nominal president of the bank since 1888, but until father's death everyone knew that he had control not only of the shares, but of me," Chauncey said.

"No, I would not say—" interjected Lyman.

"Well, I would. Fortunately, I have a strong reaction to Mr. Gould's proposal."

"As do I," said Lyman. "But please, you go first."

"I say 'no' to the deal and here is why. I have been taught since I was eight years old that the job of a bank is to loan money," Chauncey began, and then stopped to chuckle nostalgically.

"I remember when father first tried to explain to me how the banking system worked. I was flabbergasted that anyone would lend anything to anyone by choice, much less make a living at it. I had just lent my brand new baseball glove to my brother William and I never saw it again. So I confidently told my father that I would never lend another thing to anyone. His response? 'You will, son, you will.'

"There is a lesson in this digression. Banks have been lending too much of late. Credit is too easy and, just like my baseball glove, we may not get it back. I have taken a much more rigorous approach in trying to control this dangerous tendency.

"Our loan officers now know there is no point bringing me half the applications that would have been approved two years ago, because I will reject them. I have tightened up standards of credit and I stand by that decision. It has cost us some money short term, but in the long run we won't regret it."

Chauncey knew he'd best end his presentation soon, as Lyman was more than halfway through his second whiskey.

"In addition, there are signs of a slowdown most everywhere. As you know, I am the treasurer of the Chicago Mining Company, and the miners report orders are down twenty percent. Just yesterday, Martin Gaylord told me building construction is significantly behind where it was last year. And I hear that less than fifty percent of railroad shares will pay a dividend this year. We already have part of the Pullman account and it seems to me that is enough railroad exposure for now.

"The Exposition will protect us for a while," continued Chauncey, "but for every ten thousand jobs created to make the fair a reality, there will be ten thousand unemployed when the fair is over. I predict that the next five years will be hard in Chicago and in the country, maybe even traumatic."

His voice took on a sour tone that had not been there moments before. "I was forty-one when the riots broke out in Haymarket in 1886, when the city percolated with radicalism, so I know what anarchy smells like.

"Uncle Lyman, it seems to me that even today there is too much rail capacity, not too little. I cannot see where the growth is going to come from.

"So, on Tuesday, I will inform the board of Mr. Gould's proposal, allow for a discussion during which I will repeat what I have said to you. But at the end of the day, I will vote no, and I hope you will as well."

Lyman Blair smiled benevolently and said, "I am with you one hundred percent, and I am proud of you. I know your father would have been as well. But more than anything, I am beyond delight in thinking about Jay Gould's reaction when he learns Merchants Bank of Chicago has turned down his proposal. He is a first-class son of a bitch, from all I hear, so this is particularly satisfying. He will find his financing, of course, but rejecting Mr. Gould, who has bought and sold people as well as companies, will be something worthy of mention on your tombstone."

HERE LIES THE MAN WHO SAID "NO" TO JAY GOULD

A Productive Day

5

Winter 1892

HE ELITE FAMILIES OF CHICAGO had been dreaming of a World's Fair since the Great Fire of 1870. Such a spectacle would serve as a tribute to the resilience of the city. If their fathers and grandfathers were no longer alive to see the phoenix literally rising from the ashes, their sons and grandsons would create a monument to their achievements.

The cultural aristocracy of New York, who referred to Chicago as America's Second City, considered Chicago's bid as just that—second rate. They scoffed, wondering if Chicagoans really expected that millions of visitors from all over the world would be interested in going to the hinterlands of America, only to be greeted by noxious fumes from the stockyards. Could Chicago really guarantee the wind would blow only from a favorable direction for the six months of the fair?

Those who argued in behalf of New York City before the congressional committee responsible for making the final selection had sneeringly pointed out that 20 percent of all Chicago residents depended directly or indirectly on the stockyards for their livelihood. Would the municipal government mandate that Philip Armour, the meatpacking czar, fumigate his workers as they left the yards after each shift? Anti-Chicago partisans pointed out that the Chicago River flooded periodically, and the soil was too soft for significant building, forgetting to mention that Chicago had more skyscrapers than New York.

More threatening still, despite the efforts of the Protestant purifiers, there was a saloon for every 200 people, which might help explain why murder and mayhem were staples of Chicago life.

But the men who built Chicago prevailed. After eight ballots, Congress chose the city by the lake. The planning could begin in earnest.

Chauncey was a member of the board of the exposition company that was in charge of organizing the financing of the fair. As such, he took it as his personal responsibility to ask everyone he knew to be a bondholder. He peremptorily deducted proportionate monies from the wages of all the members of his staff; the Blair servants as a group were listed as investors. No other household in Chicago had that distinction.

Mim found Chauncey's action one of supreme arrogance, but he saw no problem, insisting that "none of the servants complained to me."

"Of course they have not complained to you," Mim scolded. "They know on which side their bread is buttered. But you have no right to demand that your servants support the exposition. It is the rich who want the fair, and it is the rich who should pay."

"The rich will pay aplenty, don't you worry. But if the fair is to be a true success, the whole city must play a part in it. We have sold thousands of ten-dollar bonds. I think our servants will be especially proud when they walk through the main entrance knowing that they have sacrificed something for the greater good."

Mim avoided extending the argument by ignoring the pomposity of Chauncey's tone. This took some doing.

But perhaps Chauncey was right on the merits. Their butler, Robert, had told Mim that he and Bertha were honored to be bondholders of the great exposition. It made them feel like real Americans and they were looking forward to Chicago Day when the fair would be open to only Chicagoans.

Both German, Bertha and Robert had arrived at 4830 Drexel Boulevard last May. They were honest and frugal and, most important, appreciated the critical quality in any servant—tight lips.

Robert had served in the German navy before coming to America, and though he was a mere seaman, he looked every inch the German officer—tall, dark and very handsome.

Bertha had been orphaned as a little girl and sent to live in Hamburg with a maternal aunt. Saving every penny, she bought passage to America.

Mim knew that many immigrants who sought work in service found it easier to find a job as a couple. She neither knew nor cared whether Bertha and Robert had a marriage of love or opportunity, or whether it was even a marriage at all. She liked them both and, no matter, she had a house to run, so she had never asked to see any paperwork confirming their relationship.

Mim would meet with the couple separately at the beginning of each week. With Robert she would review Mr. Blair's schedule, use of the carriage, what rooms needed special attention, any inadequately performed duties that had surfaced during the previous week, and any turmoil that had or might be brewing amongst the servants. Robert's management style meshed nicely with Mim's. He was neither an alarmist nor a minimizer and he intuitively understood which matters needed her intervention and those matters about which she need know nothing.

Mim marveled at how accomplished a cook Bertha had become, having arrived in America with no particular skill. But she was smart and resourceful, took criticism constructively and acted on it. She was "coming along nicely," as Grandmother Mitchell used to say. She could now roast a chicken to perfection, prepare a saddle of lamb and, just last week had created a beef Wellington that was equal to anything Mim had eaten at the Palmer House Hotel.

❦

"Thank you, Robert," Mim said distractedly. She looked up from her needlepoint at the envelope and instantly recognized the distinctive handwriting of Cissie Palmer on the cream-colored paper. The ink too was unique. It was an onyx-green. No one in Chicago had been able to replicate that particular color, and those who had tried were frowned upon as being too obviously aspirational.

It was hard for Mim to understand how an inanimate object like a cream-colored envelope could carry so much authority simply sitting on a silver tray. Those who counted knew that Cissie Palmer wrote and addressed her own letters when she wanted to relate something important. This note from Cissie almost certainly had to do with the exposition.

Mrs. Palmer was the president of the Board of Lady Managers for the Women's Pavilion, a board of 117 women comprised of females from each of the 44 states. There were nine on the board from Chicago, and Mary Mitchell Blair was the youngest amongst them.

It was widely rumored that George Pullman had lobbied hard in behalf of his wife's appointment to chair the decorative arts committee. One of the few people in Chicago who could withstand such forceful pressure, Cissie Palmer had appointed Mim. Her work for the Antiquarian Society for the Decorative Arts, her own reputation as a collector, her close association with Martin Gaylord and the power of the woman who selected her proved to be enough to mute any voices of public dissent.

Mim Dear:

I hope you are well. I know you must be busy as you begin to build a collection of decorative arts for display in the Women's Building at the exposition.

I have some additional suggestions for you, which I will give you when I see you.

The reason I write is that there is something important I need to ask of you. It requires the utmost confidentiality as well as expediency. Therefore, I will see you tomorrow for lunch at noon.

Appreciatively,

Cissie

Hmmm, Mim thought to herself. *Appreciatively.* This sign-off raised the probability that if Mim agreed to do whatever it was that Cissie wanted, she would be appreciated indeed.

Mim liked Cissie Palmer, who was several years her senior. They were in the same cycling club and Chauncey had handled many of Potter's real estate transactions. But more than that, Mim respected Cissie Palmer. With her wealth, she could easily have chosen a life of opulence without engagement, but Cissie instead chose to be visible in all the cultural institutions of the city. It was fair to say that without Cissie and Potter Palmer, there would have been no art institute, symphony or the recently completed Auditorium Theater. And while the major funds for the new university had come primarily from John D. Rockefeller, the Palmers had stood alongside in philanthropic support. Without these institutions of cultural maturity, Chicago would never have been considered a site for the World's Fair.

As much as Mim respected Cissie, they had very different tastes in art.

"At the moment, she is smitten with that new group of French painters you are recommending to me," Mim said to Martin. "I try to like them but they do nothing for my soul!"

Never a faddist, Mim's taste remained devoutly classical, or as Martin Gaylord would say, "unnecessarily restrained." It was a mystery to Mim what there was to admire about the Impressionists.

"How could anyone favor a canvas of colorful mush over my newest love?"

Mim had recently purchased a fourth-century Greek sculpture of a lovely young girl. There was no ambiguity about her darling's beauty. She had wavy hair, most of which was pulled back into a knot at the back of her strong neck. She posed with an ever so slight and completely enchanting inclination of her head to the left, as though she were suspicious of what she was hearing.

Mim liked this woman. Wisps of hair fell casually around her face and there was a gentle indentation in her hair where she appeared to be wearing a ribbon. *Imagine that*, thought Mim. *A ribbon. A simple hair ribbon on a young girl in ancient Greece. This simple act of a woman putting a ribbon in her hair transcended all the intervening wars, natural calamities, and empires.*

Yesterday's mail had brought compelling news for someone building a significant Medieval collection. The same dealer from whom she had purchased the statue of the Greek girl wrote to inquire about her level of interest in a magnificent fourteenth-century Book of Hours, possibly owned by Margaret of Beauford, mother of Henry Tudor. If it were authentic and as beautiful as he had described it, oh yes indeed, she would be more than interested.

"Well, Mim, you are marching through the centuries, aren't you? Quite a leap from fourth-century Greece to fourteenth-century France," teased Martin when she told him of the inquiry.

Then he looked more intently at her and asked, "I don't suppose you would consider meeting me in New York should I find another Book of Hours or something else suitable? You will need to see anything I find, for you will be the best judge of its quality."

The logic of Martin's argument was solid, but the sudden jolt she felt in her stomach at the idea of traveling to New York to meet him confused her. She had never thought of him in an amorous way.

She knew that most women found Martin very attractive. His nose was too big, but his mouth was full-lipped and his sleepy, hazel eyes were set off by eyelashes that appeared outlandish on a man. His voice was often too loud and his opinions too strong, though he got away with more than most men because he was entertaining and clearly liked women.

"Martin, until I have finished with the acquisitions for the Women's Building, I am not going anywhere."

"Mim, recognizing that a Book of Hours can be a magnificent work of art, can you tell me what explains your dogged, no, almost obsessive interest in having one in your collection?"

"Yes, Martin. I think I can. A Book of Hours is a spiritual experience for me. Vastly more spiritual than the countless hours I have spent on my knees at Grace Church. I can just picture the monks hunched over their parchments in the scriptorium, sweltering in the summer and icy cold in winter. I can feel their fingers frozen into a stylus, hour after hour, only stopping for the daily prayers. Can you see their rheumy eyes searching for the precise vertical and horizontal lines to create a letter? Can you imagine the hours the illuminators spent crushing the lapis lazuli into powder until the perfect blue was achieved? And all this for the glory of God?"

"No, Mim, I cannot," answered Martin. "But I love that you can."

Mim knew the note from Cissie Palmer was a command rather than a request. This was the woman whom all Chicago called "The Queen." Mim also knew that Chauncey would insist that she go. He never turned down an opportunity to associate with Potter Palmer and he urged Mim to develop every relationship she could with the Palmer family. Mim moved to her own desk and penned a short, affirmative response, summoned Robert and sent the message on its way.

Construction of the Palmer "Castle" was completed in 1882, and ten years later it still dwarfed any other residential structure in Chicago. There was no mistaking the message the Palmers sent when they installed no external doorknobs on the house. Even invited guests required layers of servants to admit them. Entry into the mansion required a calling card, which would be examined by an assortment of servants—twenty-five maids, butlers and social secretaries. It was said that even Mrs. Palmer's closest friends were required to write in advance for an appointment. However, as a guest who was expected, and in this case commanded, Mim gained entry with a minimum of fanfare.

The "Castle" was a mélange of styles, all exquisitely executed: a French drawing room, Victorian library, Spanish music room, and English dining room. Mim had been in the dining room many times and though today it was empty, she had seen it filled with fifty or more seated guests, footmen stationed behind every other chair. Potter Palmer's favorite portrait of his wife dominated the vast space. If Mrs. Palmer was dining in her usual place, directly below the portrait, the effect was as intimidating as if the guests were dining with two queens.

Mim's favorite spot in the Palmer's home was the three-storied octagonal entry hallway. The mosaic floor astonished her every time she saw it. She coveted every inch of it.

"I have a recurring dream," she told Chauncey every time they returned from dinner with the Palmers.

"On a summer night when the household is vacationing, I adorn myself in black and storm the Castle, delicately removing the mosaic, tile by tile. I am so happy. But then it turns into a nightmare. I try to restore the mosaic in *our* foyer, only to realize I have forgotten the pattern so that no matter how hard I try, I cannot. I awake crying!"

Cissie received Mim in her sitting room, which immediately reinforced what Cissie's note had implied. Something serious was indeed afoot. The room was not Cissie's inner sanctum, but it was close. While the formal Palmer art collection was housed in the downstairs gallery, some of the choicest pieces were displayed in Cissie's suite of rooms on the second floor. Mim recognized two Childe Hassams, not unlike the one she had recently bought. Every inch of the wall's pale yellow brocade wallpaper was filled with the frame of one masterpiece touching the frame of the next.

Too cluttered, thought Mim.

"Mim, dear, thank you so much for coming," said Cissie, rising from her desk. Mim was usually suspicious of applied Southern charm, but her previous encounters with Cissie led Mim to believe that Cissie's Kentucky roots only augmented her natural inclination to genuine warmth. Cissie pecked her on the cheek before gesturing for Mim to join her at the round red and black lacquered table set for lunch.

"As I mentioned in my note, I do have a favor, a rather large favor, to ask of you, but first tell me how you are, as well as how Chauncey and the children are faring."

"All quite well, thank you. We took Italia to the Palmer House restaurant to celebrate her birthday last week and she is still talking about the grandeur of it. We had to go back to the barbershop three times so she could assure herself there were real silver dollars embedded in the floor," Mim replied.

"I have never known a child who did not find that floor fascinating. Most of them have plans for how to extricate the money. Someone will some day," Cissie said.

"Let's just hope it is not Italia and a gangster boyfriend. She is a handful."

"Yes, but a beautiful handful, I hear," said Cissie.

"I am not at all certain I wouldn't rather have a beautiful Rembrandt than a beautiful eight-year-old. Anyway, we had a lovely evening and a delicious dinner. Italia felt quite special."

"Did they offer you our newest delicacy?" Cissie asked. "It's called a 'brownie.' It is all chocolate and the people who have tasted it think it is going to be the rage. They are not yet available for general consumption, as they will be unveiled for our guests during the Exposition. But the staff do occasionally offer them to preferred customers, and you and Chauncey are certainly that."

"In fact, we all had the brownie. The waiter even offered to pack some up to take home to the other children. They were unlike any cake I have ever tasted. I asked for the recipe so Bertha could make them, but we were told it is a state secret. So Bertha will have to experiment," Mim said with a conspiratorial smile.

"I will see to it that you get the recipe, but not until after the fair closes. We need to make every guest who eats one feel as special as you did."

No brownies were on today's menu. But the meal was lovely. The poached salmon with watercress sauce and decorative sliced cucumber was served on the Havilland china trimmed in 24-carat gold that Cissie had bought in Paris, largely for the Palmer House. But she kept some for use at home. Wine was offered and declined by both women. A few delightful anise madeleines were served as a light dessert.

Throughout lunch Mim felt more and more as if she were being wooed, but she was growing frustrated at being unable to imagine in what form the request would come.

"Well, my dear, it has been lovely catching up, but we must get down to business," Cissie said, rearranging her body as well as her tone. "Can you tell me how far along you and your committee are in the acquisition of decorative arts for our building? I am returning to New York at the end of the month, so you must let me know what pieces you still need for your displays. The collection must maintain its focus. Most, if not all of the objects, must be created by women, preferably American women. I see quilts from Kentucky, ceramics from Pennsylvania, and embroidery from every corner of the country.

"I have begun working with Sarah Hallowell. You know Sarah, do you not? If you don't, you must," said Cissie. Without waiting for a response from Mim, she continued, "Anyway, she is from Philadelphia and a graduate of the Pennsylvania Academy of Fine Arts. A first-rate eye. She will be a good resource for you."

Mim had strongly supported Cissie's idea that the art inside the building be created by and appeal to women. She had heard that Sarah Hallowell had been instrumental in convincing Cissie to consider the American artist, Mary Cassatt, to do a large mural at the entrance. Mim presumed that since Miss Cassatt was reputed to be an intimate of the Impressionists, the mural would likely reflect that genre.

Cissie stopped and Mim sensed that it was her turn to speak (not that a conversation with Cissie Palmer was a question of "turns").

"We are progressing nicely. I recently met with Mr. Ames at the Art Institute. We will be able to use many items from their permanent collection, particularly items related to interior design, which I am pleased about. We have some wallpaper samples from a woman designer in Boston to represent the growing interest of American women in decorating.

"I had an exciting piece of news in a letter this morning from Margaret Ames from California, who will loan us a magnificent chest of drawers from Washington's home in Mount Vernon. I think we should buy it after the exposition for the Antiquarian Society's permanent collection. If they don't want to buy it, I will. A piece that beautiful should not be in a backwater like San Francisco."

"Mim, dear, that is not like you. You are talking to someone who has done quite well coming from the backwater of Kentucky," Cissie teased. Then she continued, "Tell me, dear, have you been out to the site recently? If so, I would be interested in your assessment of the progress on our building, as well as your impression of Miss Hayden's work thus far."

The Miss Hayden of whom Cissie Palmer spoke was the architect of the Women's Building. Mim sensed that whatever answer she gave was connected to the reason she had been sent for. She would be honest but cautious until she could better discern Cissie's direction.

"I have been out to the site, and I think Miss Hayden's concept is stunning. You should be proud that you selected her as the architect. You took a risk with someone so untested, not to mention a woman who is only 21 years old. I think she will make all women proud in the end. I cannot imagine the indignity of having a man design the Women's Building this close to the beginning of the twentieth century."

Cissie paused before replying,

"I am glad you think so highly of her intellect and skill," Cissie said. "But as you may have heard, her personal qualities are frankly less impressive. Her strengths come at a cost. And it is this cost that brings me to ask a rather large favor of you."

Mim often observed that petitioners grow more uncomfortable the closer they get to the moment when they put their wishes into words. People look down, shift in their seats, lower their voices, as if diminished volume would lessen the significance of the favor. This was not the case with Cissie Palmer, who grew more regal the closer she got to the gist of her plea. In the few seconds it took her to utter the next words, she looked like an American Queen Victoria.

"My dear, this is not a favor for me personally, though it would certainly make my life easier. I am not exaggerating when I say that the success of the Women's Building may depend on your answer."

∽

Mim pressed the foot buzzer under the carpet in the dining room, summoning Robert.

"Robert, please tell Bertha that dinner was delicious tonight. As you can see,

Mr. Blair has finished the apple charlotte and the only reason mine is untouched is that I continue to be a little under the weather. Since I will retire early, we will take our coffee here tonight, along with some Madeira for Mr. Blair."

"Yes, Mrs. Blair," said Robert. Though it was commonly discussed among the servants, Robert wondered when the Blairs would acknowledge Mrs. Blair's pregnancy.

"Will that be all?"

"Yes, thank you," said Chauncey, "and again, extend our compliments to Bertha. You can leave the Madeira on the table. I will put it back when Mrs. Blair and I finish our conversation."

"Thank you, sir. I hope you are soon feeling better, Mrs. Blair," Robert said as he exited.

With Robert dismissed and her body aching for bed, Mim began laying the groundwork for acquiring Chauncey's approval. What a joy it would be to rule her roost the way Cissie Palmer did. How much easier life would be if she could simply say, "Chauncey dear, Miss Sophie Hayden, the architect of the Women's Building at the Exposition, is coming to live with us until she has completed her work. It shouldn't be for more than six months."

In her fantasy, Chauncey would reply, "Whatever you say, dear," and that would be that.

"Have some Madeira, darling," she said, returning to reality.

"Thank you, I think I will. I am sorry you cannot join me. I gather you are still feeling subpar."

"Better every day, but not fully free of evening ennui. I am well in the mornings this time, but by nightfall, I am spent."

"Is it time to think of names yet?" asked Chauncey.

"I think we should just name the baby Chauncey, be it a boy or a girl. There are so many Chaunceys in the Blair family now that if we simply summon 'Chauncey,' someone will likely come running."

After this light banter, Mim segued into her more serious purpose.

"Speaking of names, does the name Sophia Hayden mean anything to you?"

Chauncey took a stab, "It sounds familiar, but only distantly. Someone from the Fortnightly Club?"

"No. Actually, she is a very accomplished professional woman. She is the architect of the Women's Building. She was the first woman graduate of something called the Massachusetts Institute of Technology. I think it's in Boston."

"Close, it is in Cambridge, which is across the river from Boston. Very good school, though. Does Miss Hayden have anything to do with naming our forthcoming child?"

"Well, if she could carry it for the next five months in my place, I would be happy to name the baby Sophia," said Mim.

"At any rate, this is an enormous project for Miss Hayden. It is her first contract. Cissie took quite a chance on hiring her, but her designs carried the day and the early construction is on time and on budget, and, while not brilliant, it is impressive. I think it will be a success. But at the moment, Miss Hayden has the weight of the masculine world on her shoulders and—"

"That is a weight she took on herself," interrupted Chauncey.

"Unfortunately, she is not handling the pressure well at all, according to Cissie, with whom I had lunch this afternoon. Providing the remedy to this unfortunate development is where we come in."

Chauncey chortled and said, "Oh, I see where this is going. Cissie wants you to be the construction overseer because Miss Hayden is buckling."

Mim had to laugh at this idea. She could envision herself setting out each morning to ride herd over burly marble installers who would just love taking orders from an hysterical woman.

"Please go on, Mim. My curiosity is increasing with each passing moment."

"It seems Miss Hayden is living alone at the Palmer House Hotel and, while that sounds like a delicious luxury to me at the moment, she has broken down in the dining room twice this week and had to be escorted to her room, frail and weeping. She is not eating and is terribly thin. Cissie is worried that she is having a breakdown. That would be a personal tragedy for Miss Hayden, of course, but it would also be a disaster for the completion of the Women's Building.

"Cissie has spoken to Dr. Mills, who was called in to treat her, and both of them feel that her isolation exacerbates her fraying nerves. Dr. Mills suggests she would fare better in someone's home—some place where there was a family, children, a less impersonal existence.

"So Cissie has asked if we could accommodate Miss Hayden here for the duration of her work."

There, it was out. Mim instantly felt unburdened.

"Mimsy, if Cissie is so concerned about her, why not make her comfortable in the most luxurious house in Chicago—her own?" countered Chauncey.

Mim was ready for that one.

"Miss Hayden does not want the most luxurious house in Chicago. She is not thriving in The Palmer House, which is the most luxurious hotel in Chicago. The idea is a place with noise, activity and companionship."

"Well, we can certainly give her noise and activity. But please, Mimsy, have no expectation that *I* will give her companionship," Chauncey said.

Mim knew now that she had her victory.

"I will be happy to keep her company, because I think she will be an interesting addition here, but I doubt she will need much. She will be working all day, and I suspect most nights. Besides, while Mildred is too young to notice, I think it will be good for Italia and CB to get their first look at a modern American woman, an accomplished working woman."

"Mim, I must warn you, if Miss Hayden is one of those aggressive and masculine suffragettes, I will ask her to leave. The last thing we need is for Italia to be marching around this house with banners, bantering about society's terrible sins against women."

Best claim victory and escape, thought Mim. "Darling, I thank you for your cooperation in this matter. It will not be lost on Cissie, and therefore on Potter, that we have done them a very, very big favor," said Mim, with a warm smile at her husband. It was a smile that reflected her affection for this man, who at heart was generous and good if not enlightened. As she left Chauncey that night, he was moving both his Madeira and himself into the smoking room. And she was moving her weary bones to bed, satisfied that she had had a very productive day.

Work In Progress

6

Winter 1892

M ISS SOPHIA HAYDEN TURNED OUT to be the antithe-
sis of a firebrand. Mim found her houseguest surprisingly
insecure for a multi-talented woman. She was so remote,
so timid in asking for any attention from the household staff, that Mim
worried she was not doing right by her honored guest. The only meal at
which the family saw Miss Hayden was breakfast. There, both Mim and
Chauncey tried to engage her in conversation, with little success.

Ever since their childhood, Mim and her sister Hortense had been
warned that the rules governing manners at table were inviolable—the
clearest reflection of a woman's gentility and upbringing. Miss Hayden
had obviously learned from a different teacher, or, more likely, no teacher
at all.

To his credit, Chauncey tried to draw her out. He was quite sweet,
asking her questions about her training at MIT and when she had decided
to become an architect. He solicited her views on the talents of the architect Frank Lloyd Wright, who was making a name for himself around the

city. Most of Miss Hayden's responses were monosyllabic, and when they weren't, they were delivered with downcast eyes, as if the inquisitor were speaking to her from somewhere between the table and the rug.

Mim gave a dinner party for Miss Hayden two weeks into her stay. Purposefully, she had limited the guest list, thinking that a small number of diners would be psychologically manageable for someone so shy and socially maladroit. She had invited her younger sister, Hortense Mitchell; Daniel Armour, the nephew of Phillip Armour and, for a little spice, Edith Rockefeller McCormick and her husband Harold. Harold was a nice man who knew well his responsibilities as a dinner partner (meaning Miss Hayden need not worry about carrying the conversation. If need be, Harold would carry it for both of them).

At the last minute, Mr. McCormick was called out of town on business. Most wives would have offered to withdraw from the party altogether, but it never would have occurred to Edith that she would be unwelcome anywhere.

As it turned out, the evening was delightful. Hortense looked especially pretty and charmed young Mr. Armour. Edith was her best and worst self. Mim enjoyed both.

After a serving of Bertha's delicious strawberry trifle, while sipping some of Chauncey's best port, Edith, unafraid to engineer conversation to topics of her own interest, treated the dinner party to her observations on the steamy details of Dr. Freud's analysis.

"Really, Americans should loosen up about discussing sex," Edith stated without a trace of the embarrassment that instantly engulfed the other diners. "Dr. Freud says our sexual impulses are not only completely normal, but their suppression makes us all neurotic."

All her life, Mim had obeyed the rules of good breeding. She took pride in doing so. But every so often she longed to say or do something completely out of character. For Edith, startling behavior *was* her character.

It would have been most interesting that evening to observe Miss Hayden's reaction to the outlandish revelations of Edith Rockefeller McCormick, but that turned out to be impossible because Miss Hayden failed to appear at the party in her honor. When she arrived at the Blairs' at nine-thirty, claiming that a crisis had kept her at the Women's Building site, the dinner guests were just leaving. Miss Hayden fashioned a limp apology and disappeared into her room.

So retiring was Miss Hayden at the Blair home, Mim wondered how in the world she mustered the authority to oversee the workers at the construction site. She would soon find out, for she had an appointment the following week with Sara Tyson Hallowell and Miss Hayden. Sara wanted to review the inventory of decorative arts with Miss Hayden, in case there were any important gaps to be filled before the fair opened. Perhaps Mim would see a side of Sophia in her element that was not discernable at home.

Mim's greatest fear, when Robert asked if he and Bertha could meet with her, was that they had found employment elsewhere. She had heard the old adage that no one was irreplaceable but rejected its verity at the moment. The thought of trying to find replacements for two key household positions on the eve of the birth of a new baby and an exposition filled her with a dread bordering on panic.

"Good Morning," Mim said as warmly as she could to the couple she suspected was about to desert her. Usually she was quite good at reading a face, but today their faces defied scrutiny. "Is everything running smoothly downstairs?" Mim prompted.

"Oh yes, Mrs. Blair," they said in nervous unison. Bertha continued. "We have asked to see you because our circumstances will soon change and we wanted to give you some advance notice."

Mim heard the word "notice" and an involuntary spasm gripped her momentarily.

"Do go on," Mim encouraged, wanting this to be over as soon as possible. Already she was calculating whom she could contact and how long it might be until the house was running smoothly again.

Robert looked to be at a loss for words and nodded towards Bertha to speak for them.

"Well, Mrs. Blair, it would seem that I am expecting a baby sometime this spring. We wanted to tell you ourselves and give you the opportunity to find someone else should you wish no disruption in the management of the household.

"Mind you, you and Mr. Blair have made us feel very welcome and if we could, we would be more than happy to stay—for, well, you know, for the whole while. I am young and strong and could work until the end. Once the baby is born, I should be up on my feet in no time."

Mim wondered if they had heard her sigh of relief, and if so, she hoped now to conceal her initial selfishness with a sincere expression of congratulations.

"I am so very happy for you. You will make wonderful parents. Be mindful that it is more difficult than it looks!

"Mr. Blair and I appreciate all your good work for us, and we will do what we can to make these next months as easy for you as we can. In other words, we want you and your family here. Have you had any medical attention? Seen a midwife?"

"Oh no, Mrs. Blair," said Bertha with a smile. "I grew up on a farm in Germany. No one in Germany uses a midwife unless there is trouble, and I know of no one who has ever seen a doctor. Work is the best agent for good health."

Mim thought Bertha was likely right. She herself had delivered three babies at home, but always under the care of Mrs. Miller, the midwife. Dr. Stephens was available, should he be required, though Mim suspected that Mrs. Miller knew vastly more about childbirth than he did.

"Just the same, Bertha, I want you to share the good care that I enjoy. As you may have guessed from my weak stomach of late, I am going to have a baby in the summer. Mrs. Miller will be making several visits before then, and I will send her to check on you after she has seen me. We will take no chances with any baby coming into this house."

Robert and Bertha looked as relieved to depart as Mim felt seeing them go. Such intimacies were best kept short and to the point.

⁓

To many in Chicago, the World's Fair had come to symbolize the possibility that their city could become a modern, utopian metropolis. As Mim made her way through the building debris on her way to meet Miss Hayden and Mrs. Halloway, she despaired that the transformation of Chicago would ever be at hand. Some areas had been landscaped and from a distance looked lovely, but the manure from the stockyards had been used as fertilizer, so the closer one came, the further away one wanted to be.

Each day, as many as five thousand people observed this beehive of activity. Originally free passes had been distributed, but now the exposition authorities were charging fifty cents for the right to gawk, and still they came.

There were, however, a few signs of hope. An enormous monument by Daniel Chester French, called the *Statue of the Republic*, had recently been installed at one end of the enormous tidal basin whose waters dominated the fairgrounds. The huge female statue had been conceived as an integral component of the landscape of the fairgrounds, announcing to all who saw her that Chicago was the embodiment of American optimism.

Early for her appointment, Mim chose to be a sightseer for a few minutes. She walked west toward the lagoon and the Women's Building. The White City was the informal name given to the whole of the exposition, but in truth that term described only those buildings sited around the lagoon. Even in an unfinished state, these majestic structures looked as if the snow gods had appropriated large amounts of white powder and sprinkled it liberally. Since plans called for the exposition to be electrified, Mim could only imagine how magical it would look at night.

Exotic buildings dotted the landscape— pagodas, kiosks, pavilions and some structures for which Mim did not even know the proper term. They offered millions of Chicagoans, who otherwise would never have traveled beyond their own ethnic neighborhoods, elevated trains and daunting skyscrapers, a ticket to the wonders of the world.

The beauty of this idea touched Mim, as if her small part in the advancement of the fair were ennobling, as if it made her a better person. She sometimes wondered how she would justify herself to her maker when she approached the pearly gates. Often her prayers wandered into convoluted explanations about why she had done this or that. Though it was the only life she had ever known, she doubted that dinner parties, travel and needlepoint constituted what our Lord had in mind when he called his disciples to serve the meek and the poor. Perhaps the Lord could find some merit in her work for the fair that would offset her otherwise dilettantish life.

As she passed the Turkish exhibit, she stopped abruptly. It was unlike any other building she had ever seen. It appeared to be made entirely of wood in alternating dark and light hues, none indigenous to America.

She had heard that this building had been designed by a Chicago architect, but if that were true, he must have had Turkish blood pumped into his veins as he worked on it. She might have liked it better if only it had not vaguely reminded her of the work of Frank Lloyd Wright, whose work she abhorred. It was one thing to have an authentic replica of a Turkish temple at a world exposition. It was quite another to have Mr. Wright's work spoil otherwise gracious neighborhoods throughout the city.

Still, when it was finished, she would definitely return to see the interior of this unique edifice.

As she approached the two-story Women's Building, Mim knew instantly that it would not take its place as one of the great examples of world architecture.

Mim was no judge of accurate measurement but she remembered that the plans called for almost 80,000 square feet of space. She looked up and saw that Alice Rideout's statuary had been installed on each of the four corners of the exterior. Mim had seen them in the studio and had admired them. Each depicted an allegorical statement about women. She had been shocked by one of the statues, the Spirit of Civilization, torch and all, hovering over an obviously downtrodden woman wrapped in a cap and gown, desperately searching for an education that had been withheld from her, presumably by the male power structure.

Mim thought it so confrontational she wondered if it would survive scrutiny. The men she knew would loathe it and dismiss it as the work of an angry suffragette. Even she, who understood the validity of the point it made, thought it unnecessarily disheartening.

The women she knew were extremely well educated and would take understandable offense at this representation of all womankind. If the goal of the Women's Building was to highlight the advancement of women, surely a more uplifting statue would have been a better choice.

❧

"Good morning, Mrs. Blair," said Sara Tyson Hallowell, extending Mim a gloved hand.

"Good morning to you, Mrs. Hallowell. And please call me 'Mary,' " Mim replied.

"Only if you will call me 'Sara.' "

Mim had anticipated being engaged and impressed by Cissie Palmer's artistic alter ego, Sara Hallowell. What she was not expecting was the presence of Hattie Pullman. Like most of Chicago, or at least anyone who read Madame X's society column in the *Tribune*, Mim was aware that "a well-known railroad magnate was fuming that his wife had been excluded from a prominent role on the arts committee." Perhaps Cissie had capitulated and Hattie was now her co-chair. Such was the power of George Pullman's influence.

"How very nice to see you, Hattie," lied Mim.

"I hope you don't mind my tagging along, Mary," responded Hattie. "I have been pestering Cissie to let me help and when I heard you were coming today, I said it would be quite the daisy if I could be here with you."

Mim smiled graciously, disguising her revulsion at this banal turn of phrase.

Hattie Pullman is made of milquetoast. I could never work with her. She is a shopper, not a serious collector. Her home is unimaginative and without a point of view. A partnership with her will never work, thought Mim.

Sara Hallowell interrupted Mim's spiraling negative thoughts.

"Mim, I have worked with Mrs. Palmer for some time now, and I have never heard her speak so glowingly about another collector as she does of you."

"Well, that is most gracious of her since we do not always share the same opinion. But I respect her enormously. I hear that you and she are heading to New York for the final buying trip before the opening of the exposition."

"Yes, we are leaving a week from tomorrow, so I am meeting with the each of the committee chairs to see what omissions there may be in each collection. We still have time to fill any holes."

"There are no holes. Too much trivial hodgepodge has accumulated already," said a loud and masculine voice from behind them. It was such a strong, petulant voice that Mim at first did not recognize it. Women she knew did not speak that loudly or gruffly.

"Hello, Miss Hayden," said Mim softly, attempting to ameliorate the harshness of her interruption. In uttering her surname, it struck Mim how odd it was that despite six weeks of living under the same roof and being over a decade her junior, Miss Hayden had never asked Mim to call her Sophia.

"Mrs. Hallowell, Hattie, this is Miss Sophia Hayden, the competition-winning architect of the Women's Building. And isn't she doing a superb job?"

Sara Hallowell smiled and said, "I have met Miss Hayden on a number of occasions, and yes, I do think the building quite wonderful. I also have a feeling that it may be the first of the major buildings to be completed on time, which would add to Miss Hayden's triumph."

Sophia Hayden's workday outfit struck Mim as perfect funeral attire. She had a nice figure, and a sweet face, so Mim supposed it was a strategic but effective move to diminish her femininity. Every aspect of the architect's appearance was unrelentingly dour. She was one of those people whom one wanted to avoid lest their melancholia prove contagious.

Miss Hayden interjected, "I don't have much time to give you a proper tour of the progress we have made, but you are more than welcome to look around after our meeting. Come, I will show you both to my office."

Mim tried to keep pace with her guide down the Gallery of Honor, which ran through the heart of the building. As they approached the end of the long hall, Mim paused mid-step.

"Miss Hayden, we must stop here for a moment. I have not yet seen the fully rendered Cassat mural and I see that the installation is now complete."

Mim had stopped suddenly, as did Sara Hallowell. Remarkably, Miss Hayden marched on, trailed by Hattie Pullman.

Mim had been more than tolerant during the weeks that Miss Hayden had been a guest in her home. Several friends proposed beatification. But she was not going to be rushed past this stunning mural. She stood her ground and simply stared. Her first thought was, *Oh God, how wrong I have been.*

Years later, when recounting her reaction to Mary Cassatt's brilliant mural, the word she kept coming back to was "glee." The triptych blazed with strong color in each of the three panels. Mim had often found such color in the work of the impressionists ostentatious, but here it was celebratory. The grass, found in all three panels, was blue-green, yellow-green, green-green. It was joyful green wherever it grew. The blues, yellows and purples were equal in vibrancy. Such colors perfectly fit the exuberance of *The Modern Women*—some purposeful, some playful, some a combination of both. *If this is what the modern woman is, I want to be one*, thought Mim.

Sara could sense that Mim was in another world so she was gentle in her intrusion. "Your reaction, please?"

"Magnificent," was all that Mim could manage, so Sara continued.

"Mrs. Palmer will be very pleased. She loves the mural, but she was concerned that your eye might not see it the same way. When I see her later today, her first remark will be, 'tell me about Mrs. Blair's reaction to the mural.' "

"Magnificent," Mim repeated. "I have never admired anything quite as much. I feel as though my heart has wandered far afield from its normal classical boundaries."

What she next thought but did not say was that Martin Gaylord would be proud of her.

At that moment, a young clerk stepped towards the two women to curtly announce, with more imperiousness than his young years or lowly station deserved, "Ladies, Miss Hayden has been waiting."

Mim had had enough of Sophia Hayden.

"Please tell Miss Hayden that Mrs. Hallowell and I will be with her when we are finished here, no sooner and no later."

"Brava," Sara replied. "I understand Miss Hayden has been living in a man's world for some time. I understand she has met with hostility and cynicism since she first won the competition. But it would be so much more helpful to have her act as an exemplar of manners. Doing so would better showcase her obvious talent. I have tried to be cordial, but I am afraid we have an insecure architect who wants to control the interiors of buildings as well. Which, frankly, she has little talent for."

Mim was undeterred in her focus on the mural. She wanted to know everything about it and about Mary Cassatt. Knowing that Sara Hallowell had been the midwife to its birth, she asked, "Tell me what you know about it, will you?"

"As you may know, Miss Cassatt was not the first choice for the assignment. But when Elizabeth Gardner declined the offer, I immediately suggested Mary. I had come to know her in Paris; I believe she will become the most important American woman Impressionist of the century. I suspect there will be criticism of the work, so your imprimatur will be useful. *The Modern Women* will need allies."

"I think you and Cissie overestimate my influence, but I will be happy to lend any defense necessary—"

She paused as she saw Miss Hayden's assistant reappear. Before he had come within twenty feet of them, Mim cut him off. "Young man, please leave us be. Tell Miss Hayden and Mrs. Pullman that Mrs. Hallowell and I want some time to linger. We will be along when we are finished here."

Mim returned her attention to Sara Hallowell and observed, "It does not look to me as though Miss Cassatt has used traditional Parisian models for her mural. Can that be true?"

"Quite right," said Sara Hallowell. "She rejected urban models in their silks and satins. In fact, she had ordered some haute couture gowns for her models, and then reconsidered. Instead, she opted for country girls and women, females who worked and played with exuberance, not delicacy.

"The girls in the first panel run. They don't saunter. The women of the middle panel stretch their bodies into the trees to pick the ripened fruit. They load, heave and carry heavy baskets."

Mim, who had not taken her eyes off the triptych, said, "These women are full of life. They are hardy and happy, as if they are exulting in their growing independence. I have two daughters and I hope they grow to embody the modernity Miss Cassatt envisions for women of the twentieth century."

"I guess we have put off the tyrannical Miss Hayden long enough," Sara Hallowell said, adding, "Mim, it has been a real pleasure watching you respond to this mural. You understood immediately what Miss Cassett was hoping to achieve.

"My friend, Monsieur Rodin, will exhibit here as well. Be sure to take a look and, after the exposition, you may want to consider adding him to your collection."

Mim smiled and took a chance that she could tease her newest friend. "Well, let's not rush me to radicalism. I have made more progress today than anyone who knows my collection would expect."

"I understand. I understand," said Sara Hallowell, enjoying the repartee. "But today's radical departure need not lead to radicalism, just a fresh eye."

Mim paused. "Before we enter the lioness' den, I need to be direct with you. Is Cissie still comfortable with her choice of me as chairwoman of the decorative arts committee?"

Sara Hallowell gave a slight grin and answered, "She is as delighted as she was when she designated you. Why do you ask?"

"I was simply wondering if Mrs. Pullman's presence here today was an indication that Cissie might want us to share the responsibility. It is no secret that George Pullman has felt his wife has been unfairly overlooked."

Sara Hallowell's grin now turned into a full and warm smile. "Mary, I have no idea why Hattie Pullman showed up here today. Mrs. Palmer certainly did not suggest that she come, and I think she will find it irksome that she appeared. Without revealing too much, I can tell you that Mrs. Palmer thinks Mrs. Pullman's knowledge of and taste in art is—well, let's just say, common."

As they continued their walk, Mim's heart softened towards Miss Hayden. There was not a woman anywhere on the premises. It could not be easy to be a twenty-one-year-old woman, girl really, and to have to struggle each day giving orders to what Mim now saw as a male hunting party, each member with his weapon aimed directly at the woman in charge. Such sympathy evaporated when, after she and Sara entered Miss Hayden's office, they were informed that Miss Hayden had left the building for the rest of the day.

As Mim, Hattie Pullman and Sara Hallowell waited for taxis, Mim turned to her new friend and said, "Sara, I have a favor to ask of you."

"Nothing would please me more than to do you a favor."

Normally Mim would never have considered revealing such an important interest in front of a third party but so dismissive was Mim of Hattie Pullman's dedication to true art that she proceeded as if Hattie were a phantom.

"I would be most grateful if in your travels you would keep your eye open for something that would be very precious, and for which I would pay a great deal."

"Degas? Monet? I know them all," continued Sara.

"You will be amused when I tell you my prize comes directly from the fourteenth or fifteenth century," Mim answered.

Sara seemed sincere as she said, "Despite my admiration for the direction of the Impressionists, I can tell you that I, too, love the treasures of Medieval art. What in particular do you have in mind?"

"A Book of Hours," said Mim. She could hear the reverence in her own voice.

"What, may I ask, is a Book of Hours, and where do you get one?" asked Hattie.

"Oh yes, they are indeed beautiful works," Sara continued, completely ignoring the absurd question. "If I might ask, are you an especially religious person?"

Mim thought a moment.

"I appreciate church services and attend quite regularly, but this comes from a different impulse that I myself cannot quite understand. In a strange way, a Book of Hours reminds me of Miss Cassatt's mural—strong colors, precise execution.

"The art of the monks, like Miss Cassatt's, seeks to convey ideals. It seems to me this is the essence of art. I am not expressing myself well, but I know I would be interested in anything you find. But I warn you it must be exceptional."

7

Babies on the Way

*B*ERTHA WAS TRUE TO HER word. She worked throughout her pregnancy with no noticeable complications nor a word of complaint. As always, each Monday morning she arrived to confer with Mim on the menus for the week. Only when they completed that task would Mim inquire as to how Bertha was feeling. Each week Bertha answered the same way. "I am fine, thank you, Mrs. Blair. I hope you are fine as well." This was the only acknowledgement that the two women ever exchanged regarding their pregnancies.

The midwife Mim had hired for her previous deliveries had retired. Dr. Stephens recommended Mrs. Anna Marie Stengle as a replacement.

"She is the most competent midwife with whom I have ever worked." (Dr. Stephens was one of the few doctors who could admit that a competent midwife knew the intricacies and dangers of childbirth far better than he.)

The common practice was for a midwife to visit her patient once a month until the last six weeks of her confinement, when she visited weekly. Mrs. Stengle voiced surprise bordering on shock when Mim proposed that she assume care of not only herself, but of a servant as well.

"Mrs. Blair. This is a most unusual request. I have never before cared for both a mistress and her cook. I would be happy to see if I could find someone who would be more—well, more appropriate. I think it would make your cook more comfortable to have someone of her own— hmmmm—her own ilk to attend to her."

"Mrs. Stengle, I am reasonably certain that what would make both Mrs. Schmidt and me most comfortable would not be 'ilk' but competence.

"Incidentally," Mim continued, "It has been five years since I have needed midwifery services. What are the rates these days?"

"I charge forty dollars per patient, which covers all appointments before the delivery, my presence at the delivery itself, as well as visits until you are on your feet. I like my patients in bed for a full six weeks after the birth. I know some midwives are saying three weeks is adequate, but I am old-fashioned. Two weeks until you put your feet on the floor, and then a slow increase in activity each day."

"Mrs. Stengle," Mim said, "since your obligation here would be to two women in fairly close succession, I propose that I pay you one hundred dollars for your best effort on behalf of both Mrs. Schmidt and myself. How would that suit you?"

Anna Marie Stengle calculated immediately that this would be the largest sum she had ever earned in so short a time and delicately reversed her position.

"Your offer is more than generous, Mrs. Blair. I promise to take good care of both you and Mrs. Schmidt. Is Mrs. Schmidt agreeable to this arrangement?" asked the midwife.

"Yes," Mim assured her. "She told me she was of good farm stock and that women in your common native country use a midwife only for a difficult birth. But I think she will be very glad of your presence when the time comes."

"I will see her today after I examine you. Now, if you will please lie back so I can take a look and then listen for the baby's heartbeat. I understand this is your fourth pregnancy but we cannot be too careful. Each time is different."

Mim did as she was told, but felt sure there was nothing to be concerned about. Italia had been a surprisingly easy delivery for a first baby and, despite her inherently difficult nature, compliantly arrived the day she was due. Mim had labored for only six hours, which at the time she thought was more than enough.

CB entered the world as if he had been shot from a cannon. There had barely been enough time for Mrs. Miller to set up the catch sheet. Dr. Stephens had not arrived in time for the birth and, frankly, there had been no need for his presence.

Surprisingly, Mildred was her most difficult labor. Dr. Stephens administered a dose of chloroform, which Mim had thoroughly appreciated. She had heard that chloroform was a drug only for the wealthy, but what was money for, if not for blessed relief in extremis? She still remembered asking for another whiff and being so grateful when she saw Doctor Stephens dab a few additional drops onto a gauze pad and move it towards her nose and mouth. Mim related all this information to Mrs. Stengle and, in the retelling, she had to wonder why in the world she was doing this again.

No mistakes next time. She would take charge of the pregnancy protection, being sure to thoroughly cleanse herself with the water and vinegar solution many of her friends recommended. Coitus interruptus was not a method as far as Mim was concerned. It was a fallible technique, and it appeared Chauncey was not very good at it.

Mim watched as Mrs. Stengle unpacked her cased set of instruments. She did her best to avoid looking at them, as if denying the sight of them could deny the reality of their eventual use.

When she was expecting Italia, someone had told her that if you let your eyes fall on ugly things, you would produce an ugly child. Fortuitously, she lived surrounded by beauty. Her vigilance had succeeded. Her girls were very beautiful and CB arrestingly handsome. Really, it was such a small price to pay to the gods, why not play by their rules?

Mim loved all the *objets d'art* in her bedroom, so during Mrs. Stengle's examination she focused her eyes on the beautiful miniature sixteenth-century Indo-Persian painting Martin Gaylord had recently purchased for her.

Mrs. Stengle took out a tape measure and her stethoscope and began to take measurements of Mim's stomach, both vertically and horizontally, noting the figures in a small, black leather notebook.

"How big did you say your son was at birth?" asked Mrs. Stengle.

Not a good sign, thought Mim before she answered, "Over eight pounds as I remember."

"I think you have another big one in here," said Mrs. Stengle with a smile. "But I wouldn't worry too much about the relationship between your labor and the size of the baby. Perhaps if this were your first, but he or she should slip out quite nicely. Now let me take a listen."

The midwife spread apart the silver tubes of the stethoscope and placed the ivory tips at the ends of the tubing into her ears. She then laid the cold listening horn on Mim's white belly.

Mim allowed her eyes to travel to Mrs. Stengle's face as she searched for any sign of concern. Instead of alarm, Mim found only an intense concentration in the midwife's demeanor and a rhythmic nodding of her head, as if she were a piano teacher measuring her pupil's beats per measure.

Mim was not a chatterer, and certainly not from a prone position, so she held her questions until Mrs. Stengle said she could sit up as she finished adding notes to her log.

"What do you hear in there with that device? I have not seen anything like that before. I've always had the midwife put an ear to my stomach."

"To be sure, the ear worked well for centuries, but a stethoscope provides me a more accurate reading of your baby's heart rate. You might be surprised to know it is quite noisy in there and I can distinguish how the baby is faring far better with the stethoscope than with my ear.

"For example, I am happy to tell you that your baby not only has a regular heart rate but the tone is excellent. I detect no signs of what we call 'fetal distress.' From what I can tell, I predict your delivery will be as easy as childbirth can be. I pronounce you one of my healthiest patients. My orders are for you to stay that way," Mrs. Stengle said as she repacked her case.

"I am going downstairs to check on Mrs. Schmidt, and when I am through I will come back to report how she is managing."

Thirty minutes later, as Mim read her quarterly *Renaissance Collector* magazine in the early spring sunlight, Mrs. Stengle returned to give her evaluation of the downstairs patient.

"How did you fare with Bertha?" asked Mim.

The midwife reported, "At first I think she was a little confused about who I was and what I was doing there. But then again, so was I. She was apprehensive when I took out the stethoscope, but we muddled through. It helped that I spoke German with her, though her English is adequate. She is a bright woman. I think we established a rapport of sorts. I know there will come a time when she will look to me as an ally.

"Mrs. Schmidt is certainly correct about coming from good strong stock. She is on her feet almost all day, and yet they show no sign of swelling. The baby's heart rate is strong.

"I believe she is further along than she thought. I have told her that she could be a mother in the next two weeks. I believe her when she says she intends to work until the baby arrives, but I hope you can manage without her for a week or so after the delivery."

"I have already contacted an agency and they will send someone for at least a week," Mim replied. "But it strikes me as incongruous that there is such a disparity between when Bertha can expect to be back on her feet and when I am considered 'well.' Either her recovery is too short or mine is way too long. We both have the same 'disease,' after all."

The next time Mim saw Mrs. Stengle was ten days later when she arrived upstairs to announce that Mrs. Schmidt had given birth that morning to a baby girl, who was to be named Mary Roberta Schmidt. Mrs. Schmidt had borne her labor stoically for about twelve hours. Mother and daughter were both doing extremely well. Mrs. Stengle was most pleased to report that when she left, Mrs. Schmidt had given her the highest of compliments by saying, "Thank you, Mrs. Stengle. I am glad you were here."

A Command Performance

Late Winter 1892

"I AM SORRY TO INTERRUPT, MRS. Blair," said Robert softly as he bent to offer her the silver tray with a calling card on it.

"I presume this means that Mrs. Pullman is waiting for me," Mim replied with a weary sigh.

"Yes, Madam, she is in the foyer. Shall I ask Bertha to prepare some tea?"

"Yes, I suppose I must be gracious, though my calling day is Thursday, and this is Wednesday."

Suddenly, without apology, Hattie Pullman appeared before her, responding to what Mim had thought was a private comment to her butler.

"Mary, I know Thursday is your day to receive visitors, but I was passing this way and I have a verbal invitation I would like to extend to you. I feel certain you will be both interested and flattered. In addition, I have a few questions for you."

"Please sit down, Hattie. I have ordered some tea and I hope you will join me."

"No tea for me today. I only have tea at home. I have never found another brew as satisfying as my own."

"Well, Bertha makes some delicious—"

"No, no thank you, Mary," replied Hattie, her eyes obviously sweeping the drawing room for objects that might be of interest or, more likely, of value.

"Well then," said Mim now realizing to her relief that this would not be a long visit, "I am all ears."

"First, I would like to know if you are available in March."

"What day did you have in mind?" asked Mim, buying time to formulate any reasonable excuse to avoid what was coming next.

"Pick any day that is free for you and that is when it will be."

Mim knew a strategy of entrapment when she saw one, realizing that she could not plausibly claim no free day in the entire month.

"Without my calendar in front of me, I would say Mondays are generally best. How much time should I plan on devoting to this mysterious excursion?"

"Good. Let's pick the first Monday of the month, which I happen to know is the fifth. You should plan on spending the day. Plan to be at my house at 9 a.m. and you will be home no later than 6 p.m."

"I am sure it will be a fine outing, Hattie, but is the destination to be shrouded in mystery until we arrive?" asked Mim, more irritated than intrigued.

"We will be visiting George's workers' paradise, Pullman Village. It is just south of here. I am taking you along to take advantage of your artistic expertise."

"I would be most interested to see Pullman Village, and thank you for the compliment. But what do you mean by my 'expertise'?"

"Your eye, of course. Since your appointment as chairwoman of the Decorative Arts Committee you are now, despite your youth, considered to be Chicago's arbiter of artistic refinement. I am sure you have heard that George thinks I should have had the appointment, but as long as it is yours, I want to see what you can do."

Ignoring the sarcasm, and completely befuddled, Mim asked, "Do about what?"

"About what they say you are good at, decorative arts."

"I am still confused as to how my skills, whatever they may or may not be, can be of use in a workers' village."

"As you will see during our tour, Mary," said Hattie, preparing to depart, "the centerpiece of the village is the Hotel Florence. It is a majestic structure and thus appropriately named after our oldest daughter."

"What about the Hotel Florence?" queried Mim, attempting to lead her guest to the point of this strange visit.

"The hotel is in need of, well, let's just say some, ah, some additional refinement. Given your reputation, Mary, finding something of significance should be an easy job for you."

"The last thing, the *very* last thing I want is a job working for Hattie Pullman!" fumed Mim to Chauncey. "She is the most imperious woman I have ever met. She breezes in here, unannounced, and basically demands that I be her interior decorator. And you are telling me that I should go on this fool's errand? I will not do it. I just will not do it."

"Mimsy, all I am asking is—"

"And can you imagine, can you even imagine the idea of a sacred book, one of the sublime, sanctified treasures of the Renaissance, on display in a hotel in the middle of nowhere?"

"Mim, Pullman Village is in the city of Chicago and the Hotel Florence is where many important visitors stay," Chauncey said, though with no hope of mollifying his angry wife.

"Mimsy, it will only take a day, and I am sure any help you give will improve the décor of the hotel, not to mention that George, who has been vocal in his opposition to your appointment as chair of the committee, will be mollified. This would prove Cissie Palmer was right in selecting you over Hattie Pullman."

"I don't care a fig about proving anything to George Pullman. Neither he nor Hattie is educable about truly beautiful things. They buy. They do not collect."

Chauncey leaned his head back, swirling his port in the cut crystal glass and admiring the perfect smoke ring rising from his mouth.

"Let me say this differently but more directly. It would be a politically wise gesture and, frankly, a help to me were you to accept the invitation," said Chauncey.

Mim had grown up a banker's daughter and was now a banker's wife. She had no difficulty discerning his meaning.

※

For the entire fourteen-mile trip on the Illinois Central Railroad to the ersatz utopia that George Pullman had created in 1881, Hattie talked as if her words were synchronized with the monotony of the train wheels. All Mim needed to do was ask one question and Hattie filled the time and space, permitting Mim's mind to drift and luxuriate. However, on several occasions her reverie was broken by a question or comment to which her hostess clearly expected a reply.

"Mary, are you there?"

Scrambling to see if she could remember the last word she had heard, she took a stab at a cogent response.

"No, Hattie, I do not think it is a good idea to use Canton china for your place settings. You have told me the room gets little natural sunlight and, if Tiffany lamps are the source of the lighting, I think the blues will not come alive. You will risk using such beautiful china prosaically. But let me give you my final opinion after I have seen the room."

"By the way, Mary, what is a Book of Hours and where would I find one?"

"A Book of Hours, well, let's see how I could best describe it. It is a sacred book that was written and illustrated by a scribe, usually a monk, in the thirteenth or fourteenth century. The best are unique and spectacularly beautiful."

"What are the best of them?"

"There are many beautiful ones. Lady Margaret Beaufort, the grandmother of Henry VIII, was a paragon of piety and she commissioned several of great beauty."

"Do you know if any are for sale?"

"I would doubt it. These books are thought of as national treasures and I know English cultural officers pay close attention to sales which would take such relics out of the country."

"Well, Mary, as you must know, everything is for sale at some price. I heard you and Mr. Gaylord talking, and I know you want one, but if these books are so rigorously restricted, how can you hope to find one? There were no monks in America in the fourteenth century illustrating manuscripts."

"That's true," Mary agreed.

"So if Lady Beaufort's books are the best, would you settle for second-rate ones?" pressed Hattie.

"Actually, no, 'best' really doesn't apply. It is a matter of taste. I just mentioned them because I thought you might have heard of them," said Mim aloud. To herself she thought it implausible that Hattie had even heard of Margaret Beaufort, much less her Books of Hours.

"Well, if not any of Margaret Beaufort's books, then do any others stand out?"

"The three most famous books are the work of Dutch brothers named Limbourg. They are considered classics of the genre—"

Before Mim could finish her description, she watched as her traveling companion reached into her reticule and pulled out a small leather notebook and gold pen, which she uncapped, then sat poised to write.

"And what are those titles?"

For a split second Mim considered making up the titles of the Limbourg books, chuckling at the thought of Hattie Pullman making a fool of herself by insisting to a dealer that the names she was giving were correct, she had it on the highest authority.

"They are called, *Les Petits Heures, Les Belles Heures*, and the one reputed to be truly divinely inspired, *Très Riches Heures*."

∽

Mim saw Martin Gaylord awaiting her and Hattie on the station platform. Her day brightened considerably.

"Mary, I believe you are very familiar with Mr. Martin Gaylord."

"Yes, Hattie, Martin is an old friend and collaborator. He has helped me select some of my most beautiful things, though not without criticism of my timidity from time to time. Hello, Martin."

"Come on now, let us begin our day with a general tour of the village. We can then have lunch at the hotel and spend a couple of hours discussing your suggestions for purchases that would enhance the décor of the hotel."

Mim considered Pullman Village a vast eyesore but a valid social experiment. Thirteen hundred buildings dotted the landscape, all made of the clay from nearby Lake Calumet—factories, shops, schools, a library, and homes for one thousand Pullman employees, each with a back yard, daily garbage pickup and indoor plumbing. The clock tower could be seen for miles around, and the Pullman Trust and Savings Bank, a post office and a five hundred-seat theater dominated the arcade.

Mim was authentically impressed with what George Pullman had set out to do here, so her exclamations rang true.

"Hattie, you were right, George has created a wonderful life for so many of his employees. These workers would be in the tenements if they lived downtown. I am sure it costs George a lot of money to provide these homes, but to have happy workers—"

"Oh my dear, the workers pay rent! The village was designed to make a profit. And George sees to it that it does."

Lunch at the Hotel Florence was pleasant enough. Mim's participation was minimal as Hattie recounted the price of each item in the dining room and Martin effusively complimented her on what a remarkable deal the Pullmans had gotten.

"Yes, George is formidable negotiator. Everything you see here is just a railroad car for him. Best value for the lowest price. And sometimes his effort was, shall we say, rigorous."

Mim took a while to catch the rhythm of what role she was expected to play once the tour of the hotel began.

"Well," began Mim cautiously, "if the dining room is typical of what we are to see throughout the hotel, I would say you have all you need to make people feel comfortable. After all, this is a hotel, not a museum. What is it exactly that you are looking for?"

"Refinement, Mary. What I seek is refinement. By all accounts you have a refined eye and I want you to apply it to our hotel. I am looking for just the right piece or pieces to set the Hotel Florence apart from all the hotels in Chicago, most especially the Palmers' hotel."

Aha! thought Mim, *there it is. Art is a contest for the Pullmans and Martin and I are here to coach one of the combatants.*

Martin and Mim exchanged glances that registered their simultaneous understanding of what was afoot.

To say that the main floors displayed a potpourri of items would have been an understatement. Some of the furniture had merit but it was all so heavy—like a ponderous idea carried room to room. Where there were pieces of art, there was no point of view, no thematic order. There was one sweet landscape of an English country garden but its effect was nonexistent because it was placed between a pair of enormous oil paintings, one of the Roman forum and the other of the Tower of Pisa.

As Mim walked over to get a better look, Hattie followed closely on her heels, like a hunting dog who had gotten a whiff of blood.

"This is just where I see putting it," said Hattie.

"Putting what?" asked Martin, joining the women.

Ignoring the question, Hattie said, "Tell me Mary, do you like these Roman paintings?"

"I prefer the English flowers. It is so lovely, but it is overshadowed by ancient Rome. It is good enough to stand on its own. Is it a William Steele?"

"I have no idea who painted it. But I think this is the right spot for something more significant."

"Do you have something in mind?" asked Martin. "I just saw a Thomas Eakins landscape which might flatter the spot."

"Mr. Gaylord, I am not completely uncouth. Thomas Eakins is American, is he not? American is not what I have in mind, " said Hattie.

"Then, if I may, let me ask you directly what you have in mind so I can be efficient in finding something appropriate."

"What I want, Mr. Gaylord, is one of those Books of Hours."

౼

Hattie was spending the night at the hotel, so she did not participate in the lively dispute that dominated Mim and Martin's conversation as they returned home. The topic was not the virtues of Renaissance art over

French Impressionism. Rather, they discussed the validity of the social experiment where they had spent the day.

"I respect what he has achieved for his workers," declared Mim. "I don't think there is a community like it in the country, where the owner has created residences for his employees.

"I imagine that any employee who lives there would be everlastingly grateful to George Pullman. He has created a workingman's Utopia—newly built homes, schools, and parks for their families. Every woman I spoke with told me she had much more time in her day than she had had before she moved there. Some were even taking classes. This experiment is about the moral improvement of workers. No one can be against that."

"I beg to disagree, Mim," said Martin loudly, as if volume would reinforce his point. "It is not utopian. It is feudal. And despite the appearance of *noblesse oblige*, the real reason for George's creation of a workers' village is to keep labor costs down and eliminate the chance of labor unrest. I have heard that George's spies are embedded at every level of community life. There are no independent newspapers, no elections, no alcohol, and workers' homes can be inspected without warning.

"It is the most manipulative and paternalistic place I have ever seen. Workers are treated like children. The better they behave, the better Papa George likes it. Just wait until the residents become unruly adolescents. This social engineering will not work in the end."

"Martin, you are a cynic. Imagine being a common man living in an establishment that collects your refuse, manicures your lawn, sweeps your street, cleans up after every slothful man who drops his cigar butt on your property, and also sees to it that your family has access to a doctor when your child comes down with tuberculosis. Compare that to the way people live in the slums downtown, surrounded by filth, rats, stench and malnourished children. It seems to me an easy choice."

"It is a subversive bargain for the workers. They are trading creature comforts for total compliance with the will of George Pullman, and, mark my words, the charm will wear off."

As they left the train, Mim had her final say. "I will wager George's social engineering will be a success and a model for many other industrialists.

"But, Martin, I must extract a solemn and inviolable promise from you."

"Oh, Mim, whatever could it be?" he teased, knowing full well what oath he was going to be asked to swear to.

"Never, never, under any circumstances, are you to aid and abet the installation of a Book of Hours in the Hotel Florence."

An Alarm Sounds

Spring 1892

CHAUNCEY BLAIR WAS NOT A nuanced man. Mim saw color and shading wherever she looked; Chauncey saw black and white. Mim was a collector of art; Chauncey was often a collector of rigid opinions. Mim softened many of his rough edges and frequently had to recalibrate the household balance after one of Chauncey's dogmatic pronouncements.

At the office he was always on top of things. Despite his insecurity after the death of his father, things were running smoothly. He had the full support of his directors. He was proud to be on a path that matched his father's in the accumulation of wealth for bank shareholders, among whom he was the first among equals.

Nonetheless, the state of the modern world now inflamed Chauncey's deepest anxieties. Protected from the upheaval of the Civil War, the world of his childhood had been structured and safe. The Haymarket Riots in 1886 changed all that. Like many of his class, the anarchy had terrified Chauncey, a terror that had stayed with him to this day.

Because so much of the union movement was dominated by Germans who had fled Otto von Bismarck's rule, Chauncey was always a little surprised at the quality and apparent loyalty of the Germans who serviced his home—Robert, Bertha, and Nanny. These were fine, cultured people who, he suspected, were as embarrassed by their rabble-rousing countrymen as he was by the American politicians who encouraged their inflammatory language and violent behavior.

Chauncey knew Robert was largely an admirer of class distinctions; he believed that the upper classes kept the world in order. Robert despised the radicals who frequented the German beer halls, and, fueled by drink, fulminated against the rich and powerful. Robert had seen the same behavior in Germany and distrusted the rabble more than the rich.

Chauncey had sworn that the first person in his household found to have radical leanings would be out on the street, no time wasted, no questions asked.

"Robert, I have complete confidence in you," Chauncey confided. "Total and complete confidence. I know that your values are our values. Should an agitator make his way surreptitiously below stairs, I will hold you responsible."

So when Chauncey found a copy of *The Alarm*, that malicious rag of a subversive newspaper, tossed onto the path near the servants' entrance to his home, he exploded in full-throated, red-faced fury. Chauncey took this as a warning that the Blair House was soon to be a target. (Only a few months ago, a gang of firebrands had encamped on Marshall Field's and George Pullman's properties, yelling obscenities and singing revolutionary songs.)

"Jesus Christ! Whose is this?" trumpeted Chauncey as he stomped past Mim without a greeting, heading directly downstairs with the irrefutable evidence of venal radicalism in his fist.

He bade no one good evening as the servants sat together eating their supper.

Snapping open the newspaper so all of them who could read might see the banner and logo of the paper, speaking with more spittle than sentence, Chauncey continued his profanity. "Who brought this shit into my house?"

The servants were startled into muted immobility by the obvious rage of their employer. Thus, it was left to Robert to defuse the tension and answer the question in a way that at least acknowledged Mr. Blair's presence.

"I know what it is, Sir," said the butler. "It is a piece of trash and not one that anyone around this table would have brought into this house."

"Exactly right!" blurted Chauncey, who had lost none of his outrage in the few seconds that Robert had spent diverting everyone's attention. "Robert, would you be so good as to enlighten your fellow servants as to what *The Alarm* is and why it must never come near this house again?"

"Mr. Blair, did you find that paper in this house?" asked Robert.

"No, I did not. I found it inside the gate by the back entrance. But that is too close for my comfort."

Robert thought it was important to show his cohorts that he had faith in them even in the face of Mr. Blair's suspicions, so he calmly but firmly said, "Mr. Blair, I know everyone around this table, and not one of them subscribes to the ideas in that paper. I gave you my word of honor that I would let you know if we had a problem on that front. And I don't believe we do. You and Mrs. Blair have no cause for concern while I am here."

"That is for me to decide, Robert," Chauncey snarled. "Now please tell your friends what you know about *The Alarm*."

"*The Alarm* can be found in any German tavern in the city. I have not read it, but I have heard that it says that America would be better off if workers were in charge, and that violence is a means to that end.

"I don't agree with that. Workers are not educated. Workers don't know what is best. People who hold these beliefs are as dangerous here as they were in Germany. That is the reason Bertha and I came here."

"Well, that was the best decision of your lives. Now get this shit rag out of here," said Chauncey, hurling the offending newspaper on the floor for someone else to pick up.

Mim descended the stairs and now stood next to her husband.

"Good evening, Mrs. Blair," Robert said in behalf of the now-standing servants.

"Good evening everyone," said Mim, smiling at the group. "Forgive me for interrupting, but I need Mr. Blair to accompany me upstairs for a moment. Please continue your supper."

Though Chauncey knew that Mim's interruption was censorious, and her declaration of his being needed upstairs a ruse, he was not willing to leave without a final threatening word to his servants.

"Have I made my point?"

"Yes, sir," said Robert.

With that, Mim and Chauncey retraced their steps. Chauncey stomped up the stairs almost as loudly as he had descended them. As always, Mim left a lighter footfall.

Days later, Chauncey told the story of the mysterious appearance of *The Alarm* on his doorstep to the small group of businessmen who were working behind the scenes to elect Sam Allerton the next mayor of Chicago.

Chicago's elite would never forgive former Mayor Carter Harrison for his shamelessly cozy relationship with the trade unionists, the bomb throwers—all those whose only goal was to destroy capitalism.

The purpose of tonight's meeting was to refine the plan for the remaining weeks of what was being called the ugliest campaign in the history of Chicago—former Mayor Carter Harrison against businessman Sam Allerton.

Chauncey did not know Samuel Allerton well. More than twenty-five years Chauncey's senior, Allerton was one of the generation of men whom Chauncey had placed on a pedestal. He, like Chauncey's father and uncle, came from farming stock and was now considered the most successful stock rancher in the country, or, as Mayor Harrison liked to say, "a most admirable pig sticker."

Allerton was a director of the First National Bank, so when Chauncey and Sam's paths crossed, the conversation consisted largely of shop talk—interest rates, commodity futures, economic predictions, and the likelihood of labor unrest. Both men agreed there was no greater danger to the well-being of Chicago, as well as to their respective fortunes, than the radicals who practiced the power of dynamite.

Unlike Carter Harrison, who appeared to Chauncey motivated only by greed, Sam Allerton ran because he was committed to public service, according to his supporters. He would gain nothing financially by being mayor. He was already rich, an attribute Chauncey considered a prerequisite for elective office.

Years ago Allerton had written what was still considered the seminal treatise on the best practices for farming and raising cattle. If elected, he promised to demand best practices in city government—civil service reform, lower taxes, clean streets and expanded municipal services.

All of Chicago's most important businessmen were assembled tonight, save one: Potter Palmer. Shockingly, the Palmers were supporting Mayor Harrison. Chauncey believed the only reason for the Palmers' defection to the enemy was that Cissie Palmer, a canny politician in her own right, was confident of a Harrison victory and, as Chair of the Board of Lady Managers of the coming Exposition, she needed to be close to the center of power.

Tonight's Allerton meeting was at McKinley's, the city's most fashionable restaurant after the Palmer House. In a wood-paneled private room with oriental carpeting, tapestried chairs, silver cutlery and Irish Waterford crystal glassware, the back roomers, including Chauncey Blair, dined on braised duck, glazed spring carrots, rice pilaf, an English raspberry trifle and plenty of cognac.

The men enjoying such finery represented 90 percent of the net worth of the city. Few among them did not expect an easy Allerton victory, because that is what they deserved.

One participant was more skeptical of Allerton's prospects than his comrades: Joseph Medill, a former mayor himself and the majority owner of the Republican *Chicago Tribune*. He understood what the other men in the room did not—elective power was not in the back pockets of Drexel Boulevard elites, but in the tight knit ethnic neighborhoods.

Medill was doing his part to secure an Allerton victory. His paper had covered the campaign with a steady barrage of reportorial and editorial criticism of Carter Harrison. Day after day, the *Tribune* argued that Carter Harrison had done nothing in his previous term to improve the civic life of Chicago.

Like Chauncey, Medill blamed Harrison for the debacle of the Haymarket Riots. As a young reporter, Medill had written, after the Great

Fire, "Chicago will rise again." The riots had come close to jeopardizing that prediction.

As the Allerton partisans prepared to leave their plush surroundings, overconfident as well as overfed, Medill sought the final word.

"Gentlemen, my paper will provide all the editorial ammunition we need to make the argument that Carter Harrison must not be re-elected as mayor. However, the *Tribune* will be preaching to the choir unless we can get our message into the neighborhoods. We will lose the election if our voice remains unheard there. And the language of our message cannot be English. It must be translated into the vernacular. If we are going to win, we must organize massive pamphleteering in German, Italian, Yiddish, Polish, and even in Egyptian if we can identify more than two Egyptians eligible to vote in Chicago."

The Sunday before the election, readers of the *Daily Tribune* awoke to read a stinging rebuke of Mayor Harrison's tenure and moral character:

THE BATTLE FOR CHICAGO

No More Chances for Carter Harrison

The choice between Carter Harrison and Sam Allerton in next week's election should not be difficult for people who hold this city in high regard. Sam Allerton is the man for the job.

As Chicago prepares for the eyes of the world to be focused on the Columbian Exposition, the achievements of this great city and its miraculous renaissance after our tragic fire, do we really want those eyes to behold a city strangled by the ineptitude, vice and corruption that have always characterized a Harrison administration?

The answer should be NO!

During his dishonorable campaign, every assertion that Mr. Harrison has made touting his previous achievements is false: that the streets are cleaner, the garbage less prevalent, and the financial position of the city stronger. All, if sworn to in a court of law, would constitute perjury.

The truth is that Mr. Harrison presided over an empire of vice as a result of his self -imposed blindness to the eyesores of prostitution, gambling, and alcohol consumption. He issued more saloon licenses than the previous three administrations combined.

Mr. Harrison claims to love the immigrant neighborhoods of the city. If he truly loved the neighborhoods and the immigrants living there, he would not allow the police to ignore the wise prohibition against drinking alcoholic beverages on Sundays. Are wives and children properly cared for when their husbands use The Lord's Day as just another excuse to circumvent family responsibilities?

The worst indictment of Mr. Harrison's tenure as mayor is his mangled mishandling of the chaos in the Haymarket district during the riots. For that failure alone, the people of Chicago should not give Mr. Harrison another chance.

Mr. Harrison's control of the Chicago police department is well known. They make few moves without his imprimatur. Therefore, it is reasonable to conclude that the failure of the police to protect citizens against the violence of the anarchists is his failure. Mr. Harrison supported every incendiary and wild demand of the workers union movement.

Citizens of Chicago, Mr. Harrison has proved to be an abettor of bomb-throwing anarchists. Let our city move into the sunshine. Cast your vote on Tuesday for businessman Sam Allerton.

On Election Day, Sam Allerton and his inner circle dined at the Union League Club, confident of a celebratory evening.

They were later to learn that Carter Harrison spent the day on his white horse, galloping through the city, stopping at polling stations, urging campaign workers to spare no effort. They did not, and their work was rewarded. Carter Harrison would be the next mayor of Chicago. His would be the face of the White City at the World's Fair.

"God damn neighborhoods," hissed Chauncey when he got home to Mim.

Lord Have Mercy

June 1892

MIM WAS SITTING IN THE morning room with her needlepoint canvas as limp on her lap as she was in the chair. She was not her best self. She could not bear to be touched and every impediment made her skin bristle with irritation. Chauncey had said nothing remotely kind for weeks, and the children, for whom she had a perpetual soft spot, were better neither seen nor heard.

Her ankles were swollen, her legs twitched, she slept fitfully if at all.

Tennie found her sister touchy. She had brought her some musk soap for her bath with an aroma both strong and alluring. But after smelling it, Mim collapsed in a fit of tears.

"Mim dear, what is it?" asked a befuddled Tennie.

Mim was not a pretty crier. Her nose ran and she had a tendency to heave. She had always envied those heroines in the romances who could control the flow of tears to one or two beautiful pearl drops meandering down their blushing cheeks.

"Tennie, do you know how long it has been since I have been able to step into a bath? I am a pachyderm, a huge malodorous pachyderm." She could not go on.

Mim's official confinement began the last week in May. During previous pregnancies, she had bristled against the isolation that society, as well as her medical advisors, had imposed on her. But now, all that made her happy was a darkened room, cool compresses and bare feet.

She tried to read, but her normally good concentration quickly evaporated into diffuse reverie. She often read, reread and reread again the same paragraph in her book, and even then she could not have adequately represented to an inquisitor what had transpired.

She had purposefully saved some of the books recommended by friends for her confinement. She had started Oscar Wilde's popular novel, *A Picture of Dorian Gray*, thinking she could make quick work of it, and she had. She laid it aside halfway through. Dorian Gray was not the sort of character she liked. She found him uncomfortably effeminate and, always superstitious, she did not want any perversion to be absorbed by her soon-to-be-born son or daughter.

Instead of joining Chauncey in the dining room that night, Mim asked for a tray to be brought to her room. Despite the unusually oppressive hot weather, Chauncey would have his favorite tonight—calf's liver with both bacon and sautéed onions. Without even having to ask, Bertha knew such fare would be anathema to Mrs. Blair.

"I am all but certain that the sight of calf's liver smothered in onions and bacon would not be what Mrs. Blair would want to see in front of her," said Bertha to Margaret, Mim's personal maid. "If you could just find out what time she would like to eat, I will prepare something more appealing, more appropriate to what is likely her current disposition."

When Margaret brought her tray, Mim almost wept with gratitude— a cup of beef bouillon, lightly buttered toast with honey, an arrangement of green grapes and sliced apples and a small Scottish shortbread cookie. Not only did the choices suit her mood, each item arrived plated on her best Havilland china. The aroma wafting from a cup of steaming hot jasmine tea with lemon was pure ambrosia. The *pièce de résistance* was a single rose peony in full bloom standing cheerily in a cut glass bud vase.

So touched was she by the affection represented on this tray that Mim cried, for the third time that day.

She was almost asleep when she heard the soft knock at her door. Despite knowing exactly who it was, she asked, "Who is it?"

"Mimsy, may I come in?" asked Chauncey in a near whisper.

"Of course," she responded, meaning most of what she said.

Chauncey was a big man, so the sight of him tip-toeing across the room to sit on the edge of her bed made quite a sweet picture. Mim's eyes misted yet again.

"How are you feeling, Mimsy?" he said as he took her hand. "Though I know you are weary, you look quite content at the moment."

"I am as content as I have been in days. Bertha spoiled me with a nice dinner and I even did some reading. Is there something wrong? Something I need to deal with?"

"Nothing at all. I just came to check on you," said Chauncey, still whispering.

"That is very sweet and I appreciate your popping in. We don't spend enough time, just the two of us, just being our own company. I'm afraid that with the new baby and the exposition, conditions will get worse before they get better," Mim whispered back, mimicking his hushed voice. They were like small children talking after bedtime, fearful of waking nanny.

"I know that. After all the dust settles, how about you and I make a visit to New York? For starters, we can travel in the full luxury of George Pullman's Palace Car. We can see some theater, stay at the new Waldorf, and look for that Book of Hours you want."

"It sounds lovely, all but the George Pullman part. I like neither the man nor his wife, and would prefer to travel beholden to someone more congenial," said Mim sourly.

"But George's car is the only luxurious way to get to New York, darling," replied Chauncey, and then quickly and wisely got up to leave.

"But thank you, Chauncey, the trip will give me something to look forward to. So I shall indeed have sweet dreams tonight. Thank you."

Before tiptoeing out of her room, Chauncey held her head between his large hands and gave her a kiss on the forehead. No gesture could have been more welcome, for Mim wanted nothing more than to be a little girl who had someone to tuck her into bed with a goodnight kiss. As she readied herself for whatever sleep she would get that night, tears flowed for the fourth time that day.

Mim was awakened by what she instantly knew were the signs that her labor had begun. The first thing she did was to check the clock to be certain it was after midnight. It was 2:30 a.m. *Yes,* she thought, *this baby will thankfully not be born on June 13th, not a propitious birth date for a Blair baby.*

Remembering that she was to alert Mrs. Stengle as soon as she felt any contractions, she moved to a sitting position and pulled the bell to summon Margaret.

It was only when she put her feet over the edge of the bed to make her way to the lavatory that she felt the unfamiliar sticky substance beneath her.

Thank God we have electricity, she thought, not for the first time since they had electrified the house a year ago. Mim rolled towards the lamp and flicked the switch.

Despite her nocturnal disorientation, Mim now saw she was bleeding from somewhere. She threw off the light summer covers and traced the stains down to the midpoint of her sheets. She was not particularly worried. Her recollection of childbearing reminded her that the whole experience was a collection of demeaning positions and unattractive fluids.

"Mrs. Blair," said a gentle voice accompanied by an equally gentle knock.

"Come in, Margaret. It looks as though you had best awaken the footman and ask him to send the carriage for Mrs. Stengle. There is no need to alert Mr. Blair just yet."

Fifteen minutes later, Mim was relieved when she heard the carriage pull up to the front of the house. She could hear Mrs. Stengle's footsteps establish a quick pace up the steps and towards her room.

Her contractions were now coming more regularly, each tightening bringing with it a tiny but discernible pulse of moisture between her legs.

Mrs. Stengle did not bother to knock. She greeted Mim cheerfully as she pushed through the door. "I predicted I would see you soon. How are we doing?"

Mim disliked the pronoun "we." It was not "we" who was having contractions and bleeding with each one. Nonetheless, she was glad to hear Mrs. Stengle's voice, so full of optimism and confidence.

Mim did not know whether the bleeding was significant as she had been experiencing it intermittently for the last couple of months, but it had always abated. (Complaining about one's aches and pains was not a part of the ethic of her upbringing. Suffering in silence was considered the only acceptable way to suffer.)

Mrs. Stengle gently pulled the covers down, readying her stethoscope for the preliminary examination. Though Mim tried to avert her eyes, her peripheral vision took in the linen sheets. Crimson-brown clots were spattered throughout, as though dark summer cherries had been pressed deep into the linen. Mim was mortified that someone in her household was going to have to see this mess, much less clean it up.

She turned to see if she could glean any more information from Mrs. Stengle's demeanor. She could not. Her midwife looked as calm as if this were a routine visit.

"Mrs. Blair, I am sure you are aware that we have some bleeding here."

Mim could contain herself no longer. "Mrs. Stengle, if you don't mind, *I* am bleeding. *We* are not bleeding."

As soon as she said it, she knew her petulance must mean that she was more afraid than she thought. As always, when she was abrupt with her inferiors, she considered an apology. But these thoughts were interrupted by another contraction, accompanied by another gush of blood.

"I am sorry, Mrs. Stengle. I did not mean—"

"Mrs. Blair," soothed Mrs. Stengle, "from now until the delivery of your baby, there will be no apologies. If at the end of it all, if you have behaved badly, which I think highly unlikely, you may apologize. But for now, I am going to listen to the baby's heart and then I am going to step out and summon Dr. Stephens.

"Mrs. Blair, before tonight, did you experience any bleeding that you did not mention to me?"

"Yes," Mim replied.

"How frequently?" Mrs Stengle pressed.

"Here and there for the last three months."

"And you didn't mention it to me because—?"

"Because it would come and go. I was not in pain. I was busy. I assumed that if it represented something serious, it would get worse. Is it something serious?"

Mrs. Stengle took a long listen and reported to Mim, "I know it is easier said than done, but try to relax. If you could will yourself to sleep just a few winks between the contractions, it would be most beneficial to you and the baby. They call it 'labor' for a reason. Dr. Stephens should be here shortly."

Astonishing herself, Mim actually did sleep until she heard the door reopen.

"Hello, Mrs. Blair," Dr. Stephens said with a smile, "I am sorry to awaken you. Mrs. Stengle asked me to have a look at you to see if we can discern where this bleeding is coming from."

Mrs. Stengle stepped forward. Despite the short nap, Mim felt worse than she had before she had dozed off, and not simply because the rate and intensity of the contractions had increased. She could sense there was more blood in her bed and she felt nausea so intense that she waved her hands, hoping the gesture would signal Mrs. Stengle to move away.

"I am so sorry but I am going to be sick. I need a clean chamber pot. Is this related to the bleeding? Never mind, I just need the—"

Mim never finished the sentence, nor was she able to prevent herself from vomiting onto her now totally soiled bed. Mim was beside herself that these strangers had seen her vomit all over herself. Surely vomiting was supposed to be a solitary activity.

"I am so sorry," she said reflexively to her attendants.

"Mrs. Blair, remember, I said no apologies!" scolded Mrs. Stengle.

After taking soundings from various points on her abdomen, Mrs. Stengle turned to Dr. Stephens and with compressed lips and a slight shake of her head said, "110 with a fading tone. When I listened twenty minutes ago, it was 120. Not the direction I was hoping for. Have a listen. Maybe you will hear better news," said Mrs. Stengle, whereupon Dr. Stephens began uncoiling his own stethoscope.

"No better. 107 and the fetal tone is now erratic. I think it is time to awaken Mr. Blair."

Turning to Mim, he saw a very different woman from the one he had seen only three minutes earlier. Her face had lost its color; she had begun to sweat and she only managed to nod when asked if she were still nauseated. He now pulled down the soiled covers and, as gently as he could, palpated her abdomen. Mim winced at each application of pressure as if her stomach were severely bruised.

"Mrs. Blair, I am going to have a word with your husband. You have lost some blood, but not a lot as of yet, which is a good sign. I want to keep it that way. Mrs. Stengle will stay here with you. I will be back shortly."

Outside Mrs. Blair's room, Robert stood like a sentinel guarding the royal chamber, fully dressed for his professional duties despite the predawn hours.

"May I be helpful, sir?" he asked the emerging physician.

"Yes," replied the doctor, "I need to see Mr. Blair immediately. After you have awakened him, go and have the carriage brought around. We will be leaving here in no more than five minutes."

Within a minute a disheveled Chauncey Blair, his arms struggling to find their way into his navy blue silk dressing gown, trotted down the hall, stumbling in and out of one slipper. The second was nowhere in sight.

"Sorry to awaken as well as alarm you, Mr. Blair," said the doctor. "But I am fearful about the progress of Mrs. Blair's delivery. She is bleeding. Not a great deal at the moment, but I think we must move her to the nearest hospital in the next five minutes."

Chauncey was now fully awake, but confused.

"A hospital? Why a hospital? My wife has had three children at home. Forgive me, but aren't you being a little bit of an alarmist? Has Mrs. Blair approved your plan? May I see her?"

"Of course you may see her, but I can tell you Mrs. Blair is in no condition to weigh her options. It would not be in her best interest to include her in the discussion. That is what you and I are here for. What I hope you will do is go in there and tell her that, after consulting with me, you have decided she must be moved to Mercy Hospital, which I believe is only a few blocks away. It would be especially helpful if you could deliver that message calmly and with confidence."

Where is Mim when I need her? complained Chauncey to himself. He felt entirely unprepared to make this decision. The person he relied on in this kind of a crisis was at the center of it.

"Dr. Stephens, my wife is a very strong person. I think she would do better here at—"

"At home? Of course she would do better at home," Dr. Stephens shouted. "Under normal circumstances that is where she would be, but that is not what we have here. I suspect the placenta has pulled away from the uterus. It is called 'placental abruption.' If I am right, we will need to take the baby out as soon as possible."

"I have no idea what you are talking about, and the last thing I want at the moment, or at any moment, is for you to explain the female reproductive apparatus to me. The reason we have employed a midwife *and* a doctor is for just this type of situation. What I want you to do is to carry out this delivery here."

By now, Chauncey was literally spitting out his words.

Dr. Stephens took some time to marshal what he knew could be his last cogent argument with this clearly frightened but inappropriately argumentative man. If his patient bled to death, the only comfort he would have would be in knowing that he had made the best case he could on her behalf.

His voice ricocheted back at Chauncey with the same vehemence the banker's words had come at him. "Mr. Blair. You are right. I am being an alarmist because there is cause for alarm. I can walk you through the details that led me to my conclusion. But that would waste time. I will tell you that if we do not get your wife to a hospital, she will exsanguinate.

"'Exsanguinate' means bleed to death, Mr. Blair. It means you will certainly lose her, and likely the baby as well. We are going to have to cut Mrs. Blair open to extract the baby and stop her bleeding. To do this requires surgery. It is called a Caesarian section, and it must be done in a place where we have the best possible sanitary conditions.

"That place is a hospital. I have never performed a section myself, nor even seen one performed. I am hoping there will be a surgeon available. There is no other option, other than to passively witness the death of this young woman. There is no guarantee the surgery will work, but it is our only hope. Focus on that, Mr. Blair.

"Now you know the reasons for my recommendation. The decision is yours. And I need it in the next minute."

Chauncey was forcing himself to follow the details of Dr. Stephens' dramatic plea. The logic made sense to him. But what overwhelmed him as he stood there was the feeling that they were talking about taking Mim away from him, possibly for good. At least at this moment she was still here and he had some control over the situation. Once he relinquished it, he feared that neither the control nor Mim would ever come back to him.

As if reading his inner conflict, Dr. Stephens continued with slightly more sympathy. "Mr. Blair, none of us can influence the outcome of this emergency except for you. Please allow us to take your wife."

Dr. Stephens turned to the midwife and said, as quietly as he could, "Mrs. Stengle, please remain with Mr. and Mrs. Blair. No packing, no organizing, no goodbyes. I will go ahead and see what I can arrange at the hospital. I am not affiliated with Mercy Hospital, needless to say. It is Catholic, but it will have to do. Say a few 'Hail Marys.' Maybe it will do some good."

"I am not optimistic. I suspect an abruption of the placenta. If we are lucky, it will not be a complete one. Did she ever complain of bleeding at any of her appointments?"

"I asked her tonight, and she said she had had some bleeding in the second and third trimesters but she neglected to mention it because, among other things, she was busy!"

"Ah, the stoicism of the upper class," said Dr. Stephens as he rolled his eyes in derision. "With that kind of attitude, they will either continue to rule the world or become extinct."

"Dr. Stephens, do you want me to listen again to the fetal heart to see where we stand before we go?"

"No need. I know where we stand and the footing is perilous."

Edward the coachman, Robert, Bertha and Margaret each took hold of one corner of the filthy bed sheet underneath Mim, making it into a soiled and foul-smelling litter. They carried Mim downstairs. Like Hansel and Gretel's trail of breadcrumbs, small red drops plopped at regular intervals onto the white marble floors, tracing Mim's journey from her room, down the stairs, through the foyer, and finally down the steps and into the carriage.

The four attendants settled Mim in the back of the carriage that had been cushioned with towels to absorb the blood that, by now, had completely soaked through the sheet.

No one spoke except to make suggestions on preferred positioning or ways to keep Mrs. Blair from slipping out of the litter. The normally voluble Mr. Blair worried his servants with his intense silence. His only contribution to the procession was to urge haste and caution, which were often conflicting directives.

Bertha and Margaret held themselves together until after the carriage had pulled away, but that was all the self-control they could manage. They embraced, patting one another and saying things neither believed.

"They will fix her right up."

"She will bring us a new baby safe and sound."

Each felt hopeless about Mrs. Blair's return, based on what they had seen, but to give voice to that fear seemed disloyal.

Margaret straightened up. "Enough crying for now, I best awaken Nanny. She will need to know what has happened before the children stir."

"What in the world will she tell them?" asked Bertha.

"I have no idea," said Margaret, "but when you go downstairs, send someone to scour this floor before Mr. Blair comes back. I will attend to the bedroom. If Miss Italia comes looking for her mother and sees it in its present condition, we will have two crises on our hands, and hers would be even more dramatic than Mrs. Blair's."

⁓

Anne Marie Stengle doubted that, if Mim lived, she would remember the departure from her home or the ride to Mercy Hospital. However, she herself would never forget them. The atmosphere inside the carriage that carried the Blairs the three short blocks was a *mélange* of urgency, unambiguous terror and more tenderness than she had ever seen a husband bestow on his wife in all her years of delivering babies.

Mim was not what anyone could call "conscious." Nonetheless, her husband sat on the floor of the carriage and, holding her hand, talked to her without ceasing for the three-minute ride. Every jolt of the carriage produced a soft moan from the rear seat, which only encouraged Chauncey to ramble on. He talked and talked with no apparent concern that Mrs. Stengle undoubtedly overheard him or that his one-sided conversation was bizarre.

"Mimsy, in just a few minutes we are going to be at the hospital. Dr. Stephens assures me that this is where they will be able to take the best care of you. He said I had no choice. When you are well, I will see to it that everyone is rewarded for their efforts, even if they are Catholics."

No more than ten seconds of silence elapsed before Chauncey continued his monologue.

"Just imagine, Mimsy, one of our children will be born in a hospital. What a distinction! Do you know anyone else who has had a baby in a hospital? Oh, you don't have to answer that right now, but it will be something to tell our son—or our daughter.

"Only two more blocks—there's a girl. And the baby will have whatever name you want. Yes, I promise, whatever name you want. I was thinking we might ask Cissie and Potter to be the godparents. What say you to that idea? What a special child this one will be, not only born in a hospital but with the richest couple in Chicago as godparents! Quite a start in life!"

Chauncey paused and when he realized that he would not get even the slightest response, he continued his frightened, impotent but devoted bluster.

"And that Book of Hours, Mimsy. I will find just the one you want—maybe two. How's that? Two! Have you ever known me to be so impulsive? You can start a new collection. And we will take that trip to find it. Just you and me.

"Only another minute now. You know we are going to a Catholic hospital, don't you? Never mind, you don't have to answer that question. Of course it would not have been my first choice. No, indeed. But if they fix you up, I will never again say another bad word about Catholics.

"Do you think that everyone in the hospital will be Catholic? You don't suppose they will secretly baptize the baby, do you? That I would not stand for.

"Here we are, Mimsy. Will you look at that! There are four angels of mercy here to meet you. That is a fine start. Maybe even a divine start."

As glad as Mrs. Stengle was to see it come into view, there was nothing welcoming in the appearance of the hospital upon which so much now depended. It looked more like a fortress than an island of mercy. It had been constructed with what, in the daylight, were probably dark granite stones, but tonight, with no moonlight, Mercy Hospital stood encircled by pervasive black, save for a few peeps of light from tiny gas lamps placed intermittently in the windows.

Mrs. Stengle's imagination, stimulated by the fear that the darkness enhanced, was now spinning out of control. She half expected to hear a creaking drawbridge lowered to allow them to pass over the River Styx, as ghoulish armored ghosts held flaming torches and chanted ominous imprecations.

Stop it, she chastised herself. *If there is any hope, it will come from inside this building.*

Dr. Stephens had been persuasive in describing the emergency that would greet the nursing nuns when the carriage arrived. Four women, in starched white wimples and enormous wing-like headdresses, awaited them as the carriage halted under the portico.

To Mrs. Stengle, who did not associate with Catholics, it looked as if they had arrived at some strange religious costume ball where Mim was to be the guest of honor.

11
Interventions

*I*T TOOK FOUR ORDERLIES TO move Mim from the back of the carriage to the stretcher. Mim's muted moans turned to deep guttural groans with each movement. Mrs. Stengle had covered Mim with a blanket folded at the foot of the gurney, not only to keep her patient warm but also to preserve a shred of dignity.

At that moment, a nun whose demeanor instantly signaled "I am in charge here" came forward. Her grey eyes and bushy grey eyebrows were a perfect complement to the exterior of the building, as if she had not seen the sun since childhood.

Was everything Catholic always so pallid? Mrs. Stengle asked herself.

In a voice as cold and stiff as her headdress, the nun asked brusquely, "And who might you be?"

The midwife knew this was no time for a territorial battle. She was in an alien land and any chance she had of accompanying Mrs. Blair to whatever awaited her depended on ingratiating herself with this formidable woman. She had not completed her duty to her patient and she wanted to be with Mrs. Blair for as long as she could.

"Sister, thank you for meeting us—"

Before she could get any further, the elderly woman barked, "Don't just stand there wasting time, Sister Agnes. We don't have much of it. Take the lady upstairs immediately. Third floor. They will tell you what to do when you get there. Please remind anyone who thinks of touching my patient without washing her hands with plenty of green soap that she will have to answer to me, and it will not be a pleasant conversation."

My patient? objected Mrs. Stengle silently. *She is not her patient, not while I am here.*

When the nun concluded her instruction, the midwife began again. "Sister, thank-you for—"

"And, Sister Agnes," she called after the young nun. "Oh, never mind. I am coming myself."

She turned to the midwife and said, "Whoever you are, if you have something worthy to add, you had better walk along as we go upstairs."

Still understanding her best strategy was ingratiation, the midwife began, "I am Mrs. Anna Marie Stengle, Sister. I am Mrs. Blair's midwife. I have delivered almost two hundred babies, and perhaps I can be of some help. I promise not to be in the way but I am—"

"You most assuredly will be in the way, but it is Dr. Flannery who is in charge and he will make the final decision, he and our Lord. But first, go and tell that man, who, I presume, is Mr. Blair, it would be wise for him to go home. We will send for him when there is a resolution to Mrs. Blair's condition. After that you may proceed to the third floor."

Mrs. Stengle was more used to being in charge than being charged. But this nun had made an impression on her, and it was not all bad, so she immediately set off and did as she was told.

Chauncey Blair's countenance spoke of complete defeat. He seemed just waiting to be told what to do. Much to the midwife's surprise, he offered no objection to being sent home. He asked no questions about how long it would be until he knew something about his wife's condition, or what they would do to her upstairs, or what her likely prognosis was. He simply gestured what she took to be a thanks and shuffled compliantly away.

Mrs. Stengle had never been in a hospital before. All her training had been in private homes. Who knew if she ever would be inside one again, so she calculated that, for the moment, she would tolerate whatever subservient role this grey Sister assigned her in the interest of improving her knowledge and skills.

As she was walking back to the doorway leading upstairs, she thought and rethought about her culpability in the events that had transpired tonight. She felt confident that if Mrs. Blair had mentioned her episodic bleeding two months ago, this emergency might have been avoided. She did not feel guilty, but she did feel responsible. More than that, she had grown fond of Mrs. Blair. She was a young wife and mother who did not deserve to be this close to death.

She took the stairs two at a time to the third floor and, as instructed, gave her name to the nun behind the desk, who also barked at her.

A pack of growling wolves, the midwife thought. *There is nothing about this place that reflects its name, but if they rescue my patient, all will be forgiven.*

"First door on the right," Mrs. Stengle was told. "There is green soap at the side of the washbowl. Three-minute scrub, minimum. There is a basin of alcohol for soaking for another three minutes. There are rubber gloves to the side of the bowl. No one goes in the operating room without raw hands and rubber gloves. Don't forget the fingernails."

As she entered the operating room, Mrs. Stengle saw Mrs. Blair lying with a mesh mask strapped over her nose and mouth. The brutal surgery about to begin was not a circumstance where occasional whiffs of chloroform would be adequate. Ether, one of the few wondrous products of the Civil War carnage, was, she suspected, what had put Mrs. Blair fully to sleep. She could only pray that, if she survived the surgery, she would reawaken.

The operating room was spare, the centerpiece being the table upon which Mrs. Blair lay fully draped in white. She looked spectral, completely peaceful in her induced dream world. There was a large hole cut in the linen from which her abdomen protruded, now painted with a yellow-brown liquid.

There were two additional nuns in the room whose purpose was not entirely clear. They looked like guardian angels standing slightly back from the surgical table, not moving a muscle except to pass the rosary beads through their fingers and whisper inaudible prayers. Was their role simply to pray?

What a waste, thought Mrs. Stengle.

The three principals—Dr. Stephens, Dr. Flannery and Sister Raymonda—surrounded Mrs. Blair's abdomen, as if it were an entity unto itself, in no way related to the woman lying inertly beneath it.

Carbolic acid had been sprayed throughout the operating room to reduce the possibility of infection in case Mrs. Blair survived.

Dr. Stephens seemed almost excited by the surroundings. His voice, normally low and soothing, was now staccato and high-pitched. It became an annoying contrast to the quiet apprehension Sister Raymonda and Dr. Flannery displayed.

Moving quickly to greet her as if they would soon be late to the opera, Dr. Stephens said, "Ah, Mrs. Stengle, come in, you are just in time."

"Dr. Flannery, this is my midwife assistant, Mrs. Anna Marie Stengle."

The surgeon ignored the formal introduction. She took no offense, knowing he was seconds away from the first cut into Mrs. Blair's belly; once he began, they would all be swept into the whirlwind.

Dr. Stephens talked on, not unlike Mr. Blair in the carriage. He was undeterred by the unresponsive surgeon. "Neither of us has ever seen a Caesarian section before."

With a look that betrayed more than a touch of hero worship, Dr. Stephens spoke directly to his assistant. "We are very fortunate Dr. Flannery was here when I arrived. He is a general surgeon, one of an up-and-coming new breed of men who save lives in operating rooms. Mrs. Blair is very lucky, very very lucky."

Mrs. Stengle noted the inanity of Dr. Stephen's comment as she gazed at the inert figure lying before them.

Dr. Flannery was oblivious to everything in the room, including Dr. Stephens' flattering chatter. His lips were moving as if he, too, were reciting a prayer.

Did anyone here have skills or did they just pray? the midwife asked herself.

But as she looked more closely, she could see that Dr. Flannery was not praying. He was reviewing the implements displayed on the tray to his left. Sister Raymonda, the erstwhile commanding general of the lobby, was now a mere foot soldier in Dr. Flannery's battalion.

Now that the surgery was about to begin, Anna Marie Stengle began to feel emotional about her patient, yes *her* patient, lying there, so young, so completely vulnerable, looking like one of those medieval maidens sculpted in alabaster, an effigy on a stone tomb, so still, so resigned to her fate. In place of what she supposed should be a prayer, Mrs. Stengle silently exhorted Mim to invigorate herself to do battle. She refocused her gaze from Mim's face to the main action in the room—the vertical incision that Dr. Flannery made from just below Mim's navel to the top of her pubic bone.

"I am in," Dr. Flannery declared, apparently the least emotional person in the room.

"Let's get this baby out. Dr. Stephens, as soon as I remove the baby, I will hand it to you. There will be too much to do to save its mother for me to attend to the child."

With that command, Dr. Stephens reverted to his usual professional demeanor, grateful for a job to do. He signaled Mrs. Stengle to his side. They had worked together so often before this terrible night that their current proximity felt completely normal. It was the only thing that had felt normal in many hours.

f

In the endless and detailed replays of what happened that night, Mrs. Stengle never failed to express amazement whenever she described how quickly everything moved after Dr. Flannery began to cut.

Mrs. Blair's new son was delivered in no time.

Dr. Stephens ministered to the baby until Dr. Flannery called to him.

"Dr. Stephens, I need you here."

At that point, Sister Raymonda took the baby and, after a few tense minutes, while she held him upside down to drain the mucus, baby boy Blair began to wail. Who could blame him?

Sister Raymonda motioned to Mrs. Stengle to accompany her to a corner of the operating room.

"I assume you know how to proceed from here with the baby. Dr. Flannery is by no means finished with Mrs. Blair. She continues to lose blood, and my suspicion is that he will need to remove her uterus for her to survive. I will go back to assist the doctors," said Sister Raymonda, not waiting for a response.

Mrs. Stengle was delighted to finally be of some service to her patient, albeit indirectly. Displaying a full set of lusty lungs, the baby complained throughout his first bath as she sponged him with warm water, rubbed him with camphor oil and swaddled him so tightly that his little fists were restrained, enabling her to squeeze the drops of silver nitrate into the corners of his firmly closed eyes. The use of this liquid was now standard practice for newborns, preventing any bacteria acquired during the delivery from infecting their eyes. This baby stood a good chance of losing his mother. He need not lose his sight.

When she was finished, and the newest Master Blair looked presentable and content, Mrs. Stengle handed him to Sister Agnes, who walked the baby out of the operating room, cooing and talking to him as if they were old friends. There was no need for him to watch his mother die.

By the time Anna Marie Stengle returned to the surgical table, Dr. Flannery appeared to be suturing Mim, which meant he had successfully removed her uterus. Since any procedure the midwife would now observe would, thankfully, be useless to her in her practice, she turned and followed the baby and his temporary caregiver to the nursery.

Dr. Flannery's final act was to remove the ether mask and throw it into the nearby enamel slop pail almost overflowing with surgical detritus, including Mim's most feminine and now useless body part.

Turning to the anesthetist, he directed, "She has a better than even chance of dying, but if she awakens, she will hurt mightily. You can give her chloroform whenever she wants it. There is no need for her to die without some relief."

Dr. Stephens stepped forward and offered his thanks and praise to Dr. Flannery, whose blood-soaked white gown gave credence to the drama of the night.

"I am an 'old dog' and will never learn the new tricks you employed tonight. I don't want to learn them. I suspect that what you have done here will be seen as routine twenty-five years from now. I am grateful you were here, and I know the Blair family will be grateful as well."

The young doctor replied, smiling for the first time that night, "I hope you are right that soon we will be able to serve more women by Caesarian section. I doubt Mrs. Blair will survive to tell the tale. But she certainly would be dead without it."

The young surgeon continued, now fueled by his own pent-up adrenaline, "You, too, played a part in saving her life by getting her here, Dr. Stephens. The majority of doctors I know would not have recognized their own limitations and simply resigned themselves to the fact that there was nothing to be done to prevent her death. You are a rarity, Dr. Stephens. So I applaud you as well."

"What do you suggest I tell Mr. Blair?" Dr. Stephens asked.

"Tell him the truth. Tell him this will be a long vigil with some hopeful days and many not so hopeful. Tell him the greatest danger now is infection, which can appear just when you think all is well. Tell him she is to have no visitors, including him, for two weeks at a minimum. Tell him to expect the worst and hope for the best. And you might also tell him that the Irish nuns will pray their rosaries over her for what remains of the night, as well as during the difficult days to come. Tell him not to discount the importance of their prayers. Sometimes I think they are of equal importance to any skills you and I may have brought with us this evening."

12

Introductions

June 1892

*I*N THOSE FIRST DAYS, ON an almost hourly basis, sometimes conscious, usually not, Mim summoned strength from her most important collection: her resilience, her strong heart, and her natural optimism, even when it did not appear to be warranted. Often making those around her squirm, she insisted she be told the truth, however alarming, and she paid scrupulous attention to the details of her recovery.

Mim's insistent attention to hygienic precaution, advised by Mrs. Stengle, was greeted with annoyance by Sister Raymonda, who thought Mrs. Blair had been saved from death by herself, Dr. Flannery and Jesus, in that order.

"Mrs. Blair," she said haughtily, her grey eyebrows arched in judgment, "I have been scrubbing my hands with soap since before you were born. I never forget."

Mim always smiled her sweetest smile, graciously ignoring any rebuke Sister may have intended to deliver. "Sister, I have told you time and time again that I will be everlastingly grateful for the excellence of my care here under your direction. I will never forget who saved my son's life and my own; you all are in my prayers every night, and there you will remain for as long as I live."

Then she would lean toward Sister Raymonda and say, confidentially, "You are not my concern. You are infallible. But I remind some of the younger nuns just to be sure." Rarely mollified by Mim's charm, Sister Raymonda harrumphed and stalked out of the room.

Dr. Flannery saw Mim daily. In the most critical days of her recovery he would minister to her himself, surprising the rest of the staff by performing the most mundane medical tasks. He took her temperature, changed her dressings and applied salves to the angry-looking scar he had created.

Occasionally he turned up with medical students who scribbled furiously every word he uttered. It was clear that Dr. Flannery had V.I.P. status at Mercy Hospital, and that she somehow shared in it. Sometimes Mim would catch him looking at her in astonishment.

One day, after his fourth visit of the day, she asked him directly, "Dr. Flannery, do you come to see me and perform all these menial tasks just to convince yourself that I am not dead?"

Dr. Flannery had almost no sense of humor, but he did have a pleasant smile, which he flashed when he answered her question. "That very well might be the case, Mrs. Blair. You have no idea, no idea at all—"

"They tell me, Dr. Flannery, that the nuns prayed over me all night after the baby was born. Is that so?" asked Mim.

"I am certain it is, Mrs. Blair, and many days thereafter that, fortunately, you will never recall. Most of the Sisters who attend you believe they participated in a miracle that night. You and your son are the talk of the hospital."

"Are you a Catholic, Dr. Flannery?"

"I am, Mrs. Blair."

"And what do you believe happened to me that night? Do you consider it a miracle that I survived?"

Dr. Flannery took a long time to consider his answer, sensing that his most illustrious patient was looking for more than a casual reply.

"Mrs. Blair, after I finished your surgery, I thought the chances of your survival were slim. Maybe even less than slim. I told Dr. Stephens that the nuns would be praying for you and your son. I told him that as much good work as he, Sister Raymonda and I had done—and I think we did excellent work—I considered the prayers of the Sisters to be as much a part of whatever success I achieved as the surgical implements, anesthetic and good training that I brought to the operating room.

"There are, of course, precedents in medical literature for your case. I have performed one Caesarean section. That woman was less fortunate than you. Was your survival a miracle? I don't know. Did the imprecations of the nuns place God at my side or in my brain guiding me? Honestly, I did not feel anything mystical, but then again maybe God was wise enough not to distract me.

"I believe it was something out of the ordinary that extended your life—but now, time for some rest. These are big questions you are asking. If God is willing and we can continue to stave off infection, you will have plenty of time to review your experience and decide for yourself if it was miraculous."

The household staff at 4830 Drexel Boulevard had performed admirably, maintaining as best they could an appearance of normality.

Since Margaret was no longer needed to serve Mim, she was reassigned to help Nanny in the nursery, and the two women became an effective unit in dealing with the children, who clearly missed their mother. While the duo maintained discipline and kept to the schedule, there were more stories on laps, more sugar treats and abundant hugs given to all three children until Mrs. Blair was considered out of danger.

Italia especially sought and accepted Margaret's soothing kindness. At story time she would draw the needlepoint-covered rocker her mother had made for her as close to Margaret as she could and drape her arm around her, as if her mother's personal maid were now her personal cuddle toy. She did not believe for a minute the fable that her mother was simply resting at the hospital and awaiting "better weather" to bring their new brother home.

As all children will, in a household pulsating with tension, she absorbed the bristling anxiety in the adults around her. Italia sensed that the servants were walking on eggshells. They whispered amongst themselves when they did not think she was about. When she did appear, they immediately stopped and addressed her with a cheerfulness that she recognized as false.

When her father was at home, she could feel his unstated anguish passing directly into her own body. One evening, when he had come to the nursery to bid his children goodnight, Italia asked him directly what was the matter with their mother. Chauncey had burst into tears and left the room, her question unanswered and her sense of danger considerably heightened.

CB grew more withdrawn and Mildred, whom Nanny had cajoled into giving up the habit of sucking her thumb, had regressed, though for the time being she sucked without reprimand.

On day fifteen, Chauncey began pressuring Dr. Stephens for permission to see Mim.

"Mr. Blair, I am sorry but that is not my permission to give. The moment she entered Mercy Hospital, Mrs. Blair became Dr. Flannery's patient. And thank God for that," Dr. Stephens added, still awed by the work of Dr. Flannery.

In the weeks following Mrs. Blair's emergency, he felt a noticeable ennui when dealing with the quotidian maladies he was asked to treat every day in his office. Rheumatism, gout and constipation no longer felt remotely important, and he caught himself several times wanting to tell his patients to stop complaining until they were really sick.

Perhaps no one could have prepared Chauncey for the sight of his wife, but after two weeks, with family, friends and most especially the children clamoring for information about her, Chauncey had to see Mim. Vividly remembering how close she had come to dying, he was nervous as he approached the hospital. At least in the light of day the environment at Mercy Hospital was more reassuring than it had been on that terrible night, but he would never get used to the nuns in their foolish costumes, their clacking rosary beads, and the maudlin pastels of Christ on the cross adorning the hallways.

He wondered if there was similar artwork in Mim's hospital room. If so, he would have to insist that something be brought from home. Mim's recovery would be badly impeded if she had to look at such eyesores until she returned to her sanctuary of beautiful things.

Gaining entry into Mim's room was a little like being admitted unannounced to the Palmers' castle. There were many impediments standing between him and his wife. In order to find her, he had to stop at the information desk in the lobby, where he received a visitor's pass. Then he was stopped again at the nurse's station, where his pass was inspected. At the door to her room, a nun, who appeared to be only slightly older than Italia, shushed him. Young and slight though she may have been, this nun either innately possessed or successfully emulated the air of authority carried by her older peers.

"Lower your voice, sir. My patient is asleep, thank God. You may await her awakening, downstairs in the lobby, or go home. It does not matter to me which choice you make, but you will not be going into that room."

Now knowing where the power lay in this hospital, Chauncey used his most conciliatory voice and said, "Sister, you are correct. I too very much want Mrs. Blair to sleep. I will wait until you tell me it is permissible to enter. In the meanwhile, perhaps you can direct me to the nursery so I can get acquainted with my son."

The baby, as yet unnamed, was known throughout all of Mercy Hospital as "Angel Boy Blair." Chauncey had visited him only once in the first two weeks since his birth, just to be sure his mother's trauma had not rubbed off on him.

Evidently Mim's guardian had not been charmed by Chauncey's softer approach. Without a trace of warmth in her voice she said, "I am sorry. Seeing your son will not be possible either."

Now terrified that his son had suffered a setback and was critically ill, Chauncey lost all control. "Not possible, Sister? Let me tell you what is not possible. What is not possible is that the likes of you is going to prevent me—"

"Who and what do we have here?" said a voice from behind Chauncey.

When Chauncey turned, his fears deepened because he recognized the woman who had acted as 'Queen of the Nuns' the night Mim had been admitted.

Dear God, thought Chauncey, *if only we had lived near a suitable hospital, a place like Chicago Hospital where I have some influence. Here I have met no one but abrasive Irish women, with an undue amount of power despite their lack of social standing!*

"Mr. Blair, is that you? What seems to be the problem?" said the woman, adding herself to the growing gathering in front of Mim's door.

"You are correct, my name is Mr. Chauncey Blair and I will tell you the problem. I came today to see Mrs. Blair, who has been a patient here for two weeks. I think you know her, as you were on duty when we came in. I was told I could see her today.

"This lady here has explained to me that she is sleeping, which, of course, I understand is what she needs."

Chauncey's voice was now so constricted by a mixture of fear, anger and pent-up frustration that even he could hear in his voice that he was close to tears. But there was no stopping now.

"I then asked where I could find my son. He has not yet seen his mother,who is still gravely ill. I think he should know that one of his parents is beside him, and at the moment I am that parent. I want to see him.

"Then, without giving me the reason, this woman tells me I may not go to the nursery so I can only suppose he too is unwell, maybe seriously so. This is tyranny."

"Mr. Blair, I am Sister Raymonda. I was indeed here when you brought Mrs. Blair to us, and it is a good thing you got her here when you did. It was quite a night for all of us.

"I am in charge of this floor and I have been here every day since Mrs. Blair arrived. I have been impressed by her will to live out the miracle that God has granted her.

"In addition, I can reassure you that your son is doing very well. He was born over eight pounds, and I am sure we can discharge him as soon as your household is ready to receive him. Unfortunately, his mother will be with us substantially longer, and I am sure that makes things difficult for you and those at your home.

"Let us step over here so as not to disturb Mrs. Blair, because the one fact we can all agree upon is that she must sleep."

As she pressed Chauncey's arm in the direction of the nurses' desk, she turned to Sister Mary Martha and said, "Sister, I will take care of Mr. Blair now. Please come to the nursery to find us as soon as Mrs. Blair awakens."

Turning back to Chauncey she continued, "Your son is very handsome, Mr. Blair. He has captivated all of us and, as you may have noticed, we are not a group easily smitten. A few of us show tenderness every so often, though usually I am not in that contingent.

"I believe the survival of your wife and son is the closest thing I will see to a miracle in my lifetime, an act of grace on the part of our Lord. Such an event moves even the sternest among us."

Walking along companionably, practically old friends when they reached the nursery, Sister Raymonda beckoned one of the nurses to come outside the glassed-in chamber. Chauncey, meanwhile, was straining over their massive headdresses to see if he could identify his son among the newborns, all of whom looked the same to his eyes, each swaddled tightly in a miniature white cotton nightdress irrespective of their gender.

Though the nurse had closed the door, there was no mistaking the sounds emanating from the tiny cotton cocoons.

How could anyone tolerate being in there hour after hour? he wondered.

Then it suddenly occurred to him that he could not remember ever hearing a baby cry. Surely his children had cried. That is what babies did. One thing was certain—Italia, CB and Mildred had never cried in front of him.

"Sister Brigitta, would you escort Mr. Blair to the changing room and then bring his son in to him?

"Mr. Blair, have you ever held a baby so new to the world?" Sister Raymonda asked.

"No, I haven't. There is no need for me to hold him at the moment. I simply wish to see him. Someone else can hold him."

"Oh, I think your son would very much enjoy his father's arms around him. The nurses have too much to do to hold God's babies for very long," Sister said gently.

"We will give you a sterilized gown and, if you sit in that chair over there, I will hand him to you. Just be sure you keep his neck secure with your hands cupped behind his head at all times."

After handing the baby to his ungainly father, Sister Raymonda said, "You are a natural, Mr. Blair. Take as long as you like. He has just been bathed and fed and is not likely to wake up." She left father and son alone.

As long as his son was asleep, Chauncey did not mind holding him. *Not much to this,* he thought.

He was more fascinated than smitten with his new son, inspecting those parts of him that were not enfolded in cloth. Since the baby's eyes were tightly closed, he concentrated on his tiny but distinct nose and his remarkably intricate fingers.

Chauncey would not have called his son handsome, as Sister had, but he was interesting. He did have a tangle of black hair. Chauncey thought, *quite the daisy* and then laughed for the first time in weeks when he thought of the reprimand Mim would have showered upon him had he expressed himself thusly to her.

After about ten minutes, Angel Boy Blair began to squirm. He then gave a noticeable shudder, sending his father into paroxysms of panic, causing him to hurl himself out of the chair and, with no regard to volume, call out desperately, "Miss, Miss, no, I am sorry, I mean Sister, Sister—Can I get some help here? I think my son is having some kind of fit. Please, someone, come quickly!"

Two sisters burst through the door, one grabbing the baby from his father and the other carefully evaluating the breathing of the baby.

"What did you see, sir?" she asked, looking down at a perfectly contented and calm infant.

Baby Boy Blair began stretching again, at which point Chauncey, said, "There, see? He seems not to be able to control his movements. He is having spasms!"

"Sir, that is called 'stretching.' I imagine you do it when you first wake up as well. It puts his small frame into alignment and I imagine it feels good."

And then his son opened his eyes and looked directly into his father's. They were a deep, deep blue—a beautiful blue, more sapphire than robin's egg. There was no one in his family that he could think of with his new son's coloring. *Black hair and blue eyes,* thought Chauncey. *Damnation! He may as well be Irish.*

Before being let into Mim's room, he was ordered to wash with green soap and finish with a rigorous scrub of his forearms in alcohol. Sister never took her eyes off him, and when he had done what he considered a more than adequate job, she inspected his fingernails and told him to do it again. No woman since his mother had ever had this much control over him.

"We have our first visitor, Mrs. Blair," Sister said cheerily as they entered the room. "Your husband has come to say hello. But no more than ten minutes today."

Then, to Chauncey's horror, she left them alone. For a woman who was dedicated to hovering and giving orders, couldn't Sister Mary Martha have hovered a little longer just until he got his bearings on how he should be with Mim? He felt abandoned without instructions.

The last time he had seen Mim, her face had at least looked familiar. He could no longer say that was true. He had been told her eyes were open, but so heavy were her lids, it was difficult to tell if she absorbed anything she saw. Her face was yellow-grey except for the purplish tint under her eyes. These were not colors that enhanced any woman. Her normally shiny brown hair was stringy, oily and, frankly, as he leaned over to kiss her forehead, gave off an unpleasant odor.

As if to distance himself from the reality of his wife's condition, Chauncey instinctively stepped back, placing himself close to the one grimy window in the room, so it was from a distance that he tentatively began to speak.

"Mimsy, you have given us all a terrible fright. I imagine you have given yourself a fright as well. How are you feeling?"

What a ridiculous question, he thought to himself, *just look at her.*

Mim stirred as if she had heard something, if not his exact words. She turned her head ever so slightly, as if seeking out a familiar sound rather than a person. Then she closed her eyes again and fell back to sleep.

Chauncey felt a streak of anger course through him. If he had given voice to his thoughts, he would have told her that he had been alone and terrified for two weeks, much of the time not knowing if he was to be a husband or a widower, that her children were ragged with worry and he did not know how to soothe them because he did not know how to soothe himself, and that he had not been able to focus on work since her surgery. He would appreciate it if she could muster just a little appreciation and stay awake.

But what he said was, "Mimsy, everyone at home misses you, and that includes me. The children have been as well behaved as can be expected, but they want their mother back. I have brought you some notes from Italia and CB and a drawing from Mildred to cheer you up."

He reached into his waistcoat pocket and took out some papers, which he smoothed out on her bedside table as if stalling for time.

"But Mimsy, we, I mean you, must pick a name for the boy, who is being spoiled by all the nuns in the nursery, hard as it is to believe that those nuns could spoil any creature, young or old."

"William Mitchell Blair," came a voice from the direction of the bed in a voice so strong that Chauncey at first thought it must be a ventriloquist's trick.

"Yes, yes," shouted Chauncey back at the voice. "That is a fine name, a name as strong and as handsome as he is. Excellent choice."

Moving closer to her bed, no longer fearing that he was approaching a cadaver, he took Mim's hand, shaking it exuberantly, as if he had just concluded an important business deal.

Now Mim's eyes were more open than they had been since the night she had arrived at Mercy Hospital, and though Chauncey sensed she had more to say, he could not restrain his excitement at finally having his conversation partner back.

"Have they allowed you to see him, Mimsy? I have just spent ten minutes with him, which is all they will allow me with you, and he is very much a Blair. Yes, a strapping William Mitchell Blair," Chauncey enthused.

Without as much as a knock, the door opened and Sister announced that twelve minutes had passed and it was time for Mrs. Blair to get some rest.

Two whole extra minutes, thought Chauncey. *Who says these nuns are inflexible?*

But, no matter. He could now leave with a lighter mind than he had had in weeks because of his certitude his world would once again spin on its proper axis. He leaned over and once again kissed Mim on her forehead. To his surprise, her eyes were still open.

"Goodbye, Mimsy. You have no idea how glad I am to see you coming along. I will come back as soon as they allow it. I must say, they appear to be taking very good care of you and William Mitchell Blair.

"You are my girl, Mimsy." He did not expect a response, so he was surprised when he heard her voice call back to him. He could not quite make out what she said, but it did not matter. Or did it?

If he had heard her correctly, it sounded as if she had said, "I had him baptized."

"What did you say, my dear?" he asked as he walked back toward her bedside. But by the time he looked at her, she had secured herself in sleep.

$\mathcal{R}$evelations

Fall 1892

$\mathcal{B}$Y SEPTEMBER 1892, MIM HAD been home for more than a month, though her activities were limited. Dr. Flannery encouraged her to walk five minutes a day, gradually increasing the regimen to thirty minutes by early October.

Mim was compulsive about spending time with Billy. She bathed him each evening, put him in his cot, and even changed his soiled diapers, duties she had never performed for her older children.

After he began smiling and laughing, the competition grew fierce among his siblings as to who could perform the most outlandish tricks to encourage his beguiling reactions.

"Billy, Billy, look at me," Mildred would call out as she pirouetted and leapt in front of him.

CB had been desperate for a brother. "It's you and me, Billy Boy," he would whisper conspiratorially to Billy, who would reward CB with a wide drooling grin as if he understood the full implications of CB's promise.

Mim appreciated that it was her life, not Billy's, that had been im-
periled during those critical days at Mercy Hospital, but that did not diminish her obsessive belief that he was only completely safe when he was
with her. Her superstitious mind conjured up black clouds even on the
sunniest days. Her magical thinking, formerly under control, sometimes
felt as if it were taking over her whole being. Dozens of times a day, she
promised behavior and attitudes designed to protect those she loved. And
after every bargain, she vowed to stop such ridiculous gamesmanship, but
she could not. She decided it was better to continue the talismanic thinking than face the irrational but threatening consequences.

Mim had still not sorted out all that had happened to her since the
night she left Drexel Boulevard. But every so often little pellets of memory
dropped into her consciousness. Some of these caused her a physical sensation of panic, as if the current moment might be the dream and she
would soon be dragged back to the reality of Mercy Hospital.

Friends and even vague acquaintances asked to visit, eager to be
with one of the medical wonders of the world. Edith Rockefeller McCormick had sent her several beautifully hand-printed notes with enigmatic
aphorisms, designed, as best Mim could interpret, to reinforce the idea
that no one should be troubled by what happens in this inconsequential
life, since there would be other lives to follow. This was not a message that
resonated with Mim, as she had spent months and endured considerable
pain to ensure that this particular life continued.

Even Madame X noted in her column, ". . . Mrs. Chauncey Blair's
midnight rush to the hospital and her victorious battle over death."

Martin Gaylord's letters to her had been such a relief because they
rarely mentioned her illness. While her women friends wanted to talk of
nothing but the details of her crisis, Martin focused her attention on the
world she most missed. A serious man about most matters, none more so
than about collecting art, he had the good sense to keep his communication with Mim light and occasionally capricious. He entertained her with
news of his trips to New York and his tangles with artists, dealers and
customers:

If I gave you a million opportunities to guess, you
would never suspect who bought the newest Hassam.

*There is a new hotel on West 10th Street with a chef
who has created a superb dish with oysters and
spinach and for some reason named it after the
Rockefellers. Can you imagine? You must taste it
when you are next here.*

*I was broken-hearted to lose the Titian, but I was not
about to pay more than...*

*I made a side trip to Boston to meet with Mrs.
Gardner, who is always looking for more acquisitions
for her museum. What a character she is! When I
arrived she met me wearing...*

Finally, in a more serious tone and with a special tenderness, he had written:

*Mim, I have not forgotten about the Book of Hours
I promised to find for you. Your recent illness has
fueled my resolve to make you happy with the
most exquisite example of Renaissance devotional
material available.*

He concluded by saying,

*Speaking of which, you will be amused to know I
received a letter from Hattie Pullman saying she
was also interested in a Book of Hours, specifically
one by the Limbourg brothers. I wonder where she
got that idea? Perhaps you are curious as to my
response to her. It was non-existent. She has no
right to such a treasure. I hope this little piece of
news makes you laugh rather than impedes your
recovery.*

With Fond Regards,

Martin Gaylord

Mim's telling of her story, over time, became mechanical—her inflections, pauses and emphases repeated in the same places each time. Mim added no unnecessary embellishments.

There was one part of her story she had told no one. She could not even convince herself that it had really happened. Her mind tried to replay the experience many times during the day. But it was in the dark of night that she came closest to capturing the magnitude of what happened at Mercy Hospital.

Mim recalled nothing of the carriage ride to the hospital. Vaguely (and perhaps only because others had told her about it), she could conjure up the image of being carried out of the house. All else was a blank until she was in that strange white room with more people around her than had been with her during her previous deliveries. In addition, several surreal, white-robed angels hovered, fingering beads as their mouths moved without sound. She remembered shivering, shaking with the cold and asking if someone would please fetch her more blankets. But no one seemed to hear her.

Then it happened. She saw, no, that was not correct, because her eyes were closed, she *experienced* being pulled into a luminous shaft of light. Not only was it beautiful, it was comforting and most blessed of all, it was warm. She was no longer cold. She was no longer ill and she was no longer scared. All she wanted was to be a part of it. And then she was.

As though animate, it drew her into itself and she was blissfully folded into its vortex. Everything inside the light was good. Everything outside was irrelevant. She was able to look down at the woman on the operating table, whom she recognized as her previous self, for whom she now had a kind of detached affection. She felt no emotional investment in this woman's well-being. It was the light she yearned for. And what was most amazing, the light yearned for her too—a gentle mutual attraction like two magnetic souls who have at last found one another.

The light encouraged her to travel within it. As she moved along its path, multitudes of apparitions, all of whom she sensed loved her, encouraged her onward. Though none of them had a defined corporeal shape— no faces, no bodies, nothing distinguishing one from another—she knew them all, and at the same time, she knew no one. Her emerging soul ached for only one thing and that was to stay in this place.

But, at the very moment she acknowledged this desire, she heard a voice calibrated in the strangest audible tone, somewhere between a lion's roar and a lover's whisper, say, "Oh no. Not yet. She is not ready. She must go back."

And so she did. With a heavily laden heart she returned, only to feel the abrupt absence of light, the return of the cold, and some restraint clamped over her face.

∽

Ever since her illness, Mim felt her attitudes and reactions changing. She now found encounters with friends tiresome at best and, at worst, irrelevant. She simply didn't care about who had been seen, who had not been invited, who had behaved, who had been daring—all tidbits that would have held her attention a year ago.

Her social skills had been finely honed over years of practice and familial reprimand, so she knew precisely when to laugh, when to express disbelief, and when to sympathize. Nowadays she found herself play-acting her way through most encounters.

Even so, she was looking forward to May and the fair. Whether the country re-elected President Harrison or voted for Grover Cleveland, the President of the United States was sure to serve as the officiator for the opening ceremonies. Every day the paper listed names of celebrities who had announced they would be arriving for the fair—Annie Oakley, the cowgirl entertainer; actress Sarah Bernhardt; Polish piano sensation Ignacy Jan Paderewski.

Mim pledged she would not treat her full recovery and the opening of the Exposition as a coincidence. If the beautiful light had let it be known she was not yet ready to stay in its divine cocoon, then she was determined to fill her earthly life with whatever adventures would make her ready the next time. The Chicago Exposition of 1893 would be the perfect place to start.

14

Revelations

Early Spring 1893

*A*S MIM HURRIED ACROSS THE World's Fair's East
Lagoon Bridge on her way to lunch, she saw Cissie Palmer's
black carriage come through the main gate at full tilt. Mim
paused to wait for her under the front portico of the Women's Building,
where she was also expecting her sister Tennie.

They were on their way to the café for a formal luncheon and a presentation by Swami Vivekananda. Mim was excited and more than a little
curious to hear this strange Eastern monk who had created such a stir
at the recent Parliament of Religions here in Chicago. Tennie needed
convincing.

"Tennie, it will be 'efficacious for your mind,' as Grandmother
Mitchell used to say," Mim told her sister. "He brought seven thousand
people to their feet for a two-minute standing ovation last month at the
gathering of religious leaders."

"Mim, the last thing I want is a new religion! I have never been in a church other than Saint Matthew's Episcopal Church, and I don't intend to shop around now.

"At least the Swami is not Catholic. Other than being responsible for your survival, I found nothing to admire about those Mercy Hospital nuns hiding their bodies underneath their angel costumes, pretending they aren't women, yet somehow married to God. All that ghoulish statuary with Christ on the cross, painted blood trickling over his nailed hands. Horrifying!"

"Tennie," said Mim with exasperation, "I am asking you to keep an open mind— not become a Buddhist, a Hindu or, God forbid, a Roman Catholic."

Mim was frustrated about the anti-Catholic bias her family expressed during her stay at Mercy Hospital. To a person they praised her recovery, called it miraculous, but not one of them ever managed to credit the Catholic doctor, the Catholic hospital or the Catholic nuns. This ridicule of the place and people who had produced her miracle was one of the reasons that, even after almost a year, she had told no one about her encounter with the beautiful light.

Mim's preoccupation with her near-death experience continued. Usually inspired by beautiful music, she was occasionally overwhelmed by a feeling of enveloping goodness—a feeling that she was completely loved and loving. It was pure, unconditional and abiding, the way love should be but seldom is.

Often she was embarrassed by these moments; they happened at the oddest times and caught her completely unaware. Just last week she was en route into the parlor thinking only of the quotidian errand at hand. She stopped at the sliding door and saw two of the parlor maids who, assuming they were unobserved, were singing a lilting melody and dancing a little jig. So absorbed were they by their own gaiety that when they saw Mim, they did not stop, but rather turned to her and clapped her into their little circle. Completely comfortable with their entreaty and with herself, Mim accepted their call and for a few seconds the three of them were laughing and dancing hand-in-hand as if they were girlhood friends, all social barriers temporarily broken. Within those brief moments there were hints of the light.

Originally, the skeptics, including her husband, had been certain a café catering to women would fail. Mim pointed out to Chauncey that the café would bring women of all classes together, a rare event in Chicago society.

"That is the whole point of the Exposition!" she challenged Chauncey. "This cafe will not simply be for the gatherings of our set. Women from all strata of society are welcome. All of us need a little spoiling."

With a delicious menu at reasonable prices, the cafe evolved into a successful enterprise, serving as many as two thousand women a day. Reservations had become so difficult to arrange that the Board of Lady Managers had to set aside a room for those, who by virtue of their social and financial status, would expect to be seated instantly.

One of the younger women managers suggested the private room be designated the "Isabella Room," "Isabella" being the nickname given to the radical feminists who were agitating for a woman's right to vote. Cissie Palmer, though she favored many rights for women, vetoed that idea out of hand.

"Ladies," said Cissie Palmer, "are you going my way?"

"I wager we are. Nice to see you, Cissie," said Mim, giving her friend a kiss on each cheek. "I want to introduce you to my sister, Miss Hortense Mitchell. Tennie, this is Mrs. Potter Palmer."

Hortense made a quasi-curtsey as she greeted her sister's illustrious friend. "How do you do, Mrs. Palmer? I love your building!"

"My building? If you mean the Women's Building, it has been a team effort.

"I hope you will have a chance to visit what I consider the best exhibit at the fair, which you will find in the Hall of the Decorative Arts. It is not to be missed. There are hundreds of exquisite pieces there from all over America."

With a wink she teased, "I am told the collection was assembled by the most discerning collector in Chicago. I stop in every day, and every day I find something more astounding—flushing toilets, faucets, things called 'zippers' that will eliminate the need for buttons.

"And while I don't think you will ever have a need for a map of the United States created out of pickles, that should be noted for sheer vulgarity."

Mim had not seen Cissie since the fireworks at the dinner party the Palmers had given for the Infanta Eulalia, the younger sister of the late King Alfonso of Spain. She had come to the exposition as a special guest of the American government.

Most of the invited guests, including Mim, had expected to be charmed by Her Highness. The early newspaper stories had depicted a woman of some spunk. She smoked cigarettes in public and was quoted as envying the liberty of American women. She loved to escape her bodyguards, leave her luxury suite at the Palmer House and walk incognito through the busy Chicago streets to watch what she called "the normal woman." She was gracious at the many ceremonies she attended, showing up promptly and with a smile on her rather pretty face.

But the first blush of appreciation was not to be the final hue of the royal visit. Princess Eulalia's initial enthusiasm for her tour waned quickly and obviously. By the end of her stay, she was absent more than she was present at scheduled events, and when she did appear, the smile was missing and she spent as little time as possible performing what were supposed to be her royal duties.

Her final insult to the fair and to Chicago was to its own royal family, the Palmers, when she behaved every bit like the "infanta" her title portended. She refused to attend the reception in her honor at the Palmers' residence, complaining that it would be demeaning to herself and her country to dine with a simple "innkeeper and his wife."

"Cissie, I just want you and Potter to know that, despite your lowly status, Chauncey and I always feel honored to be invited to a party at your home, and would be particularly delighted if you would be so kind as to set up the platform and throne you had built for Her Majesty. Chauncey is partial to elevated status," said Mim mischievously.

"Believe me," replied Cissie as smoothly as if she had rehearsed her response repeatedly, "We removed all signs of monarchical deference within minutes of the departure of the peevish princess."

Cissie turned to Tennie and, with her control quickly reclaimed, asked, "Miss Mitchell, will you be able to stay for the presentation by Swami Vivekananda?"

Mim seized the opportunity to answer for her ambivalent sister. "We were just talking about that. Yes, my sister has agreed to accompany me. She is very open-minded and is anxious to hear what the Swami has to say. Experiences like this are the heart and soul of what this fair is all about."

"Excellent," observed Cissie, heading towards the main staircase. "Now let's go see if our lunch today will feature the new dessert everyone is raving about that I think is called Jell-O. I understand it is as much acclaimed as the Palmer House brownies. It comes in all colors and jiggles wildly—just like the belly dancers on the midway.

"By the way, have you seen them? I am going to be sure to sneak a peek, just in the name of expanding my horizons."

The three women fell into easy conversation as they bypassed the line for the ordinary cafe diners and made their way into the Founders Room that was already filling up with curious Chicago matrons, as anxious for a good story to tell as they were to explore the realms of Eastern meditation.

As lunch was being cleared and coffee served, there was a stir at the rear of the room. Fashionably hatted heads turned toward a small coterie of dark-skinned men. At the center was a man who comported himself with such stately dignity that Mim knew that, if he was not Swami Vivekananda, he must be the god Vishnu himself. The manner of this man was so powerful that many of the women, Mim included, reverently bowed their heads as he passed, much as Episcopalians did each Sunday as the crucifier moved towards the altar with the cross.

Mim made an ungainly hybrid motion, something between a curtsey and a genuflection, which made her feel a little foolish but it was always better to err on the side of decorum than disrespect.

She had read every word of the newspaper accounts of the Swami's life. The god Shiva had come to his mother in a dream and predicted that her son would be a great messenger from God.

The Swami had fulfilled Shiva's instructions. He became a monk, wandering throughout India preaching tolerance and harmony.

Displaying genuine empathy for the sufferings of the poor, he carried only a staff, water pot and his two favorite books, *Bhavagad Gita* and Thomas a Kempis' *The Imitation of Christ*.

His entourage took seats at the back of the room. Well, not seats actually. They sat crossed-legged on the floor. She watched with admiration as one of the women at the luncheon boldly went over to the men and gestured to vacant seats, suggesting they would be more comfortable in the chairs. Smiling broadly in what could only be understood as polite appreciation, the junior swamis made return hand signals indicating they were perfectly comfortable as they were.

"Tennie, close your mouth, you are gaping," said Mim, accurately describing not only her sister's demeanor but that of most of the women in the room.

Swami Vivekananda was an imposing figure. He had a strong, swarthy face. Mim supposed his coloration was the result of years of traveling the rugged terrain of his native country. His good looks were enhanced by the naturally flattering bone structure inherited from his aristocratic Bengali family.

In her introduction, Lydia Watson, Chair of the V.I.P. Luncheon series, made the mistake of trying to seem more enlightened than she was about the Swami's mastery of the Ramakrishna tradition, flinging around terms such as "non-dualism" and "harmonic detachment" with an air of unconvincing erudition. Mim felt embarrassed for her and was relieved when the introduction ended.

The audience then rose to its feet. Some women clapped their gloved hands, others curtsied, a few deeply genuflected as if meeting Queen Victoria herself, which to Mim looked completely incongruous. She herself simply stood in place and then sat, pulling Tennie down with her.

Swami Vivekananda wore a long black linen tunic over matching trousers. His jacket had a square collar rising only slightly underneath a stiff white collarless shirt. His red and saffron-yellow turban was wound multiple times around his head, the remaining material cascading over his left shoulder.

Once on the stage, the guru gestured in appreciation of the warm reception by placing his hands in a typically Christian prayerful position—fingertip to fingertip—and bowing deeply. Motioning for everyone to sit down, he made his way toward the podium, but never reached it. Inches in front of it, he sat down on the stage and crossed his legs over one another in what looked to Mim like an excruciatingly uncomfortable position, though one that looked completely natural for Swami Vivekananda.

"Good afternoon, my sisters of America," he said in a simultaneously strong and lilting voice. With this greeting, he repositioned his hands and bowed as he intoned what sounded to Mim like "No Mast Day."

The Swami repeated the greeting and explained, "This, my friends, means that the divine spirit within me acknowledges and reveres the divine spirit which is within each of you, and it is that divine soul that must guide you on your journey towards God. All the great religions of the world lead to our Maker so that we are no longer separate from one another, but are part of the great whole. Our job in this life is to search for knowledge of the divine light. And when you have found the truth of the light, you will want to live within its embrace always."

Mim was fully focused on the words of the cross-legged speaker. She had brought a pencil and small notebook to record the Swami's wisdom.

The more he spoke, the more certain she was that this man had something to say to her. She was just not yet sure exactly what it was. One lesson she was able to record urged all men and women to "take up one idea. Make that one idea your life. Think of it, dream of it, live on that idea. Let the brain, muscles, nerves—every part of your body— be full of that idea, and just leave every other idea alone. This is the way to success, the way great spiritual giants are produced."

This simple statement of philosophy struck Mim forcefully. Was the swami suggesting that she now dedicate her life to the light of unconditional love? That was such an awkward quest in her social circles. How could a wealthy Chicago matron with a husband, four small children, and a reputation for solidity in the most elite echelon of society integrate the Swami's philosophy and her glimpse of God into her conventional life?

It was certainly more socially acceptable to make art the unifying force in her life. There were many wealthy women in New York and Chicago who were passionate about collecting precious pieces of art, either because they truly cherished them or because valuable possessions enhanced their status. Ever since she was a little girl, mentored by her grandmother, she had applied her intelligence and intuition to acquiring knowledge of painting, sculpture and the decorative arts. Beautiful objects had entered her life, enriching and fulfilling her, capturing her imagination and sense of history. Her mind was completely engaged when she researched a prospective acquisition.

But, unlike art, the light was not something one could study or master. How was one to learn the light? When those rare sightings came to her, her mind shut down. It was not her intellect that was engaged. It was her soul. If the Swami could just tell her which choice to make, she knew she could bring her natural discipline to its mastery. She understood the concept but she needed a road map.

Her discomfort grew when he said, "You have to grow from the inside out. None can teach you, none can make you spiritual. There is no other teacher but your own soul."

When the lecture was over, Swami Vivekananda arose and left the building, bobbing and chanting the sounds that still sounded like "No Mast Day."

It was clear that this strange man from the East had made diverse impressions on the women in the room. Some positively glowed with admiration. Others left the moment he had finished speaking, huffing and harrumphing as they pushed brusquely through the crowd.

"Ghastly man."

"Why would the Board ever let those people in here?"

"Worse than the Irish."

"Do you think that is his real skin color, or is he just dirty?"

Tennie and Mim parted company, Tennie no more enthusiastic about the Swami than she had been before the lecture. She decided to take a few hours and walk the midway by herself. Despite her admiration for her sister's accomplishments and artistic sophistication, she was more attracted to the exotic characters of the fair. Two in particular, starting with a young magician and contortionist named Houdini who, word had it, could miraculously slither out of stupefying, strong chains. Mr. Houdini, if you could call someone named Houdini "mister," was a new talent, but already he was the most notorious sensation on the midway. Tennie would have much preferred watching a human pretzel than listening to one of Mim's eccentric spiritualists.

Buffalo Bill Cody's Wild West Show was the other attraction Tennie vowed not to miss. Technically, he was not officially inside the fair, because his dozens and dozens of tents had been placed outside the thirteen-block midway – a colossal financial mistake on the part of those in charge, who could have quadrupled their revenue if they had placed the "Pilot of the Prairie" inside the fairgrounds. To Tennie, Wild Bill with his flowing hair, white buckskin coat and silver medals was far and away the man of her wildest dreams.

When Mim arrived home later that day, she did her best to tell Chauncey about the holy man. But because she still had not told her husband about her original transcendental experience, her description of the swami's words fell on puzzled ears.

Fear of a censorious or dismissive reaction to an intimate peek at her soul overtook her the few times she had thought she might reveal herself to her husband. Talking to Chauncey about being "enfolded in light," not wanting to come back to reality (which meant to him and the children), swamis, and ideas to which one should dedicate one's life would risk his considering her as eccentric as Edith Rockefeller McCormick.

Her experiences as a child had taught her that the more you told people about your secrets, the greater the risk of ridicule. Perhaps someday she would trust her husband, but at the moment it was simpler for them to live in the worlds they expected of one another.

For now, Mim would pray for glimpses of the light and would continue to surround herself with beauty. She would ask Martin to reinvigorate the search for the Book of Hours, which embodied both the beautiful and divine.

Family Outing

15

Fall 1893

*T*HE BLAIR FAMILY HAD BEEN looking forward to this outing ever since the fair opened. Mim was insistent that the fun would come in the afternoon, only after they had toured the Palace of Fine Arts in the morning. Chauncey had summarily decided they would then separate, Mim taking the girls to the Women's Building and he shepherding CB to the Manufacturers' Building.

"Chauncey," said Mim, "CB should see some of the items in the Women's Building, not to mention that I would like him to at least see the exhibit of decorative arts. It is a good lesson for him to learn—that while his father works hard at the bank, his mother can work hard at something as well."

"Yes," agreed Chauncey. "But then you and the girls can meander through the other exhibits while I show CB the dynamism of American capitalism. That, I can assure you, is something he will need to know."

"I don't doubt he will be appropriately well-schooled in banking and finance, but appreciation of the arts will give him a depth that all humans need, to be fully happy."

"Has such exposure made you happy, Mim?" asked Chauncey quietly. "I used to be sure about what made you happy, but you seem different of late, more unsettled," pressed Chauncey.

Mim considered before she answered. "You are probably correct. Ever since Billy's birth I am a little different. I feel it myself."

So unusual was Chauncey's inquiry into her emotional sensibilities that Mim felt she owed her husband a deeper explanation. But she was still unsure of her ability to express herself well enough to make her experience of the light adequately vivid. And if she failed to do that, she would likely encounter his skepticism and possibly his derision. That she could not risk. So she decided to divert his attention, a technique that had always served her well in moments of indecision.

"If you are asking whether or not I am happy, the answer is yes, I am happy. I am happy in this house. I am happy with our family. And though it sounds frivolous, my beautiful things make me happy. They are my treasured friends, collected over the years; every time my eye alights on one of them I feel happy.

"Speaking of beautiful things," she continued "Martin Gaylord has several sculptures he wants to show me before the fair closes next week. Would you like to see them with me?"

"No need. I trust your judgment," Chauncey replied.

Mim sighed. "By the way, I am going to hold you to a promise you made before Billy was born. Remember, you said you would take me to New York to search for a Book of Hours? Martin says he may have found an exquisite fourteenth-century one for me to look at, and you did promise—" said Mim, more coquettishly than she had planned.

"Unfortunately, Mimsy, it can't happen anytime soon. I am sorry. This exposition has stolen an enormous amount of my time. If you want to go in the next month or so, why don't you see if Tennie would like to accompany you?" And he was off.

Of the 27 million people who passed through the gates of the Columbian Exposition, most arrived on foot, including, today, the Blair family. They marched with the multitudes.

The fair would close at the end of the month. They had waited until October because both Mim and Chauncey had had so many social obligations. Mim was a guide at the Women's Building two days a week and a hostess on Drexel Boulevard at least three nights out of ten.

Chauncey was invited to breakfasts, lunches and dinners at the various clubs around town, helping clients to entertain visiting financial dignitaries. So the summer had sped by.

Another reason for delaying a visit to the fair was the fear created by the menacing news reports of what were called "the vanishments." Almost daily there was another report of a young woman who had come to Chicago to look for work—girls only slightly older than Italia—girls who arrived but whose families never heard from them again. While none of Chicago's children of privilege had disappeared during the summer, it was not uncommon in the elite world of the Blairs to overhear whispers of "kidnap," "ransom," "bodyguards" or, amongst the men, "arming," "pistols," and "shotguns."

By October, either the crime rate had diminished or the press had been silenced in the interest of attracting the final coterie of ticket buyers.

Today signaled the approach of winter, chilly and windy, enough so that Mim and the girls wore their heavy coats.

"Mother, we need to walk a little faster," said Italia, who was sniffing the air like a hunting dog newly onto the scent of its prey. "I can smell those beastly stockyards. It is disgusting."

"Ity, no one will smell anything but the crispness of fall today. Even this summer there were few complaints about the yards. Consider that your idol, America's most famous actress, Sarah Bernhardt, asked to visit them while she was visiting the fair, and reported the experience fascinating."

Rarely admonished to the point of changing her behavior, Italia continued to accelerate her pace while surreptitiously holding her nose.

Italia's mood had soured since she had learned that this day, the day she considered *her* day at the fair, had also been designated Waif's Day by none other than CB's hero, Buffalo Bill Cody. Italia had not known what a waif was before her father had read her the article in the paper. Apparently the officials at the fair had rejected a request that would have allowed poor children to attend the fair at no cost. Mr. Cody had subsequently and unilaterally invited all the city's waifs to attend his show as his guests.

"Why would he do that?" asked Italia sincerely. "I agree with the officials. If I cannot afford a ticket to something, I cannot go. Those are the rules."

Her father, naturally sympathetic to his daughter's argument, said, "I agree with you, Ity, but apparently Buffalo Bill does not."

"But today is *my* day at the fair."

"No, darling, it is *not* your day at the fair. It is our family's day at the fair," Mim broke in.

"What if people think I am a waif?" whined Italia. Mildred, understanding nothing of her sister's complaint except her tone, mimicked her sister's alarm.

"Mother, I don't want to be a waif," she howled.

"Girls, you have fur collars on your coats. I can assure you, no one will mistake you for waifs."

In the end, the day was a grander success than its beginnings had augured. The walk itself might have ranked as the most exciting part of the day, given the sights and sounds they took in on the grand midway. Several times Mim caught Italia and CB pointing and snickering at what they saw. Chauncey had jested that perhaps they could save the entry fee and simply walk home for entertainment, so exotic were the characters they met along the way.

"Eye-popping" was how Mim later described the walk to Edith.

Edith McCormick was normally unshockable when it came to matters of decorum. She stayed true to that impulse when she replied to Mim.

"Come now, Mim, this is a new world. Children must be exposed to new and different facets of life. As you have said yourself, it is an exposition. Its duty is to expose, both inside and outside the gates. Dr. Freud would find the whole experience efficacious for your children's psycho-sexual development."

"Well, perhaps Dr. Freud would like to explain to my seven-year-old son why, in broad daylight, those voluptuous doll-faced women were whistling and calling to his father, 'hey, hot stuff, come to Babette.' I actually had to laugh. I mean, Chauncey is a nice-looking man, but, 'hot stuff'?

"And you should have seen Mildred. It was she who stole the show. She made quite a spectacle of herself and it was all done in complete innocence, which made it even funnier. I suspect she thought those paint-ed women were clowns or simply part of the entertainment.

"All of a sudden we looked around and there she was, waddling behind a woman with ringlets of red hair, a face caked with cheap make-up. For a full block, until we could get to her, she followed the floozie, mimicking her walk perfectly, swishing her four-year-old hips and little *derrière* in perfect rhythmic synchronization with the harlot. It was too funny. She performed a completely accurate rendition of what it means to 'sashay.'

"Finally, the 'lady' stopped and turned, almost toppling Mildred over, and said to her, 'Hey, baby girl, want to come home with me?' at which point Italia, surprising all of us, pushed her way through the crowd and pulled her little sister away muttering, 'Next time, we take the carriage.'

"I don't know where the vice squad was," Mim continued. "Maybe they only patrol at night. Chauncey intends to speak with the police commissioner, and with good reason. I am sure other families have complained.

"By the way, did you see in the paper this morning that the London reporter for the *New York Times* said something about Chicago making more of an open display of evil than any place he had ever visited? After all the fine effort of so many, it seems a shame for the city's underbelly to be what people write about."

Taking a more worldly perspective, Edith said, "I am sure the hooch-ie-coochie girls are not what most women will talk about when they re-member the exposition, but it will be what every man I know will be thinking about if he were being honest. They posture and lie about true love, but believe me, they think with their genitals. Dr. Freud said—"

"Edith, please spare me another vicarious trip to Vienna."

Edith complied, but continued, "But worse, we have to endure the other extreme. The Moody evangelical Christians are everywhere now. I detest those dour black-bonneted women preaching hellfire and damna-tion and pushing their sanctimonious literature into our hands.

"The irony is that, in their ardor, they completely miss the fact that most of the young men who come to their tent are there for only one reason: to pick up the pamphlets which are veritable guides to the "dark places" of the city night life. The faithful think they are saving souls when in fact they are aiding and abetting carnality by giving out the best pornographic guidebook ever printed.

"Their abhorrence of liquor will never amount to anything. I promise you, they will have no effect. Americans like to drink and it will ever be thus. I would choose a little vice over piety any day of the week.

"But tell me about the rest of your day. Other than the hookers and the Jesus people, what did the children enjoy?"

Mim proceeded to recount the family's journey through the cultural exhibits and the midway. True to his word, Chauncey guided the children into the Women's Building and, with obvious and endearing pride, told them that their mother was the most impressive woman in Chicago.

In addition to the Palace of Fine Arts, Mim had insisted they go to Cairo Street. Luckily, they had arrived just in time to see the recreation of an Egyptian wedding celebration that was performed several times a day.

Cairo Street was arguably the most elaborate of the many ethnological stagings at the fair. It was a successful mixture of the principles of the fair—edification and entertainment, just as the guidebook had promised. The wedding procession had something for everyone—tom-tom drummers, camels, tambourine and flute players, twirlers, spangled and turbaned Arabs in long multicolored robes atop donkeys. As the procession danced before them, Mim, Chauncey and the children were applauding enthusiastically along with the rest of the crowd.

Chauncey, in a rare moment of spontaneity, had agreed to the pleas of the children and spent the extra ten cents a person for a private tour of a replica of the Temple of Luxor.

The vicarious visit to Egypt had inspired Mim as well. She remembered the many hours she had spent as a girl making lists of precious objects she wanted to be able to enjoy in her tomb. At the time it had made her less afraid of death. Now she knew that the only protection she needed was to be reunited with the reassuring light. And if she ever purchased a Book of Hours, she would have a real moral dilemma as to whether to take it to her grave or leave it to her children.

As she thought back on the family outing, she mused that very few experiences in life were as thrilling as they were predicted to be, but the ride on the Ferris Wheel was every bit as glorious as they had expected.

Mim and Chauncey were occasionally like children themselves. There were several unguarded moments when holding Chauncey's hand was the only tonic for her unsteady nerves.

The Ferris Wheel was Chicago's answer to the Eiffel Tower that had been the sensation of the Paris World's Fair. It too had been considered by many to be unsafe. Mim knew that the first visit to this bizarre contraption had been delayed until its public safety could be guaranteed, a delay that cost thousands of dollars in lost revenue. That fact notwithstanding, her fears about taking her family on so perilous a ride were not allayed. As she stood in its shadow her fears only grew more pronounced.

"But Chauncey, we will be over 250 feet above ground and there are over 100,000 parts to that mass of wood, glass and spokes. What are the odds that all of those parts will be working correctly at the same time?"

"I have no idea what the odds are, but the fair is almost over and there have been no lives lost," Chauncey assured her. "I will grant you there have been occasions when debris has fallen onto the spectators below, but no serious injuries resulted. Cissie Palmer was on the initial ride. What did she say?"

"She went with Mayor Harrison and the entire city council, so she had to put on a brave face however she felt. Nonetheless, she said it was not to be missed."

"Had I known of the passenger list, I would have seen to it that Cissie was in another car and then prayed fervently that that particular car did not complete both its rotations unscathed," huffed Chauncey, who was still disdainful of the Palmers' support of Mayor Harrison.

"Chauncey Justus Blair, that is the most uncharitable sentiment I have ever heard come out of your mouth. You had better be on your knees for a good long time on Sunday."

Each of the Blairs loved the ride on the Ferris Wheel in ways that were as different as their personalities. Chauncey, standing in the rising compartment and inspecting the nuts and bolts, was fascinated by the aerodynamics of the capsule in which they arose. CB fantasized about flying, telling himself and anyone who would listen that he would fly someday, maybe even around the world. Italia was busy trying to locate her house from the air and Mildred was simply gleeful about the whole experience, clapping and squealing with every turn of the car.

Mim was torn by two competing impulses that day—one was to simply rest her gaze on the magnificence of the view—the lagoon edged by the beautiful white buildings of the fair, the city skyscrapers, and the river with its miniature boats so busy in the harbor below. The second impulse was to simply watch her children watch the world. She was absorbed in their wonder and felt contentment in this moment of family unity and tranquility.

Italia was a particular joy to observe. It was as if the centrifugal force of the Ferris Wheel were spinning all the pretense out of her. She was beaming with the same childish jubilation she had shown when she was five years old, a relief and delight even for the short time it lasted. *Maybe she will be a happy person after all,* Mim thought hopefully.

Not wanting to end such a wonderful day by retracing their exotic morning journey, they rented two hansom cabs for the happy trip home.

"Mother," Italia said, dreamily leaning her head against her mother's shoulder, "does the Ferris Wheel operate at night?"

"I think it must," replied Mim. "I read that there are over three thousand electric lights strung around the exterior, all of which come on after dark and, with flood lights trained on it, the Wheel can be seen from sixty miles away."

"Can CB and I come back with you and father tomorrow night to see it? Please? Please? Please? I promise I will be my best self all year. I promise. I will not tease anyone. I will share all my things. Please? It will be the most beautiful sight I will ever see in my whole life. I know it will."

Mim was touched and amused by her daughter's enthusiasm. She replied that she and her father "would think about it," a phrase that any child as smart as Italia knew meant "no."

Mim knew her daughter would be proven right. The answer would indeed be "no." A nocturnal trip to the fair was out of the question. If there were any danger of "vanishments" during the day, the fairgrounds would be more menacing at night, even with parental accompaniment. There were simply no circumstances under which Italia and her brother would be allowed to go at night.

The final verdict was just as Italia predicted.

The Duet

16

"*M*RS. BLAIR, I JUST CAN'T do it," Bertha said as emphatically as Mim had ever heard her. "I hate to disappoint you and I know how much this dinner party means to you— means to all of us—with the famous people coming. But I just can't cook from this book. I can certainly prepare the scrapple. We have something like it in Germany, so I could make that. But it is a breakfast food. There is nothing I could do to disguise that fact. It would sit on the plate looking like there should be scrambled eggs next to it."

"That makes sense, Bertha. We will forego the scrapple. But is there no other recipe from the *Columbia Cookbook* that you could serve?" asked Mim.

For a moment Bertha just stared at her mistress with incredulity and then, coming as close as she ever had to challenging Mim's authority, said, "Mrs. Blair, have you actually looked at the cookbook?"

"I can't say I have. All the lady managers received a copy of it in appreciation for our work. I thought it would be entertaining for our guests, especially our international guests, to be eating authentic American food. But perhaps you are trying to tell me something important, so please go on."

"If that is authentic American food, then I have been living in the wrong country all these years," said Bertha.

"Bertha," said Mim calmly, "I am sure we can find a solution. Your dinner will be a great success, so please, tell me what choices we would have if we were to serve something from the *Columbia Cookbook*."

Anticipating this moment, Bertha had brought the offending cookbook with her, holding it as far from her as she could, as if it were a soiled diaper. She began to leaf through the pages, reading aloud some of the possibilities—baked calf head, how to skin and debone a raccoon, a blackbird pie, with real blackbirds.

"I had thought that a fricassee might be a way out of the dilemma, since I can disguise many sins in the heavy cream. But, see for yourself, the only fricassee recipe they have is for squirrel fricassee and I just will not do that. Even during the worst times at home, only beggars ate squirrel."

With this, Bertha closed the book and practically thrust it at Mim saying, "If you can find something to your liking, I will do my best. I always try to do my best for you and Mr. Blair, but I have my standards, Mrs. Blair."

"I know you do, Bertha, and I am not going to ask you to lower them even in the interest of culinary inventiveness. Trust me, Bertha, I will not allow this party to undermine your reputation as the finest cook on Drexel Boulevard."

"Thank you, Mrs. Blair. I appreciate that."

This dinner party was to be the most formal of the dinners that the Blairs would host during the fair. Mim had taken great care and gone to not inconsiderable expense to ensure its success.

Later in the day, she sent a message to Bertha, asking her to prepare a menu for dinner for fifty people, which they would review in the morning. "Perhaps Beef Wellington would be nice—"

Mim entered the dining room, savoring the moment she most enjoyed when she gave a dinner party of consequence—before the guests arrived. The room was as perfectly dressed as she was.

I am quite good at this, Mim thought to herself.

She had had the large table removed to make way for five round tables, allowing each guest more intimate conversation with his or her fellow diners. The flowers on each table included baby's breath and peonies in full spring splendor—their pale pink and white offering an elegant contrast to the dark purple iris and cascading ivy. No one arrangement was like another, but all the displays were complementary, like beautiful siblings in a family photograph.

Mim had chosen her Meissen china. Though it was not her most valuable, its crimson floral pattern and fluted edges sat exquisitely on the solid gold chargers that had been wedding gifts from Grandmother Mitchell. Each place setting was set off by four crystal goblets trimmed with gold leaf—one for water, one for the white wine to be served with the poached trout almandine, another for the red which would complement the Wellington, and, finally, the champagne flute to accompany the dessert Mim had left to Bertha's discretion. She hoped it would be a sacher torte, which was Bertha's *pièce de résistance.*

Chauncey and Robert had spent a great deal of time selecting the wines for the evening, and Mim was confident they would perfectly enhance the meal.

Normally strict conventions guided the behavior of well-bred guests, but Mim wondered, with a certain playfulness, if, when one had the American cowgirl Miss Annie Oakley and the Polish pianist Mr. Ignacy Jan Paderewski at the same dinner party, protocols could possibly be maintained.

One protocol that could not be overlooked was the selection of dinner partners— assignments that were made with more precision than a bank merger. Personal idiosyncrasies—long–standing animosities, clandestine romantic involvements—were all details that could be overlooked only at the hostess' peril.

The highest-ranking men of the evening would flank Mim. Tonight her dinner partners would be Potter Palmer and Mr. Paderewski. (Though she both liked and admired Potter, she wished she could have put Martin Gaylord next to her. She had several matters to discuss with him, the most important of which would be any new information on Hattie Pullman's quest for a Book of Hours. Nothing could convince Mim that Hattie had genuine artistic enthusiasm for this treasure of the Renaissance. She was simply being competitive.)

Mim was eager to have the Polish pianist as a dinner companion, but she worried about Chauncey being seated next to Annie Oakley.

"What in the world am I to say to her? We have nothing in common," said Chauncey with genuine if somewhat exaggerated uncertainty.

"You were from a farming family before you were from a banking family," said Mim with a smile. "Ask her about stud fees for her horses and continue from there."

Chauncey ignored what he assumed was sarcasm. "There is no chance she will be carrying a gun, is there?"

"I certainly hope she does," said Mim. "I promised Italia and CB they could come to greet the guests, and CB will be crestfallen if she has not brought her gun."

Tradition would prevail tonight despite the diverse guest list. Normally, for example, when Mim signaled that dinner was over, Chauncey, as the host, would rise and lead the men into the smoking room for port and cigars. The women would follow Mim to the front parlor for Sauturne and petit fours. The separation of the sexes after dinner, though a time-honored ritual, annoyed Mim, particularly if, after a desultory conversation with the gentleman on her left, she was finally immersed in an invigorating conversation with the gentleman on her right.

Tonight, however, unbeknownst to her guests or even to Chauncey, there was a secret plan, which by the end of the evening would obliterate all prevailing traditions, conventions, and protocol. Only she and Cissie Palmer, her co-conspirator, knew that the party would be remembered for only one thing—a stunning challenge to a cardinal rule of elite life. *Une scandale*, thought Mim with a mixture of fear and titillation.

Normally, the first thing people observed when introduced to a world-class pianist were his hands, as if genius were embedded there. Ignacy Jan Paderewski was an exception. It was his hair that arrested the eye. It was profuse and wild, so much so that Mim had to exercise extreme discipline throughout dinner to focus on his witty and intelligent conversation so as not to stare at the bottlebrush atop his head.

His Polish accent was thick, but years of listening carefully to Chester Hibner, her tailor, had prepared her ear favorably for understanding her dinner partner.

Mr. Paderewski took delight in telling Mim about his recent New York concert where, he proudly told her, the demand for tickets was so great the program had to be moved from Carnegie Hall to Madison Square Garden.

"This Garden is not a garden, Mrs. Blair. Madison Square Garden is an arena. Imagine hearing Chopin in an arena. But, do you know, Mrs. Blair, the audience was *fantastique*. *Absolutement fantastique!*

"In Europe, so full of pseudo-cultured people, I sometimes must stop my playing to tell the audience, '*SILENCE, s'il vous plaît!*' *Mais pas aux États-Unis. Le publique américaine a politesse musicale.*' Mim laughed at the thought of this musical lion roaring to his audience to be quiet. But she was patriotically pleased to hear of American audience supremacy.

Meanwhile, Chauncey seemed to be having no trouble conversing with Miss Oakley, or "Annie," as she told everyone to call her. As an accomplished hostess, Mim always kept her peripheral antennae alert to be sure all her guests were suitably engaged, and Chauncey appeared smitten. In defiance of proper etiquette, he had talked to Annie Oakley straight through the fish course, and they were now chatting through the beef course as well.

Miss Oakley had arrived with disappointingly little fanfare as far as the Blair children were concerned. They had been peeking from the upstairs window long before they were summoned to greet the guests. CB had been certain that Annie Oakley, the only woman he truly admired, would arrive guns a-blazing, on a horse that would be tied to the front porch during the duration of the dinner, giving him ample opportunity to befriend it. Perhaps Buffalo Bill's show could use a child stunt man. He would ask her directly should he be allowed to speak with her.

Miss Oakley was every inch an American cowgirl, and a pretty one at that. Her long, curly hair was an undistinguished acorn brown, but it cascaded gracefully down to her waist. She was surprisingly feminine for a woman leading such a masculine life. Mim honestly could not tell if she came in costume, or if what she wore was her dinner party best. Mim knew nothing about cowgirl outfits, but this appeared to be some kind of polished leather, the fullness of which allowed the sharpshooter to move with ease. The bodice was close-fitting, a bevy of colorful medals covering her chest. Her skirt was heavily fringed and she sported black and tan leather boots with pointed toes and high heels. Mim had been told that, among her other talents, Annie Oakley sewed all her own clothes.

"Annie is quite wonderful," fawned Chauncey even before they went in to dinner. "She has been traveling for more than five years as the only woman with a battalion of Indians, soldiers and cowboys. And she is the best shot in the group."

"Is that what all the medals are for?" asked Mim.

"Indeed. What you see is only half her collection. She can fire the ashes off a cigarette tip with a .22 caliber rifle, and she once shattered 90% of five thousand glass balls thrown into the air. Think of that!"

Mim knew someone who was star-struck when she saw him. She was resigned to hearing more about Annie Oakley over the next few days than she might want.

"And to think," she said, "I have just been handling babies while I could have been learning to handle a gun as well."

"Well, you might be able to do something about that. She told Philip Armour that she held classes for women. She would like to see every woman know how to handle firearms as naturally as they handle babies. And I thought you might want to sign up—"

"Suspecting where he was going, Mim cut him off quickly. "Chauncey, don't even consider my doing anything of the kind."

"By the way, Mimsy, this is an excellent party. You look lovely and all our guests appear to be having a wonderful time. You can now relax."

If only I could, said Mim to herself. She was growing more and more anxious about what was to come after dinner.

With that in mind, she detoured to have a private word with Robert. "Robert, I wanted to alert you that sometime before the dessert, say around eight o'clock, another guest will be arriving. He will come to the front door and I had better warn you that he is a colored man. A Negro, that is. Please show him into the drawing room and then come and get me, so I can receive him properly."

"Yes, Mrs. Blair," said Robert, betraying no reaction to the unusual news.

"Remember, Robert, the front door and then the drawing room."

A seasoned hostess knows from the earliest moments whether or not a party is a success. Mim knew this one was going very well. The dining room was buzzing with chatter, laughter, the clink of cutlery and crystal. There were no conversational wallflowers.

"Mrs. Blair, your guest has arrived and is awaiting you in the drawing room as you suggested," whispered Robert with a bow.

It was not unheard of for a hostess to leave the table, presumably to see to some detail. But what was a complete surprise to the guests at Mim's table, and to any other guest who happened to glance up, was that Mr. Paderewski stood, pulled the chair for his hostess, then accompanied her from the room. As if that were not enough to puzzle onlookers, it was not thirty seconds later that Mrs. Palmer smiled demurely, excused herself, made her way through the tables and also left the room.

Several minutes went by and the pulse of the party returned to its earlier liveliness. The sacher torte had been served, coffee poured, and the guests were expecting that at any minute Chauncey would invite the gentlemen to join him in the smoking room.

Curious guests speculated that something was badly amiss, and, truth be told, many were enjoying the speculation of an impending disaster.

With perfect timing, but sans Monsieur Paderewski, Mim and Cissie Palmer returned to the dining room and stood in front of the sliding doors. Cissie took a knife, which had been unused at Mim's place, and sharply tapped it against the champagne glass. It took no time at all to get everyone's attention, most particularly that of Chauncey Blair and Potter Palmer.

"Ladies and gentlemen, if I may interrupt your dessert for a moment," began Cissie. "Before I tell you what lies ahead for this evening, which I guarantee will be an unforgettable experience for all of us, I want to say a word of thanks to our host and hostess. Potter and I have known the Blairs for many years. We share many interests, especially enhancing the arts in this city for all its citizens to enjoy."

Chauncey had a ghastly feeling that what Cissie and Mim might consider "an unforgettable experience" would not be one he would have supported. His familiar distress about events spinning out of control was running silently but rampantly deep.

"During this last year, Mary Blair and I have become true friends. I have watched as she has masterfully supervised the decorative arts exhibitions in the Women's Building. When you applaud the exhibition, as I know you will, please remember that it was our hostess, whose exquisite and intelligent eye, made it the best exhibition in the building. Please join me in tribute to an astute collector and true friend of the arts, Mrs. Chauncey Blair."

"Here, Here," chorused the dinner guests, accompanied by an ear-splitting whistle from Miss Oakley. Now it was Mim's turn.

"Thank you, Cissie. There is no artistic eye in Chicago, nor in the country, that I admire more than yours, so I have learned from the best," Mim said, although as soon as she said it, she knew that it was an untruth, because the person who truly held that place of esteem in Mim's mind was Martin Gaylord.

"You must all be wondering about tonight's uncharacteristic informality. Tonight we are suspending the traditional separation of the sexes, and instead now ask the gentlemen to escort the ladies into the living room."

Mim knew that if she looked at Chauncey, she might lose her nerve. She had never considered letting him in on tonight's secret entertainment, as she knew he would have opposed the idea, and forcefully so. But she hoped by the end of a wonderful evening, and after he had received complimentary reviews for his open-mindedness, he would be mollified, maybe even proud of Mim's daring.

"I hope many of you have had a chance to speak with our two honored guests tonight, both of whom are visiting our city and its exposition. First, America's most accomplished cowgirl, Miss Annie Oakley. I am told that Annie, as she has asked us to call her, has been known to best any marksman in the country." Applause and whistles shattered the formal setting in exuberant appreciation of the feat and the woman.

Annie Oakley had been an entertainer long enough to know when to seize the spotlight, so she stood, executing both a crisp bow and then a deep curtsey. At that moment, Chauncey bounced off his chair and gave his dinner partner a solo standing ovation.

"I am certain you all know of our other illustrious guest. He is the great Polish virtuoso pianist, Mr. Ignacy Jan Paderewski, who has come to the exposition directly from a triumph in New York, where it was almost impossible to get a ticket for one of his performances. Tonight, many of you will literally have a front row seat. He has agreed to play for us, and when he has finished, he will introduce our third very special guest who is now, as they say in the theater, waiting in the wings."

Dutifully, and with a certain detectable group apprehension, the guests arose and walked arm-in-arm with their escorts into the living room. The only sounds were murmurs of curiosity and the rustling of expensive silk and taffeta gowns.

The great man himself was seated at the lustrously polished black piano. Because his head was bent over the keys as he softly played while the guests took their seats, most people could only see a figure that looked more like an aging feline than the world's most renowned pianist.

When the guests were seated and quiet, Mr. Paderewski arose from the bench and made a low bow. "Ladies and gentlemen, tonight I will play for you three short pieces by my fellow countryman, Frederick Chopin. I have selected three dances—two waltzes and a mazurka—in honor of the festive spirit of the glorious exposition that has brought me to your wonderful city, as well as to this delightful evening sparked by the charm of our hostess.

"Regrettably, Monsieur Chopin died at a very young age, but he loved to compose for the piano, a proclivity for which we should all be grateful. His music is romantic, poetic, often gay, and sometimes heartrendingly sad. You will hear all those emotions in these works tonight.

"All I ask is that you listen with an open ear, an open mind and a firmly closed mouth. I do not tolerate talking during my concerts and will stop playing if I hear any conversation. Please spare Mr. and Mrs. Blair that embarrassment."

With that command (and it was definitely a command, not a

request), Mr. Paderewski played. Those who knew anything about music knew they were hearing a virtuoso at his most brilliant. He interpreted the *vivace tempi* quite literally, leaving Mim almost breathless and decidedly awestruck. She had placed herself purposefully on the left side of the room so she could see his fingering; often there seemed to be hundreds of fingers playing, not ten.

At the conclusion, the audience hesitated before making a sound, concerned that the time had not yet arrived for applause and fearing castigation by the master. Mim had heard the *Valse* before so she knew its conclusion and rose to her feet, clapping vigorously and calling out "bravo," which was picked up by the others and echoed within the room. After a sustained ovation, and multiple bows, Monsieur Paderewski motioned for the audience to sit.

Everyone, except Mim and Cissie Palmer, was expecting an encore and settled easily, grateful for more music. Mim could not vouch for Cissie's nerves, but hers were electrified.

Mr. Paderewski spoke.

"Thank you, my friends. I thank you and Monsieur Chopin thanks you. His music will last through time and his reputation will blossom.

"Tonight I have a surprise. I will present to you a very different but no less exceptional musician.

"Last week, in a club in your city, I had the pleasure of hearing a young artist playing the most extraordinary music I have ever heard. It is, I am told, an authentic American sound called ragtime. It is happy music, filled with melodies as infectious as those I have just played for you.

"Let us think about this music as an experiment. After all, is it not true that the reason to hold an exposition is to expose? Yes, to expose us all to new ideas, new inventions and new talents. That is why I asked for and received permission from Mrs. Blair and Mrs. Palmer to invite a different kind of virtuoso here tonight. I, for one, will never forget that it was in Chicago, your great city, that I first heard the American ragtime. I ask you to keep your ears and minds open and, of course, your mouths shut. Ladies and gentlemen, may I present my new musical *protégé*, Mr. Scott Joplin."

Mim sat catatonic looking at the side door. The knob turned, the door opened and in walked the darkest man ever seen as a guest in any reputable living room in the city. Chauncey did not move a muscle. He did not even try to search Mim's face for an explanation. Italia, now sitting between her parents, openly stared at the man, wondering if he were dangerous.

Mr. Joplin was indeed dark. But he was also very handsome. He was dressed more like a banker than an entertainer—in a dark suit, formal white shirt with a rounded collar above a white silk tie. He had a smoothly shaven face and Mim, who had a front row seat, noticed his deeply intelligent eyes. He spoke in a baritone with little trace of his Texas roots.

"Ladies and Gentlemen, may I present to you a taste of American Ragtime."

With a nod to his benefactors, the courtly Negro settled himself at the piano and began to play. And did he ever play. Piece after piece exploded from the piano, coupling bold syncopation with energetic melodies. Mim noted with delight that many of her guests were smiling in appreciation of the performance, although possibly not of the performer.

It was hard to get a sense of what Chauncey was thinking as she was sitting next to him and could not see his full face. At the moment she did not care. This music was fun, simply spirit-lifting fun, and if she had to soothe him later, she would happily pay that price.

When the music ended, Mr. Joplin's Polish promoter rushed to the piano and almost lifted his protégé off his feet, clapping him on the back, raising their entwined hands in the air and bowing simultaneously, as if they had just finished a duet. Cissie Palmer and Mim made their way toward the artists and privately thanked them profusely for a wonderful evening of entertainment.

"Gentlemen, I thank you both for the most varied and interesting musical evening I have ever experienced," said Cissie as she extended her hand in congratulations to both men.

Turning to Mim, Mr. Joplin said, "I hope your guests feel the same way, Mrs. Blair. It is not easy sometimes to introduce traditional audiences to new musical forms and sounds."

"I am sure some will like it and others will not," Mim replied candidly. "Speaking for myself, I was thrilled by *all* the music and I would appreciate it, Mr. Joplin, if you will send me word of where you will be playing while you are in Chicago. I need to hear your music more than once."

"I will be delighted."

The days following the party were not pleasant ones at 4830 Drexel Boulevard. Mim had never seen anger smolder as deeply as Chauncey's. Close up and directed at her, it was intense and intimidating. Their words behind closed doors were rooted in what each felt was irrefutable and logical disappointment in the other. Chauncey was snappish at everyone and everything. Mim was quiet and felt bruised all over.

"Mimsy, what you have done is unforgivable. You should have warned me about who was coming through our door last night. I live here too. My name was also on the invitation and I have a position in this community that may now be besmirched by a colored boy being treated like a guest here."

"What would you have said if I had told you?"

"I would have told you no, of course."

"That is precisely why I didn't tell you. And Mr. Joplin is not a 'colored boy.' He is an artist. Most of our guests thoroughly enjoyed hearing him play."

"And some of them did not. I don't suppose you considered that."

"Of course I considered that. But I, too, have a position within the world of the arts. That is what happened here. People were exposed to something new.

"Cissie Palmer came to me and asked what I thought of Mr. Paderewski's idea of presenting ragtime to our guests. I told her I thought it was risky, which of course she already knew. She said, 'Mim, to be timid in the midst of all the talent that the fair has brought to Chicago is a waste of a unique opportunity.' If you look at it from her point of view, inviting Mr. Joplin made perfect sense."

"Did Cissie ask Potter what he thought?"

"Yes, she did, and he was none too pleased, but—"

Chauncey interrupted, "Everyone knows Potter is a sissy with a small 's' when it comes to Cissie with a capital 'C.'"

"So you are saying a man is considered a sissy if he supports his wife even though he disagrees with her judgment? Is that what 'for better or worse' meant to you when we exchanged vows—better for you and worse for me?"

"You, Mim, might do well to review those same vows, specifically the part about honor and obey."

"I did not disobey you, Chauncey. I simply chose to exercise my independent judgment."

"That judgment apparently falls somewhere between terrible and outrageous when you exercise it without me. You are sounding like one of those damn Isabella suffragettes who think they know everything about the world that men have been managing for centuries. It will be a long time before I am able to trust you again.

"Oh yes," he fumed, "and if you won't apologize for your willful error, which it seems to me you won't, then try to make amends with Italia. She knew it was an embarrassment to this house. Next time, when in doubt, ask her. She will lead you back to the straight and narrow path."

Mim was stung by his last belittling sarcasm. "Chauncey, don't you dare discuss this with Italia. And as to the 'narrow path' you value so highly, have you ever considered that narrow paths are seldom wide enough for couples?"

17

The Great Escape

October 1893

"IF YOU BREATHE ONE WORD, if you give one little hint, for the rest of your life I will consider you the most loathsome, awful boy in Chicago," said Italia, as her hand encircled her brother's wrist. Laying her other hand on the already reddening flesh, she once again squeezed them counter-clockwise, giving CB a deep burn to re-enforce her verbal threats with physical pain.

"Stop!" implored CB, tears forming across his long black eyelashes.

"I will not stop. Not until you promise me you will tell no one."

"I promise. I promise. But it is a dumb idea, Ity. What if you get kidnapped or killed? Mother says bodies wash up in the river all the time. One of them will be yours if you do this," wailed CB. Tears now flowed down his blotched face; mixed with the goo running from his nose, he looked an effluvium of misery.

"Cry Baby, Cry Baby," Italia jeered. "That is what CB will stand for forever. I will introduce you as my brother, CB, but what I will really mean is this is my brother, 'Cry Baby.'"

175

Italia was unused to being beholden to anyone, least of all to one of her younger siblings, who, in truth, were afraid of her. So now that CB had some measure of power over her, she felt an unfamiliar vulnerability.

Italia had not expected her brother would actually turn her down, but now that he had, he was a serious liability. Consequently, she would have to implement her plan this very night. It was the only way to lessen the chances CB would give her away. The longer he knew her secret, the greater the danger. So tonight was the night. Tonight she would ride the mechanical aurora borealis into the night sky and see the magnificent White City lit up like a thousand Christmas trees.

Italia had chosen her blue velvet frock both for the way it flattered her black hair and grey eyes and for the warmth it would provide on this late October night.

At teatime she was talkative and winsome, inquiring after her mother's day and general good health. Showing uncharacteristic patience, she spent the better part of an hour teaching Mildred the rudiments of playing jacks, which Mildred had been begging her to do for months. She ate heartily from the platter of thin tea sandwiches and shortbread biscuits and, after her mother left, put several extra nibbles into the pocket of her pinafore.

After supper, she excused herself from the table and bade her family good night, saying she was just about to finish a particularly engaging book and was anxious to see how things turned out. In truth she could not concentrate on anything at all, as she systematically reviewed each detail of her plan. One could not be over-prepared.

All her life, Italia had had no need to develop habits of tidiness because someone either prepared her clothing or picked up after her. So tonight she had to mimic the servants' routines as best as she could remember them. She carefully folded her escape garments into small piles, which she then distributed evenly under the covers at the foot of her bed to avoid obvious lumps. After checking and rechecking to be sure all three dollars she had saved were stuffed into her black patent leather boots, squirreled underneath her bed, she felt quite calm about her imminent departure.

When Mim came into the room on her way to bed, Italia feigned sleep, her face turned away from her mother's good night kiss. At the

risk of waking her daughter, Mim planted the kiss atop Ity's newly sham-
pooed, sweet-smelling dark curls and then, as she did nightly when tucking in each of her children, she whispered her most devout prayer. *Lord,
keep my Italia through the night. Bring her safe into morning's light.*

Since Italia knew her mother to be completely predictable, she knew
it was exactly 9:00 p.m. When the clock on the landing struck 10:00, it
was time to move. So organized was she that at the first chime she began
to dress and, by the tenth, she stood at the top of the back stairs, furtively
peering down into the dimly lit kitchen.

During the countless times Italia had reviewed her escape route, she
found herself most concerned about the moments in the servants' hall
that adjoined the kitchen. It was here, she predicted, she might be discovered. Knowing little about the private lives of the servants, she had no
idea if one of them might be lurking.

Italia saw that the top of the door to the outside had two bolts. One
was positioned just above the handle and posed no problem. It turned
easily and noiselessly. The other, which was at adult eye level, would require her using a chair. Placing her boots on the bench beside the door,
she glided noiselessly in her stockinged feet over the highly polished floor.
She picked up the closest chair. Understanding that she must lift rather
than drag it, she summoned all her strength and placed it directly under
the targeted upper bolt. She needed both hands to turn it. Louder than the
first lock, the sound froze her in place as she listened for anyone stirring.
Hearing no one, she regained her nerve and set the room in its original
order. She then transferred the money from boot to pocket, and, as an
after-thought, selected a banana from the basket on the marble side table
in case she was gone longer than expected.

Because this was the last week of the fair, closing time had been extended until midnight to encourage last-minute revisits and additional
revenue. But not daring to overreach, Italia had pledged to herself that she
would spend no more than an hour. In addition, she knew it would be
too dangerous to wander the fair as she would have liked, so she limited
herself to riding the Ferris Wheel—just the Ferris Wheel. Taking only
enough money to cover admission and two rides was the most disciplined
decision of her young life.

Thinking ahead, Italia had rehearsed her responses to any questions posed by inquisitive adults. If she were stopped on her way into the fair, she would say that she was going to fetch her parents because nanny had fallen and they were needed at home immediately. If any of her fellow passengers in the Ferris Wheel cabin pressed her for conversation, she would simply smile and gesticulate, and say the few words of German she knew, thus appearing to be foreign and unable to speak English.

Once out the door, Italia moved quickly. She met few people en route, and when she did, she kept her head low to avoid grown-up eyes recognizing eleven-year-old eyes for what they were. She passed no policemen, which both reassured and frightened her. Mercifully, none of those hideous painted women who had loitered in the walk with her family were on the street. Her brother and sister might not know what they were and why they were calling out to their father, but Italia did and she never wanted to think about them again. They were disgusting.

The weather was an accommodating accomplice. Chilly, but not cold, the night was overcast, eliminating the stars that would have competed with the ambient lights of the White City.

Long lines snaked toward the admission window, a fact that Italia correctly concluded would distract any ticket agent from paying undue attention to each customer.

"We want you all to enjoy one of the last three days of our great exposition. There is plenty of room for everyone. Please, just keep moving," said the guard marshaling the crowds into an orderly queue. As her turn approached, Italia kept her head down and her money out. "Peaze to haf a ticket," she said, using an accent she had practiced in front of her mirror. The sounds she made were loosely based on Bertha's heavy German accent, though the cook would have been offended had she heard Ity's imitation. The agent shoved the ticket at her without so much as an upward glance and through the turnstile she went.

Her mother had said that thousands of electric lights illuminated the fair at night. But as Italia took in the twinkling heaven she saw before her, she knew there were millions and millions of them. There had to be. Though her better judgment told her she should step lively, she stopped in her tracks, unable to move beyond the view of the lagoon. This could not be the same place she had been days earlier with her family. No, some magical creature must come each evening to sprinkle the White City with fairy dust. Giant searchlights swept the vast fantasy kingdom, showing each building, each walkway, edged in miniscule lights, as if every star in the galaxy had been assigned to a particular inch of the fair with the sole responsibility of illuminating its beauty. Everything gleamed white until her eye took in the enormous jewel-tinted bursts of water that spewed from the fountains that rose at the far end of the lagoon. Arced rainbows formed, as if recalling a giant thunderstorm.

The colorful gondolas in the lagoon, which had looked so pretty during the day, now looked like lighted lily pads gliding languidly through the dark waters. The strong, swarthy gondoliers wore brightly colored tunics and pointed jeweled slippers just like the ferrymen in the Grimms' tale of the *Twelve Dancing Princesses*.

Italia's equanimity dissolved at the magnificence of what she saw. She felt her heart pounding in a way it hadn't during the most daring parts of her journey. She told herself that whatever they did to her, however they might punish her, this moment was worth it.

✑

Italia was not the only member of the Blair family fully awake at this hour. But she was the only one who was having any fun. After CB had been tucked in and prayed over by his mother, he had tried counting sheep and then baseballs, but he was still wide awake, not to mention very worried.

CB knew Italia was not one to make empty threats. If he told Mother and Father of her whereabouts tonight, he could fully expect to be called "Cry Baby" for all eternity. She neither forgave nor forgot. Maybe it would be for the best if she *were* kidnapped, he considered, trying mightily to replace fear with logic. The household would, after an appropriate period of mourning, be a happier place. Perhaps his silence would be a gift to them all.

At the moment, CB couldn't know if Italia had carried out her plan. Maybe she had had a change of heart. If he woke his parents before he knew for sure, he would face double danger—Italia would know he had broken his word, and his parents would think he was simply trying to get her into trouble. No, he decided, he needed to gather more information before he took action. As much as he hated Italia at this moment, he could not erase from his mind's eye those women who had accosted them on the way to the fair. He was not sure what they were doing, but they were ogres. Ity was beautiful and those uglies might grab her and turn her into one of them. In fact, they might have done it already.

Though his room was dark, the hallway was lighted, a help as he sneaked down to Italia's room. Unlike his sister, he had no well-thought-out plan, other than to reassure himself that she was still in bed and a "fraidy cat" herself, which of course would be his new name for her had she not gone and was asleep in her bed.

Pulling the door slightly inward, he turned the knob quietly but quickly. It did not take long to see no head on the pillow and no body in the bed. Just to be certain, he inched cautiously to the edge of the bed and smoothed the spread, hoping against hope that he would feel her form.

Despite the conclusive evidence, CB remained indecisive about what course would now be best, though he found his feet moving downstairs toward his mother's room.

In all his nine years, day or night, he had never knocked on his mother's door. Since he and the other children slept on the third floor and his parents slept on the second, there was no easy access. Through bad dreams, fevers, and vomiting, he always called for Nanny. It was Nanny who pressed a cold cloth to his face and Nanny who reassured him that he had had a nightmare and all would be well.

The first several knocks were little more than a whisper of knuckles. When they produced no response, he began knocking with something approaching authority.

"Chauncey, there is someone at the door," he heard his mother say.

Surprised to hear his father's voice coming from his mother's room, CB heard his father reply, "I didn't hear a thing. Go back to sleep."

Not wanting to risk that possibility, CB knocked again and for emphasis he spoke for the first time.

"It's me, CB," he said.

Hearing the rustling from within, CB knew that, for better or worse, he had acted.

"Coming, coming," said Mim and after what seemed to be hours, his mother opened the door. "CB, what in the world are you doing here? Are you ill? Where is Nanny? Has something happened upstairs?"

Giving him no time to respond to any of these questions, his father, who was now sitting up in his mother's bed, began with his own set of interrogatories. "Who sent you down here? Do you know what time it is? Where is your sister?"

Finally giving him a question he could answer, CB said, "Well father, that is the problem. She is missing."

As most people do when they are instantaneously confused and deeply frightened, Mim and Chauncey needed to hear their son's message again and, hopefully, differently.

"What did you say?"

"I know I should have told you before, but she said she would—" CB, all his composure gone, was sitting on the floor of the hall, crying openly.

"What did you say?" repeated his father gruffly.

Mim, sensing this was not a winning approach, made a shushing motion to her husband and gently pulled CB into the bedroom where she seated him on the edge of the bed.

"CB, you must stop crying and tell us all you know about your sister's whereabouts. We are not angry with you. In fact, you have acted very bravely. Now, please start from the beginning."

"Mimsy, don't assure him we are not angry. We may very well be angry when we hear his story," interrupted Chauncey, drawing a withering look from his wife.

"CB, please tell us. Is Ity in her bed?"

"No, Mother, she is not. She has gone to the fair. She went to ride the Ferris Wheel. Remember, she asked you nicely, but you said 'no.' She asked me to go with her but I was too scared."

"No, CB, you were too sensible. Do you know when she left?"

"I am not sure, but it was sometime after you and Father went to bed. She had her clothes tucked into her bed and she had her own money."

Chauncey sputtered, "Her own money? Where did she get that?"

Mim could not believe her ears. "Chauncey, that is completely irrelevant at the moment. Who cares where she got the money!"

Turning back to her son, she asked, "CB, did she say how she was going to get to the fairgrounds?"

"Yes. She said she had memorized the route we took the other day. She promised me that the lights from the fair would show us the way."

Eschewing slippers or dressing gown, Mim rose and went downstairs to the recently installed telephone in the foyer. Chauncey and CB followed.

"What are you doing?" demanded Chauncey.

"I am calling the police," she said in firm reply.

"No, Mim, you will not call the police."

"Oh yes, I will call them. I believe that is why we have police, to find people when they are missing, and at the moment our daughter is very much missing."

Chauncey placed his hand over the small black mouthpiece into which Mim was preparing to speak and then, taking it from her trembling hand, carefully replaced the phone back into its cradle.

"Listen to me, Mimsy. I am as worried as you are. But if you don't want to see your daughter's picture on the front page of every newspaper in Chicago tomorrow morning, give me a chance to find her first. CB said she has gone to the Ferris Wheel, so I will have no trouble discovering her whereabouts if she made it that far."

"Don't say 'if she made it that far,'" Mim shouted, belying her earlier calm.

Then remembering that CB was at her side, she lowered her voice and began again. "I know she has made it that far. Ity is a clever girl. I know she made it that far. I know it. But promise me that if she is not on the Ferris Wheel, you will waste no more time and alert the police."

"You have my word," promised Chauncey, who was now moving at full throttle.

Taking the steps two at a time, he ascended the stairs in his nightwear and descended in his street clothes. He was out the door in less than two minutes.

Turning to CB, Mim saw in front of her the saddest face she had ever seen in a child. He looked every inch the street urchin—disheveled, his face a vision of tears and trauma—which corroborated her instinctual feeling that, at the moment, her son needed tending to, not scolding. Pulling him to her, she said nothing, just rocked him and rubbed small concentric circles on his still-shaking back.

∽

Italia had never known such exultation as when the door of the Ferris Wheel carriage slammed shut, closing her in the glass box that would lift her into the air. As each carriage stopped to disgorge those whose ride was finished and to receive new passengers, Italia inched closer and closer to the top of the giant wheel. No one could stop her now. She had won.

Not wanting to engage in conversation with any of the other passengers, she pressed her face hard against the carriage window, made cold by the night air. Then, as if to memorialize her triumph, she stepped ever so slightly back from the glass and let her index finger trace her initials in the moisture created by her breath.

After endless stopping and starting, her dream ride began in earnest. Delighted by both the ascents and descents, she loved stopping midair so her carriage could swing back and forth. She loved the intoxicating mixture of fear and anticipation at the tippy, tippy top. She was beginning to think she would need one more ride.

More than anything, Italia had been driven to return to the fair to see the lights— the lights of the Ferris Wheel, the lights of the fair itself and the lights of the city. She was not disappointed. As her carriage began moving, she felt as though she were ascending from the underworld and through the middle kingdom to the celestial realm where few humans ever travelled. She could hear the music from the midway singing her into the air. Through twinkling lights her imagination searched for a glimpse of her fairy godmother who surely had brought her this far.

When her carriage was fifth in line to release its passengers, she felt a thunder-clap explode in her stomach.

She saw him standing at the foot of the Wheel and she instantly realized that the end of her nocturnal joy ride was imminent. There would be no second ride, much less a third.

She had no doubt about the identity of the man who awaited her. What was in doubt, for the briefest of seconds, was whether there was any way she could evade her father. Perhaps if she turned around and flattened herself against the back of the cabin, the guard might not notice her and think her an entering rather than an exiting passenger. If she could gain just one more rotation, it would give her the time she needed to plan her excuses, if not her escape.

Now, only two carriages separated her from what would certainly be an unpleasant rendezvous. Panic fostered a better idea. When the door opened, she would simply run out, pushing her way through whoever stood in her way. She did not think Father could possibly outrun her. With the same kind of luck that had brought her this far, she might make it back to the house ahead of her father, reclaim her cozy bedroom, feign sleep and assert that of course she had not been at the fair and please leave her alone as she wanted to go back to sleep. Yes, she could see this might play out nicely, and it was her only hope.

As it turned out, luck finally failed Italia in the last moments of her incredible journey. Paternal instinct allowed Chauncey to spot his daughter before her carriage made its swaying stop. Obviously he had deputized the ticket-taker, as the uniformed man and Chauncey stood like overgrown tin soldiers blocking the doorway. Escape would not be possible. Vowing to leave the Ferris Wheel as proudly as she had entered it, Italia took off her hat, folded down her collar and made eye contact with Chauncey.

"Ladies and gentlemen," said the ticket-master, "I hope you enjoyed your ride tonight. Might I ask that you exit quickly, one by one, so that this gentleman can escort his daughter home."

Her father spoke not a word on the walk home, but he never let go of her hand and the pressure had hurt. Nor did her mother speak to her. She simply enfolded her daughter in a long and tearful embrace.

But Italia's experience in the nursery, to which she was summarily relegated "for the foreseeable future" was torture. She was forced to eat every meal with baby Billy while Mother and Father made a grand production of inviting CB and Mildred to dress every night and join them in the dining room for formal dinner. Italia was made to apologize to CB for putting him in such a compromising position. The indignity for Italia was stinging but she knew any retribution against her brother would bring her further punishment.

And then, after a week of indignity, the hammer fell harder.

18

A Premature Portrait

Fall 1893

*I*TALIA ALWAYS MAINTAINED THAT THE exhilaration she felt that magical night at the fair overrode the punishment she had to endure, though it had been extraordinarily humiliating.

It came as no surprise that her mother was shocked and outraged by her behavior. She was expecting that and, being a realist, she knew she would not be able to avoid some small measure of chastisement from her adored father whose blind devotion was acknowledged by everyone in the house. Unable to look his daughter in the eye as he laid down the law, Chauncey's voice left no doubt that this time he would not be susceptible to any of Italia's attempts at manipulation.

"Italia, your mother and I speak with one voice on this matter. You will not be able to divide and conquer us. You must accept that your transgression was grave— almost unpardonable. Consider yourself lucky to receive a punishment instead of a mortal wound in a back alley. No, my girl, we are doing this because we love you."

What a perfectly ridiculous thing to say, thought Italia. When I have children, I will certainly punish them, but I will never say anything that silly.

❦

Chauncey and Mim had agreed the time had come to commission portraits of their children. Initially they considered waiting a few years and including both of their daughters in the same painting but Chauncey's sensitivity to property rights argued for only one child per portrait.

"Having more than one individual in a portrait only makes life more complicated when dividing estate assets. We will have each of our children painted separately. You have to remember that a portrait is really just property," declared Chauncey.

"I had thought of them as representations of our children," Mim mumbled, then continued, "We will start with Italia. I want to capture her with as much of her child-self as possible. She is like a snake, each day shedding the few child-like qualities that remain. We must move quickly."

❦

Mim had met the artist Robert Vonnoch at a reception at the Antiquarian Society in early 1893. Their encounter was brief, but she had admired his work, particularly his portraiture. When Mim had asked Chauncey at the reception if he wanted to meet the man to whom they would entrust their daughters' beautiful face, he replied, "No need, Mimsy. I trust you. You can tell me what you know of him. Your endurance at these events far exceeds mine. My legs turn to rubber after thirty minutes and my legs tell me we have been here long past that."

Mim had ambivalent feelings about the freedom her husband gave her when it came to additions to the Blair collection. It was not that she lacked confidence, but how she would have welcomed a partner with whom she could exchange opinions and even enjoy the repartee of disagreement, as she did with Martin.

Mr. Vonnoch got off to a good start with Mim by arriving at 4830 Drexel Boulevard precisely at 10:00 a.m., as scheduled. Robert ushered the distinguished-looking gentleman into the morning room, which looked its best today, dappled sunlight lending fluttering energy to the otherwise sedate room.

"Mrs. Blair will be down momentarily. She asked me to tell you to please make yourself comfortable," said Robert whose pleasant smile complemented his simple politeness. *What a relief,* thought the waiting artist. Often butlers in elite homes appeared to have taken classes in the art of odious pretension, likely designed to create the impression that they were a mere half-step below their employer's station in life, while the guest's social status was yet to be proven.

Robert Wells Vonnoch felt no unease in the Blairs' morning room. His wife Bessie was originally from the Chicago area and had begun her training as a sculptor here before their marriage. Bessie's family was not wealthy, but her work at the Fain Galleries had led her, and subsequently her husband, into the mansions of many private collectors.

Just last week, George Pullman had selected Vonnoch to begin preliminary sketches for an enormous oil painting of him and his wife and their two purebred water spaniels. After the initial meeting, the artist predicted that the dogs would prove the easier subjects. High-spirited though they were, the dogs at least showed some warmth, unlike their pinched and petulant owners.

"Mr. Vonnoch, thank you for coming and for being so prompt. I apologize for keeping you waiting. My grandmother used to say only unimportant people are late so we now know that by her standards I am irrelevant and you are a person of the highest value." Already delighted with her forthright manner, Mr. Vonnoch gave his new client a compliment of his own.

"Mrs. Blair, while I doubt you are irrelevant, your collection certainly is not. I can see from my brief moments in this one room that you have an exceptional eye for beauty. Your reputation has preceded you, and I can see it is well deserved."

"Well, it is a bit eclectic, a mélange of the classical and Oriental, but I can honestly say I love all the pieces I have purchased over the years. And as sentimental as this may sound, they are my friends, each and every one.

"Tell me about yourself, Mr. Vonnoch, and then I will tell you about my daughter. I understand you studied at the Pennsylvania Academy of Fine Arts. Is that correct?"

Yes," Vonnoch replied, "I then went to France for additional study, most recently with Claude Monet who is the—"

"Oh indeed, I know the works of Monsieur Monet, Mr. Vonnoch. I am working hard to keep an open mind when it comes to the Impressionists. Instinctively, I am not enamored, but some people whose taste I admire are schooling me in their merit."

Mim pressed further, "Mr. Vonnoch, how would you characterize your style?"

Robert Vonnoch laughed again at Mim's directness and answered, "Well that depends on with whom you talk. Monsieur Monet tells me I have not sufficiently abandoned the traditional. He would never think of me as a true representative of his school. On the other hand, American reviewers often label me as the man who brought French impressionism to the United States. I love color, particularly when juxtaposed against white. In my landscapes, I make abundant use of natural light and broad-brush strokes.

"But let's talk about what you contemplate for this portrait, and we will see if we can come to a meeting of your mind and my style."

After only forty-five minutes, Mim and Mr. Vonnoch came to terms. The artist left with a deposit for half the agreed upon price. He would begin the following Monday. If their daughter was compliant, the sketches would take only a day or two and, if approved, he could begin painting her by mid-week. The Blairs' daughter was a little younger than he would normally recommend for a portrait. But while painting Miss Blair would be a challenge, if he pleased Mrs. Blair, he would surely earn the favor of her many well-placed friends.

For weeks Italia had been looking forward to what she considered her initial passage into womanhood—sitting for her first portrait. She and her mother had spent hours considering what she would wear, how to fashion her hair, and whether or not she would be allowed to redden her cheeks.

Still relegated to the nursery, presumably to reinforce that she had behaved like a child, Italia thought she sensed a thaw in her parents' attitude. At least they were now responding to her comments and questions in full sentences instead of monosyllabically noting her presence. Perhaps the worst was over.

By the Wednesday preceding her sitting, she was surprised she had heard nothing about the details. By Friday, she was more than curious.

"Mother," she probed, "when is Mr. Vonnoch coming?"

"On Monday morning," Mim answered her daughter without embellishment.

"Oh goodie," Italia replied, her eyes lighting up with the first good news she had had in almost two weeks.

"Maybe on Sunday, after church, you can help me try some different arrangements of my hair."

"Oh darling, I don't think that will be necessary," said Mim, focusing all her attention on her needlepoint, as if she were sorting out an especially complicated pattern.

"Thank you, Mother, but I should at least have—oh, what do people call it when they dress as if it were opening night?"

Mim knew the drama of her daughter's punishment was drawing close to its denouement. Thus, she was both attracted to and repelled by the prospect of delivering her upcoming pronouncement.

"It is called a dress rehearsal, and I think you have a good idea. We will do it this afternoon at teatime, so when you come down, please do so dressed in the frock we have picked out," Mim said encouragingly.

"Yes, Mother. But don't call it a 'frock'. That sounds frightfully babyish. I call it a gown."

"Yes, Ity, I am sure you do."

Italia began preparing for her dress rehearsal immediately after the chat with her mother. She was still in love with the dress they had selected. Mauve had always been one of her most flattering colors, and when she added the simple strand of graduated pearls and matching drop pearl earrings her mother kept in the downstairs safe, she would be transformed from being simply pretty to ravishing.

Wanting a more adult look, Italia wished the gown fell to the floor instead of to mid-calf, but the length of the dress was unlikely to be represented in the portrait. Now that she thought of it, there were many other details as yet unknown and about which she had hoped to be consulted—what room would they use for the sitting? What would Mother select for the background? How would Mr. Vonnoch position her? How many sittings would be required? Would she have to remain completely still? Could she talk with the artist? Would Mother remain in the room for the whole time? She must press her for more information at teatime.

Mim intercepted her older daughter in the hallway outside the library. Italia was pleased to see her mother had not forgotten to bring the jewelry, which she handed to Italia. Needing no mirror, Italia fastened and straightened it into perfect alignment on her neck and in her ears, as if she had come into this world similarly adorned.

"You look simply lovely," said Mim, and she meant it.

As mother and daughter entered the room, Italia was besieging Mim with questions, which showed how much she was anticipating her starring role in next week's event. So animated was she, it took her a few seconds to notice that Mildred had preceded her into the room.

"Millie, what are you doing here dressed like that?" asked Italia with authentic curiosity.

"Mother said I was doing a dress rehearsal for Monday and that I should wear the dress she bought me," Mildred replied innocently.

If Italia were on the verge of becoming a Mediterranean beauty, Mildred would be her English counterpart. In years to come, beaux could choose their particular ideal of beauty by favoring one of the Blair sisters. If you liked dark, exotic and sultry women, Italia would be your choice. If you liked a delicate English rosebud, it would be Mildred.

Mildred's complexion was all peaches and cream, framed and complemented by auburn ringlets that cascaded to her waist. Today, the tresses were pulled back from her face and secured with a lavender bow, as if an enormous purple butterfly had appeared.

She wore a dress unknown to her older sister and, although Italia considered it childish, she had to admit it was a beauty. The underskirt was sheer white linen, starched so crisply it looked as though it might stand on its own. But it was the overlay that arrested Italia's eye. The lace was magnificent, looking as though dozens of Spanish mantillas had been delicately woven together, using the thinnest silken threads from the world's most intricate spider web. Mildred looked like an angelic postulant, all purity and ethereal innocence. What added to her aura was that she betrayed no self-consciousness, no trace of vanity, either in the way she held herself or how she looked at her mother and older sister.

"Why are you looking at me like that?" asked Mildred.

Italia was beginning to sense there was a twist in the plot, which would not be to her advantage.

"Mother," she echoed, "why is Mildred dressed like that?"

Taking a deep breath and trying to remember to keep her voice even, Mim proceeded to answer each question at the same time.

"Well, girls, there has been a slight change in the plan regarding the portraits. Your father and I have decided that you, Mildred, will sit for your portrait first, beginning on Monday morning."

There, thought Mim, with a mixture of relief and dread. *It was out.*

As if lurching for a ray of hope that all was not lost, Italia asked with a hint of desperation in her voice.

"Mother, do you mean that Mildred and I will be sitting together in the painting? I thought you favored one-at-a-time portraits. I would go first, then CB, then Mildred, and then Billy, when he is old enough?"

"No, Ity. Your father and I have decided, for reasons you will understand if you think back carefully to your recent behavior, that Mildred is to sit for the first portrait. The only reason I have included you in Mildred's dress rehearsal today is because you are going to be accompanying your sister to the sitting to watch Mr. Vonnoch work on his rendering of your sister. Mr. Vonnoch will, if he has time, and you are on your best behavior, make a sketch of you, for use when we get around to commissioning your portrait."

Mildred felt bewildered as she tried to comprehend what part she played in her selection as the subject of the first portrait. Whatever it had been, she was excited. She loved her dress, the bow in her hair and the most exquisite adornment of all—the undivided attention of everyone in the room.

Her mother may have felt relief and her sister may have felt confusion, but Italia felt volcanic anger. A powerful hurricane of tears ensued, followed by tirades and hysteria and then, true to form, she collapsed onto the floor in a spasm of weeping and groaning.

As Mim and Mildred watched this performance, Mim could sense from her younger daughter's face that Mildred's natural sympathy was about to complicate matters.

"Ity, don't cry. Please get up. I will let you go first," Mildred said as she moved towards the mound of misery folded on the floor. "Mother, do something. Please let Ity go first. It does not matter to me. Please, Mother."

Mim had never felt less maternal than she did at this moment. Over the years, Italia had accrued and wielded power over the household. Now, Mim could feel an almost gleeful hardness encrusting her heart. As difficult as it was to admit, she was enjoying this visible demonstration of her rightful dominance over her daughter. Mim knew, however, that she would be wise to leave the room immediately, lest she weaken and before Mildred became a pawn in the drama that Mim suspected would not end any time soon.

"Come along, Mildred," said Mim softly, "Your sister needs some privacy to collect herself."

Italia's deportment during the painting of Miss Mildred Mitchell Blair was exemplary, and therefore, astonishing. For eight days she sat, dressed in her finery, reading quietly as Mr. Vonnoch sketched, dabbed and brushed oils on the large canvass that slowly bore the likeness of her little sister.

Until Mildred was married and the portrait was sealed, carted and sent to New York, it hung over the fireplace in the library as a constant reminder to Italia of the unfairness of life.

A Premature Portrait

19

Fall 1893

*M*ARTIN GAYLORD FLIRTED WITH MIM and she flirted back. But their badinage lacked the overt sexual innuendo he sensed with many of the women he knew—so obvious, so common and therefore so boring. There were far more beautiful women available to him in Chicago, New York and Paris, but Mim's exposure to the arts at such an early age had made her an astute companion.

When he and Mim disagreed, as they often did, Martin admired the way she took a position and defended it knowledgeably. In refreshing contrast to the typical rich American woman, interested in buying in bulk, wanting to purchase culture to adorn her drawing room, Mim was a cut above all the others. Martin might not agree with her conclusions, but her point of view was always worth hearing.

The newly rich were transactional. They hired Martin to find a piece, verify its preferably European provenance and assess its likely rate of capital appreciation. Only then would they sign the check. This approach by unsophisticated shoppers, personified by Hattie Pullman, infuriated him.

They made no effort to understand a work of art. They made no effort to learn why it represented something beautiful, or something interesting, or even something risky. "I don't know why, Mr. Gaylord, but I just don't like it," they would say, shaking their heads and smiling weakly. He had never heard that kind of blanket banality from Mary Blair.

Mim was a collector at heart, and she was gaining legitimate respect from the true cognoscenti, certainly in Chicago and increasingly in New York. But more than that, she was not afraid to fall in love with something.

By now Mim's devotion to classical art had become almost a joke between them. She would never be avant-garde in her taste, but moving her toward more modern sensibilities was part of Martin's challenge and delight in spending time with her.

Today he was taking her to the exposition to see several sculptures by Auguste Rodin, the French sculptor whose earliest roots were in Mim's beloved Greek tradition.

Sara Hallowell, who was the chief buyer for the Potter Palmers, was Monsieur Rodin's representative in the United States. She had met the artist in Paris several years ago, and it was she who had asked him to submit his work to the exposition so he could become known to American audiences and, more importantly, to wealthy American buyers.

Technically, Sara Hallowell, and not Martin Gaylord, should have been the one to bring Mim to see the sculptures. Martin certainly knew the proper courtesies and he was perfectly happy to give Mrs. Hallowell the lion's share of any commission that might accrue from today's visit. But Sara Hallowell had agreed to let Martin introduce Mim to Rodin because, "We are two weeks away from the close of the fair and I have had not a single bid on any of the pieces. So be my guest. I have been so very disappointed in my Chicago clients. I thought they—"

"For God's sake, Sarah," Martin interrupted, "how could Monsieur Rodin possibly expect to secure a bid when such splendid statues are behind draperies, being treated like objects in a peep show?"

"You are right. Americans still operate with a seventeenth-century puritanical disposition. If they don't change, the rest of the art world will always think of them as cultural Neanderthals, though don't quote me on that," scoffed Sara Hallowell.

"Can it be that none of them has seen a Michelangelo or a Reubens? Christ, if the *David* himself came to Chicago, they would probably send him to Marshall Fields to be outfitted before putting him on display," said Martin dismissively. "If they don't sell here, you should take the sculptures to Isabella Stewart Gardner in Boston. She has expressed an interest and she is not the least bit timid about nudity."

⁓

"I think you will find this worthwhile," Martin said, handing Mim a brochure. "After you read it, you will better understand why I asked you to come today."

"I don't need to understand why you issued the invitation. I spent a glorious but exhausting day here yesterday with Chauncey and the children, and I am looking forward to adult company, your company most of all."

"Will you allow me to buy you some lunch after we have looked at the Rodin?"

"I certainly will," said Mim, thankful for the care she had taken in choosing her outfit.

She immediately felt the pleasure of sharing a compatible pace as she and Martin set off. It always irritated her that Chauncey charged ahead whenever they were looking at a possible purchase together. He was a man on a mission—find the piece and come to a quick decision. For Mim, most of the enjoyment came from circulating through a gallery, pausing, evaluating, and admiring.

"Aha, now I see why you think I will like Monsieur Rodin's work!" said Mim, reading the brochure. "I thought you wanted me to leave fifth-century Greece and the Renaissance behind. I suppose you have read what Monsieur Rodin says?"

"I have," answered Martin with a smile.

Despite his affirmative response, Mim decided to read the sculptor's words aloud:

"For me the Greeks are our masters. No one ever executed sculpture like they did. They knew how to make blood flow in the veins of their statues."

Despite the provocative subject matter, Mim felt no embarrassment looking at the sculptures with Martin. Although he stood by her side, he carefully positioned himself at a respectable distance, which she appreciated. So there they were, she and Martin Gaylord encircled by naked bodies—polished, luminous, begging to be stroked.

All three works were nudes. By far the most titillating and the most beautiful to Mim's eye was the statue of *Cupid and Psyche*. Rodin had drawn forth from the white stone both erotic passion and tenderness. What he captured was infinitely more than an embrace. What struck Mim most forcefully was that Psyche was by no means the passive recipient of Cupid's kiss. Her strong arm was firmly around his back, right beneath his wings, and her small breast came tantalizingly close to his muscled thigh.

She felt an urgency to separate herself from Martin. On the one hand she wanted to be frozen into this day, and on the other she wanted to flee. The ease of their ambling had passed and she could feel the long-forgotten, aching, moist arousal begin to paralyze her movement as well as her ability to think clearly.

Mim spent almost an hour considering the Rodin sculptures. In the end, she decided to buy none of them. She loved the Cupid, but it was just too provocative. In her mind it would always be associated with her day with Martin. She was not ready to be known as the woman who had such erotic tastes.

By lunchtime, their normally comfortable conversation had turned awkward, filled with double entendre and innuendo. And upon later reflection, and to her horror, she realized she had initiated most of it. Several times there was an unusual heavy silence between them, which had never been there before. Sensing the silence had an obvious meaning, they would both try to fill it simultaneously, thereby tripping over one another. She felt untethered from the safety of social stricture, much as she had felt untethered by centrifugal force on the Ferris Wheel.

Only because of the discomfort she was feeling was Mim relieved to see Hattie Pullman approaching their table.

"Well, look who is here? Are you looking or buying, Mary? Do tell."

"Don't tell her anything," hissed Mim under her breath.

Martin rose to greet Hattie, making no motion toward the prominently empty seat at their table. Not surprisingly, she sat down unbidden.

With little choice but to be minimally polite, Martin answered the question that had been directed at Mim.

"I can't speak for Mary, but I am here to see the Rodin sculpture so I can figure out what all the fuss is about. Having seen Monsieur Rodin's work, I am frankly disappointed in the puritanical hysteria with which the people of Chicago have greeted some of the most beautiful sculpture I have seen in years."

"I think they are disgusting," countered their uninvited guest. "But I am especially glad to see the two of you together today because I have a piece of news."

Knowing further debate on the place of nudity in art would only attenuate the length of this unpleasant interruption, Mim and Martin simultaneously asked, "What is it?"

Pulling back from her tantalizing revelation, Hattie became more coy saying, "Now that I think about it, I think I shall wait until you receive an announcement of a major work George and I have acquired. Invitations go out later this week. We will welcome something very special to Chicago. But I had best leave it at that, just in case something goes awry at the last minute. But I know you will both be very happy for me."

I doubt that, thought Mim. Normally a woman who genuinely liked people, there was something she detested in Hattie Pullman, a feeling further enhanced when Hattie collected her things, rose from her chair, looked directly at Mim and said, "Mary, I assume Chauncey has no cause for concern over your artistic assignations with Martin. Maybe you two will come as a couple to our party."

On her way home, Mim had to restrain her impulse to run the last part of the way, feeling relieved and safe only when she walked through the door, instantly but not completely comforted by the normality of her surroundings. She was almost hysterically happy to see the children and was overly animated when Chauncey came home from the office.

Mim did not like her current persona. In her discomfort, she began the tedious but predictable cycle of constant worry over how God, who judged the smallest of missteps, would treat these bold transgressions. She was certain He would punish her—and she deserved it. She must tell Nanny to increase her vigilance over the children in the coming days, for that was where God was sure to strike.

When they were at dinner that evening, Chauncey asked about her impression of the Rodin sculptures.

"They are interesting, but there were none I admired enough to take you to see. I can certainly understand why there has been such a hullaba-loo over their display," said Mim. "The powers that be, whoever they are, did the right thing by securing them behind the drapery. They are not appropriate for general viewing."

"I am surprised you say that, Mimsy," said Chauncey. "You normally tilt to the side of artistic freedom. You were certainly all in favor of artis-tic freedom when you invited that colored man to play his minstrel show right here in our home.

"I presume Mr. Rodin is French, is he not? How like a Frenchman to submit pornographic sculpture to a public fair."

Ignoring the jab aimed at her invitation to Mr. Joplin, Mim replied, "No, they are not pornographic, but they are, shall we say, well, loose. Monsieur Rodin has talent. And he may well be the sculptor of his gener-ation. I will keep my eye out for something more suitable."

꿍

The next morning Mim carefully crafted her thank-you note to Martin for the outing and lunch. She was painstakingly careful to infuse propriety, even primness in every line she wrote. The salutation read, "Dear Martin," and then continued textbook perfect, "Thank you very much for. . . ." She tried several different ways of closing the letter, settling on, "Sincerely, Mrs. Chauncey J. Blair."

A Letter

20

November 5, 1893

Miss Hortense Mitchell
Milestone House
Kansas City, Kansas

Tennie Darling:

Oh how I have missed you these past dreadful weeks! I am sure you will remember that when we said goodbye, I told you that you were making a mistake in not being here for all the activities, parties and balls marking the end of the exposition. How wrong I was!

Every day, since Mayor Harrison's assassination, I have wished to join you to be as far away from this miserable city as possible. Naturally all the closing festivities were cancelled, and, though I never had much affection for Mr. Harrison, no one—not even Chauncey—would have wished his life to end this way.

I sometimes think it has all been a bad dream or the work of a melodramatic novelist—the bleeding mayor dying in his son's arms, calling out for his fiancée who was racing to him before the moment of death. If you or I had read this in a novel, we would have scoffed and pronounced it 'trash.' But that is what actually happened.

I was sorry to miss your phone call yesterday, especially since it was long distance and must have cost you dearly, but it was the day of the burial, and we were among the mourners walking behind the casket. I felt somewhat hypocritical walking with the dignitaries, who, almost to a person, loathed Carter Harrison. But there we all were, a bleak sea of black solemnity, as if the dirge was for one of our own.

I myself would not have gone because I really did not know the mayor well, but Cissie asked all the local members of the Board of Lady Managers to participate in tribute, and most of us did. (Death is classless, after all.)

Though it annoyed Chauncey to hear me say so, the mayor has to get some of the credit for the success of the fair.

Whatever one might say of him, Mayor Harrison was beloved in the neighborhoods of the city, and they did him proud yesterday. Thousands and thousands of what the newspapers referred to as 'real people' fell into line behind us; thousands more stood at attention on the sidewalks, saluting and openly weeping as his casket passed by. Reporters estimated there were over two hundred thousand people crowded along the route to Graceland cemetery, not including those who travelled by carriage or hung from the windows.

Most touching was the honor guard of Chicago firemen who walked beside the casket—strong burly men, tears flowing, their white-gloved hands tenderly placed on the American flag covering the casket. The Pipers of the Royal Scots piped Mr. Harrison into his grave.

If you have read the newspaper accounts, and found yourself disbelieving the bizarre account of the actions of the perpetrator, I can confirm they are all true! This venal little Irishman is insane. Apparently he had sought the job of Corporation Counsel—a position for which he had no credentials—and, when rejected, plotted his revenge. He appeared at Mr. Harrison's home, was admitted by a maid, marched into the room where the mayor was resting and shot him three times in his stomach. Just like that! And, to cement the validity of his insanity, he ran directly from the scene of his crime to the police station where he confessed it all.

Clarence Darrow has agreed to represent him but most informed people say he will face the death sentence. I certainly hope so.

At any rate, I miss you. It always feels lonely without you and never more so than in times of calamity. Despite your being my much younger sister, I find myself quite dependent on your company.

I hope my description of these events does not upset you. I will write more cheerful news tomorrow or the next day.

With much love,

Mim

There Must Be Some Mistake

21

January 1894

*H*ATTIE PULLMAN WAS MORE BULLDOG than woman when she set her mind on something. Recently that something was a Book of Hours, not because she valued Renaissance art, and certainly not because she hoped it would deepen her spiritual life. She simply wanted one. Why, she asked herself, did she need more reason that that?

She no longer believed she had an ally in Martin Gaylord. If Martin were going to look for a Book of Hours, he would put Mary Blair's interest ahead of her own.

Hattie harbored several resentments against Mary Blair, most especially her overstated reputation as a cultural maven. By wealth and notoriety the Pullmans' status should have eclipsed the Blairs', whose wealth came from financing the entrepreneurial energy and creativity of people like George. Manufacturers were the drivers of American ingenuity because they actually made things that people wanted. To Hattie, banking was a second-rate route to riches. Yet in so many social situations, she and

George were shunted aside by people courting Mary Blair's opinion on what constituted cultural quality.

In addition, Hattie's suspicion was that Mary Blair, who had a perfectly adequate husband at home, used the guise of artistic collaboration for more prurient reasons. The hypocrisy! Everywhere Hattie went, there were Martin Gaylord and Mary Blair, moving as a single muse for each other, like Siamese twins conjoined by shared brain waves.

She, on the other hand, lived in the tyrannical and immense shadow of George Mortimer Pullman, with no apparent Lancelot lying in wait.

Soon it would be her turn to take center stage.

⚭

While he was not considered in the same league as Martin Gaylord, Samuel Drucker had been an art dealer in Chicago for several decades. His knowledge of art was adequate but, more importantly, he had cultivated a capacity for attentiveness and alacrity to which many, most recently Hattie Pullman, easily succumbed. Within a month of meeting with Mrs. Pullman, he sent her a note informing her that he had found what she was looking for.

My Dear Mrs. Pullman:

First, let me say that meeting with you gave me a joy I don't often feel with other clients. Your eye has a unique ability to discern both the beautiful and the valuable.

I think I have found both in my successful search for a significant Book of Hours. Its distinguished provenance will perfectly match your own status in society.

The Book belonged to Margaret Beaufort who, as I am sure you know, was the grandmother of Henry VIII. She was the richest woman in England and the dowager queen. She was renowned for her piety.

This book was her personal devotional.

The manuscript is currently secured in a fourteenth-century monastic library outside London. My guess is the monks are in search of new revenue.

While the book is available for sale, foreign governments are making it difficult for "national treasures" to leave their country. Your husband is known to have many connections both in the United States and abroad. Is it possible he would be willing to bring his considerable influence to bear in securing the Beaufort Book?

Please let me know if you wish to proceed, as we will need a deposit to hold the book in your name. This is a rare opportunity and no time should be lost.

Sincerely Yours,

Samuel Drucker

Dear Mr. Drucker:

I am enclosing a check for five thousand dollars as a deposit on Margaret Beaufort's Book of Hours. However, I do wish you to continue your search for one of the books illustrated by the Limbourg brothers, whose work I know to be superior to any in Margaret Beaufort's library.

That said, I do want the Beaufort book if I must settle.

Finally, I am sure my husband can pull any string necessary to acquire whatever you find for me. He is, as you know, influential both here and abroad.

Sincerely,

Hortense Pullman

Dear Mrs. Pullman:

I have investigated every lead to find a Limbourg

Books of Hours. You are correct that their work is seen as the pinnacle of the genre, but their books are somewhere in France or Italy, the two countries *with the most rigorous restrictions on foreign sales.*

The Beaufort book is located in England, which also has restrictions on the removal of national treasures. However, and this is where your husband comes in, I have contacts who would be amenable to facilitating the transfer of this property with a well-placed word at the Ministry of Culture.

Sincerely,

Samuel Drucker

Hattie had gotten close, very close to purchasing her own Book of Hours, but she needed George's intercession to break the logjam before the book would be hers.

After almost thirty years of marriage and four children, one should not require a strategy to get a simple favor from one's husband. How nice it would be to emulate Cissie Palmer, who simply asked Potter and then proceeded to get what she wanted. Or to be like Mary Blair and have her own bank account. But neither of those scenarios applied to her situation, so she had to work with what she had. Luckily, she knew exactly to whom to turn.

"Florence, the hotel has your name on it! Everyone knows Papa named it after you. All I am asking you to do is tell him that the Beaufort Book of Hours will ratify the reputation of *your* hotel beyond anything in any museum or personal collection in Chicago."

"Mother, I don't care a fig about the prayer book of some lady who lived almost five hundred years ago. I know Papa will do it if I ask him, but I just don't care about this enough to waste my power."

"I am not asking that you care. I am asking you to pretend that you do," Hattie said. "As you might imagine, it is not easy for me to have to implore you like this. I would like to be able to ask your father myself. But those days passed long ago."

"What exactly does this Book of Hours add to the hotel that makes it worth owning? If it is so valuable, shouldn't we have it here at home?" asked Florence.

"Status," said her mother. "It adds status to my name and your father's name and, by extension, to yours."

⤝

Mr. and Mrs. George Mortimer Pullman
Request the honor of your presence

Wednesday evening
April 23, 1894
6 p.m. to 8 p.m.

The Florence Hotel
Pullman Village
Chicago, Illinois

Installation of The Book of Hours
of Lady Margaret Beaufort

⤝

"It's a charade! It's like a parlor game where I write 'A Book of Hours' on a piece of paper, Hattie Pullman picks it out of the hat by mistake, and now she is acting out the part that was meant for me. It was supposed to be *mine*. I collect.

She acquires."

With Chauncey standing beside her, she turned the invitation back to front and front to back as if looking for the correction she had missed.

"You know I am not going to this," Mim stated, brandishing the offending invitation in the air.

"Yes," answered Chauncey. "But you also know that by not showing your face where it would be expected, Hattie wins."

"Chauncey, she has already won. I have never thought of the purchase of a Book of Hours as a competition, but at the moment this feels like a victory for the enemy."

"Mimsy," said Chauncey, now in possession of the invitation, "This says that the Pullmans have purchased Margaret Beaufort's Book of Hours. I thought you wanted one by some Dutch brothers."

Scoffing at her husband's ignorance, Mim said derisively, "Anyone would *prefer* one of the Limbourg books, but they will never be available for purchase in America. Make no mistake about it. George and Hattie have the prize. They have my prize."

Mim heard the phone ring, but since she had not slept a wink until dawn arrived, she felt entitled to the little bit of sleep she had just dozed into. Moreover, she had no interest in speaking to anyone about anything.

"Forgive me, Mrs. Blair, I know it is early, but Mr. Gaylord is on the phone," said Margaret from the other side of her bedroom door.

Mim's first thought was that Martin had called with the clarification she had been looking for, a rectification of the ruse that the Pullmans had secured Margaret Beaufort's Book of Hours.

But her hopes sank. Martin's opening words were more a rhetorical question than a reassurance. "You got the invitation, I assume."

Tensions Abound

May 1894

M OST OF MIM'S FRIENDS FELT relief as the fair and the burdens of constant entertaining, outings and busy schedules diminished. But the exposition had allowed Mim more social and intellectual freedom than she had ever known. She missed the charisma of fascinating new people, many of whom she had entertained at her table.

Mim did not expect to feel so alive ever again.

Before the closing of the fair, Mr. Paderewski had returned to Drexel Boulevard to play duets and she had attended three of Swami Vivacananda's yoga classes—stretching and lunging, all the while trying to figure out what in the world these contortions had to do with spiritual enlightenment.

She had traveled vicariously to dozens of countries—eating indigenous food, marveling at local costumes and, most thrilling of all, experiencing art from cultures with which she had no familiarity. Most of what she saw she admired as "intriguing," even if she did not especially yearn to possess it.

Routine and the blow that Hattie Pullman had rendered to her spirit had left her feeling deprived and, from time to time, weepy. She forced a smile when friends noted that it was Hattie Pullman who'd orchestrated the biggest coup the Chicago art world had seen in many a season.

"Mim," said Malvena Armour, "If anyone were to purchase a Book of Hours, I thought it would have been you. You've talked about it for years."

"Mim, have you seen the Pullman's Beaufort Book of Hours? Tell me what you think of it?"

Each comment like that, and there were many, literally left a putrid taste in her mouth. *I think it is beautiful and I think it should be mine*, is what Mim thought.

Chauncey was hard-pressed to understand what was ailing her, suggested that she had a case of "nerves," and recommended that she take to her bed for a few days. That was the last place Mim wanted to be. What she really wanted was more excitement.

Chauncey still had not forgiven his wife for her betrayal of their shared values— inviting that colored man into their home. Mim knowingly and defiantly exacerbated his anger by a trip to a "club" with that "lunatic" Edith Rockefeller McCormick, to hear Joplin play again.

Mim saw every minor flaw in her husband as evidence of his provincial dogmatism and narrow view of life. It was visceral. Few mannerisms escaped her critical notice, though she bit her tongue. Even the selfish way he made his choice out of the bowl of mixed nuts at cocktail time set her teeth on edge. *Really,* she thought to herself as she watched Chauncey pick only the cashews, *the differences between us are found in that nut bowl. Wasn't the joy of life in the mélange of what came our way? To eat only one kind of nut, where was the fun in that?*

The exposition had given Chicago a temporary immunity from the virus of economic depression that had infected America. But after the closing festivities, Chicago got sick. Thousands of fair workers joined the ranks of those whose employers had already been forced to cut labor costs for lack of consumer purchasing. More than ten thousand workers flooded into the general labor market at the end of 1893. Few were absorbed and Chicagoans grew desperate. As banks closed and orders fell across all sectors of the economy, the city tried to dull its pain in cheap pleasures.

Michael (Mickey) Finn had begun to tend bar at Toronto Jim's on Custom House Place, experimenting with a magic potion he would use to knock out and then "roll" unsuspecting customers.

Men so inclined could be serviced for a nickel by "cribs," the name for the rooms that housed opium-addicted prostitutes who sat in the windows of cheap houses in the Levee district, making suggestive gesticulations to passersby.

Rich men had access to more sanitary sexual pleasures. The Chicago police, handsomely rewarded for episodic blindness, encouraged a fierce competition among madams, including Vina Fields, a Negress whose forty colored "employees" serviced a whites-only clientele. But if Miss Fields' and Mr. Finn's workers were fully employed, they were the exceptions in 1894.

State Street, the center of Chicago commerce, was still chaotic— throngs of people, clanging El trains (the wonder of urban transportation). But inventories remained high and the craving of shoppers to buy was meager. Marshall Field continued to recruit farm girls to run the elevators in his department store and hired boys to run cash transactions, but in far fewer numbers than before. He no longer hired theater set designers to decorate his windows—a wrenching decision as far as Mr. Field was concerned because he had insisted, and been proven correct, that display was the key to successful enticement.

Preceding the fair, innovation infused his store. Field opened the first-ever bridal registry and expanded the men's department to cater to the needs of the well-appointed traveling man—silver saddles for western travel, outfits for an upcoming safari or dapper yachting haberdashery. Men forced to accompany their wives into the store found the smoking room a satisfying place to pass the time, nibbling on smoked baby alligator and quail eggs.

In peak seasons and prosperous times Marshall Field employed as many as nine thousand workers. Now, as he walked his customary route through the store, he knew profits were down by almost half and the store's ability to 'give the lady what she wants' had been badly compromised.

As worried as he was about plunging orders, he was apoplectic about union activity among his staff. Allegedly, though not surprisingly, it was said that Marshall Field had spies sprinkled throughout the building to catch even the softest whisper of employee organizing.

Because the balance sheet at Blair bank was strong, the family was immune to the difficulties of the workingmen and women of Chicago. As yet they had laid off no staff and, insensitive to the cause, Mim viewed the less crowded aisles at Marshall Fields as a blessing. But Mim did read the newspaper and she could tell that her husband was worried.

"Chauncey, you would tell me if the bank were threatened, wouldn't you?" Mim asked after a particularly quiet dinner.

"Of course I would, but there is no need to worry on that front. Unlike the failed banks, we are well capitalized, something the banks that have failed have not been. They have taken risks I would never sanction," Chauncey replied with an ever-so-slight edge of sharpness. "There is simply no reason for you to worry. In fact, there are benefits to the larger banks because when weak banks fail, we just buy them up."

As he reviewed the evening's mail, Chauncey reached across and handed Mim a letter, commenting, "Here is a letter for you posted from New York, but the return address says its author is a guest at the Union League Club."

While Chauncey may not have known the name of the correspondent, Mim did. It was from Martin Gaylord. She took the envelope, but to gain some time and distance from Chauncey, as well as to compose her nerves, she walked to the desk and picked up the letter opener. When she extracted the letter, she was relieved to see it was little more than a postal card and that the message was a short one.

Dear Mim:

I have returned from Paris. I think I have found your Book of Hours. It is sensational, but the transaction may be complicated.

I cannot obtain it for you in the normal way. You will have to come and see it for yourself.

Sincerely,

Martin Gaylord

Mim handed the note to Chauncey, gave him a few minutes to read it and then asked him, "Chauncey, please tell me, can we go to New York soon?"

"This is unlike any transaction I have ever heard of. No price, no description, no dates attached, no artist. It is as if Martin does not want to commit any information to writing," Mim said as Chauncey read.

"I agree," said Chauncey.

"That is why I want you to come with me. If Martin wants me to travel all the way to New York to see this Book of Hours, and I buy, this will be a significant purchase, potentially the most significant of my collection. You must come."

"Mimsy, I have told you. I am not going to be able to get to New York for at least another six months."

"I have the feeling I cannot wait six months to see it," Mim replied.

"Then you will have to wait until the next opportunity comes along. I simply cannot manage it," said Chauncey, becoming more adamant as the conversation progressed.

"I have waited years for a letter such as this. You know that, Chauncey. If Martin says it is sensational, I must take him at his word."

"That is precisely my point, Mimsy," said Chauncey. "You *have* waited for years to buy a Book of Hours. Surely you can wait another six months." Softening his tone a little, he added, "Believe me, I want you to have it. You deserve it, especially since—"

Neither needed to mention Hattie Pullman by name. But her presence was in the room, just as it was wherever Mim went, at every social gathering where she ran into someone who pressed her on her reaction to the Pullman purchase.

Mim was not proud of her animosity at being bested by Hattie Pullman. But she had wanted a significant Book of Hours for years. It was literally her heart's desire.

Ever since she was a little girl, Mim had needed to feel an emotional connection to the things she bought. She had been known to pass up valuable pieces because they did not delight her heart as well as her eye. She knew she would love a Book of Hours like nothing else in her collection. It represented a combination found all too rarely in artistic expression—beauty and heavenly inspiration. It embodied the phenomenon where the limitations of human creativity meet some kind of divine force and transcend those limitations. She was convinced that there was such a force and that only *it* could extend beauty beyond what was possible for mere mortals to achieve.

The monks who ornamented these books were not interested in self-expression or self-aggrandizement. They illuminated for the glory of God with their exquisite calligraphy, vibrant colors and gold-leaf binding. Mim romanticized the monks, vividly seeing them hunched over the prepared vellum, working for months to create a small human paean to their Lord. The monks must have been held in the light as they worked, the same light that she had been held in at Mercy Hospital.

In the end, the best Chauncey could offer was to allow Mim the freedom to go with her sister Hortense. Mim wrote to Martin to see if he was still planning to be there in two weeks time when she and Hortense could arrive.

Dear Martin:

Thank you for your intriguing note about the Book of Hours. Without question I am interested in coming to see it! I had hoped Chauncey would be available to travel with me in the next two or three weeks, but he is not. However, my sister, Hortense Mitchell, who has never visited New York, has agreed to accompany me.

I have several matters to attend to here in preparation for my trip, but I have made a reservation on the Pullman Palace Car (yes, you will understand the irony of that unpleasantness. I would rather take a cattle car, but there is little choice from here to New York).

We leave Chicago on May 11 and will arrive in New York on the 12th.

We will be staying at the Waldorf Hotel.

In order that I may be better prepared, I would appreciate any details about the book that you can send me—dates, coloration, provenance, condition, to name just a few of the hundreds of questions that are floating through my overly excited mind.

Appreciatively,

Mary Blair

Mim was normally a patient collector, understanding the value of circumspection before buying any art. Rarely did she make an impulsive decision. But since receiving Martin's note, her caution had turned into a concentrated commitment to join him. She spent several nights in turmoil, her mind spinning, as if she had unloaded her brain onto Mr. Ferris' wheel and then stood as an onlooker, wondering when the wheel would stop so she could put her mind back into her head. Her agitation was exacerbated by the mysterious tone of Martin's letter—no price, no provenance, no description, no facts, just hints at something wonderful.

She would go to New York and, unless something were truly amiss, she would be buying.

23

Preparations

*D*ESPITE A RITUALIZED COCKTAIL HOUR, the Blairs were not heavy drinkers. Mim applied strict rules to her own imbibing, repelled by the sight of people whose personalities changed from attractive to ugly when spiked with too much liquor. She would never drink to excess, for fear of losing the control she had carefully cultivated over the years.

Currently, many touted the virtues of living a life free of alcohol. A whole movement had sprung up urging complete "temperance," as devotees called it. They demonstrated in the streets, always carrying sanctimonious signs urging all who encountered them to accept their view that alcohol in any amount was a vice.

Last week on her bicycle club outing, she had ridden past a particularly large group of the austere members from the Women's Christian Temperance Movement. They banged their drums, shook their tambourines and chanted, "Serve the tyrant alcohol no more," while blocking the entrance to McEntee's Saloon.

"In reality, there is nothing temperate about their views," said Mim to Chauncey one evening.

"Listen to this," she continued. "I received it in the morning mail."

Chauncey looked up from his paper, curious as to what in the world had put, yet again, such a sour look on the face of his wife.

"First of all, Mimsy, who is the letter from?"

"It is from Malvina Armour, the president of the new Women's Athletic Club. The issue is whether wines and spirits should be served at the club. Can you imagine such a restriction at any of your clubs?"

"Only when hell freezes over," answered Chauncey with a disparaging chuckle.

"Well, it is going to get plenty cold at the Women's Club if this ban is allowed to stand. If Malvina has her way, we will never be able to attract new members and will likely lose the ones we have."

"Malvina is a teetotaler?" asked Chauncey.

"She does not drink herself, if that is what you are asking. But therein lies what annoys me so about issues like this. The Women's Athletic Club is a club. It is not her home. We all pay to use the trapeze, the pool, take fencing lessons and work the dumbbells. And after an energetic workout in the gymnasium, nothing feels better than a Turkish bath, a hair wash and a light lunch made complete by a glass of sherry."

"Mim, why is this so important to you?" asked Chauncey, quite surprised at the fervor of her reaction. "You don't even drink very much."

"I am taking this seriously because I hate being ruled over by people who impose their personal values on the rest of us."

"By the way," Chauncey said distractedly, "Do you have a date yet for your trip to get that book you are after?"

"It is a Book of Hours, Chauncey. You refer to it as if it were a romance novel. And yes, Tennie and I are planning to leave on May 11th. I think we need only be there a week. We will take in some sights, wander the new collections at the Metropolitan, and maybe go to the theater. I am very much looking forward to it."

"What might you expect to pay for a Book of Hours?" asked Chauncey.

"That is a good question. It is curious that Martin has said nothing about price. In fact, he has shared few details at all, despite my inquiries.

But if the book merits Martin's lavish praise, I am prepared to spend what I must to have it."

"Do you have any guess as to what the Pullmans paid?"

"Well, I suspect that there were two prices. One that they paid by cheque and another they paid behind the scenes."

"Are you saying that George bribed someone?"

"Not with money, perhaps, but there are many forms of bribery," said Mim enigmatically.

"Mimsy, I have never before interfered with your purchases. I admire your taste as well as your sensibility. But for some reason, I feel apprehensive about sending you off in search of your heart's desire."

In preparation for her journey to New York, Mim had been operating at full tilt for days. She had packed and repacked, only to take her trunks apart and start from scratch. Margaret, her personal maid, had seen to it that her wardrobe had been laundered, pressed and wrapped in tissue paper but her mistress needed to make decisions she seemed unable to make. Claiming that her indecisiveness was merely a result of the unknowable weather in the east, Mim disrupted Margaret's normal efficiency.

"Margaret, I am afraid this blue suit will have to be re-pressed. I have decided to take it after all, and the tissue has come off with all the in-ing and out-ing. I am so sorry to trouble you, but linen withstands so little handling."

Despite her official, "Yes, Mrs. Blair," Margaret groused aplenty to her compatriots downstairs. "Lordy, if I did not know Mrs. Blair better, I would think she had a secret admirer awaiting her in New York. It has taken us a week to do what could have been done in an afternoon."

"You know Mrs. Blair better than that," scolded Bertha. "How many trunks is she taking?"

"At last count, four. But by the time I get back up there again, it may be six. At the moment, there are two trunks for ball gowns and the opera, one for day dresses and coats, and one for lingerie and toiletries."

With that, the bell rang, summoning Margaret back upstairs. "Off I go to see what needs to be redone for the third time."

Mim's trunks finally packed, she completed the necessary conversations with Robert, Bertha and Nanny regarding the running of the household in her absence. All she needed to do today was spend time with the children. She had even allowed Italia a day off from school—a rare indulgence.

Italia had grown more petulant in recent days. Having been the most aware and therefore the most frightened during Mim's extended hospitalization and recuperation, Italia was always on edge when her mother left the house for more than a few hours, as if Mim had no right to do so.

CB was almost blasé about his mother's departure, or at least he appeared to be. His natural still waters ran deeper now that he was eight. Whatever he was feeling was not going to be apparent to anyone, least of all to his mother.

Mildred did not fully understand what it would mean for her mother to be gone for ten days. Nevertheless, she used her new colored pencils to draw Mim a *Bon Voyage* card with a remarkably accurate representation of the tall buildings of New York.

Chauncey was puzzled by the epic investment Mim was making in planning this trip. He had never seen her so intent, so frenzied. During the fair, she had handled all her duties, most of which were highly visible, involving her name and reputation, with calm efficiency. Now he found her emotional and snappish, behavior that was not especially endearing. If he were honest, he would admit that he occasionally wished her gone.

But the news today would be a blow. He wondered if she had had time to read the paper. If she had, she would know that George Pullman had serious labor troubles on his hands, and those troubles might easily derail Mim and Tennie's trip, to say nothing of creating turmoil nationwide. While Chauncey did not know how to tell Mim that her journey was in serious jeopardy, he did know he must handle her gently.

This fellow Debs had given a statement to the press this afternoon claiming that he opposed a strike, arguing that the union was willing to negotiate with management. Chauncey did not believe a word of it. He hated the unions as much as George Pullman did, but the last thing the country needed at the moment was a major railroad strike, so he hoped there was room for accommodation, though Chauncey was not sure that George was a man who ever compromised.

Mim felt her stomach constrict when she heard the phone ring. It was 7:45 a.m., too early for good news. When she heard a gentle knocking at her bedroom door, she knew it was not Chauncey who summoned her.

"Who is it?" Mim asked.

"It's me, Ma'am, Margaret. There is a phone call for you from Miss Hortense. She asked me to awaken you. Shall I tell her to stay on the line?"

"Where is Mr. Blair?" asked Mim, understanding there was little relevance to this question.

Tennie was calling her and she'd best go. But if this were yet another trivial question about gowns, she would start the day more annoyed than she would like.

"I will take it in my sitting room. Tell her I will be there shortly. And, as I am now awake, may I trouble you for some coffee? Thank you, Margaret."

"Good morning, sister dear," said Mim, greeting Tennie more warmly now that she was up. "If this is about borrowing my—"

"Mim, have you seen the newspaper this morning?" an agitated voice came through the line, awakening Mim further with a sharp shot of fear.

"No, I haven't seen it, but you sound upset. Is someone hurt?"

"It is not someone. It is our trip."

"What about our trip could possibly be in the newspaper? If it is some piece of gossip in Madam X's column, it cannot be worth your concern. She always writes on our comings and goings. Tell me what page it is on and I will call you back after I have read it."

"Mim, you will not find out what is upsetting me on the society page. It is on the front page. I am so angry I could spit. All that preparation, all the new clothes, all the adventure, all the fun."

"Here comes Margaret with my coffee and the paper. I will call you back when I can make sense of what you are talking about. At least it is not someone we know who has died."

"Our trip has died, and it is all George Pullman's fault. It is *all* his fault. I hate him. I will never get to New York. I will die never having been to New York."

"Tennie, stop this drama. I am sure it will all work out," Mim soothed. "Let me read it and then we will speak again."

By the time Mim finished reading the first several paragraphs, she knew Tennie was right to be worried.

STRIKE LOOMS AT PULLMAN

May 10, 1894- Hopes dimmed last night for a peaceful resolution to the labor unrest roiling the workers at the Pullman Palace Car Factory. Any possibility that there would be an accommodation on the part of the Company disappeared when three members of the workers' Grievance Committee were fired, shortly before they were scheduled to negotiate on behalf of workers.

Mr. Eugene Debs, President of the American Railroad Union, said, "Mr. Pullman is a felon as well as a hypocrite. The railroads make money every mile. And what does he do? He lays off thousands of workers, reduces wages for the remaining few, refuses to lower prices in the company store and refuses to lower rents in his village where he claims everyone is happy. And all the while he is padding the pockets of management and shareholders.

"Today he showed his true colors by issuing a stringent message of disrespect as he fired the members of the committee who came, in good faith, with their hats in their hands, to plead for what should be their right. Shame on you, Mr. Pullman," said Mr. Debs.

There was no reply from anyone in senior management at the Pullman Company. However, Mr. Pullman has made it clear on many occasions that he will not negotiate with unionists under any circumstances and, if a strike comes, he will ask President Cleveland to back him up with federal troops. Further, during an earlier job action against the company, Mr. Pullman hired non-union workers for the duration of what turned out to be a brief action.

"I like scabs," he was quoted as saying. "Scabs show that the wound is healing. I will use them when and where I must for as long as I run railroads."

Later, speaking at a meeting in Kensington, several miles away from Pullman Village, Mr. Debs tried to dampen the workers' insistence that a strike be called immediately. But, in the hall, packed with intense and angry workers, some still smeared with dirt from a day at the plant, others wearing a look of desperation, Mr. Debs appeared to be arguing a minority position.

"Let's give Mr. Pullman five days. If we have heard nothing from him or his representatives by then, we will act."

A statement issued this evening by the Civic Federation, a group made up of influential business and civic leaders, urged both sides "to negotiate for the good of the city and of the country."

※

Only three minutes had passed before the phone rang again. It was Tennie, who was sure she had given her sister enough time to digest the news and formulate a plan that would make it all work out.

"Well? Do you have a plan yet?" she demanded.

"Tennie darling, be calm. I agree it looks complicated. But we are not unpacking our trunks just yet. The trains are still running and, until we hear otherwise, we will be, as planned, at the station tomorrow at 4:30 pm. sharp. I have not given up hope that in 36 hours we will be on our way to New York."

"But, what if—" protested Hortense.

Mim cut her off mid-whine, "I will talk to you later. Go and recheck your luggage. We will prevail."

Mim's *Bon Voyage* dinner that night should have been more jubilant than it was. She and Chauncey joined Cissie and Potter Palmer in the Grill at the Palmer House Hotel. The palpable tension on the city streets permeated the restaurant and seemed to pull up its own chair at the Palmer-Blair table. Words like, "strike," "scab," "Pullman," "unions," "delays," and "stranded" struck ears that did not want to hear them.

Cissie tried to distract the others by focusing the conversation on the details of Mim's trip to New York, but Mim was reluctant to discuss her search for a Book of Hours because she wanted no one to know about it until she had it in her possession and could relish the luxury of presenting it to the Chicago art world in her own way. The only thing she knew for sure was that her presentation of her book would have all the class that

Hattie Pullman's lacked.

Mim and Chauncey were surprised, and Mim delighted, at the force of Cissie's comments about George Pullman. "He is being pig-headed," she declared. "He is a vain martinet, with no ability to see or hear any other point of view than his own. This will not end well."

"What other point of view can there be but his?" protested Chauncey. "The workers are making a huge mistake if they think George Pullman will give an inch. And why should he? His profits are down. What choice does he have but to cut his costs?"

Cissie was ready for this argument.

"He has had plenty of choice when it comes to showing the public that he at least understands the worker's circumstances. Shave five percent off rents and food staples in Pullman Village for a start."

"But that is merely a gesture," proffered Chauncey. "Mr. Debs would scoff at such a paltry offer."

"If anyone should know about gestures, it would be George," countered Cissie. "The Pullman empire would be a little putt-putt company today if George had not seized the opportunity to let people know of its existence by making a big show of bringing President Lincoln's body back to Illinois for burial. Believe me, George knows the value of gestures.

"But at least the public should see that George is willing to acknowledge the concerns of his employees. At the moment, public sentiment is entirely with the workers. He must at least appear willing to talk."

Mim was getting more and more edgy as this conversation continued. Had she not been so invested in this trip, she might have had an opinion to share but, at the moment, she simply wanted the next fourteen hours to pass so she could get on the train and leave for Grand Central Station in New York City. She gave Chauncey a cease-and-desist look across the table, which should have told him to talk of something else.

"I am one hundred percent with George," proclaimed Chauncey adamantly, not seeing or simply ignoring her message and thereby further convincing Mim that he either had a completely tin ear or that he enjoyed getting her goat.

She would be on her way soon.

24

Running the Gauntlet

May 1894

"I WILL BE BACK AT 2:30 to accompany you and Tennie to the station," said Chauncey as he pecked his wife's cheek absent-mindedly. "Shall I call if I hear any news?"

"No," replied Mim. Hearing the sharpness in her voice, she softened her response, "No, thank you, darling. I am intentionally going to put my head in the sand until I am on that train."

"And a pretty head it is," said Chauncey, purposefully returning to Mim for a fuller kiss. "I will miss you."

"I will be back in no time. And if the collection gods are smiling on me, I will return with treasure."

"Perhaps when I see it, I will better understand why this bee has been buzzing in your bonnet so insistently."

Mim checked her impulse to lash out against the triviality that his words routinely conveyed about her beloved Book of Hours. She merely replied, "Darling, this is more than a 'bee in my bonnet.' If you keep an open mind, I know that, finally, you will see its beauty."

"Tell Tennie we will be round to pick her up no later than three."

"You do think we will be able to make this trip, don't you?" asked Mim as Chauncey departed, knowing full well that he had no better idea than the rest of the world whether or not the Pullman workers would allow her journey to begin.

At the meeting the night before, Eugene Debs surprised many by recommending that they delay a strike vote to give negotiations one more chance. Having been dependent on George Pullman all their lives, the workers were willing to return to the false cocoon the rail magnate had created, even if it meant reduced wages, higher rents and soaring food prices. Only when two rumors began to circulate, one true and one false, did cautious optimism collapse.

On the morning of May 11th, the Pullman plant was operating smoothly. Little chatter circulated over the machines that clanked and hissed, as if emulating the noises they would eventually make on the rails.

By eleven-thirty the rumors began:

"He is going to lock us out."

"This is the last shift."

"Motherfuckers."

"Closing the plant."

"No work anywhere." Mumbles passed from man to man, like an angry version of the familiar parlor game.

Soon the machines were quieter than the men who operated them as the workers slowed and then stopped their equipment. Three thousand whisperers became chanters.

"You lock us out. We strike you down. Strike! Strike! Strike!" they repeated rhythmically as they packed up their belongings and made ready to leave the factory.

The union floor managers turned towards the office a floor above, looking for guidance, but none was forthcoming. Two or three of the most ardent aggressors took the stairs two at a time, invaded the office and roughly hustled out those who, while not senior management, were nonetheless part of the Pullman hierarchy.

With the forcible expulsion of the hapless executives, the mood on the factory floor changed from one of anger to one of ebullience. Once outside, the crowd immediately doubled in size as men arriving for the new shift joined their comrades. The workers of the Pullman Palace Car Company were now on strike.

As the men poured out of his factory, Pullman's assistants were carrying out the robber baron's orders and stationing Pinkerton men around his South Prairie Avenue mansion, directing that his valuables be secured in the vault of his downtown skyscraper. Meanwhile, George Pullman was on his way to his summer home in New Jersey.

At Blair House, the departure plan was in full motion. Chauncey saw no reason why the children should be a part of the farewell entourage, but he acquiesced because he wanted harmony between himself and his wife. Good-byes edged with acrimony unsettled him.

Great excitement invigorated the children at the prospect of being allowed to accompany their mother and aunt to the station. Italia had overdressed, looking as though she were going to tea at the Palmer House Hotel. CB had given polite voice to wanting to spend time with his mother before she left, but he was clearly more interested in the train she would be taking, peppering her with questions about engine size, miles per hour, and routes, all of which she was unable to answer.

"CB, I promise to return with answers to all your questions."

"Who will you ask?" pressed CB.

"I will ask the porter, and if he doesn't know, I will ask the conductor, and if he doesn't know, I will find the engineer and ask him. If he doesn't know, I think we should get on another train," teased Mim, as she gave her freckled-faced son a kiss on his cheek which he promptly wiped away.

Amidst the gay group of carriage occupants, there was one who was very, very sad. Mildred made no effort to hide the fact that she would miss her mother. As she was waiting to be dressed, she asked Nanny if she could wear her black velvet party dress.

"Do you want to wear black because the train station is so dirty?" wondered Nanny.

"No," said Mildred with a pout.

"Why then, dear? This is not a party."

"Sad people wear black when they put people they love in the ground and then they stand around and cry. That is what I shall do when Mummy goes on the train."

As predicted, Tennie had more trunks than Mim. Five were standing in the vestibule when the Blair carriages pulled up. She had also packed three handbags with last-minute items.

Hortense "Tennie" Mitchell was considered the prettiest of the Mitchell girls. Other than an occasional pinch of her cheeks she needed no beauty aids. Painting her face would have been a disservice to her natural loveliness.

Though five years separated them, Tennie and Mim were as alike as any sisters could be, considering that one was the mother of four children and the other was little more than a debutante. They could talk and laugh together just as easily as sit silently reading for hours.

Tennie had been schooled in the arts, though not under the rigorous tutelage of Grandmother Mitchell. Like Chauncey, Tennie had no idea why Mim was so intent on this Book of Hours, but she knew how much its acquisition meant to her sister, and if a search for it meant that she could get to New York, she would feign interest even if she had to exaggerate genuine enthusiasm. She looked forward to the museums, theater and opera that awaited her. But most of all, she looked forward to her freedom.

"Mim, tell me why you want to see this book so much," Tennie queried.

"You'll see," replied Mim.

As the Blair carriage caravan made its way to the station, Mim was trying to explain to her younger daughter how many days there were in two weeks. Tennie, ever the indulgent aunt, riding in the second carriage with Italia and CB, was asking them what presents they might like to receive upon their mother's return.

Chauncey was a fussy traveler even when he travelled alone. With two passenger carriages brimming with children and chatter and a third filled to capacity with trunks, he was very nervous about the whole chaotic production.

"Workers Walk," yelled the paperboy hawking a copy of the afternoon paper.

"Stop the carriage!" Chauncey barked to the driver. "Stop right here!" he repeated.

Without waiting for his carriage to come to a full stop, Chauncey jumped out, ignored Mim's questions, and nimbly crossed the busy street to buy the afternoon paper. He scanned it and, with all the information he needed to make a decision, he re-crossed the street, his mental wheels spinning as he wondered how he was going to tell Mim that there would be no trip to New York City today.

"What is it, Chauncey?" Mim called to her husband. "Chauncey, what are you doing? Surely you would have had plenty of time to get a paper at the station."

Instead of answering her directly, or looking into what he knew would be her anxious eyes, Chauncey tossed the newspaper with its alarming headline into Mim's lap. Allowing her time to read and absorb the message, Chauncey went back to the second carriage carrying Tennie and his two older children.

"Tennie, I am afraid your trip to New York must be postponed. The Pullman workers have declared a strike, and in a matter of hours it is likely no trains will be moving in or out of Chicago."

With nothing more to add, he made his way back to the carriage carrying Mim and Mildred. He expected and understood Mim would be disappointed, perhaps even angry, but, being a sensible woman at heart, she would be readily compliant. What he encountered, however, when he climbed back into the carriage, ready to comfort or perhaps cajole, was a woman who, after overhearing Chauncey's words to Tennie, was not close to compliant.

"Chauncey, there is nothing I see on this page that helps me understand why we are stopped here in the middle of the street and not proceeding directly to the station. When we left home, we had plenty of time to spare, but now we are in danger of missing the train. We must go."

"Mim, I understand your disappointment, but we cannot continue to the station. The Pullman workers have called a strike against the railroad on which you were to travel. In addition to being futile to proceed to a train that likely will not leave, it might well be dangerous. Did you read the whole article?"

"I did read the article. But just because they have stopped making engines does not mean existing trains are idle. My guess is that our train will leave on time and we are now in jeopardy of missing it. Please get in and tell the driver to proceed with haste."

By now, Tennie had arrived at the door of the lead carriage.

"Mim, are we going to New York? Chauncey said there is a strike. I am confused. Why does that mean we cannot go?"

"Of course we can still go. Now get back in your carriage. We are wasting time."

Feeling events slipping out of his control, Chauncey grew more aggressive. "Mim, you at least owe your sister the truth about the danger involved in proceeding."

"You mean your truth. I see no danger."

"One of you must explain," begged Tennie. "I want to go to New York, but I am not interested in courting danger to do so."

Chauncey did his best to explain the situation without giving a hint of his inner turmoil. He was as frightened as he had been the night he took Mim to the hospital to deliver Billy. As much human blood as had been spilt that night, he had a sense that much marital blood would be spilt in the resolution of this situation.

With her eyes fixed stonily on Chauncey, Mim spoke from a deep reservoir of implacability.

"Tennie, I am going to the station and have every reason to think we will get to New York just as we have planned. I will understand if you do not wish to join me. But decide in the next minute, as I need to proceed."

"Mimsy, you may indeed be able to get on your train. You may even get to New York. But there is no guarantee you will get back. Please, come home with us now. You can go to New York as soon as the strike is over. I will take you there myself. Please, please come home," Chauncey pleaded.

By now CB and Mildred were both crying and Italia was standing outside the carriage with her hands on her hips and disapproval on her face.

"Mother, we are making a scene here. People are staring as they go by. Let's go home!"

"All of you are over-reacting," Mim scoffed. "The paper says the workers have stopped making new engines. They are not working on ours. It is sitting in the station, waiting to pull our train, and I will be on it."

Lowering his voice so the children could not overhear him, Chauncey said, "Mim, I don't think you fully understand the way a strike works. You may not remember the turmoil of the Haymarket Riots, but I do.

"At this very moment, my guess is that the station is filling with sympathizers who are urging passengers not to board the trains. You should not be among these people. They present danger, especially to women like you who look every inch what you are—upper class and rich."

Resolutely facing her family, Mim said calmly, "I am going to the station. I give you my word that, if I encounter anything even remotely alarming, I will turn around and come home. But I think this brouhaha has been blown out of proportion to sell newspapers. I appreciate your concern, but I shall be fine and I will call you from New York when I arrive. Tennie, what is your decision?"

Absorbing all the tension of the last few minutes, Mildred was now crying hard and clinging to Mim, who had to pull Mildred's clenched little hands from around her neck and hand her to Chauncey.

"Chauncey, please try to understand. I am not a crazed woman. I will return shortly if I sense menace of any kind."

Hortense Mitchell joined her sister in the carriage and Mim called to the driver to proceed. Knowing that if she turned to look at the hurt and anger she was leaving in her wake, she would lose all the courage she now felt. She sat stiffly in her seat looking straight ahead.

"Mim, is this fortitude, or foolishness? Whatever you call it, is it really about a Book of Hours?" Tennie asked as they rolled on.

Mim knew that she needed to reassure Tennie. "You know very well that collections are built by a combination of prudence and risk. You do not enhance a collection like mine without some risk. But, I promise you, nothing bad will happen to us, and if the situation appears to be dangerous, we will come home."

Train stations, those monuments of steel, glass and stone, are strangely emotional places. On a stage supported by massive iron girders, thousands of human dramas take place every day—joyful reunions of fathers and sons, tearful farewells to those who may never be seen again, anxious moments when the expected visitor may have missed the train or, disappointingly, was not coming after all.

Grand Central Station was part of the downtown loop sitting at the southern edge of the Chicago River. Completed in 1890, it was an extravagant masterpiece. The marble floors and Corinthian columns were bathed in southern light filtering through beautifully arched windows. The station's most prominent feature, a two hundred foot clock tower, was as central a meeting place for railway passengers as the clock in front of Marshall Field's store was for shoppers.

The two remaining Blair carriages pulled up to the passenger entrance easily enough and the drivers sprang out to summon the three porters they would need to carry the trunks to the departure track. Once inside, Mim felt a wave of relief, as nothing appeared to be amiss inside the station. While it was certainly not quiet, the sounds were purposeful as people were busy going about their business. In an act more of self-congratulation than affection, Mim linked her arm in Tennie's and patted her hand. The gesture made words of triumph unnecessary.

Mim looked up at the departure board and reassured herself that, though no gate had yet been designated, the Pullman Palace Car was scheduled for an on-time departure to New York City.

Mim took out the small pad of paper and fountain pen she kept in a silver holder in her purse and wrote Chauncey a note of reassurance.

Darling:

The rest of the trip to the station was as uneventful as the first part was dramatic. Please tell the children that Tennie and I are here and are just fine. I will call from New York. Imagine that,

being able to be in New York and call halfway across the country!

I am sorry for the little tempest.

Love,

Mimsy

She knew their exchange had been more than a "little tempest," but she wanted to give herself peace of mind while she was away, and she wanted to calm Chauncey, who hated confrontation. Handing the driver the note and a dollar tip, Mim instructed him to take the note "directly to Mr. Blair."

Tennie, fear now gone, was enjoying herself, floating in and out of the shops adorning the concourse. She bought the latest copy of *Vogue*, paper tissues and several packages of lemon drops.

Mim, on the other hand, was seated in the waiting area by the ticket windows, lost in thought. She had been sincere in her note to Chauncey. She was sorry for the hostility she had leveled at him when he really was only trying to protect her. He precipitated such ambivalent feelings. When he was at the office, or away on business, she could bring him to mind and a warm feeling would come over her. In those moments she was sure she loved him and would never love another. But hours later, when he came home full of commands, bluster and strong opinions, those gentle feelings fled.

Mim was heading to New York with a million questions as yet unanswered. She had had only one additional note from Martin since his first one. His second, equally enigmatic, had done little more than reiterate the flimsy facts of his earlier letter—the Book of Hours was "sensational," it was for sale, the purchase arrangements might be "tricky," and she best come quickly. Not that she minded, but Mim wondered why she had to go to New York to see the book. Normally the dealer would simply mail the object for her approval.

No matter, thought Mim as she checked and rechecked the time. *Think of it as a great adventure.*

Time freezes in the strangest ways. Mim would always remember that she was looking at an advertisement for Hershey Chocolate when she heard the first rumblings of the coming chaos. Throughout the rest of her life, whenever she saw a Hershey's Chocolate Bar, she would give a little shudder as if her body had never quite left the scene that was almost upon her.

Suddenly, as if thrust open by a gust of wind off the river, the doors to Grand Central Station slammed open. Man after agitated man poured in so fast that Mim could not easily read the signs they carried, but most displayed the word "Pullman" in one form or another. As the men swarmed onto the concourse, they shouted at no one in particular:

"Where is he?"

"Find him."

"Try the train shed."

"Palace Car."

Instantly, Mim acquired two important pieces of information—that the men were in search of George Pullman, and that they were headed to the same platform she was. Her first thought was that she must find Tennie immediately. Other than her reticule with her tickets, money and valuables, she gave no thought to whatever other possessions she might have to leave behind in order to be out of this chaos and safely reunited with her sister.

Many times Mim had heard Chauncey use the word "hooligans" to describe unruly street boys, but the men who were now directly in front of her were in an entirely different category, seething with malevolent anger. Dressed in grease-spattered overalls, which only partially covered their sooty grey work-shirts, these men were filthy. None appeared to have bathed in weeks. Their caps and bowlers were worn akimbo over straggly hair, and when they opened their mouths to froth, she saw more gums than teeth.

Standing up, her eyes futilely scanned the crowded perimeter of the concourse for a glimpse of her sister. Travelers near the doorways escaped. Those whose way was blocked shrank fearfully to the edges of the terminal.

Mim was now at the center of the swirl, completely surrounded by ugly, shouting beasts. Two angry antiphonal choirs were now serenading one another. The workers stomped their feet and rhythmically clapped in unison, "Pullman scum! Pullman scum! Find the bum and make him run."

The other voices, notable for fear rather than rhythm, begged for the police for protection or escape. Shouts of suspected bombs and guns sprayed staccato-like through the air.

In order to traverse the main concourse to find Tennie, Mim would have to make her way through the agitators, whose numbers grew by the minute. It was like trying to cross Dearborn Street just before the stores closed on Christmas Eve. She was ready to elbow and shove her way through, if only she could see a little open space. As Mim's fear approached hysteria, she no longer resisted the urge to shout for Tennie, despite knowing it would be futile, given the cacophony surrounding her.

Please God, I want to get out... Please God, get us out. Let me find Tennie and get out, she prayed to a God she hoped could see her predicament.

Finally, she began to push and fight her way through, all the while muttering the language of conventional politeness. "Excuse me... Please sir, I have to find my sister... Please let me through... I am sorry, please let me through."

And then down she went. Hard. Chin first. Stars. A noise reverberating in her ears told her she had taken a blow somewhere above her neck. She pushed up on to her elbows and began to crawl through the dirty boots. *God, these people smelled.*

Like an injured snake, she dragged herself, coil by coil, through a jungle of giants who would step on her without even feeling her beneath them. Mim no longer felt frightened. She simply kept moving across the floor.

And as she did, she felt her loathing mix with bizarre amusement. If she was not mistaken, she, Mrs. Chauncey J. Blair, who, only hours earlier had been on her way to New York to buy, to spend more money than these people could ever imagine, was now crawling along the floor of Grand Central Station. As she lifted her head, she felt a gush of warm blood spurt from her chin. Soon she smelled its familiar, musty, vile aroma. Within seconds she gagged and vomited. *Good,* she thought. *I hope it dries and cakes on them. I hope they never get jobs. It serves them right.*

She was bleeding, vomiting, and now crying, not with pain but with anger. *I hate these people. I hate these people. I will always hate these people.*

She must have dragged herself within sight of those on the perimeter because several of the horrified onlookers spotted her and pulled her to safety. Unfortunately, she never had a chance to thank them properly because when she was next conscious she was in her bed with both

Chauncey and Tennie looking down at her. Tennie held her hand and smiled at her. Chauncey did not.

After seven sutures under her chin and ten days of a largely liquid diet to spare her broken jaw, Mim tried to put the attack behind her, if not entirely out of her mind.

Chauncey remained furious. Not even the sight of Mim, banged and bruised, softened his heart. It was the angriest he had ever been with her. He never uttered the words, "I told you so," but he may as well have.

In the first few days he deliberately avoided her and responded monosyllabically to any of her comments. Even accidental propinquity caused him to edge away from her.

"Chauncey," said Mim, when she could stand the frosty isolation no longer, "can you linger just a few minutes longer before you go off?"

"Isn't Tennie coming by today?"

"I suspect she is, but it is you I want to talk to," answered Mim.

"What about?"

"Just talk. You know, as we used to in the mornings." Mim was almost pleading now.

"Well, those were the days when you actually would listen to me. That was the delight of those moments. One of us would talk and the other would listen."

"Chauncey, if your point is that you were right about my going to the station, I have already acknowledged that. And I have said I am sorry."

"Yes, you have said you are sorry for the way things turned out, and that you regretted putting Tennie into harm's way. But what you have not apologized for is your willful defiance of my recommendations."

"What you are really saying is that I disobeyed your orders and until I admit that fact and apologize, you will not forgive me. Isn't that it?"

Chauncey did not answer, so Mim continued. "I was not aware that the foundation of our marriage was based on my following your orders. If that is what you are saying, you had best tell me now, so I can begin to adjust to that notion."

Once again, Chauncey did not answer, and this time his silence was accompanied by his departure from the room.

Martin Gaylord was one of thousands of people who had been stranded in New York during the strike, but when Chauncey had called to tell him about Mim's injuries, he told Chauncey to tell Mim to take her time healing because he had plenty to keep him busy. It was late enough in the season that he would not return to Chicago and, in fact, planned to go directly to Maine for the summer. He would return to New York for a week in early September. Perhaps she could join him then.

In response to his message, Mim immediately wrote a note asking about the status of the book and its availability. She offered to send a check to hold it until she could get there.

Martin answered quickly, "No need for a deposit."

How perplexing, thought Mim.

She completely trusted Martin's judgment. What she did not trust was her own ability to wait all summer for another opportunity to go to New York.

⁓

By the end of the strike, thirty people had died. For a time, a false calm settled on the city. In the early days, public sympathy was allied with the strikers. Even members of the Blairs' social circle conceded that the combination of their peer's retreat to his summer home and his refusal to allow management to meet with the union representatives weakened his public image.

By the end of June, Eugene Debs, leader of the American Railway Union, grew impatient with the stonewalling tactics of the Pullman Palace Company. In July, the union voted to discontinue building and maintaining Pullman cars all across the country. While the porters and conductors did not support this action, more than a quarter of a million workers in twenty-seven states brought commercial and passenger travel to a halt.

Management began to hire strikebreakers, most of whom were Negroes and therefore not permitted to become union members. What had been a local labor dispute, albeit in the crucible of American commerce, now turned into a national crisis. Food prices rose, and even mail delivery was threatened.

United Sates Attorney General A.G. Olney prevailed upon President Cleveland to nationalize troops.

The union was served with the first injunction ever issued against strikers; it ordered them to move the mail and protect the food supply. Federal troops rode shotgun on the trains with orders to shoot, if necessary.

On the night of June 29th in Blue Island, Illinois, events spun fully out of control. Debs refused to obey the injunction and called for a rally of union workers. Peaceful at first, by the end of the evening, strikers had set fire to railway cars, smashed switches and pulled up rail ties.

On July 7th in Chicago, a mob attacked a soldier guarding the trains, hurled bricks, and burned all the railroad cars they could find. Thirty people, mostly strikers, were killed that night; fifty-seven were wounded. Damage was assessed at over $80 million. Martial law did its job, and by mid-July the strike was over.

Despite Clarence Darrow's defense, Eugene Debs was sentenced to six months in jail, and public sympathy had turned against the violence of the unionists.

At the end of July, Mim had secured new tickets to New York for herself and Tennie. She told herself that the only way to endure the next six weeks would be to stay busy.

The Jewel Thief

May 1894

Mrs. Chauncey Justus Blair
Misses Italia and Mildred Blair
Master Chauncey Buckley Blair

Cordially Invite You to a
Sunday Afternoon Taffy Pull

August 12th, 1894
3:00 p.m
The Blair Residence
4830 Drexel Boulevard
Chicago, Illinois

R.S.V.P.
Informal Dress Recommended

"Mother, pulling taffy is a messy, childish form of entertainment," scoffed Italia when she saw the invitation. "Why not just buy the taffy and invite people for a formal tea dance? How about an at-home theatrical? I love those."

"Because, Ity," her mother replied, "A taffy pull is great fun. People like getting their fingers into the taffy, pulling and shaping the candy and then eating the fruits of their labor. I did it as a girl."

Mildred's and CB's excitement more than made up for Italia's dismissive attitude. They were like conspiring elves, spending hours gluing together paper chain decorations to festoon the kitchen. CB showed endless patience with Mildred as her six-year-old fingers tried to cut the colored paper into strips and then apply just the right amount of glue to the interlocking circles. When Mim looked into the nursery, even Italia had joined in the fun and, unobserved from a distance, she looked just like the little girl she desperately no longer wanted to be.

For elite Chicagoans, Sunday was the servants' day off. Mistresses of Mim's ilk had varying strategies for coping with their abandonment. Some went to their clubs for Sunday lunch after church and ate their way through the equivalent of two meals. Pluckier ones learned to boil eggs and viewed the experience as an adventure. Bertha always took care that the Blair pantry was filled with cold meats, fresh fruit, cheeses, breads and a pudding.

Mim chose Sunday for her taffy pull with every expectation that she would manage all the arrangements so that Bertha, Robert and Roberta, now almost two years old, could simply do whatever they liked to do as a family. But when Bertha heard of the party, she hinted that perhaps she could stay to help, just this once.

"Mrs. Blair, I would be happy to help you this Sunday," she said.

"Bertha, there is no need for you to feel obligated to stay. You do so much for us during the week," Mim replied. "I did not plan this party on a Sunday to entice you to give up your day with your family."

"I am sure you did not," said Bertha firmly. But, Roberta and I—"

"Bertha, would you like to come to the taffy pull?" asked Mim delightedly.

"Yes, Mrs. Blair. I think we would. Roberta overheard the older children talking about candy, and all week she has asked me if she could make 'canny.'"

"I think Roberta is a little young still, but, unlike Billy, she is a careful child. So if you would like, please come on Sunday."

"Thank you, Mrs. Blair. We would enjoy that very much," said Bertha as she gathered her notebook after their usual Monday morning meeting.

"I would be happy to order the ingredients for you if you give me a list," said Bertha with a happy smile. "We do not make this taffy in Germany, and, though I think I could figure out what goes into making it, I would prefer to follow your direction."

"That would be a big help. Thank you, Bertha. I will send a list to you later this morning."

Just as Bertha was about to open the door to leave, Mim called to her, "Bertha—"

"Yes, Mrs. Blair?"

"As I said, thank you for offering to order the ingredients. But when you and Roberta come up to the party on Sunday, I want you to come as guests."

"Oh, Mrs. Blair, that is very kind of you, but I don't know if—"

"As guests, Bertha," said Mim firmly. "This is a family taffy pull, and you are part of our family."

What Bertha did not know, and Mim only vaguely realized, was that she felt uncomfortable remembering her vehement reaction to the mob that had almost trampled her in Union Station. Her thoughts at the time were, and continued to be, ugly and unkind when it came to immigrants. But she wanted to reassure herself that she did not hate them all. Inviting her cook to be a part of this party was proof. She did not find it the least bit awkward to be entertaining Bertha and Roberta as guests, and no one else was likely to pay attention amid the pending chaos.

The children, particularly the younger ones who were doing this for the first time, were gleeful at being allowed to get so messy. It was sweet to see Mildred help Roberta try to master the art of 'canny'-making. Mim smiled as she watched her younger daughter assume the role of older sister and teacher.

In the end, twelve children and six mothers participated—scrubbing little hands, donning aprons and finally seating their progeny at stools around the kitchen table.

As the molasses, milk and sugar began to blend under the low heat, the smell catapulted Mim back into Grandmother Mitchell's kitchen as if she were in a lovely dream, visions of sugarplums dancing in her head.

"Be sure," called Mim to the women within earshot, "to take off your rings. Taffy gets so sticky it can be surprisingly harmful to jewelry."

Three separate workstations were set up around the kitchen so everyone could take part. Children over six were allowed to add ingredients, and each helped stir the mixture into a ball, which they were delighted to see take shape before their eyes as if it were magic.

"Be sure to scrape down the sides so all that delicious sugar mixes in," called Mim to the group.

"Now comes the best part," Mim said. "I am going to show you how to pull the taffy, and then, each of you, pull off a handful from the ball and replicate what I do."

"What does 'replate' mean?" asked Mildred.

"It means to do just as I do," answered her mother. "First, you will need to grease your fingers, and Roberta's, so that they are slippery enough that the taffy will not stick to them."

As the children proceeded to follow directions, they sounded like a litter of little pigs, all squealing with delight at the rarity of being encouraged to get as messy as possible.

"It will work better if you use only your finger tips," cautioned Mim.

The pulled strings of taffy were then twisted into strips and laid on wax paper to harden.

Yes, thought Mim, as everyone put on coats and hats, thanked her and left, the day had been just what she had hoped for—diversionary for her and great fun for the children. She wasn't sure that she did not prefer an afternoon like this to all the formal entertaining she did. So it surprised her when, just as she had put her very tired feet up on the chaise, Bertha appeared in the library with tears coursing down her cheeks.

"Mrs. Blair, I am sorry to disturb you, but—"

"That is quite alright, Bertha. I can see you are upset. Is it your family?"

"No, not directly."

"Then, please be seated," said Mim, gesturing to the seat across from her, "and we will see if we can solve whatever has come up since I last saw you. Does this have anything to do with the taffy pull?"

"Well, ma'am. Yes and no," Bertha replied as she took her handkerchief from her apron pocket and gave a resounding blow to her reddened nose. Though Bertha had come to her, it appeared it was going to take a little work to draw out the reason for her visit.

Mim was of two minds. The first, her irritable mind, wanted to be done with whatever this crisis was and she felt like saying, "out with it." Fortunately her second mind reminded her first mind that Bertha's distress was completely out of character. She was not one for frivolous complaining, so Mim owed her an honest listen and some patience.

"Bertha, did anyone say anything to you at the party? Were you or Roberta made to feel uncomfortable in any way? I was busy, but it seemed as though you both were having a pleasant time. Please tell me so I can try to help."

Bertha's only reaction to Mim's entreaty was to sniffle, wipe and blow again. *One more try,* thought Mim, *otherwise we will be here all night with no resolution.*

"Bertha, after all these years, I hope you know you can trust me with your confidences. Whatever it is that has so upset you will remain between you and me. You have my word," soothed Mim.

Never having taken a seat, Bertha now stepped forward and, taking her hand from her pocket, thrust it at Mim and simultaneously barked out her news. "It's gone, Mrs. Blair."

Mim understood that whatever it was she was supposed to see involved this hand, but for the life of her she could not unravel the mystery. What she saw was a hand—a hand with closely cropped, unvarnished nails, a hand that was slightly red and chaffed, a hand with a simple wedding band.

"Bertha, forgive me. I can see nothing that should upset you so. I see five fingers. Nothing is missing. Have you injured your hand in some way?"

"Mrs. Blair, it may not seem much to you, but the ring on my hand is my most treasured possession."

"It is your wedding band, is it not?" asked Mim.

"Well, yes and no."

Within an inch of showing her growing frustration, Mim said, "Please, Bertha, tell me more about this ring."

"It *is* my wedding band. But just before Roberta's first birthday, Robert asked to take it, as he wanted to add something to it. I assumed he wanted to put some kind of inscription on it." There she stopped again, trying to collect herself.

"Go on, Bertha," encouraged Mim.

"At Roberta's birthday party I saw an unopened box."

"And it was your ring?" asked Mim.

"Yes and no."

"Bertha! Was it your ring or something else?"

"It was my ring. Robert had added a diamond to it. He said it was to honor me on our daughter's first birthday. I called it 'my Roberta diamond.'"

After another round of crying, Bertha managed to control herself and finished her story. "Mrs. Blair, it was a tiny, tiny diamond, just a chip, but it was so beautiful. I have never taken the ring off. But now it is gone."

"But Bertha, it is not gone. I see it," said Mim, now genuinely curious as to where this story was going.

"You see the band, but look—" and here she again thrust out her hand.

Bertha twirled the band around her finger until she came to what Mim could now see was a tiny hole in the center of the band. What she could not see was a diamond.

"Where is the diamond, Bertha?" Mim's question was completely sincere, but the minute it was out of her mouth, she knew she had the answer.

"Bertha, were you wearing the ring when we made the taffy?"

"Yes, Mrs. Blair. I told you, I have never taken it off since the day Robert gave it to me."

Mim thought better of asking Bertha if she had heard her warn all her guests to take off their rings, as taffy pulling was a well-known jewel thief.

Mim felt a great tenderness for Bertha, as well as acute shame for having too many prized possessions. In front of her was a woman who had only one, and it had been stolen from her.

"Bertha, I think your diamond is in the candy. Come with me."

Bertha, her eyes still wet, but with a new touch of hope in her voice asked, "Mrs. Blair, there are five pounds of candy in the kitchen. Most of it is wrapped. Are we going to unwrap each piece?"

"We will if we have to," said Mim, enthused now about the chance to make something right.

Mim learned an important lesson that night. It is much easier to pull taffy than it is to re-pull it. By the time they were done, most of the household had been engaged in the hunt. Italia, CB and Mildred joined the search party and unwrapped each piece of candy as though it were a butterfly whose wings needed separation, then gently placed it into a bowl that Mim put into the oven to soften.

Once the ball of taffy was malleable, Bertha, with practiced expertise, applied the rolling pin to it until she produced paper-thin oblong pieces. Then the search began for Bertha's missing diamond.

Marshaling her forces, Mim commanded, "Everyone, come and wash your hands and have your fingers greased. Use just the tips. They are the most sensitive part of your fingers and they will feel something more easily. Now, pull your stools up to the table.

"Come quickly, we have not much time until the taffy begins to harden again. Finding the diamond is very, very important to Bertha. Diamonds are rare and expensive. I will give a reward to the person who finds it."

"If I find it, I want a—" said Mildred.

"We will discuss that after you find it, Mildred," said Mim sharply.

As the search went on, Mim fine-tuned the instructions to her search team. "Lightly, CB, you will not find anything by pressing so hard. Try closing your eyes. I find I can concentrate better if I am not looking, just feeling."

The search of the first batch produced frustration, but no diamond. By now, Bertha had taken herself to a corner of the kitchen and sat with her head in her hands.

"Mother," whispered Italia, "look at Bertha. She is so worried. How big is this diamond?"

"Your fingers are looking for something quite small, but let your heart understand that for Bertha, it is the largest diamond in the world."

Bertha did come back to the table to roll out the second batch of warmed taffy. Re-greased, all the fingertips went back to work. Though unspoken, everyone, from oldest to youngest, realized that only one batch remained for inspection before the search party had to be called off—failure.

"Mrs. Blair," Angela, the new upstairs parlor maid said quietly. "I feel something."

All hands stopped as Mim, followed by Bertha, made their way over to Angela's stool. Others began to cluster around as well.

"Please, God," said Mildred, her hands in bedtime prayer position, expressing what everyone else was feeling.

Mim remained calm as she ever so lightly brushed her fingers over the whole oblong of dough to get a sense of the contour. Oh yes, there was something in there. Her fingers went back to have another feel.

Before allowing herself to say anything that would give false hope, Mim repeated her manual probing and finally said, "I too feel something. Bertha, please start some water boiling, and someone please, hand me a pair of scissors."

She cut a wide circle around the spot where she and Angela had felt the bump, and then, as if she were a surgeon excising a malignancy, she dropped the cropped circle of taffy into the bowl of boiling water. The taffy began to dissolve, sending clouds of brown liquid to the edges of the bowl. The water was too hot for anyone to scoop out the small diamond chip, which lay at the bottom of the bowl. But there was no doubt about it. The search was over.

"There it is, Bertha," shouted a gleeful Mildred. "We found it!"

Bertha's hands were not delicate. Unlike Mim's, they had not been smoothed by years of fragrant and restorative creams. Without waiting for the water to cool, she plunged her hand into the hot water and picked up the diamond.

Bertha now turned to the group and, with tears rolling down her face, she said, "Thank you, everyone. My heart is full."

The servants, the children and the mistress of the house began clapping and congratulating one another. Robert, whose role in the drama had been to distract Roberta, now moved in and put his arm around his beaming wife.

After Bertha had dried the tiny stone, she laid it lovingly on the kitchen table, which had been cleared and cleaned. Everyone gathered around to see it up close.

As the Blair family made their way towards the stairs, Bertha trailed them and called, "Mrs. Blair," at which point Mim stopped. "Thank you, Mrs. Blair. You did not have to take the trouble."

"Yes, I did, Bertha. For years, you and Robert have helped this family. It was the least we could do."

When Mim and her children had reassembled in the library, there was a congenial sense of family unity among the group. "I was proud of you all tonight," Mim cooed.

"I was the first to see it," exclaimed Mildred. "Are you the proudest of me?"

"Mother," said Italia, "I was happy to help tonight, and I am glad Bertha has her diamond back, but really, did you see it? I am glad I don't need glasses; otherwise, I would never have recognized it as a diamond. Such a fuss over something so small."

A Boy's Life

August 1894

C HICAGO WAS OPPRESSIVELY HOT BY the end of the summer, but frost was still permeating the foundation of the Blair marriage. Mim had made several attempts to engage Chauncey in a discussion of her behavior at Grand Central Station and, in her opinion, his overreaction to it. Each effort had resulted in a replica of their first argument.

She had repeatedly told him she was sorry, and she was. But Chauncey continued to make the issue one of disobedience. While it was true that Mim had never before looked him directly in the eye and defied him, she had never considered that she had an obligation to click her heels at his commands. Their last conversation, if one could call it a conversation, ended by Chauncey accusing her of being a secret suffragist, which in his mind was the worst epithet he could hurl.

"Defiance of family values is where it all starts," fumed Chauncey.

"Don't be ridiculous," Mim calmly replied. "If I were a suffragist, I would have returned to the station on the day the strike ended and

249

boarded a train for New York instead of spending what I hoped would be a nice summer here with you and the children. And it has been a good summer with the children. I wish I could say the same about being with you."

"If you truly had your children in mind, you would never have behaved as you did," Chauncey said snidely.

"The children are no longer the central issue in this disagreement," Mim replied. "The issue has become whether it is your right to exercise power over me. Because if my submission to your authority is what you insist upon, you will soon see me with a placard at the front of a line of militant women."

Once again, Chauncey turned on his heel and left the room. Not knowing whether she wanted him to hear her or not, Mim said the first thing that came into her mind. "Thank God I have my own money."

To say Mim was counting the days until she could leave for New York was an understatement, but also an act of faith. She had not gone to the installation of the Beaufort Book of Hours in the Hotel Florence and, now that Martin had found her something "spectacular," she smelled blood in the water, making her days interminable.

The only late-summer activity Mim was looking forward to was the long-planned trip to West Side Park to see the Chicago Colts play baseball. Mim enjoyed baseball, as much for the atmosphere as for the action itself, but she was mostly excited because CB had been looking forward to it with an enthusiasm that was infectious.

The Colts were mediocre this season. Any hope of their making it to to the playoffs had ended weeks ago for everyone but Chauncey Buckley Blair.

Like every other nine-year-old boy in Chicago, CB's favorite player was number 82, first baseman Cap Anson. Anson was a player-manager and the best hitter on the team. Each morning, CB, sporting his proudest possession, a Chicago Colts baseball cap, flew into the dining room and, bypassing even the funny papers, went straight to the sports pages.

"Father, did you look yet?" asked CB.

"No, I leave that to you these days," answered Chauncey, enjoying his older son's entry into the men's club of sports.

"We won!" trumpeted CB after he had scanned the sports page.

"What was the score?" Chauncey asked.

So focused was CB on absorbing the thrill of the victory, Chauncey received no response.

"CB? The score?"

"Oh, sorry, Father. Let's see... We were behind 3-2 going into the home eighth, and, wait a minute, okay, here it is... There were two outs and Jiggs Parrott drew a walk."

"CB, the score? The final score? I don't need a play-by-play. I need to leave for the office."

"The final score was Colts 4, Boston Red Stockings 3, but don't you want to hear how they did it? That is the best part."

"I will hear all the details when I get home tonight."

"Please, Father, this will take only a minute. Please?"

"Bring it with you while I put on my jacket and hat, though it's too goddamned hot to wear them today," said Chauncey, capitulating easily to CB's plea for more attention. "Read it as fast as you can. I am late as it is."

CB stood straight, squared his feet, adjusted his baseball cap, and began reading, not only with speed but with the delivery of the man in the announcer's booth. "Ladies and Gentlemen," feigned C.B, "The Chicago Colts looked like a playoff contender

yesterday in their come-from-behind victory over the Boston Red Stockings."

"Father, did you hear that? It says the Colts could make it to the play-offs," said CB, eyes shining with excitement.

"Well, well," muttered Chauncey distractedly as he tussled CB's head and walked out the door.

"Father," protested CB.

"Tonight, CB, I promise."

CB continued to read the article, which went on to say that, had the Colts played all season as they did yesterday, they *might* have been in contention for a playoff slot, but since they had not, their victory was "statistically insignificant." But since CB did not understand what that meant, he had the luxury of living in a child's fantasy world for a few more days.

"Mother," whined CB. "I do not see why Italia and Mildred are coming to the game. Ity said she doesn't want to go and Mildred knows nothing about baseball. She will get bored or ask a lot of stupid questions."

"CB, if you use the word 'stupid' again, not only will you not be going to the game, you will not come out of your room for days," reprimanded Mim.

"Fine," he said. "But she will ask a lot of questions that do not make any sense, and I will have to stop and answer them. This is an important game if we want to make it to the play-offs, and I want to watch it, not talk to Mildred."

"CB, we are sitting in Mr. Spaulding's box. He is the owner of the team and I am sure you will have plenty of space in which to sit as far away from us as you want."

"And another thing," CB said, "I do not see why we cannot miss church just this once. We go every Sunday. If we are late for the game, it will spoil the whole day."

CB's protestations continued on game day. In one of the few moments of tenderness that had passed between them in weeks, Mim and Chauncey smiled at one another in mutual affection for their older son. Mim nodded at her husband as if to tell him that this was his decision to make. Chauncey stood his ground. "We are going to church, CB. We will not be late, I promise you."

CB's infatuation with baseball soured his normal inclination to comply. "Father, I know we may not be late for the game but the best part is watching the Colts warm up and take batting practice. If we are there early, I can get the other four autographs I need. Four more and I will have the whole starting line-up," he persisted.

"Remember, CB, we are sitting with Mr. Spaulding. I am sure, if you ask politely, he will see to it that you get what you need," said Chauncey.

"Well, you can make me go to church, but I will pray for what I want," huffed CB.

"As you will, CB," interjected Mim, "but just remember that while God hears all prayers, He likely sorts them by degree of importance."

"Then why does the Bible say, 'If you ask, it shall be given to you?'"

"He has a point there," said Chauncey, pleased with his son's logical argument.

"And another thing," said CB, pressing his hard-won advantage, "I already prayed that Cap Anson would get a hit yesterday, and he did!"

Baseball fever had gripped Chicago for more than a decade. In 1888 the Chicago White Stockings, who later became the Colts, had embarked on a world tour to promote international interest in this new American sport. The Chicago team had even played a game in the shadow of the pyramids in Luxor, and while it was unclear what the Egyptians thought of these curious players with their balls and their bats, when they returned, Chicago fans celebrated with a rally at the Palmer House, complete with fireworks.

The West Side Park stadium was completed in 1893, part of the World's Fair complex. Baseball fans paid twenty-five cents to sit in the double-decker grandstands. But it was to the prestigious private boxes that the Blair family headed.

Albert Goodwill Spaulding had owned the Chicago Colts since 1882. As an owner, he showed himself to be cut from the same cloth as George Pullman. Like Pullman, Spaulding felt that ownership of a team was tantamount to owning the players. In order to protect his investment, he instituted no-liquor, no-gambling, no-whoring policies and, when he suspected violations, he hired detectives to gather evidence.

More than anything he hated unions. When several National League players quit the team because of the overbearing rules, Spaulding labeled them anarchists. Spaulding's animosity toward the players was surprising because he himself had been one of the best.

CB Blair would tell anyone who would listen and many who would not that Spaulding's best season was in 1875 when the Red Stockings finished 71-8 and Spaulding had 54 wins. He put together winning streaks of 22 and 24 games in a row—an unheard of achievement for pitchers.

The former pitcher had turned his athletic prowess into entrepreneurial acumen by building A.G. Spaulding & Brothers into the most complete sporting goods store in America, with fourteen branches around the country. Originally limited to supplying baseball bats to major league teams, by the late 1890s the company produced uniforms, baseballs, tennis equipment, bicycles, sports shoes and gym outfits.

As they made their way into the Park, CB was the walking definition of "awestruck." Mildred and Italia were eating their hot dogs and drinking orange crush, all the treats the girls needed to make it a wonderful day. CB was not to be distracted by such incidentals. No true fan would be.

CB spent most of the first few minutes at West Side Park with his attention riveted on his copy of Spaulding's 1894 Baseball Guide, given to him on his last birthday.

"Chauncey, is it?" blasted a voice from behind him.

Assuming that the inquiry was meant for his father, CB did not bother to take his nose from his almanac.

"CB, Mr. Spaulding is talking to you," prompted Mim.

Jumping up from his seat, CB came around the railing and greeted his host with the firm handshake he had been taught to extend to adults.

"Young man, come with me," commanded Albert Spaulding, making his way down toward the field.

"The *field*!" sputtered CB. "You mean this one here?," pointing at the clipped emerald green grass directly in front of him.

"Yes, this field, boy. It is the only one I own. Your father said you wanted some autographs, so bring your book with you. But you won't get a better pitcher's autograph than from yours truly, Albert G. Spaulding," he boasted as he took a pen from his jacket pocket and wrote his name so that it covered an entire page of CB's autograph book. CB then shook hands with each of the players, ending with his idol, Cap Anson.

As Mim watched her son, still all freckles and shy smiles, absorb this momentous event in his life, she closed her eyes for several seconds as if she were a camera that had just taken a precious photograph which she would cherish forever.

And just as CB had predicted, as soon as the Colts took the field, Mildred asked the first of her many questions of the day.

"CB, why are all the Colts wearing different colors?"

Controlling, at least for the moment, his impulse to be irritated, CB answered, "Because each position player wears a different colored shirt. All the shortstops wear maroon. All the pitchers wear blue and the first basemen wear red with white stripes. Anyone can tell what position a player plays by the color he wears."

"Then I would be a pitcher," asserted Mildred. "Blue is my prettiest color."

"*Mother!*" exclaimed CB. "Did you hear that? Make her stop! This is just what I was afraid of. Please, please, I hate all these stu…silly comments. Who cares about the prettiest color? Do I have to listen to this for the whole game?"

"CB. I am disappointed in you. No other boy in this ballpark is as lucky as you are today. It will not hurt you to answer a few questions from your sister."

Turning to Mildred, Mim said, "Mildred, you may ask CB one more question before the game starts and then save the rest for when we get home tonight, or ask your father."

Mildred scrunched her face and then surprised them all by turning directly to the man next to her and saying, "Mr. Spaulding, why is that man putting that thing on his face? He looks like he is in a little jail."

"What an excellent question, young lady. That is called a catcher's mask. The catcher is the only player who wears one because he plays the most dangerous position. The pitcher throws the ball so hard, the catcher needs to protect his face. When I was pitching, I pitched so hard that—"

"Mr. Spaulding, does everyone have to wear that thing on his hand?"

"Mildred, let Mr. Spaulding watch his team," said Chauncey.

"No, Chauncey, I like this young lady. What they wear on their hands is called a glove. In the old days when I was playing, most of the players did not wear them."

"I have gloves, but not like those. I wear them when I get dressed up to go out. Mine have fingertips."

Some time passed before Mildred asked the most direct question of the day.

"Mr. Spaulding, if you are the owner, does that mean you own the players, or do their mothers and fathers still own them?"

That stopped the conversation in the box for all the adults except Albert Spaulding. "You are damn right I own them. Each and every one of them." Slowly, taking his time to point to every member of his team, all of whom were on the field, he said, "I own that one…and that one, and that one…"

Gotham Bound

September 1894

*M*IM HAD BEEN DISTRACTED FOR weeks as she prepared for her second attempt at a journey east. When she thought of the trip, which she did almost continually, it was as if the trip were a rock tossed into a pond, and the ripples were her fantasies. She found it hard to focus on simple tasks like organizing her wardrobe, arranging for life at home in her absence, and reviewing her New York plans. She made list after list, crossed off tasks accomplished and then remade the list, still unsure if she had covered everything.

When she was able to rein in her mind, she had to admit that there were only two points of real worry. Would the Book of Hours come home with her? And, would Martin become more to her than a congenial confidante and mentor? Though superficially straightforward, both questions generated hours of sometimes delightful and sometimes anguished perseveration.

The day of Mim and Tennie's second attempt at a trip to New York arrived. This one came quietly. Unlike the dress rehearsal months before, there was nothing celebratory, ebullient or emotional about this departure. The children were in school and Chauncey at the office when the carriages arrived for them. There were no flowers, no toasts when they arrived at the station to await their departure. But, as if their unconscious minds were conjoined without a whisper of conversation, the sisters never left one another's side.

Chauncey had bid her good night and farewell simultaneously as he left the dining room the night before, though on her breakfast tray that morning there had been a note.

Mimsy,

I wish you a successful trip.

Love,
Chauncey

First-class passengers could expect the finest in hotel living aboard the Pullman Palace cars that carried privileged passengers across the American continent. Plush Belgian carpets, gleaming crystal chandeliers and walls of highly polished inlaid wood delighted travelers as they settled in.

Negro porters closed the velvet curtains each night to keep the intrusive morning light from the eyes of the sleeping rich. Private car bathrooms were en suite with gold fixtures dispensing hot and cold running water for the travelers' toilette. Gentlemen who wished to shave need only pull out a drawer from the mahogany cabinet to find all he would require, including warm towels and a small filigreed guard rail to bar any spillage of oils and after-shave should the train encounter the occasionally rough road bed.

After a breakfast of eggs, kippered herring, grilled tomatoes, sausage, bacon, muffins, kidneys, stewed prunes or fruit compote, ladies might retire to the salon to read, do needlework or simply look out of the enormous picture windows while gentlemen—and gentlemen only—had the option of setting up for the morning, cushioned in the handsome red leather chairs in the smoking car. Brass spittoons were strategically placed to receive the brown liquid projectiles shot their way.

Though cocooned in a traveling paradise, passengers who needed or wanted to be kept abreast of the news or the status of financial markets had access to continuously clattering stock market tickers that clicked out information, reminding them of what they were missing.

"Queen Victoria or the Czar of Russia could not possibly have a car as beautiful as this," exclaimed Tennie, after being escorted to her suite by Cyril, whose only job was to see to it that Mrs. Blair and Miss Mitchell enjoyed every conceivable comfort.

Both Mim and Tennie had left their lady's maids in Chicago, as the Pullman Company provided two personal attendants to serve them. These women had unpacked their luggage and hung, folded and arranged their things before Mim and Tennie entered their separate suites, connected by a glass doorway etched with the initials GMP just below the image of the rising sun.

"George Mortimer Pullman," said Mim, tracing the letters with her gloved hand. "I feel like a hypocrite being on this train."

"Why do you say that, Mim? I for one am going to love every delectable minute between here and New York," said Tennie as she fell into a tapestried chair, grabbing two lavender-flavored macaroons from the silver plate next to her and, in quick succession, popping each into her mouth.

"Because I neither like nor respect George Pullman. He is pretentious, arrogant and competitive to the core. And his wife is worse."

Ignoring her sister, Tennie admired the silver chalice filled with ice water in the center of the marble table across from her chair.

"And look at this. I will drink a glass of cold water whenever I feel like it and when the ice melts, I shall pull this little cord here and summon Cyril."

"Tennie, you sound like a common charwoman who has never encountered luxury before."

"Mim, where has your sense of humor gone? Over these last few weeks, you, who are normally most agreeable, have been, well, let me choose my word carefully here...you have been..."

As if her guardian angel were looking out for her, there was a knock at the door, allowing Tennie to avoid her search for a word she really didn't want to find.

"Yes, who is it?" asked Mim.

"Mrs. Blair, it is Cyril and I have some flowers for you," replied the voice behind the door.

"Please come in, Cyril."

George Pullman hired only Negroes as porters on all his trains for two reasons. First, he believed they were temperamentally better suited to serving, and, secondly, Negroes were not allowed in the union, a fact that suited him to a tee.

But butlers were another matter. Cyril was tall, lean, and mustachioed and he spoke with either a natural or a practiced British accent. He worked exclusively for Mr. Pullman and he was assigned only to this car and to whoever might be a guest.

"Mrs. Blair, where would you like me to put these beautiful flowers that arrived a few minutes ago?" the butler asked, his white-gloved hands around a handsome Chinese patterned vase.

"Indeed they are beautiful. Thank you, Cyril. They can go over there," Mim said, gesturing with her head to a table almost obscured by the potted fern at its side.

After he had placed the yellow chrysanthemums, each the size of a small butter plate, on the table, he handed Mim the note that accompanied the gift, made a deep bow and exited.

"I think Chauncey is missing you already," speculated Tennie.

"Highly unlikely," said Mim. "He has made life quite miserable since our last effort to get to New York. There have been times in the last two weeks when I thought he could hardly wait for my train to leave."

Card in hand, Mim made her way to the mahogany writing desk, adorned with a silver magnifying glass, ink well, fountain pen and letter opener, all monogrammed with the swirling engraved letters GMP. As she ran the letter opener through the crease of the envelope, she too thought perhaps Chauncey had had a thawing of the heart.

Have a safe trip. I am looking forward to 'our hours.'

M.

As instantly as Mim knew from whom she had received the note, she also knew that Tennie was reading over her shoulder. Sensing that some modest explanation might deflect whatever suspicions her sister may have, she made an ostentatious show of handing Martin's note to her.

Shaking her head, she said nonchalantly to her sister, "I think Martin Gaylord is as excited about seeing this Book of Hours as I am."

"Mim, tell me why this Book of Hours is so important to you."

"Oh, that is easily done. It is, quite simply, the most beautiful book in the world. Any collector who could have it would want it for that reason alone," answered Mim.

"So there is only one book in the world and Martin Gaylord is the only person who can secure it for you?"

"There are many Books of Hours in the world, but for some time Martin has known of my interest in buying a significant one, and the one he has found he believes to be exquisite."

"Mim, tell me something. Did you invite me along on this trip as a big sister showing a little sister New York or am I supposed to act as some kind of chaperone for you and Mr. Gaylord? That note sounds like he has a crush on you."

"Mr. Gaylord and I like and respect each other very much. That is not a crush, that is a friendship. As to why I asked you to join me on this trip, it is because I cannot think of anyone with whom I would rather spend this time."

Tennie had read the note and seemed to recognize its flirtatious innuendo, so, despite reassuring her sister that there was nothing romantic between her and Martin, the last thing Mim wanted to do was to dine alone with Tennie and endure any more of her girlish questions. What did Tennie know of the frustrations of a married woman with four children or the excitement of being free? Tennie and she were close, but they were not yet confidantes.

"Tennie, let's dine in the first class car tonight. It will be more festive than you and I dining alone in this compartment listening to the wheels of the train," Mim suggested.

Always one to enjoy dressing up and, remembering her trunks full of beautiful frocks, Tennie readily agreed.

"Yes, let's do that. I know just what I will wear. I will ring for Cyril and tell him that we will not be needing his services for dinner," enthused Tennie.

"And ask him to make us a reservation in the dining car for 8:00," called Mim as she turned into her suite. "I am going to have a lie down and read for an hour until it is time to dress," said Mim.

They were no more than an hour out of Chicago and she already felt the awkwardness of obfuscation and dissemblance. *I am not cut out for this,* she thought.

In the end, Mim and Tennie took all their meals, save breakfast, in the first class dining car. It was a beautifully appointed room. Going through the smoky glass doors that separated all the first class cars, Mim had the sense of stepping into a moving forest primeval. Lovely deep green carpets flecked with gold and crimson felt welcoming underfoot. Heavy pine green velvet drapes were pulled at night, allowing the gold tassels of the valence to swing in time to the movement of the train. Lush potted palms separated the tables, creating an illusion of privacy while still allowing guests to survey one another by peeking through the fronds.

Decorative Tiffany glass leaves resembling small buttercups muted the light of the signature lamps. The gas flame could be adjusted to whatever level enhanced the diner's desired ambience.

Each section of the arched ceiling painted with midnight blue enamel perfectly complemented the gold leaf scenes depicting the huntress Diana giving chase through the night sky.

Mim and Tennie chose the 8:00 p.m. seating both nights, thinking the ten o'clock seating too late for women traveling alone.

The first night, a patrician gentleman, who introduced himself as James Marshall, asked to join them. Mim and Tennie felt obliged to accept, being that he was standing right in front of them. He was ten or so years older than Mim, and, in the small world that was elite Chicago, turned out to have been a young banking associate of their grandfather's.

"Ladies, if you will allow me, I will order the wines for our dinner tonight. I take this train to New York with some regularity and I know there are some excellent ones in the cellar."

"By all means," said Mim, pleased to be in a gentleman's care for the evening.

"Let us get the ordering out of the way so we can attend to good conversation. Have you had a chance to review the menu?"

"Yes, I am ready," said Tennie.

Not waiting for Mim's concurrence, James Marshall signaled to the maître d'hôtel, who arrived at the table and, without benefit of notepaper, took their orders. Mim began with green turtle soup and Tennie ordered the ox-tail offering. For their fish course, they both chose red snapper with piquant sauce. As an entrée, Tennie selected the stuffed roast quail. Mim was delighted that on the menu there were sweetbreads, which she adored and which Bertha did not prepare well. For side dishes, Mim chose orange fritters and Tennie, the chicory and lobster salad.

Before turning to general conversation, Mr. Marshall asked for and was granted permission to order a Grand Marnier soufflé, which needed to be ordered an hour in advance. With the delicious details of dinner taken care of, Mim and Tennie's elderly escort ordered a collection of Chablis, Burgundy, Champagne and port.

"I think that should do," he said with a smile and a dismissive wave to the sommelier.

"Mr. Marshall," flirted Tennie, filled with the exuberance that comes from knowing you are pretty, free and relatively safe with this old man. "If we drink even half of what you have ordered for us, we shall not be responsible for our actions, much less for making our way back to our car. What would the ladies of the temperance movement say of our imbibing?"

"Them." chortled James. "Had I thought for a moment you were one of those humorless prissies, I would not have asked to be seated at your table."

Normally the Mitchell girls, rigorously trained and well-practiced in conversational responsibilities, would have seamlessly carried out their duty to maintain the repartee, even with a self-invited guest. The unwritten rules of social engagement were that when one of the ladies had finished the appropriate number of conversational niceties, the other would pick up the invisible thread and move the talk to another topic. Ideally it was balletic.

But Mim recognized that tonight she was abdicating her duties and had left Tennie as a solo performer. She knew it was not fair, but tonight she could not shake her preoccupation with the emotions Martin's note had piqued. Each time she managed to drag her mind back to the dining table, she trembled at the realization that she was on a train to meet a man for whom she had "improper" feelings. And as if that were not unsettling enough, she recalled that she was also on her way to purchase the most significant piece of art she had ever considered.

A Book of Hours had become much more than a mere addition to her collection. It had become an obsession. So why, she asked herself, was she doing this? Simply, because it would be beautiful. What more justification did she need? She had always been a collector. But was she now behaving no better than Hattie Pullman? Was she now merely a competitive shopper?

Her feelings about being with Martin were more frightening. No sooner would she envision their scouring the galleries of New York, talking knowledgeably and professionally about the pluses and minuses of a purchase, than her prurient imagination intruded. It was not a comfortable diversion. She did not like herself this way, all jittery and occasionally snappish.

"I am so sorry," mumbled Mim as she recognized that Mr. Marshall and Tennie were looking at her expectantly. "Were you talking to me?"

"Well, who else can explain to Mr. Marshall why we are heading to New York?" asked Tennie.

Their dinner companion was more gracious. "Wherever you were, Mrs. Blair, it appeared from your face to be a lovely spot."

"I do apologize, Mr. Marshall. There are so many details crowding one's mind when travelling alone."

"You are not traveling alone, Mim," said Tennie churlishly, perhaps a reflection of Mim's conversational dereliction.

Ignoring her sister, Mim turned to Mr. Marshall and asked, "Forgive me. What were you asking?"

"First of all, I think now that we know one another better, we are all adult enough to use first names. Mine is Jack. Secondly, I was wondering, what is the purpose of your journey to New York? Hortense was telling me you are about to make a significant purchase."

Not wanting to jettison all formality just yet, Mim decided to maintain a little distance. "Yes, please call me 'Mary.'" Then she continued, "and yes again, I am considering the purchase of a Book of Hours to add to my collection. I am a devotee of Medieval and Renaissance art."

"I know that, as do most people in Chicago. How does one come to know of such an opportunity, if I may ask?"

Mim's initial thought was to say, *no, you may not ask.*

"Of course, you may ask. My husband and I are close friends of Mr. Martin Gaylord, who is an eminent collector himself. He knows my collection well and generously keeps an eye out for items with the appropriate provenance to match my collecting proclivities. Do you know him?" Please let him say no, she thought.

"No, I do not know him, except by reputation. You cannot have a finer eye than his, searching on your behalf. I would expect he hopes that when the time comes, you will give everything to the Art Institute. So I suppose he wins out in the end."

"That is a cynical perspective, but likely a correct one," demurred Mim.

The arrival of the soufflé put an end to the banter between Mim and Jack Marshall. The dessert was a golden confection, each soft tier collapsing into the one below until the last puff of egg whites and sugar crowned the top.

As Mim, Tennie and Jack Marshall finished their demi-tasse and sipped post-dinner cordials, their conversation returned to the details of their New York plans. Mim was now more attentive, as if the mingling of dinner, dessert and alcohol had settled her peripatetic mind.

Turning to Jack, Mim asked, "Now that you know what takes us to New York, how about yourself? You say you take this train often. Do you live in New York and travel to Chicago, or vice versa?"

"I do most of my business in New York, though I have homes in both cities."

"And are you still a banker?" asked Mim.

"Yes, after four years at the Corn Exchange, where I worked with your father and grandfather, I moved to the Bank of New York. But I still have enough business in Chicago to make it my second city."

"And, do you know my husband, Mr. Chauncey Blair?"

"I don't, except by reputation, which is an excellent one. I imagine,

Mary, you are likely to know as much about banking as I do. A husband, a father and a grandfather, all in the great enterprise of capitalizing America."

Pushing his chair back from the table and standing, Jack Marshall said, "And now, I think we should all be gone," seguing nicely to bring the pleasant evening to an end.

"But before we go our separate ways, and disembark, I will leave you with my card so we can make plans to see one another in New York. I think I can find some interesting places for you to visit, sites unfamiliar to most tourists."

"Thank you, Jack," said Tennie, still unaccustomed to applying a first name to one as old as Jack Marshall. "I have slightly less tolerance than my sister for poking my nose into every art gallery in New York. I would very much enjoy absorbing a little of the unusual."

Once inside their suite, Mim and Tennie were treated to a footbath, prepared for them by their maid. Sitting side by side, their feet immersed in the perfectly heated water, the two sisters chatted amiably about their evening. Mim was the most relaxed she had been in weeks. She gave Tennie an especially close hug as they said good night, wanting to convey how very glad she was that they were together.

Impediment

September 1894

SENSING SOMEONE STIRRING IN THE outer room of her suite, Mim came fully awake at the gentle knocking on her door.

"Yes?" said Mim, trying to disguise the fact that she had been in a deep sleep.

"Mrs. Blair, Miss Mitchell thought you might wish to be awakened."

"What time is it?"

"It is a quarter past ten, Ma'am. I have your breakfast tray here. Might I come in and open the curtains? You have a lovely day and a lovely view."

"Yes, please do come in. I am sure I have never slept this late in my life! Do you know if my sister is still in her room?"

The maid stepped through the door, and, setting the breakfast tray down, pulled open the drapes.

"No, she is not, Ma'am. She asked me to tell you that she would meet you in the parlor car."

"Excuse me, but can you remind me of your name?" asked Mim.

She chastised herself when she did not remember the name of someone who was serving her. It seemed insensitive to simply lump all servants into a class instead of recognizing them as individuals.

"My name is Sarah, Ma'am."

"Thank you, Sarah," said Mim. "Since I have been shamefully lazy, and lunch is creeping around the corner, I think I will settle for coffee and toast."

"Yes, Ma'am. Are you sure that will be all, Ma'am?"

"Yes, thank you, that will be all. I hope I have not kept you too long from your other duties."

"My only duty is to you."

Mim took very little time dressing, packed her reticule with needlework, a book, and handkerchiefs, and made her way to the first class parlor car. En route she passed a conductor who was as smartly dressed as many of the male passengers. He resembled a toy soldier—stiffly starched white shirt, bow tie, three-quarter length black coat adorned with brass buttons and embroidered with the crimson red insignia of the Pullman Company. Tipping his cap to Mim, he flattened himself against the wall to let her pass.

At first glance it was hard to see Tennie because the parlor car was constructed as if in imitation of boxes at an opera house—spring green velvet alcoves arranged for maximum privacy.

"Good morning, sleepyhead," teased Tennie when she saw Mim approach.

"I know. I was embarrassed when Sarah knocked with my tray. Did I appear to have too much wine last night?"

"Well, if you did, I would not have noticed. I awoke with a considerable thirst and a vague headache. I am feeling much better now, as I have just been sitting and watching the beautiful green hills of Ohio go by."

"How do you know we are in Ohio?" asked Mim.

"Jack Marshall was here earlier and he told me. He seems to know every hill and valley between Chicago and New York and is intent on sharing every point of minutiae with anyone who will listen. This morning I was the only set of ears around. He was so excited about passing from Indiana into Ohio that, had he had champagne handy, he would have opened it to celebrate."

"Where is he now?"

"He went off to the observation car and suggested that we come along when you appeared. What do you make of him, by the way?"

Mim was not quite sure how she felt about Jack Marshall. He was charming, informed and cultured—all qualities she admired. But if he really knew all the people whose names he dropped, then she and Jack had many acquaintances in common, and while she was not exactly traveling incognito, she did not intend to become cozy with their new traveling companion.

"I am not sure. Did he mention anything about a family? Wife or children?"

"No, but he must be relatively free. He has offered to take us to the theater one of the nights we are in New York."

"What did you tell him?"

"I told him yes, of course. We have planned on seeing some theater while we are there and I did not see the harm of our having an escort. He thinks he can get tickets for *A Bunch of Violets* which, according to him, every critic in New York says is the best play in several seasons."

Later in the day, Mim and Tennie explored the train more thoroughly. Mim's favorite room was the library, a mobile literary treasure trove of green leather books arranged with great precision on rosewood shelves that ran floor to ceiling. Each title was embossed with gold letters. But to make sure that all browsers knew who was providing them with a copy of a particular book, the initials GMP could be found on every front cover.

Lord, scoffed Mim to herself. *Apparently George suspects that people who have the means to travel in his cars are prone to book theft.*

The most dramatic feature of the room was a massive standing marble oval writing desk embellished with carved effigies of great literary figures—Shakespeare, Milton, Chaucer—implying that any words written here would likely be inspired.

Mim had seen a good deal of impressive furniture, but she had never seen anything like this. Sprouting from the center of the oval, as if it were the tree of knowledge itself, was a flourishing potted palm tree. Each separate writing area offered writers an elaborate collection of gold fountain pens, crystal inkwells, engraved writing paper and a silver magnifying glass presumably to explore the many leather-bound dictionaries, encyclopedias and atlases on the bookshelves. Mim stepped up and claimed one of the sections, where she wrote her first letter home.

Mim had shown the older three children the route of her trip in the atlas, so that days before she left, even Mildred could name all the states and major cities through which Mim would pass. She also purchased a large wall map and they were excited to use their new wax crayons to mark it so they could keep track of her whereabouts.

CB had been disappointed in the route that Mim would travel.

"Those are the most boring states in the union," he had scoffed. "What can possibly be interesting in Indiana, Ohio, Pennsylvania, New Jersey and New York?"

After she had written to her children, Mim also sent Chauncey a letter, which she found difficult to write. *How can I find myself so constrained with a man I have known almost fifteen years?* Wanting to create just the right tone, neither overly hostile nor intimate, she labored over each word. Should she say she missed him when she was not sure she did? Should she wax enthusiastic about the magnificence of the journey thus far?

Should she tell him about meeting Jack Marshall?

Should she make reference to her planned time with Martin? If she did mention him, he might be suspicious. If she did not mention him, he might be suspicious. It took her an inordinate amount of time to decide whether to make her salutation, "Dear Chauncey," or the more intimate, "Chauncey Dear." Strange how the arrangement of two innocuous words could be so freighted with import.

Dear Chauncey,

I hope this letter finds you well. It is being written from the ever so comfortable and sumptuous library George has created in his first class cabin. I can tell you it would have been more dignified to put the Beaufort book here than in that hideous hotel.

Tennie and I are ensconced in the private sleeping car, but we find the first class cars more collegial, though of course we really are not seeking company. (She wondered if this last sentence sounded too defensive). What I mean is that we are not trying to make new friends en route, we simply do not want to be isolated in our suites.

We had dinner last night with a man. Jack Marshall is his name. He worked as a young associate at the Corn Exchange when both grandfather and father were there. He now works at the Bank of New York but has enough business in Chicago to keep a home in both cities. He seems nice enough.

He has offered to show us some of the sights in New York that tourists might not otherwise see. I would feel more at ease abou accepting his invitation if you knew something of him. Tennie is flirting with him, trying out the part of femme fatale, but she is

young enough to be his daughter, and I hope Mr. Marshall is wise enough to know the limits of a schoolgirl crush.

I do miss you all. (Should she single him out or lump him in with her feelings for the family? She settled on closing with a variation of the sentiment).

I miss you and the children already, but it will all be worth it if I come home with my treasure.

Bye for now, darling. (no) Bye for now. I am off to meet Tennie in the observation car to watch our beautiful country glide by.

Mim

Once Tennie discovered the observation car, she made it her primary outpost for the rest of the trip. True to its name, it was designed for the finest viewing money could buy. Other cars had all glass windows stretching their entire length, but none had the multicolored glass dome that gave passengers the sensation of being jumbled within a moving kaleidoscope.

She was also captivated by the outdoor platform at the back of the car. Truly the last outpost on the train, it offered the strange sensation of travelling to your destination, while at the same time enjoying the opportunity to look back to where you had just been. She also loved the fresh air and the illusion of wild freedom while still being confined on a train.

"Tennie, you have driven away all of our fellow passengers with your running back and forth to the platform."

Ignoring her sister's warning, Tennie opened the door and stepped onto the platform. A few minutes later, she popped her head and called to Mim,

"You are being a hothouse plant as well as a worrywart. Come out here. This is too beautiful a valley to observe and not experience. The air feels wonderful."

Considering that she lived in a city not known for its clean air and was travelling to another sooty city, Mim thought it might indeed feel pleasant to be outside for a few minutes.

"Oh good," said Tennie when Mim stepped out onto the platform. "You will not regret this."

When she and Tennie were alone on the platform, they both took off their hats. With the warm autumn air cocooning them into feeling like the only people on earth, the two Mitchell sisters stood silently watching the hills roll by. In the beauty of the moment, Mim put her arm around her sister's waist and pulled her closer, in a kind of hip hug. A current of mutual understanding passed between them. They were on an adventure together and, without saying a word, each understood that Tennie became just a little older and Mim a little younger.

To underscore that narrowing of barriers, Tennie reached up and pulled the pins out of her hair and then from her sister's hair, giving the wind permission to do what it would. Within seconds, anyone able to see would have sworn that there were two disheveled and possibly mentally impaired women standing with their arms around one another at the end of the train.

The moment was broken by a sudden jolt of speed, enough so the two adventurers now clung to one another more in anxiety than amusement. As the roadbed grew rougher and pebbles began to spray, they had little choice but to retreat into the car. Once inside, Mim and Tennie repinned their wild hair, reset their proper hats and within minutes presented themselves in the dining car fully returned to the refined women they remembered they were.

After lunch, and despite the embarrassingly late hour of her awakening that morning, Mim went back to her suite for a lie down. Telling Sarah to awaken her in an hour should she happen to fall asleep, she shed her clothes down to her petticoat, lowered the shade so the room was as dark as night and climbed between the freshly laundered sheets.

For the second time that day, Mim was awakened from a deep sleep by a gentle rap on the door. "Thank you, Sarah, I was not asleep. Just resting," she lied.

The minute she sat up she sensed something was very wrong. When she tried to open her left eye, she felt the pain. Her instinct to close it rewarded her with recurring discomfort. It felt as though there were a boulder in her eye. Unable to control her impulse to expel whatever was irritating her eye by rubbing as hard as she could, Mim walked to the window and lifted the shade, hoping the afternoon light would allow her to see what was wrong by looking in the nearby mirror. She lifted her upper lid and then her lower one, but she could see nothing that would cause this much pain.

"Sarah, would you please fill a basin with warm water," she called. "I think something has lodged in my eye. I want to see if I can flush it out."

"Do you need me to come in and help you, Mrs. Blair?"

"No, thank you. I shall be right out. Just make sure the water is neither too hot nor too cold. It should be only slightly warmer than room temperature."

Attempting to keep her head back and her eye closed proved a challenge as she tried to dress, so she settled for simply slipping on her dressing gown. She stumbled into the sitting room and, leaning over the bowl, she splashed a cupped handful of water into her eye, and while it felt refreshing, the eye bath did not relieve the feeling that there was something deeply imbedded in her eyeball. It felt so big that she was more than a little surprised that she could not see it when she looked into the mirror again.

"Sarah, can you please fetch Miss Mitchell and bring her here? She is most likely in the observation car."

Mim had no idea of what value her sister would be other than to keep her company. On a cruise ship there was always a doctor, but she had no idea if there were similar medical staff on a train.

"Damn, this hurts," she said aloud, unashamed of the profanity.

"Mrs. Blair, I am staying here with you," Sarah called into Mim, "but I summoned Cyril, and he is fetching Miss Mitchell."

Not only did Cyril find Tennie, the chief conductor found a doctor and, though he was a pulmonary specialist, he had a confident air, a comforting manner and a black bag, which always conveyed authority.

"Mrs. Blair, my name is Dr. Warren Ames and although I am not an ophthalmologist, I think I can help you. But first, you must move your hand so I can see more deeply into your very sore-looking eye."

Mim found that if she kept her eye firmly closed and pressed the heel of her fist into the socket, she could dull the pain. Dr. Ames was very gentle with Mim's puffy, red, oozing eye. He curled back the upper lid and then the lower. He then retrieved a small flashlight from his bag and asked her to look directly at him. In order to do so, she had to blink once again which caused more pain. Her stoicism was beginning to crumble.

Mim asked, "Do you see anything, Dr. Ames?"

"One more minute of your patience, Mrs. Blair. There we go. I can now see what is causing you so much discomfort. You have a very large corneal abrasion. Whatever particle caused this abrasion is no longer in your eye, but it has done some considerable damage to the cornea.

"Since we have all been sequestered inside this train for the last twenty-four hours and typically there are no flying pebbles or stones in Mr. Pullman's first class railway cars, I cannot think of how this happened to you, but it did."

Instantly, Mim and Tennie, who had been listening to every word, knew exactly where and how she had damaged her eye.

"I am most grateful you have given me a diagnosis, but am I to live the remainder of my life like this?"

"No, Mrs. Blair, the good news is that the cornea heals itself."

"Is there bad news to come?" asked Mim apprehensively.

"Only if you care about wearing an eye patch for three to five days," replied the doctor as be began to reassemble his black bag.

"An eye patch," cried Mim and Tennie in unison.

"We are about to arrive in New York City. We have plans, parties, receptions, and the theater. She will look like a Halloween pirate!" howled Tennie.

"Well, if she wants relief from the pain and quicker healing, she will wear one," said Dr. Ames, who had done the best he could and was wearying of the vanity of his patient or, more particularly, his patient's sister.

"When you get to New York, you can ask the hotel doctor to prescribe some soothing drops which will help. But finding you a patch in the meantime is very important."

"I don't suppose you have such a patch amongst your medicines?" asked Mim.

"No, Mrs. Blair, I do not."

At that moment, Sarah came forward trailing something white over her arm.

"Mrs. Blair, I think I can fashion something for you. Put these cotton balls in your eye socket so it keeps your eye from blinking and then let me wind this around your head."

At the end of the process, Mim's eye, firmly closed, did feel better, but when she looked in the mirror, her other eye shed sympathetic tears as she now looked exactly like Swami Vivikananda. Needless to say, the Mitchell sisters took dinner that night in the privacy of their suite.

Some Answers

New York City, Autumn 1894

MARTIN GAYLORD LONGED TO RETURN to Chicago. He had grown tired and edgy. The Pullman strike had trapped him in New York, making it inefficient to return to Chicago before his traditional summer holiday in Maine. Now his internal travel alarm clock was ringing. It was well past the time to go home. It was only the imminent arrival of Mim and her sister that prevented him from packing up his personal belongings, buying a railway ticket, calling a carriage and making his departure.

Despite his weariness, it had been a productive stay for Martin. He had spent a considerable amount of his own and other people's money, using the better part of last week to supervise the packing of twelve crates filled with paintings, sculpture, antique frames, porcelain—modern works for certain clients, traditional pieces for those like Mary Blair who preferred the classic.

When in New York, Martin preferred to stay at the Union League Club on East 39th Street. No hotel could match the majesty of the décor.

The dining room was first rate if unimaginative, and the club's private art collection was on a par with most museums in the city. Walking down the grand staircase of the Union League set a man off in the morning with a spring in his step, feeling as though no obstacle would obstruct what he could achieve that day.

Like other Union League clubs around the country, the New York branch had been established by the political elite to encourage support for the Union cause during the Civil War. To this day, members still congratulated themselves on the fact that they had trained, armed and clothed an infantry regiment of colored boys, who had marched proudly past the club before boarding the trains that took them into territory where they would have been lynched had the South been victorious.

Nowadays, Gaylord's appreciation of the value of the club grew each time he stayed there, as he never failed to rub elbows with one of the luminaries who passed in and out of the reading rooms, dining rooms and gymnasiums. Last week he had seen Theodore Roosevelt. (The membership committee had blackballed Roosevelt when he first applied to the Union League in the early 1880s, as it was well known that his mother had Confederate sympathies.) But here he was, cossetted in a rich leather chair in the dining room, eating his breakfast.

Martin had had an entertaining evening just last night when he had been invited by Joseph Van Rensselaer to join his group for a post-dinner brandy. At the end of the evening, Van Rensselaer had offered Martin a private look at the newest acquisitions at the Metropolitan Museum, where he was a director. Naturally Martin accepted with pleasure and took the liberty of asking if he might bring a guest.

"I am expecting a friend and client early next week," he said. "Mrs. Chauncey Blair, a Chicago collector, is en route to New York. Might I extend your kind invitation to her while she is here?"

"Of course you may bring her," replied Van Rensselaer enthusiastically. "I know of Mrs. Blair and think that she would find these paintings very much to her liking."

Martin Gaylord gave a soft chortle. "I am afraid the French painters do not stir her soul. She has passed up many chances, too many, to buy them."

"Time will tell whether or not your Mrs. Blair has made a wise decision in abstaining from purchasing the French painters. But I suspect she has missed an important opportunity."

"Well, maybe you can convince her of the error of her ways when I bring her to the Museum. She has told me many times that she is a collector, not a shopper, and she collects only what she loves. She focuses almost exclusively on antiquities for which she has a near-perfect eye. As a matter of fact, she has come to New York to see an exquisite Book of Hours I have found for her."

"Any collector would appreciate a chance to buy a Book of Hours if she had the opportunity, so I can understand her impulse to travel halfway across the country for it. How old is it?" asked Van Rensselaer, with just a touch of predator in his voice.

"Mid-fourteenth century," answered Martin.

"Ah, the height of the brilliance of the genre. But I am curious where you found one for sale," pressed Van Rensselaer. "European governments are very particular now about national treasures leaving home. I know Continental dealers are feeling the pressure not to let antiquities leave. Auction houses here are frightened of running afoul of the authorities. I would be interested myself to know how you found a Book of Hours."

One didn't have to be a genius to see where this conversation was going, thought Martin, who was relieved when several other guests interrupted their *tête-à-tête* to say goodnight. He had said too much already.

∽

Martin had been surprised and mildly affronted when he learned that Mim had been in New York for two full days without calling him. Her explanation that she was recovering from an injury sustained on the train was hard for him to understand. He had never heard of a corneal abrasion, and, anyway, what kind of injury did one get riding in a George Pullman car?

They had made a date to meet at noon for lunch in the dining room of the Waldorf hotel; he walked there now with very mixed emotions. Normally a man who compartmentalized easily, Martin Gaylord realized that these days Mim was maddeningly present in many of those compartments. Martin felt several emotions—admiration for her taste, appreciation of her company, amusement at her spirited view of the world, and attraction to the sexual potency of that mélange.

Martin had had liaisons with many women both before and, if truth be told, during his marriage. He really could not predict what would happen now that Mim was here (albeit shadowed by her little sister).

More surprising was his anxiety about the Book of Hours itself. He had been buying and selling valuable art for years, both in America and on the Continent, and he was as sure-footed as any man when it came to negotiations and transactions. He had made mistakes, but very few. He was skilled—knowing how far he could push a client both artistically and financially. But because of how he felt about Mim, he feared this obsession of hers had already pushed him beyond the traditional boundaries that surrounded the purchase of antiquities. That he had summoned her from Chicago, and was now walking to the Waldorf, an appointment set for her to see the Book tomorrow, represented more potential risk in one purchase than he had taken in a lifetime.

Mim had spent two frustrating days in her suite at the Waldorf. After the first twenty-four hours, her eye was pain-free. Now she was finally going to join Martin; she was restless, excited and more than a little off-balance.

With Mim's encouragement, Tennie did not hover over her older sister during her confinement. Instead she set off early for the shops. Mim was relieved not to have to accompany her sister on what would have been hours of poking into the enticing boutiques along Fifth Avenue. At the end of each day, Tennie would burst into the suite, arms filled with colorful packages, each of which had to be opened, admired and then resealed. This was just how Mim enjoyed shopping—vicariously.

True to his word, Jack Marshall had secured tickets for the Broadway production of *A Bunch of Violets*, which, according to the concierge, was an almost impossible feat. Tennie was thrilled.

Mim had had misgivings about allowing Tennie to be escorted to the theater by a man they had encountered on a train. However, she had heard back from Chauncey that, while he did not know Marshall personally, his reputation was solid. *Solid*, thought Mim, as she dressed for lunch with Martin.

When Tennie returned after the theater, she was subjected to a thorough interrogation, the net result of which was that they had had the best seats in the house, the play was delightful, but that Mr. Marshall was "boring."

With mixed emotions Mim had invited Tennie to join her for lunch with Martin.

"Do I have a choice?" asked Tennie.

"What do you mean, do you have a choice?" said Mim, surprised at her sister's challenging question. "I am sure Mr. Gaylord would enjoy your company as much as he does mine, but if you have other plans—" said Mim.

"Of one thing I am sure, he would not enjoy my company as much as yours. I have seen you together, and as I said when the flowers arrived on the train, I think he has a crush on you," said Tennie as she initiated a mock swoon, fluttering her hands close to her heart.

"Don't be absurd, Tennie," said Mim, trying hard not to sound defensive. "I have a reservation in the dining room for the three of us at noon, and I mean, sincerely, that I would love to have you join us."

"Very well, I will go and change and await the arrival of Mr. Gaylord. But I must leave at 1:00 to be at my fitting at R.H. Macy & Co. at 2:00. I will likely be there for several hours. If you and Mr. Gaylord have plans after lunch, please keep them without me. I will meet you back here at the hotel at 4:00 p.m. in order to change for the opera."

"Martin is sending a carriage for us at 6:00," Mim replied, "so don't be late. We are seeing *Romeo and Juliet*, with Lili Lehman, which I promise you is a far more enlightening way to spend an evening than at that melodrama on the New York stage."

Reprising her teasing swoon, Tennie fluttered her hands again and left the room saying, "Two meals in one day with Mr. Enchanting. Be still, my heart."

One of Martin Gaylord's charms was his ability to put people at ease. Everlastingly grateful that he applied this charm at lunch, Mim had a pleasant time and began to relax as soon as she saw him.

"Mr. Gaylord, perhaps at dinner tonight you can explain to me more fully than my sister can what is so very special about a fourteenth-century religious book," Tennie offered as the salad was served. "I have enjoyed every minute of my stay in New York, but I have yet to develop an understanding of the passion that drives our journey, though as I said, I am not complaining."

"I will try to explain it to you," replied Martin, "but I will be very surprised if you don't understand immediately when you see it for yourself."

"I very much look forward to your tutelage, but at the moment I will say goodbye and go in search of the more ephemeral pleasures of high fashion."

"Neither of you has touched your Waldorf salads," Martin observed, gesturing at the still full plates of the Mitchell sisters. "I ordered them particularly because it is considered by many to be the special delicacy of the house."

"New Yorkers may consider a mixture of apples, celery and grapes a delicacy, but it would never pass muster as a delicacy at the Palmer House restaurant," said Tennie as she gathered her reticule. Martin laughed so loudly that several diners looked sharply at their table.

"I must agree, Miss Mitchell. And I thought the fanfare of the two waiters making the mayonnaise tableside was a bit pretentious. They looked more like circus performers than waiters."

By the time Tennie bade them both goodbye, Mim was fully reminded of how attractive Martin Gaylord was. After taking a moment to let Tennie's jolly spirit fully diffuse into the somewhat charged air, Mim became intensely serious.

"Martin, I can wait no longer. It is time for all the ambiguity about my Book to dissolve. I am literally itching with curiosity. Begin, please. I promise to let you talk, uninterrupted, which will be *very* hard for me, but, look," she said, "I am placing my hands firmly over my mouth," which she then proceeded to do.

Martin beamed a smile at her, which most definitely would have been correctly interpreted by anyone watching as more than polite.

"First, Mim, I am so very glad to see you. Take a deep breath and let us just enjoy the moment of being together. How is your eye?"

Mim answered tersely, "I too am glad to see you and my eye is as discerning as ever.

"Despite my best efforts at interrogation, you have given me no information about this Book you have found. Is it as mysterious as all that? Tell me all of it."

With that comment, she firmly replaced her hands over her mouth and awaited the information for which she had come.

Martin signaled the waiter and ordered two more demi-tasses and then maddeningly, since the waiter had already done it, he began sweeping his hand across the table, brushing imaginary crumbs off the linen covering.

Mim mimed that she was about to explode, but, true to her word, she remained silent until Martin began.

"I will answer your last question first. Yes."

"Yes, what?" Mim all but hissed between her fingers.

"Yes, the circumstances surrounding the Book are indeed mysterious. Your transaction, if it takes place, will be unlike any other I have been involved in, so from now on, we talk about it only with one another."

Gesticulating now so as to keep her promise of silence, Mim motioned for Martin to commence.

"Three months ago, I was at M. Knoedler & Company gallery. I believe you know it. It is the most important gallery in the city with the most elite client list in America."

"Yes, I know it," said Mim, her voice now as conspiratorial as his.

"I have known Michael Knoedler for years and, if anyone were likely to know where to look for a Book of Hours, it would be Michael. Recently I received an invitation to a private reception at his gallery for a show of Claude Monet's most recent work. It is impressive and I think you should see it, by the way."

"Martin, at the moment, I have no interest at all in Messieurs Monet, Manet, Degas or any others of the new French school. I give you my word that if I get my Book of Hours, I will go to see them and look with the eye you want, but for now, tell Cissie about them. Tell me about the Book."

"You are right, I digress," said Martin. "Michael was kind enough to give me a few minutes of his attention, though there were plenty of people who wanted time with him."

Seeing Mim take her hand from her mouth, Martin put his own hand gently atop hers and, brushing her cheek as he did so, guided it back into place as if to stop whatever words were about to come out.

"I know, I know, I am sorry, I just don't need to know about the other guests," said Mim.

"Au contraire. You do need to know about one particular guest, as you shall soon see," countered Martin, more amused than annoyed at Mim's tenuous hold on self-restraint. With her hand firmly re-placed over her mouth, Mim sat back in her chair and nodded for Martin to continue.

"When Michael spotted me, he motioned me to join him and two other gentlemen to whom I was introduced. I cannot remember the name of the older of the two and he plays no part in this story, but the other gentleman was introduced as Mr. James Hanson.

"After pleasantries and my compliments on the quality of the show, I told Michael that I had a client who had a very special interest in a four-teenth-century Book of Hours and was willing to pay handsomely for it if it were deemed to be of the highest quality. Did he have anything current-ly or, if not, did he know where I might find a suitable dealer.

"Usually, a gallery owner is going to take some time to answer a question like mine and do whatever he can to at least give the appearance of interest in what might prove to be a significant sale. I had purposely told him that my client would pay handsomely for such a book, to pique such interest.

"Instead of at least pretending to ponder the question, he answered immediately that he neither had such a book nor did he know of any such source. With that, he gave me a friendly pat on the shoulder, thanked me for coming, and moved on to another conversation group, leaving me with the distinct feeling that I had offended him in some way, though I could not think what the offense might have been."

Mim had again removed her hand from her mouth, but she remained silent, appearing to be completely drawn into the inherent tension build-ing within the story.

Martin continued, "Sensing the awkwardness of the moment still hanging in the air around our small conversation group, one of the gen-tlemen excused himself to refresh his champagne."

Martin took a faux sip from his all but empty demi-tasse, subtly signaling to the oncoming waiter that they were not yet done. He then continued his story.

"Shortly thereafter, the gentleman who had remained at my side asked me if I thought my client for the Book of Hours was a serious one. Since I was having trouble hearing him clearly, I suggested that we move into the anteroom, which was less crowded. Much to my surprise, he said, 'No, I think it best we talk right here where our conversation looks most natural and is least likely to be overheard. I will speak as loudly as I dare.'"

I replied that my client had the utmost seriousness of purpose in finding such a Book, and I repeated that she would be willing to pay top dollar should the manuscript prove to be of the highest quality.

"Without another word, he wrote out something and handed me a piece of paper with an address on it and suggested that, if I wanted to see something truly astounding, I was to meet him the next evening at 5 p.m."

"And did you?" Mim blurted out.

"Be patient, my dear. I am almost done with part one of this extraordinary tale, and then, together, for I no longer intend to be alone in this, we must set about to plan part two.

"The first thing I noticed, when I examined the note the gentleman had placed in my hand, was that it was a scrap of paper rather than the kind of formal business card one would have expected from an authentic dealer.

"The other item of interest was that the address he had selected for our rendezvous was—I guess you could call it a gallery—in a part of New York with which I am unfamiliar."

"Where?"

"It is called Yorkville. It is like Lincoln Square in Chicago."

"You mean to tell me that my Book of Hours, the one I came halfway across the country to buy, and for which I am willing to pay more than for any single item in my collection, is in a poverty-stricken German neighborhood?" asked Mim, unable to hide her incredulity.

"That is exactly what I am telling you," replied Martin, appearing to delight in extending the mystery of the story.

"Martin, is this some sort of cruel trick you seem amused to play on me?"

"Oh no, my dear. This is no trick nor, if you decide to buy it, would it be a purchase without risk to both of us."

"Martin, you are frightening me with these nefarious implications. I have bought hundreds of pieces of art. Occasionally, I was a bit fearful that I had made an uninformed or hasty choice, but never have I felt that there were danger involved."

"Well, Mim, very soon, tomorrow in fact, you will have to decide how much risk you are willing to take to be a world-class collector. Buying the book I saw will separate you from every other collector I have ever known. It may separate you from your own code of conduct.

"And, I have vowed to myself that I will not try to influence you in any way—no opinions, no hints at what I would do in a similar situation—though I have to confess I have never imagined I would be in a situation like this."

"Martin, have you seen it?"

"I have."

"And—"

"It is the most magnificent piece of Medieval art I have ever seen."

"And do you know anything about its provenance, its origin, or why, given what you say, it is being offered in an ersatz gallery in a slum?"

"I believe it to be an authentic Book of Hours, illustrated by the Limbourg Brothers, the most renowned artists in fourteenth-century France. Do you know of them?"

"Oh, indeed I do, Martin. Was it painted when they were in service to Jean de France, Duc de Berry? If that is the case, then this is more than I ever could have hoped for in my wildest dreams. But my question remains, why is it not at Knoedler's gallery?"

"Oh, that is an easy question to answer. This Book of Hours is not at any reputable gallery because no gallery I know would ever risk its reputation by handling what is almost certainly stolen property."

Since Mim and Martin were now the last people in the restaurant, Martin assumed that the waiter, whom he spied en route to the table once again, was coming to apply some pressure on them to depart.

"May I get you anything else, sir?"

Surprising Mim as much as the waiter because, though it was almost teatime, Martin was clearly not finished with his lunch.

"Yes, as a matter of fact, I think I will have a brandy," he responded.

"Mrs. Blair, would you care to join me?"

Mim experienced her second surprise in as many seconds, when she heard herself say, "Yes, yes, I think I would."

30

Another World

New York City 1894

B Y THE TIME TENNIE POPPED her head into the dining room at the Waldorf after returning from her fitting, Mim and Martin had been lunching for over three hours.

"I have had five gowns fitted and you two are still here?" chided Tennie. You are the only two people I know who actually could have been talking about a Book of Hours for an entire afternoon."

"As I told you earlier, you will understand when you see it," countered Martin.

"And when might that be?" asked Tennie, more distracted in gathering her packages than she was interested in the answer.

"We are to see it tomorrow at 3:00," said Mim, moving abruptly to the elevator in order to curtail any further conversation about the next day's plans.

During the hours she and Martin had conferred, she had decided at least a dozen times to forgo the opportunity to even *see* the Book of Hours. After all, if she never saw the book, she need not take action. She

289

could stay another few days in New York, distracting herself with the pleasures of the city and basking in the moral superiority that comes with making the right decision.

True to his word, Martin was a sphinx when it came to offering any opinion on what course she should take. It was maddening.

"Martin, if you were I, would you even bother keeping the appointment?" Mim had asked, hoping that this more subtle line of inquiry would be productive.

"Well, Mim, I am not you, so all I can tell you is, should you decide that you want to see it, I will accompany you."

"Martin, you know my tastes. Will I like it? I mean, maybe it will not inspire my imagination. My expectations are so high, I could very well be disappointed in it," pressed Mim.

"Mim, it will exceed all your expectations. It is astonishing. You will fall in love."

"Then, I will go to see it. But I will not go as a buyer, merely as a window shopper. I cannot miss seeing it, but I will most definitely not be taking it home."

In the end, neither the opera nor the elegant staging sustained Mim's attention that night. Rather, her imagination flung her wildly to the Lower East Side of New York, escorting her through dirty back alleys en route to meeting a one-eyed, toothless old man handing her a Book of Hours wrapped in a paper sack tied with frayed twine.

Mim could imagine the newspaper headlines announcing her arrest. "Society Collector Admits Knowing Priceless Book Was Stolen Property. Claims *She Had to Have It.*" Certainly that would be plenty of justification for Chauncey to divorce her and assume custody of her children. That prospect, which now seemed perfectly possible to her peripatetic mind, refortified her resolve not to buy this Book of Hours.

No, for the sake of her family and her conscience, she would not consider purchasing what might be a stolen national treasure. She only wanted to see it, to be near enough to absorb its history and maybe, just maybe, touch the Holy Spirit within its pages.

When Martin returned Mim and Tennie to the Waldorf that night, he gently squeezed Mim's hand as he helped her from the carriage. It was a delicate tightening and a slight caress, signaling his support and confidence, much like a school drama teacher would encourage her protégé before she went on stage.

Martin Gaylord spent a restless night nursing brandy and soda in the empty library at the Union League Club. He did not have any degree of confidence in Mim's ability to leave the Book of Hours behind. He had seen it. He knew that its luminous colors and its originality would capture Mim's heart, no matter the firmness of her current assertions of resolve. The power of the book had shocked him into an instantaneous comprehension of why Mim wanted to own it—the astonishing depiction of its sacred characters painted with refinement and vivacity simultaneously.

And it was a masterpiece you could hold in your hands. Most art he dealt with made that impossible. You hung it, or placed it, or enshrined it. The Book of Hours allowed a sensation that was tactile, experiential, and spiritual. If you owned it and wanted to keep it near you at all times, you could. You could explore page after page, run your fingers over the exquisite calligraphy to remind yourself of what you possessed—what you owned forever.

Martin was not a religious man. Yet, holding this Book of Hours stirred a faint hope that maybe, just maybe, Christian faith could be justified. When he looked through the lavish illustrations, he shared Mim's awe at the devotion of those who had labored for hours, maybe days, to perfect a letter, to apply the gold onto the halo of the virgin, to mix just the right tempura for the blood red pouring from Christ's open wounds.

The expression "For the love of God" was commonly used to express frustration. But in his brief encounter with this Book of Hours, Martin saw it as the perfect phrase to describe what he saw on every page—the love of God. But no sooner was Martin at a distance from the book than he realized that its magnificence in no way compensated for the risk he and Mim would be taking, should Mim decide to make an offer. In the thirty years he had been in the business of procuring art for himself, museums and clients, he could remember only two other incidents when he suspected that the transaction was not above board. In neither case had he been even remotely tempted to pursue the initiative.

Martin had real affection for Mim, but he knew he was not deeply in love with her, nor, he suspected, was she with him. Yet, here he was, knowingly placing in jeopardy his reputation by keeping the initial appointment to see the book.

⁓

Mim was aware that the amount of time she had taken dressing was excessive. But, after all, there was no etiquette book in the world that advised on the proper couture for viewing a stolen work of art.

"Is today the day you buy the Book?" asked Tennie.

"Well, today is the day that I will see what is being offered. But there is little chance that I will buy it."

"*Not buy it!*" exclaimed Tennie. "You have thought of little else since you heard of its existence. We have traveled more than a thousand miles, escaped a riot, and you have suffered bodily injury. I thought it was just days away from resting on your bedside table. Is it flawed in some way?" asked Tennie incredulously.

"No, it is not that. Martin confirms that it is magnificent."

"What then?"

"Tennie, stop badgering me. I will make a decision when I see it. Now I must go. Enjoy your next-to-last day here."

"No need to bark at me, Mim," said Tennie, equally snappish in her response. "I was going to wish you well, but you have poisoned the sincerity of that impulse."

With the conclusion of that unpleasant exchange, unprecedented in their relationship, the sisters went their separate ways.

⁓

Mim and Martin decided to forego lunch. Martin had had a late and full breakfast and Mim knew her nervous stomach would not welcome anything. Once in the relative isolation of a carriage, Mim started to speak until Martin turned to her and placed a finger on her lips, telling the driver to take them to Tompkins Square Park, where, declaring it a fine day, they would walk to their destination.

"Now, may I talk?" asked Mim, after she and Martin were seated on a park bench.

"Yes," replied Martin.

"I have so many questions, but when assembled together, they all boil down to one. Is the Book of Hours that I am to see in a matter of minutes, that I have come all this way to see, stolen property? And, well, I guess I have two questions. How do you know that for certain? And, well, then there is number three, are you sure the illustrations are the authentic work of the Limbourg Brothers? If it has authentic Limbourg illustrations, there are only two or three extant books it could be. It would be a superb find."

"I am not sure of the answers to any of those questions, to tell you the truth. That is what the owners claim, but everything about this—" Martin paused. "I don't even know what to call it, this adventure, no, it is much more serious than that. Everything about this 'transaction' has had a deleterious odor to it since I was first approached. A whispered contact, no formal business card, and that was even before I made the trip down here to see it."

Mim concurred and said, "I am expecting gangsters greeting us and leading us blindfolded into a back room. Will we be safe with these people?"

"We will certainly be physically safe. After you make your decision, safety is a matter of point of view."

"Martin, I have told you, I have made my decision. I am here only to look at what my esteemed friend tells me is a magnificent Book of Hours. If it turns out that it is a genuine Limbourg Brothers Book, being in its presence will be enough for me."

Martin took a deep breath, looked at his watch, and announced that there were only ten more minutes until they must begin the walk to their destination.

"With whom are we meeting?"

"When I was there to preview the book, there were two men, neither of whom introduced himself, which, I suppose, if you are dealing in stolen art, is a smart strategy. As to the provenance, I am going to have to leave it to you to evaluate. You know infinitely more about this genre than I do."

"Did they present anything in writing?" pressed Mim.

"They handed me a one-page evaluation. Here it is," he said, taking it from his breast pocket. "It gives very little information for a piece of this importance. It states that it was painted sometime in the early fifteenth century and—"

"Not the kind of specificity that a reputable gallery would provide," Mim interrupted.

"Mim, we must get started in a minute. But before we do, let me—"

"I am sorry, Martin. Do go on. You have shown me more patience in all of this than I deserve. You have risked a great deal for me, just accompanying me on this journey. I want you to know, I appreciate that consideration and I appreciate you," said Mim with gratitude in her eyes that matched the tone in her voice. "Now, let's be off."

When Mim rose to go, Martin gently tugged her down again, turned her shoulders so she faced him, looked at her a moment and said, "Mim, I told you I would accompany you today and that promise holds. I will escort you back to the hotel. But after that, you will be on your own as to how to proceed.

"I have seen this book and I know your heart. If you cannot resist the temptation that overpowering beauty offers, there is no one who will understand better than I. But for us to maintain a relationship, I prefer not to know whether the Limbourg book remains in an unmarked office in New York City or in your dressing room in Chicago.

"I hope you know that were it not for you, I would have immediately walked away and had nothing to do with Mr. Hanson, whom, for the record, I will never see again. He is obviously the front man for an illicit group of art thieves.

"But back to you. Your quest for the Book of Hours has intrigued me. In part that is because I love the chase, but the more compelling attraction has been your passion. It has been infectious.

"I have worked over the years with hundreds of clients, many of whom were friends. Many are knowledgeable, a few are discerning, and all of them are rich. Most of them preen, dressing up in culture as if preparing for a costume ball.

"You are unique, Mrs. Blair."

Mim had never been spoken to with as much tender understanding. Now it was her turn for the intimate gesture, made possible here in

Tompkins Square Park by the certainty that no one they knew would see them. She placed her finger on his mouth and slowly traced the outline of his lips.

"Martin, I feel as if we are making love right here in Tompkins Square Park."

"We are doing just that and it feels wonderful. But you and I know this is as far as it should go. More than this becomes too complicated. But allow me this," with which he kissed her, an extraordinary kiss placed just close enough to the corner of her mouth to allow the point of his tongue to enter, if only for a moment, as if her mouth were a sealed envelope of secret pleasure that he dared not fully open. "Come now, fine lady, we are about to enter a whole new world."

Martin firmly held Mim's hand as they walked through the park, flouting every convention instilled since childhood about public displays of affection. So wobbly were her legs from the thrilling trauma of Martin's kiss, so anxious was she about the encounter to come, that Mim held on tightly, questioning her ability to cross the busy avenue, much less engage in high stakes negotiation with a crook.

It took them no more than five minutes, each of which was filled with hundreds of impulses to flee. Mim was reassured of their safety by the normalcy of the neighborhood through which they now hurried. Pavements in front of each small shop were scrubbed clean, the produce displayed by the many grocers en route looked fresh and succulent. She had no idea of the possible uses for the hooves, tongues, tails, ears and snouts hanging in front of the butcher stalls. But being a Chicago native, the odor told her that she was closer to a Swift and Company than to a Marshall Fields.

The diversity of sights, sounds and smells was a welcome, if temporary, distraction until Martin stopped at the unmarked door. He held it, politely signaling for her to precede him. Mim shook her head, no. For a few more minutes she preferred to be the follower.

They spoke not a word as they ascended to the fourth floor. There were several offices along the hallway, all but one of which were marked with the name of the enterprise within. So it was no surprise to Mim that Martin took his silver-handled cane to tap at a door with no lettering.

After waiting for a full minute, with neither the sounds of responding feet nor voices inviting them in, Martin repeated the rapping, this time with more force. Another full minute passed. The door finally opened, revealing the most austere room Mim had ever seen. There were few chairs, comfortable or otherwise, no curtains, and one desk. Another door appeared directly in front of them, presumably leading to an inner office of some kind where any business would likely be transacted.

From behind the door came the person who undoubtedly had opened it. To Mim's astonishment, it was a woman. If she had been dressed in white, Mim would have been certain it was a ghost, but as she was appointed from head to toe in black, "gypsy" was the more appropriate moniker. Of indeterminate age, she was no more than five feet tall with luminous grey-green eyes, so like Italia's that Mim almost asked her what she was doing here.

However, there was nothing slovenly about this gypsy. Her hair looked recently coiffed, and her perfectly curled ringlets did their job of softening her long, thin face. She wore a stylish black hat with a modified veil covering her forehead. At first Mim thought this woman was an assistant to whoever was behind the inner office door. But it appeared as though she had walked in only shortly before Martin and Mim, as she retained her velvet gloves and wool walking coat and never did ask if she could take her guests' outer apparel.

In fact, when Mim thought back on the encounter, she could not remember a single sound that the woman uttered. Gesturing for them to follow her, without knocking, she opened the remaining door as if she were completely familiar with what lay behind it. Enveloped in unnerving silence once she and Martin had closed the door, Mim grew increasingly uncomfortable. She longed for the busy normality of the neighborhood, or the bustle of an office—something to ground her in reality.

"Madame, I am delighted to meet you," said the distinguished man who rose from the beautiful mahogany desk at the center of the inner office. Though his diction was perfect, his accent was thickly German, reminding her of Robert when he had first joined her household.

If the outer room had been somewhere between bare and bleak, the inner sanctum could have been any elegant drawing room on the southside of Chicago. The ecru-colored walls were a subtle background for the oatmeal, green and tangerine oriental carpet, which, when Mim stepped on it, cushioned her footfall. Two sofas, each covered in heavy silk brocade, formed an L that faced the desk; two deep green velvet chairs with gold braid trim sat opposite one another, closer to the desk.

The arrangement of the furniture presaged no conviviality. Clearly people who met in this room were invited to participate in a business relationship and nothing more. Mim sat on one of the sofas and Martin took a side chair. Though there were several other seating options available, the woman chose to stand by the gentleman.

Mim immediately noticed the walls. Perfectly hung, as though by a seasoned curator, were two small sketches, which she recognized as those of Michelangelo. But behind the desk was the *pièce de résistance*, either a perfectly executed forgery of Peter Paul Reuben's *Adoration of the Magi* or the exquisite original which had always been one of Mim and Grandmother Mitchell's agreed upon favorites, for the richness of the dark colors and exotic personages paying homage to the Christ child.

"Madame, I see your eye has found, and, if I am not mistaken, admired, the second most important work of art that is currently in this office," said the man behind the desk who, at least from the front, was as elegantly turned out as the woman who had let them in and was now positioned as a sentinel.

Are they brother and sister or husband and wife? wondered Mim, unable to restrain her rudeness by staring at them until she realized that it was she who had been addressed.

"May I know whom I am addressing?" asked Mim, embarrassed by her obvious distraction.

"Alas, that will not be possible, Madame," said the gentleman, with a slight bow and an expression of either real or fabricated disappointment that he could not oblige her request. "I am afraid that within these walls, I have found it advisable to restrict appellations to the more formal "Madame" and "Sir." I suspect your friend here would agree with the application of that rule while we are here."

No amount of time would have been sufficient for Mim to construct the perfect response to the gentleman's statement. Nonetheless she said,

"Well, Sir, I have always loved all of Monsieur Reuben's work, particularly his religious paintings. If this one is authentic, you have a treasure, though it seems to be in a strange location to fully admire it."

"Would you like to see it more closely? I think you will see, with your trained eye, that it is indeed a Reubens."

Summoning more courage than she ever thought she had, she said, "Thank you, I would like to examine it, though my eye is less reliable than my instinct."

Mim rose, as did Martin. The gentleman moved gracefully to allow them enough room for closer inspection. Neither Martin nor Mim expressed any opinion about the painting's authenticity. Mim knew that she did not know enough to make that determination. She thought Martin might, but she did not want to be discussing it with him in front of these two odd but elegant overseers.

"Beautiful," was all she said as they returned to their seats.

"But, Madame, if you recall, I said that the *Magi* was the second most beautiful work of art in this office at the moment. Are you not curious as to the piece that would outshine it?"

"I am, yes. And I do not suppose you are referring to those sketches by Michelangelo, interesting though they are."

"You would be correct. I am referring to your Book of Hours."

"Sir, it is a long way from being 'my' Book of Hours," Mim replied with just the right amount of frostiness to remind any one who may have forgotten that she was the cautious customer, not the designated buyer.

"Would you care to see it and then we can talk, or would you like to have our conversation first?"

"I would prefer to see it. There may be no need for further conversation."

Acknowledging for the first time the woman who had been standing silently at his side, the gentleman spoke to her.

"Helene," he said, all the while looking at Mim and Martin, "*S'il te plaît.*"

Te? wondered Mim. Though his accent labeled him a German, this man of the world should know better than to use familiar French in formal or professional situations. This small slip made Mim edgy. It was her first hint that this was not a top tier enterprise despite the sumptuous decorative accouterments.

No small talk accompanied Helene's entrance into the inner sanctum. When she returned, she carried a rectangular object, about the size of a *Book of Common Prayer*. With gloved hand she carried it to a standing desk at the end of the room away from the windows, presumably to protect it from the bright sunlight.

She then handed Mim and Martin grey cotton gloves. After they had put them on, she gestured for them to approach Mim's Holy Grail.

31

Decision

New York City 1894

*A*ND THEN, THERE IT WAS. She knew that the red leather cover would not be the original, but it was clearly centuries old. A leather strap held the pages together just above a seal, which could have been that of Jean de France, Duc de Berry, patron of the most famous collection of medieval manuscripts in Christendom.

Mim knew that among his fifteen Books of Hours, fourteen Bibles and sixteen Psalters, only one reached the pinnacle of artistic achievement. If the book she was about to open was the Limbourg *Tres Riches Heures*, she had indeed found her treasure.

"Monsieur," said Mim archly, "I at least need to know when this manuscript was completed, otherwise I cannot possibly be certain of its authenticity."

"Of course. The brothers began the one you now see before you after their earlier masterpiece, *Belles Heures*. Sadly, *les freres* were carried off by the plague before its completion, leaving some of it for colleagues to finish.

301

"But please, Madame, you said you wanted to talk after you examined the book. May I suggest that you do that for thirty minutes or so to take in the magnificence of the manuscript and then I will answer any and all questions you may have."

"But," continued Mim, "I need to know how you—"

"There will be plenty of time for conversation. I am going to leave you now and go into the anteroom. Helene will not disturb you. When you are ready, I will return and we will talk."

Mim felt thwarted by the presence of this strange woman. There was no need for her to police the viewing. It was inconceivable that the gentleman thought she would harm the book.

For the next thirty minutes, Mim devoured the manuscript, forcing herself, under the pressure of time, to turn the pages, each one of which she would have stared at for hours had she been alone with it.

Most Books of Hours were illustrated compilations of sacred stories which, when assembled, served as a guide to a direct personal relationship with God and the Virgin Mary. It was believed that a devoted Christian, using its format, could pray directly to God, obviating the need for an intercessor.

Mim knew right away that what lay before her was first and foremost a work of art. She had seen other medieval manuscripts but this one's realism and perspective broke new ground. It was breathtaking—almost literally breathtaking. What struck her most forcefully was the vivacity of the colors—brilliant blues, deepest mossy greens, reds and russets—all set off by gold leaf. Only the mixture of rare and therefore expensive pigments could have achieved these hues.

Most of the illustrations were religious—saints, prophets, and angels, but there were also landscapes, castles, animals, exquisitely painted human figures at work in the fields. The fifteenth century came alive and drew her deeply into it. If one never saw anything but this startling Book of Hours, it would be all one needed to know about the Middle Ages.

Sensing that Mim had been rendered incapable of turning the pages on her own, every so often Martin would nudge her and she would force herself to move on. Suddenly Martin realized Mim had stopped altogether.

She took a hushed but audible inward breath that sounded somewhere between "oh" and "ah," a sound that was a gasp of disbelief that anything could be so beautiful, a sound that was almost one of sexual satisfaction.

The painting that evoked this response was the first of the calendar pages typically found in Books of Hours. The script read, *"Ianaurius,"* which Mim knew from her schoolgirl Latin translated as January.

A sumptuous banquet of images lay before Mim and Martin in the panorama of a literal banquet overseen by a figure who was likely the Duc de Berry himself. Without a word, Mim's gloved finger touched the bright orange-red colonnade that remarkably was both in the background and yet prominent enough to be the first form to catch her eye. The red-orange was the perfect contrasting color for the two blue moon discs ornamented with gold-patterned fleurs-de-lis. Silver-white cygnets swans were entwined in swirling golden tendrils of vine.

Three women hovered in the background. One was draped in heavy black robes as if in mourning; the heft and richness of the fabric, the softness of the folds allowed the viewer to feel as well as see it. Two other women wore pink gowns, one the dark pink of a robust sunset, the other the palest pink of a summer rose. The women clung to one another with their delicate alabaster fingers. Their gold-embroidered turbaned heads were close, perhaps whispering the gossip of the court.

There was no mistaking the Duc who, despite being seated off to the side, was the central character at the banquet table. He sat erect in a fulsome tunic in two shades of vibrant blue, enhanced by embroidered gold filigree. Rich brown-black fur cuffs matched his hat, which properly dwarfed those of his decidedly lesser guests. Only the Duc was adorned with jewelry, a gold neck chain and pendant looked almost too heavy for a mere mortal to bear. His authoritative stare at the red-robed priests who were giving the blessing left no doubt that the Duc was not intimidated by the presiding clergy.

Gold dominated the feast table—gold plates, goblets, samovars, and bowls were piled high, awaiting the guests who would fill them with the wild game and wine pictured on the table.

For all the celebratory ambience of the banquet, a wholly different scene played out in the top third of the painting. Colorful pennants fluttered around a battalion of helmeted and chain mail-draped medieval warriors thrusting lances into their enemies.

Mim was no longer an observer. She found her place in the tableau. She was Alice down the rabbit hole. If she owned it, she could live many lives, real fifteenth-century lives. She could be a miller's wife supervising the milling of the grain, one of the rebel angels expelled from heaven, now burning in a fiery pit. She could be the veiled lady of the manor accompanying her lord to the hunt, or she could be one of the comforters of the Virgin at the Disposition of Jesus from the cross.

With one word her fantasies were jarringly interrupted.

"Madame," came the soft but insistent voice of Helene, the first word she had uttered since she had ushered them in. A feeling of violence arose in Mim at the interruption.

"Do you need more time?" asked Martin, sensing Mim's frustration.

"Of course I do, but there is no amount of time that would be sufficient to take all this in," Mim replied.

Turning to the sphinx in black, Martin said ingratiatingly, "Is it possible for my client to have more time?"

"*Bien sûr, Monsieur,*" she said, but Mim countered, "Never mind, Martin, since days will not be possible, I think it best to begin our conversation."

The gentleman returned and the three principals took their seats. It never was clear to Mim whether or not this woman was a principal in the business, but she remained standing erectly by *Tres Riches Heures*, like a sentry fully on duty, expecting someone to make an inappropriate move.

"Well, Madame, is it not an astonishingly beautiful work?"

Mim had come today with no intention of engaging in a discursive conversation on the merits of the Book. But now she was convinced that this book was *Tres Riches Heures*, considered the jewel in the crown of medieval manuscripts. Should she walk away, she would never see its likes again, and that very thought shattered her resolve. Who knew into whose hands it might fall should she not make the purchase? She would treasure it in a way no other collector could. She was sure of that. This book was beyond any other Book of Hours in the world and certainly eclipsed Hattie Pullman's Beaufort manuscript.

"Monsieur, can you please tell me as much as you know about its provenance?"

"Actually, Madame, I know a good deal about this work, more than I normally know about a piece that comes to me."

"Well, let's start there. How did this piece come to you?"

"The owner, a gentleman whom I have known for some years, approached me, Madame, and authorized me to offer it for sale."

"And who might that be?" asked Mim. "It is unconventional, one might even say suspicious, for a buyer not to know the previous owner. It has long been considered a form of protection for the buyer."

"Sir," interjected Martin. "A manuscript of this significance is considered a national treasure in the country of its origin, which in this case is France. I have had many, many dealings with French authorities and, believe me, I have found them understandably protective of works such as *Tres Riches Heures*. In Italy, you can be imprisoned for selling national treasure. How is it that the owner is permitted to own it privately, much less offer it for sale?"

"Monsieur and Madame, rest assured this book is the finest piece in my client's renowned collection and is legitimately for sale by the rightful owner. That is all you need to know."

Mim responded coolly, "Forgive me, and I cast no aspersions on your offices but it does strain credulity that the owner, even if he came by *Tres Riches Heures* in the most reputable manner, would not seek the wider clientele that a large gallery would be able to generate."

"Again, I repeat, Madame, all I am authorized to tell you is that my client is a very private person, reclusive almost, and under no circumstances will I break my word that his—or her— identity will be revealed. Have you any further questions?"

"What CAN you tell me about the authenticity of this Book of Hours? What kind of certification is there that this is indeed the one and only *Tres Riches Heures*, commissioned by the Duc de Berry, and illuminated until their death by the Dutch brothers?" asked Mim, wanting to draw this conversation to a close. "I have sold many pieces of art over the years. I too prefer anonymity. But I also understand that potential buyers expect more than faith as the basis of a sale."

"Come with me," said the gentleman, rising from his chair and making his way to the standing desk upon which the book still lay.

"Helene," he said.

Helene silently redistributed the gloves she had recently collected, and with her own protected hand, reopened the book, this time to a complete page of manuscript.

Mim could not shake the feeling that the gentleman and Helene were actors moving through a scene that had been well rehearsed.

Fortunately, Mim knew enough to know that what she was seeing was an exquisite rendering from the Renaissance. The vellum had been so carefully prepared, the calfskin scraped so amazingly thin that each page was almost transparent, and these were the most beautiful letter embellishments she had ever seen.

She also knew that in any acquisition, the collector took some risk, but buying what was offered here would be beyond anything she had ever done before. Martin's presence was becoming less and less comforting. He moved with her and occasionally she felt his hand brush against her, but he was largely mute. While he had warned her that he would offer neither comment nor opinion once they were inside, she now felt the full weight of acting on her own.

"Madame, let me point out a few additional distinctive features that I think will ease your mind. To begin with, note the basic dimensions of the manuscript. *Tres Riches Heures* is well known to be eleven and a half vertical inches and eight and one-quarter horizontal, the exact measurements of this book."

As he spoke, he took a small measuring tape from his waistcoat pocket and showed Mim that this book fit those proportions exactly.

"Secondly there were 206 leaves in *Tres Riches Heures*, as there are in this book, 66 large illustrations, and 65 smaller ones. You are more than welcome to count these yourself, but I can assure you, I have counted them and that is precisely the number contained herein.

"Of course you might say there are other such books that might coincidentally share the same specifications, or even been copied to match *Tres Riches Heures*, but none has the technical and artistic sure-handedness of this work. No painters, other than the Limbourg brothers, could have achieved what you see.

"Third," he said, turning to a panel dominated by a castle looming in the background. "This particular illumination is entitled *The Temptation of Christ* but most importantly, to your question, the castle is known to be *Mehun-sur-Yèvre*, the favorite castle of the Duc, where the most important pieces of his collection were housed during his lifetime. Only the Limboug brothers had an eye for the architectural design and detail displayed here.

"In addition, perhaps you noticed the abundance of animals in the paintings. The Duc had fifteen Books of Hours in his collection. One characteristic of them all was the abundance of animal life. It is reasonable to assume that when he commissioned a work, no matter how much latitude he gave his artists, his preferences would be reflected in the final product as they are here," he said, as he turned several pages to prove his point.

Whatever else this man was, he was knowledgeable. Mim now had little doubt that she was looking at the original work with its distinct markers of greatness.

"Remarkable," whispered Martin, the first words he had spoken in many minutes.

"Remarkable," concurred Mim.

"Quite the right word, Madame et Monsieur. This is the Limbourgs at their best."

Originally Mim had coveted a Book of Hours not only for its beauty and its historical significance, but also for its devotional inspiration. She had hoped it would bring her closer to the glory of God, re-infuse her with the feeling of the divine presence she had felt when she had given birth to Billy. She had not felt spiritual euphoria since then and she yearned for the Book of Hours to return her to its wonder.

But as she looked at the paintings of quotidian life, she found that they were among the pages she most favored.

Turning to the calendar page for February, Mim found a winter's tale of fifteenth-century French country life. In the deep background under various shades of leaden grey skies was a town, en route to which a stooped peasant trod on an amazingly realistic path of heavy snow, wearily prodding a mule carrying wood.

"The light," said Mim. "The light is exactly right for a sunless winter evening. I can feel the cold of the snow as if I were wearing the man's boots myself."

The scene's middle ground was spare, and appeared very, very cold—brittle, defoliated winter trees outlining a wood to the right of the path, looking as though a sharp gust of wind might snap branches at any moment.

"Have you ever seen birds scrounging for seed painted with such realism?" asked Mim.

"No," said Martin. "I have not."

Three exhausted peasants sat before a hearth, the evidence of fire inferred only because of the exquisitely painted wispy smoke coming from the chimney. Two men sat catatonic, as if the day's fieldwork had brought them close to collapse. The blue-robed woman has lifted her skirt to show her white pantaloons, not in coquetry, but in an unselfconscious effort to absorb as much warmth as the fire could give.

"Madame, is there anything else I can show you, any other questions I can answer?"

"I have two," Mim replied with more self-assurance in her voice than she felt in her still queasy state.

"Please," said the gentleman, gesturing for her to rejoin him in the sitting area of the office.

"Monsieur, your exposition has convinced me that this is the authentic Book of Hours from the collection of the Duc de Berry, illuminated by the Limbourgs. The book itself has convinced me that it is a treasure beyond anything I thought I would see here today.

"Yet, I still require two more pieces of information before I make a final decision. First, I will need in writing, verification that *Tres Riches Heures* is being offered by the rightful owner and that it is neither stolen property nor procured in any other nefarious scheme that would put either my purchase or my conscience at risk."

Martin's face registered nothing, but he knew exactly what Mim was doing. From a woman of such experience and intelligence, this was not a serious question. No, she asked knowing full well what the answer would be. This was a ploy that told him two things. Mim would buy *Tres Riches Heures*, and she would then set about convincing herself that she had made all the proper inquiries to ascertain its legitimacy.

"Madame, I hope that I have already given you that assurance. The best I can do is give you a testament upon sale, signed by me, that this manuscript is being sold by its owner. I have said the owner must remain anonymous. If your decision to purchase is contingent upon that information, then I am afraid there can be no transaction. And your final question, Madame?"

"The price, Monsieur. What amount is the owner—"

"Asking for the book? Thirty-five thousand dollars."

Not a full second passed before Mim answered, "Monsieur, I have bought and sold many pieces of art, though admittedly none as majestic as *Tres Riches Heures*. It is my opinion that thirty-five thousand dollars would be a fair price for a work of this importance, were I to receive a full disclosure of its provenance. But you have made it clear that that is not to be forthcoming. Given that restriction, I can see paying no more than twenty thousand dollars for it."

Martin did not know whether he felt appalled or proud as he listened to Mim negotiate. She took a sensible position. He was now certain that she was not playing an abstract game. She meant to buy. He had watched her many times over the years and he knew her pattern. She was not an impulsive buyer, but neither did she dither. And having come this far, she would not make this a prolonged transaction.

"Madame, I could not possibly sell you something of this value for as little as twenty thousand dollars. My client is indeed a wealthy man, who actually does not want to part with *Tres Riches Heures*, so he set a minimum and that number is above twenty-five thousand dollars. I suggest you make another offer so we can continue."

Mim wanted the book. She wanted it more than any piece she had ever bid on before. But she also wanted to be out of this room and away from this unctuous man and his ghoulish assistant.

"My final offer is twenty-eight thousand dollars, Monsieur."

Another long silence, and at last, "Madame, you will never regret your decision."

"Madame, there is one more thing. Payment is required in cash."

"Cash!" said Mim and Martin in spontaneous unison.

If there were any lingering hope in Mim or Martin's minds that this transaction was above board, it now shattered.

"Monsieur, that is not possible. I am from out of town. I have no way to generate that amount of cash here in New York. I can write you a check and I assure you that it will be honored, but I cannot see how I could get the cash before I leave the day after tomorrow."

"Do you not know any banker in New York who could arrange this for you? After all, these are modern times. Monies are wired in and out of banks frequently in circumstances like this."

"Monsieur, I have never found myself in such a circumstance. Turning to Martin she whispered, "Would this even be possible?"

"Possible, yes. Easy, no," replied Martin. "It will depend on your access to a trustworthy New York banker. I take it then you have decided to buy *Tres Riches Heures*."

"I must."

Martin nodded, giving no visual clue as to what he was thinking.

"Monsieur, allow me twenty-four hours to try to make the arrangements. This will not be easy, and it puts me in a difficult position in a city where my contacts are limited.

"I will be at the Waldorf Hotel tomorrow afternoon at 3:00. Go to the reception desk where, if I am unable to secure the cash, you will find a note from me telling you I have failed to do so. If there is no note, you will know to meet me in the tea parlor adjacent to the reception desk. I too desire anonymity, so please refrain from using my name at the desk."

"Madame, I do not even know your name," said the gentleman with a slow shake of his head.

Mim knew if she did not marshal her courage immediately to try to find the cash, her fortitude might fail her.

"Mr. Marshall's office, please," said Mim into the receiver of the telephone in her suite.

"May I say who is calling?"

"Mrs. Chauncey Blair from Chicago."

Mim had convinced herself that her travel acquaintance, who had squired Tennie to the theater, would never remember who she was and that her request to speak with him would be brusquely denied. Instead, within seconds, she was greeted by the smooth and gracious voice of Jack Marshall.

"Mrs. Blair, I have been thinking that you and your sister were swallowed up into the social swirl of New York. I was hoping I would hear from you again before your departure."

Mim relaxed ever so slightly, and tried hard to match his warmth with her own.

"I do apologize, Mr. Marshall—"

"I thought we had agreed to 'Jack'," he said.

"Well, Jack, I do apologize. It took me longer to recover from the injury I sustained on the train, and then, when I had fully recovered, I did get very busy with galleries, shopping and enjoying the city."

"Do you and your charming sister have time for me to take you to the Opera? There is *La Gioconda* Thursday night and I happen to have two seats available in my box."

"We would both love to see you, but by Thursday evening we will be on our way back to Chicago."

Mim knew that, pleasantries over, it was time to reveal her real reason for calling. He seemed to realize that as well as he made no attempt to fill the void of silence that now enveloped their conversation.

"Mr. Marshall, Jack, I was wondering if you could help me arrange a financial transaction."

"I will help if I can. What is it you need?"

She must now dig into the reality of her intention.

"I am making a purchase of a significant piece of art, and I, well, I need to find a bank to which I can wire twenty-eight thousand dollars from my Chicago account so I can pay for it."

"There should be no impediment to that, Mrs. Blair. I can have my assistant set up a temporary account for you. We will wire the money, provide you with a cashier's check, you can make the purchase and then we can close the account, or keep it open so it will be available to you on your next trip to New York, which I might add, I hope will be very soon. I am happy to help."

Now it was time for her to drop into their conversation what she was sure would come as a surprise to Jack Marshall, just as it had been to her and Martin.

"Jack, my purchase is an extraordinary piece, almost half a millennium old. And, I will admit, financing it is also quite unusual. I will be paying for it in cash."

"In cash!" exploded the voice on the other end of the phone. "Why would you do that?"

"Because the owner of the piece insists on remaining anonymous. It is the condition of sale."

"Mrs. Blair, do I need to tell you that this demand for cash suggests some maleficence on the part of the owner. You are going to hand over that much money, in cash, to a person you do not know? Have you consulted your husband about this?"

"No, I have not. I have always had my own account from which I draw funds for my art purchases. I can assure you, though it is a great deal of money, I can more than cover it."

"I am certain you can. That is not the part of your request that is worrying me. Mrs. Blair, let me ask you directly. Can you be sure that this is an authentic work, indeed can you be sure that this is not a stolen work of art?"

In preparation for uttering the biggest falsehood of her life, Mim took a deep but inaudible breath and said, "Yes, I am sure on both counts. I have been a collector for many, many years, since I was a girl, in fact. I need no protection on that score. Now, will you be able to accommodate my request?

"I am leaving tomorrow evening, and I am hoping to take possession of my purchase at three o'clock tomorrow afternoon and then go directly to the station."

Jack Marshall answered in a voice mixed with incredulity and suspicion of her sanity. "I will do my best, Mrs. Blair," reverting to the formal address of their introduction, as if to distance himself from any intimacy with this eccentric woman.

"I should know for certain by the end of business today. I will leave word at the hotel. If I am successful, I ask that you come here by yourself to collect it. I would prefer not to take responsibility for transporting that much cash through the streets of New York."

"Yes, I understand, and I do appreciate your willingness to help," said Mim, eager to end the call.

"Well, frankly I am not entirely willing, not because the technicalities of the transaction are particularly complicated. As you know, this is what banks are set up to do. No, my reluctance is that I fear you have fallen into an unsavory arrangement. But you have much more experience in the art world than I do. I just hope you do not come to regret your decision."

"Thank you, Jack. I appreciate, if not your imprimatur, then your indulgence. Of one thing I can assure you. I will never regret my decision. I have purchased perfect beauty."

From the moment Mim replaced the receiver on the hook, events organized themselves quickly in her favor. Jack Marshall surprised her by calling her directly that evening, long after business hours were over. He said she should present herself at the bank tomorrow, Tuesday morning, at eleven o'clock. She should take the elevator to the fifth floor and ask the receptionist for his office. Once there, his assistant, Mr. Gardner, would have her "requirements."

"Is there someone, other than your sister, who can accompany you from my office back to your hotel?"

"I shall be just fine. Thank you for your concern," said Mim with more confidence than she felt. Not wanting another extended conversation with someone who clearly questioned her judgment, she repeated her thanks and hung up.

Tennie, thoroughly absorbed in her own world the last several days had asked only two questions of Mim as they prepared to leave New York.

"Where has Martin disappeared to? It is now Tuesday, we leave tomorrow and I have not seen him since last week's dinner." She continued, "Have you seen your Book of Hours?"

Mim replied honestly to each of the questions. "Martin left for Chicago this morning and I have indeed seen the Book of Hours. In fact, I have purchased it."

Tennie smiled generously at her sister, knowing what this acquisition meant to her. "I am genuinely happy for you."

And being preoccupied with not missing her final fitting, she was off in a flurry of her own happiness.

Mim had a surprisingly restful sleep and was actually quite calm as the hour of her possession of *Tres Riches Heures* approached. As instructed, Mim presented herself at Jack Marshall's office the next morning and, as promised, she was given two surprisingly small leather canvass satchels, which she carried to the hotel with less trepidation than she had anticipated.

After lunch, Mim feigned exhaustion and the need for a cup of tea at precisely 2:15.

"Allow me to call room service for you, Ma'am," offered the maid.

"Thank you, but I would prefer a change of scene. Besides, you have your hands full with Miss Mitchell's things. I think you will be more productive if I am out of the way."

Leaving no room for discussion, Mim made her way to the tea salon, taking her needlepoint bag with her not only for distraction but to hide the two satchels of cash. Seated in the salon, she began her needlework rather than stare at the reception desk, which she could clearly see.

For all the years she had coveted a significant Book of Hours, for the endless days of waiting once Martin had told her he had found her heart's desire, for the agonizing minutes of the encounter in lower Manhattan, the final steps to ownership happened literally overnight. Mim spotted Helene, who had just entered the tearoom.

"Madame," was all she said in acknowledgement of Mim's presence.

Both women were well aware of their respective assignments and proceeded to carry them out. Each woman opened her bag and produced exactly what the other one wanted. There was no need for conversation. In perfect synchronicity the two women bent over their respective parcels and replaced what they had carried in with the treasure each would carry out.

"Merci, Madame," said Helene with a nod as she wafted away.

Both Mim and Tennie were bubbling with excitement at the prospect of going home. Mim had given little thought to her family since she began her trip, though she wrote postcards to the children, telling them of all the things she had done and would do with them when she brought them to New York. Her letters to Chauncey were less frequent and more emotionally erratic. But now that she had avoided a sexual commitment to Martin, now that she had experienced the most stirring kiss of her life, she could think of her reunion with Chauncey with affectionate anticipation, if not genuine excitement. But *how* she would present the details of her purchase, or *if* she would, would require a good deal of thought. She was thankful she had a third of America to cross before she need decide.

Once aboard the Pullman Palace car westward, Mim repeated the same ritual both nights. When at last she was alone in her berth, she opened the outer box in which the Book of Hours lay. Delicately she pushed aside the multiple layers of tissue paper revealing the red leather cover. She simply stared at it, caressing it with her thumb as if to welcome it into her now-perfect world.

$\mathcal{A}$ $\mathcal{P}$olitical $\mathcal{A}$ttack

Summer 1896

$\mathcal{M}$IM HAD NOW OWNED *TRES Riches Heures* for almost two years. This fact would have come as a shock to those within her artistic circle with whom she normally exchanged news and attended viewings of major purchases.

Chicago patrons of the arts were on a buying spree of late. Cissie Palmer continued to devour the work of the French Impressionists. She had enhanced her collection recently with the acquisition of *Acrobats at the Cirque Fernando* by Renoir, bringing her total number of Renoirs to ten. If, under penalty of death, Mim had been required to purchase from the French School, she would have bought a Renoir. There was a depth to his work that she did not find in Claude Monet, twenty of whose paintings were currently in the Palmer gallery.

Chauncey's cousins, the Watson Blairs, had hosted an elegant reception to unveil their newest acquisition, *The Boating Party*, by Mary Cassat. Mim was enchanted by it, just as she had been by Cassat's mural in the Women's Building at the fair. She could never articulate why she appreciated Miss Cassatt's work, except that it always made her smile. The enthusiasm of Chicago's cultural mavens over the Pullmans' purchase of the Beaufort Book of Hours had subsided everywhere except in Mim's still embittered memory.

Mim had made a conscious decision to hold no introductory celebration for *Tres Riches Heures*. There would be no announcement that the world's most beautiful and significant medieval manuscript was in her dressing room.

On the train home, while her sister was slowly moving the magnifying glass over the pages of her treasure with an intensity Mim had not seen her apply to many things, Mim had told Tennie that she would not soon be putting "my Book of Hours" on public display.

"Tennie, do you understand what I am asking of you?"

"Mim, have you picked a favorite illumination yet?" she replied irrelevantly.

"No, I have not spent enough time with it and just when I think I have picked the most beautiful, I turn the page and I am fickle again. But did you hear—?"

"Yes, yes, I heard you," said Tennie distractedly. "And yes, I will not spoil your surprise. Do you want to know my favorite?"

Chauncey loved Mim enough to be genuinely happy that she had secured her prize. He made no mistakes in his reaction to *Tres Riches Heures*, never calling it "quite the daisy" or any other of his customary trivializing phrases that he knew would annoy her no end. Just as he was about to refer to it as "your little treasure," his better linguistic self intervened.

"Mimsy, it is magnificent," Chauncey said sincerely. "Once again your eye has guided you to an object of rare beauty. My dearest, you should be proud of yourself. You knew what you wanted and you went after it. You would make a very successful businessman."

Mim was touched by Chauncey's sincerity, though she felt a twinge of discomfort when he suggested that she had a right to be proud of herself. The moral ambiguity that accompanied her purchase of the manuscript did not deserve such fulsome praise.

Nonetheless, it felt soothing to be home with Chauncey. They had been genuinely happy to see one another.

"Where are you planning to display it?" asked Chauncey.

"I don't know," she had replied. "although the Pullmans would never understand such subtlety, it was not intended to be stared it. A Book of Hours is meant to be used."

"Does that mean no formal reception? Your friends will be disappointed not to meet your new love," teased Chauncey.

"Not yet," teased Mim in return. "My new love is all mine for the moment."

And still, two years later, no one outside Mim's household had seen her heart's joy.

"I cannot abide having these goddamn Democrats crawling through town all week," sputtered Chauncey, flinging aside the newspaper that had reminded him of the imminent arrival of such unwelcome invaders.

"They are at the Coliseum, Chauncey. We won't even notice them," said Mim.

"Not notice them? You may not notice them," spat Chauncey. "I can spot them a mile away."

Chauncey's deepest predilections were immutable. He was an Episcopalian, a banker and a Republican. He had ruined several dinner parties with explosive vitriol against William Jennings Bryan, the likely Democratic nominee for president. He was largely forgiven his outbursts by his elite peers, all of whom believed as he did, but Mim's forgiveness was slightly more difficult to earn. Moreover, she was worried about how this petulance was affecting his health. His voice would rise and so too the flush on his face.

Though Chauncey denied that he was hot-headed, Mim knew better, and she also knew what was at the root of Chauncey's agitation. All his outbursts were aimed at the people that he feared above all others—unionists, populists and terrorists—words that he used to describe supporters of William Jennings Bryan.

The gathering of Democrats at the Coliseum dominated the newspapers for days, which meant that mornings started badly for anyone in the

Blair household within earshot of Chauncey's daily ritual. He considered cancelling his subscriptions for the duration of the convention, but in the end he enjoyed the *Tribune*'s editorials, which were delectably hostile to the Democrats.

Rising earlier than normal for a meeting at the Art Institute, Mim made the mistake of joining Chauncey at breakfast the morning after Mr. Bryan accepted his party's nomination.

"He is a socialist," thundered Chauncey. "Didn't I tell you he was a socialist?

These people are *not* Democrats. They are socialists and they have only one goal. They are out to destroy those of us who create capital, those of us who finance the expansion that has made this country great. If America stands for anything, it stands for getting rich. What is wrong with that? I hate these people!"

"Perhaps Mr. Bryan is simply trying to—" injected Mim.

"What he is trying to do is very, very simple. He is trying to get people to see you and me and all our friends as evil. I promise you, the Haymarket riot will look like a convivial community gathering if Mr. Bryan is elected. Listen to this."

Without Mim's direct assent, Chauncey continued reading from the newspaper.

"I am not making this up. These are his words. 'I come to you in defense of a cause as holy as the cause of liberty—the cause of humanity.'"

"Holy cause? Holy Christ!" said Chauncey, now fully fuming and pounding both of his fists on the table, causing the breakfast china and cutlery to make their protests.

"Chauncey! Please stop. What if the children hear you?"

"It would be a valuable lesson for them. They must be trained to know a charlatan when they see one. In fact, why don't you call Italia and CB to come in here?"

Mercifully not pausing for Mim to dispute his directive, Chauncey continued in full, roaring bloviation. "'The income tax is a just law. It simply intends to put the burden of government justly upon the backs of the people. I am in favor of an income tax.' The money he wants to steal is *our* money. I hate these people!"

"So you said," murmured Mim.

"But here is the worst of it. Mr. Bryan thinks we are all the same. Right here he says so. 'The man who is employed for wages is as much a businessman as his employer.' How is that possible? Can you imagine considering Robert a businessman? Robert wouldn't consider himself a businessman! There is more—"

Oh, I am sure there is, thought Mim. She had never seen him this agitated.

"Enough, Chauncey," said Mim forcefully. "You are worrying me. No more reading. You are turning redder and redder with each sentence. I understand your point. Please, put the newspaper down. It does you no good to excite yourself over something you can do nothing about. You support Mr. McKinley. That should be your answer to Mr. Bryan."

"You are right," Chauncey said, rising from the table. "I am going to send Mr. McKinley another check this very minute."

But the McKinley campaign did not get another contribution from Chauncey Blair that day or for several weeks thereafter.

"He is very, very lucky," said Dr. Stephens, joining Mim in the morning room. "It was not the miracle you gave us when your son was born, but he was fortunate nonetheless."

"I am not sure I see that a heart attack, no matter how 'minor,' as a lucky consequence. How can you be sure that he will not have another where the outcome will not be as 'lucky'?"

"I cannot promise that he will never have another heart attack, Mrs. Blair. But he is responding nicely. When I first arrived, his blood pressure was 170 over 100. Way too high. It is now considerably lower and his heart sounds strong enough," answered Dr. Stephens.

"Strong enough for what?" asked Mim.

"Strong enough for a successful recovery. But a successful recovery will mean bed rest and then a slow reintroduction of activities, much like the program after your surgery."

"That long?" asked Mim, trying her best to fathom what it would mean to have Chauncey at home for months.

"No, no, not months, but certainly for weeks. And when he does recover, his life should be a little less full of cigars, rich food and brandy."

"Those are some of the very things that give my husband pleasure. He is not the kind of man who complies easily with curtailment," Mim replied, almost instantly checking off in her mind the many changes Chauncey's attack would make in her life.

"May I see him?" asked Mim.

"He was just dropping off to sleep when I left him. Nurse Drake will sit with him until she is sure he is asleep and then she will come and get you when he wakens."

"Thank you, Dr. Stephens, for coming as quickly as you did and also for arranging for nursing care. I am certain that neither my skills nor my energy would be sufficient."

"Mrs. Blair," said Dr. Stephens with his most reassuring beside manner, "your husband will need fulltime care for at least a month. During that time, you should simply be his loving wife as he was your loving husband during your recuperation. Your husband has had a scare and that is a good thing. His fear will be a natural sedative that will ameliorate the impulse to do more than he should. But as he recovers and grows less fearful, you will need to be firm with him. If you'll remember, we had to practically order restraints for you when the invitation to the Exposition Ball came.

"Meanwhile, I prescribe some bed rest for you as well. I will see you tomorrow."

Mim did go upstairs, but she did not put herself to bed. Instead, she went to the marble table in her dressing room where she picked up the Book of Hours. She had created a routine, no, it was more than that, it was a ritual that governed her when in the presence of her muse.

Mim was still in love. But over the last year she had almost entirely changed the way she viewed her acquisition. She began to think of the manuscript the way others thought of an orphan. She had anthropomorphized *Tres Riches Heures* into a beautiful but homeless waif, cast aside into a hostile world, rescued by the only person in the world who would value her as she should be valued. The orphan and the collector needed one another to survive.

Though her ritual viewing of the book was typically in the late afternoon, she needed its calming effect immediately. She knew Chauncey would recover, but it had been a terrible shock to see him go down. She rang for some tea, placed herself on the grey satin chaise and covered herself with the peach pastel cashmere throw she now needed for the chills that had overtaken her. Placing the Book of Hours unopened in her lap, she repeated the prayer of Thanksgiving she always said before she opened the book.

Thank you, God, for the privilege you have bestowed on me. Let the beauty and wisdom I now hold in my hands bring me closer to Thee. Amen.

Moving in no particular order, she selected a scene and after a general appreciation for the whole page, she lifted her magnifying glass, moving it slowly both vertically and horizontally, inspecting the illumination as if she were a scholar. To her astonishment, she realized that after looking at the minutia and then back at the entirety of the painting, she could commit what she saw to her visual memory as she had been trained to do so many years ago by Grandmother Mitchell. Thus, someday, it might be possible for her to carry *Tres Riches Heures* with her wherever she went by merely closing her eyes whenever she needed its balm.

A knock on her door ended the few minutes of peace she had had since Chauncey had fallen to his knees. Jumping to her feet thinking there would be some news, she opened the door without inquiry.

"I am sorry to disturb you, Mrs. Blair, but Dr. Stephens said to fetch you when Mr. Blair awakened."

"Is there any change?"

"Only that he is sitting up, he has been bathed, he is about to take some broth, and he asked me to tell you that he would very much like to see you."

Hunting Parties

Fall 1896

NTICIPATING THE ARRIVAL OF "UNDESIRABLES" who would be visiting the World's Fair, the wealthy families of Chicago began purchasing home vaults. Chauncey had been insistent on installing one.

"But, darling, you work at a bank. Isn't there sufficient vault space there in which we could keep valuables?"

"Mimsy, it would be impractical and perhaps dangerous for me to ferry your jewels back and forth on Chicago streets that are filling with common criminals. The anarchists keep records on where people like us live. They track our movements. No, we should have one here."

"Where would you put it?" asked Mim.

"Here, in the library," said Chauncey, gesturing towards the mahogany paneling.

"Here!" said Mim incredulously, as she tried to imagine an unsightly steel box marring the effect of all her beautiful things in her favorite room.

"Mim, give me some credit for appreciating the aesthetics you have worked so hard to establish here. I am not suggesting that we simply place it on the floor in the middle of the library."

"Where then? Can't we put it upstairs in your dressing room?" suggested Mim, hopefully.

"My dear, that is the first place any burglar would look for valuables. If you read the police reports in the newspapers—"

"Why ever would I do that?" interrupted Mim. "It would only upset me."

"Well, I can assure you that burglars always enter through an upstairs window."

"Stop, Chauncey. I will not sleep another wink if I have to listen to this line of conversation."

"Then, trust me to see to it that the safe will be installed without sullying your decorative brilliance."

In the end, the safe was successfully installed in the wall over the fireplace behind the portrait of Mildred. The complete innocence of the portrait acted as a protective shield against the idea that there could possibly be any secrets obscured behind it.

Mim ritualized the habits of her life. So now the last thing she did before leaving on a trip of any length was to place the valuables she did not need into the new safe. In her persistently superstitious mind, she believed there was a reassuring congruity between keeping her valuables safe and keeping her children safe while she was away. When she heard the click of the lock in the vault, her mind clicked, as free from worry as her mind would ever allow itself to be.

Since owning *Tres Riches Heures*, she had included it with her most precious things; its small size allowed it to be locked safely away. She kept a supply of tissue paper in which she double-wrapped her darling orphaned manuscript, then tucked it into a special black velvet satchel with the same affectionate care she gave when tucking Billy into his bed.

Each year, in late October, Mim and Chauncey eagerly anticipated attending Philip and Malvina Armour's annual hunting party at their country estate on Lake Geneva in Wisconsin.

Mim looked forward to getting away for the weekend, but she did not look forward to the effort it took to make it happen. The pace and variety of the festivities required multiple changes of clothes each day, and as a woman shooter, Mim needed everything from long underwear and plus fours to her very best gowns and jewels.

Chauncey enjoyed the masculine camaraderie of the hunt. Mim was a fine shot herself, thanks to her father's insistence that his daughters not be timid sportswomen. She usually distinguished herself at the Armours by winning what was called "The Distaff Award," presented at the farewell banquet to the woman who felled the most birds.

Chauncey derived great pleasure from Mim's shooting achievements, swelling with pride when she was toasted last year as "having the best eye in Chicago for paintings and partridge."

Once they arrived, Mim loved the days in the open air and the pleasure of being with Chicago friends, enjoying the physical activity that city life prohibited. The lake was lovely at this time of year; the trees hugging the shore put on a spectacular show with their leaves of red, gold, and orange.

A special treat for Mim was seeing her oldest friend, Gwendolyn Goodyear, with whom she had grown up. "Gwennie," as Mim called her, now Lady Gwendolyn Griswold after her marriage to Lord Howell Griswold, lived in Devonshire, England. Mim teasingly called Gwennie "Lady Lineage," since she had produced more than the requisite number of male heirs.

Shooting days began with a knock on the bedroom door. One of the household staff arrived to announce that breakfast was ready and that shooters needed to be in the foyer promptly at eight o'clock to meet their loaders and to select their shooting position number. (Though they were in Wisconsin, all the traditions of the hunting party were British. By the end of the weekend most guests were speaking as though they were strolling through Piccadilly Circus.)

Breakfast was plentiful—eggs, blood sausages, kippered herring, toast, marmalade and broiled tomatoes. Lunch, served after the morning shoot, was a hearty meat stew or Welsh rarebit, followed by English cheeses and port. Dinner, always at least five courses, was served to the thirty diners on a table glittering with crystal and silver.

Mim's favorite taste treat in the whole world, the one that made her feel thoroughly pampered, was the midmorning arrival of the 'Shooter's Wagon,' driven to each hunter at his or her designated place in the field. It came just at the time when energy flagged and the cold was seeping deeper into the bones. The wagon was laden with hot soup, sherry, melted cheese on toasts, and Mim's favorite—miniature frankfurters wrapped in perfectly browned pastry.

Mim and Chauncey each brought a shotgun that upon arrival was given over to be cleaned and polished before the first shoot and then again at the end of every day. The Armours' kennels provided the retrievers—magnificent dogs, beautifully trained to their task of bringing back any downed birds and laying them at the feet of the proper shooter without as much as a feather disturbed.

The weekend in Wisconsin had been great fun although she had disappointed herself and, despite his protestations to the contrary, Chauncey, by placing third among the women shooters. The years of living in Devonshire had sharpened Gwennie's marksmanship so this year she won the "Distaff Award" by a wide margin. Her initials would be engraved on the cup until next year, when Mim intended to reclaim her rightful place at the top.

Mim had a sore throat the first day of the shoot but did not mention it to anyone who might construe it as an excuse for missing more birds than she normally did. By the time she and Chauncey disembarked from the train, she had not only a sore throat, but a pounding sinus headache, and, in all likelihood, a fever.

Seldom had Mim been happier to be inside her house. Once she had said "Hello" to the children and pretended to be listening to their weekend tales, she intended to take to her bed and nurse a cup of tea laced with lemon, honey and a shot of bourbon for extra warmth.

She had just reached the second floor landing when she heard Chauncey bellowing her name. *"Oh dear God, no, no, no! Mim, Mim, Mim, come here! Come right here! Hurry! Mim! I can't believe this! Robert, where are you?!"*

Now frozen in place, imagining a dead body on the floor, she called, "Chauncey, what has happened?"

"Just get here! No, call the police first! No, don't call yet! Just come in here!"

"Where is here?"

"The *library!*"

And then she knew. Even before she entered the room, she knew.

Total disarray had destroyed the stately order of the library. The floor was strewn with leather-bound books, pages maliciously ripped out. Broken pieces of porcelain mingled with shards of glass from shattered objets d'art. Not a shelf had been spared. The enormous Chinese fern pots had been overturned, black soil scattered across the rugs and ground in by feet that appeared to want to emphasize what they had done. Every chair, save one, had been slit open; stuffing spurted onto the floor like white lava.

After the cacophony that had accompanied Mim and Robert into the room, it now was eerily quiet, as if their tongues had been stolen along with everything else. The portrait of Mildred had been cast aside and was resting precariously, half on the floor and half on the settee. Mim went to it first as though to inspect any injuries to her daughter herself. A rip in the canvas tore through the bow in her hair but that could be repaired.

"Her face is unharmed. Her face is fine," Mim reassured herself.

It was not a surprise to any of them that the door to the wall safe was flung wide open, nor was it a surprise that the safe was empty.

"But why, oh why, did they have to destroy the room?" choked Mim, tears pouring down her face as she pled for someone to make sense of what she saw.

"I'll tell you why," said a frighteningly calm Chauncey as he stepped through the detritus that had been their library. "Because destruction is all they stand for. We should be grateful that they did not burn the house down with our children sleeping in it!"

"Chauncey," asked Mim, "who is 'they'?"

"Who is 'they'? You *know* very well who 'they' is," said Chauncey, gathering the steam that moments before had evaporated.

"You saw them, Mimsy. You saw them with your own eyes at the railway station when you first tried to go to New York. They stepped on you. They battered you. That is what anarchists do to rich people. They squash and steal and destroy property, until there is nothing left for us and they own everything!"

"But how do you know it was them? It could have been burglars, thieves who have no connection to the anarchists."

Robert had lost his erect military demeanor and was now slumped against the doorframe, appearing as devastated as Mim and Chauncey.

"Mr. and Mrs. Blair, I am so, so sorry. This is my fault."

"What do you mean, Robert?" said Chauncey, "Unless you pried open the safe yourself and our valuables are hidden in your apartment downstairs, I do not see that you have a responsibility for any of this."

"In the German navy, if something happens on your watch, then you are responsible. It is as simple as that. While you were away, I was the senior person in charge. I did not hear a sound. I am sorry and I will understand if you wish to call for my resignation."

Something about the dignity of this honorable man touched Chauncey, who walked over to him, put his arm around him and said comfortingly, "Robert, I know I can speak for Mrs. Blair when I assure you that neither of us thinks of you as responsible for this. As I said, I am dead certain I know who did this. We reject your offer of resignation. Now please stay here with Mrs. Blair while I call the police."

It was only after the initial shock had abated slightly that the deeper shock registered with Mim that *Tres Riches Heures* was gone too. Hoping against hope, she went to the safe to be sure, feeling inside it to be certain it was indeed picked clean. She had never been punched in the stomach but she was certain that she now knew the feeling.

As if by unstated agreement, Mim and Robert began to collect the scattered mutilated books, putting them into illogical but neatened piles. But for every second she attempted to create order in the library, her mind dissolved into complete disorder. Her eyes scanned the room, frantically looking for any sign that the book had been overlooked, hiding completely intact in its velvet case, like any lost child just waiting to be found.

By now the visceral tension among the adults on the first floor had permeated through the walls and floorboards and the entire household made its way to the scene of the all-too-real crime.

The burly Irish detective who had arrived only minutes after Robert had placed the call gave the impression that he was intimidated by his elegant surroundings. He said little, and maddeningly slowly picked things up and studied them as if he were considering a purchase rather than investigating a robbery.

"What are you looking for, Chauncey?" asked Mim as she stepped carefully through the mess with her eyes glued to the floor.

"I think your jewels are gone."

"I am not looking for jewelry. I don't remember exactly which pieces were there," she replied, never lifting her eyes from the floor.

"Was the sapphire and diamond bracelet I gave you last Christmas there? It cost a for—"

"Chauncey," snapped Mim. "I told you I was not looking for jewelry. Now leave me alone so I can concentrate."

"What then are you looking for? You would think that one of our children was hidden somewhere in this mess."

Before Mim had a chance to either answer him or stomp away in anger, the formerly lethargic detective blew his police whistle, instantly bringing everyone in the room to silent attention.

"Ladies and gentlemen, I need some order in here. No one is to touch anything in this room. It is a crime scene. Sergeants Monaghan and Curley, please escort the servants downstairs and take a statement from each of them. I want everyone interviewed separately."

Turning to Mim and Chauncey, he said, "Mr. and Mrs. Blair, I realize that walking into this room must have been a shock." Handing a pen and paper to Chauncey, he continued, "You can help by making a list of the items that have been stolen."

Mim was in a quandary as to whether or not to tell the detective anything about *Tres Riches Heures*. The manuscript was undoubtedly the most valuable item that was missing, and yet she most certainly did not wish to see it listed on any public police register. Who knew where that might lead? But she wanted it back. If she had followed her heart, she would have told the detective that his investigation should focus on the manuscript and never mind about the rest.

It was almost incomprehensible to her that it was gone. She could understand jewels being stolen—any common thief would recognize their value. But other than being encased in a velvet bag, the Book of Hours was an unlikely target for a burglar.

"I think that does it," said Chauncey. "I believe you have a description of each item that is missing."

"If you will excuse me. I want to go upstairs and be sure my children are settled in bed," said Mim, wanting to escape the reality of her loss. "They have had a scare, as have we all."

"I understand. I have little ones of my own. We have plenty of information to get started," said the detective, rising when Mim did. "If you think of anything else, please do not hesitate to call."

Despite police reassurances of likely success, Chauncey thought they would never see any of the jewelry again. He continued to believe that this was not simply a heist, but an anarchist's attack on the wealthy. It was not money they were after but the desecration of the symbols of wealth—the mansions on Drexel Boulevard. There was no other reason for the violence.

The detectives told Chauncey not to touch anything or try to restore the library. His men would be back in the morning to see if daylight revealed any more clues.

Wearily, Chauncey finished turning out the lights, the last of which was on top of the piano. What flashed through his mind was the oddity that the lid of the piano was raised. As a rule, the lid was not open unless they were having a musical evening at home, which had not occurred since last spring. The lid was never open when the children practiced. *Strange*, thought Chauncey as he went to close it. But what he saw was so much stranger than an opened lid on a grand piano. Peering inside, he realized that every one of the piano strings had been snapped and the green felts torn off.

"I'll be goddamned," he said aloud.

To the extent that Chauncey had seen Mim's Book of Hours, he had seen it open and in her hands. He had not often, if ever, seen it in its velvet cocoon, so Chauncey did not make the connection between the black object lying amid the destroyed piano and *Tres Riches Heures*.

He walked to the stairs and called to Mim to come down, worried about how he would break the news to her that her piano could never be used again.

When Mim entered the library ,she looked as bereft as Chauncey had ever seen her.

"Mimsy, come see this."

Almost literally dragging her body to the piano, Mim did not have the energy to be particularly curious as to what Chauncey had discovered, quite certain that it was more bad news. So out of place was the black velvet case amid the jumble of strings inside the piano that she almost lashed out at Chauncey's summons. And then Mim clasped her hands over her mouth, looked Chauncey directly in the eye and began to sob.

The discovery of an undamaged *Tres Riches Heures* convinced Mim that there was a God in heaven and that he wanted her magnificent Book of Hours to belong to her.

34 Omens

*M*IM HAD SEEN MARTIN GAYLORD frequently and companionably since their trip to New York. Given the intersecting arcs of their social and cultural circles, it would have been impossible to avoid one another. Happily their encounters were not awkward and over time they were able to return to the days of their respectful and occasionally jousting friendship.

Martin continued to bring her potential acquisitions, two of which she had purchased—a Persian miniature painting from the seventeenth century and an exquisite turquoise vase, the origin of which was likely older. Martin's deportment was punctilious, although an occasional double entendre kept Mim ever so slightly off balance. True to his word, he never directly mentioned their time together nor her decision to buy *Tres Riches Heures*.

Reflecting on her behavior over those highly charged, flirtatious months, Mim could only conclude that Eros himself had shot into her solid, reliable heart a romantic potion, causing her to be temporarily rewired as a coquettish, single-minded woman courting danger in pursuit of an obsession. She was relieved and deeply grateful that the beguiling winged Greek had finally relinquished his hold on her. But, she had to admit there were few days when she did not remember Martin's kiss at the edge of her lips. She would shudder with arousal at the memory of the most sensuous moment of her life.

Mim and Martin now found themselves again intimately aligned, as both had been named honorary judges of the annual Hull House art show. Each year the settlement house displayed the work of Chicagoans who had attended painting classes—a mix of affluent supporters and poor immigrants.

The mission of Hull House, founded in 1889, was the dream of its founder, Miss Jane Addams, who had grown up in an upper middle class family in Cedarville, Illinois. Her mother had died when she was young, a trauma that directly and profoundly led to her lifelong compassion for the plight of orphaned children.

Her father had surrounded himself and his daughter with books, in fact, his personal library and the town library functioned as one. Jane attributed her early reading of Tolstoy to her deep understanding of Christianity's demands—a life devoted to the poor.

Jane believed that simply donating money or volunteering was an insufficient commitment to bringing about her ultimate goal—the total reconfiguration of Chicago society. Rich and poor would not come together by building a bridge *to* one another, but rather by destroying the bridge itself and walking in each other's shoes, living in community with one another. Many of the sons and daughters of the most privileged families in the city would come to Hull House to live cheek by jowl with "the least among us."

Because Miss Addams had been brought up in comfort, she was not cowed by wealth nor was she afraid to ask rich Chicagoans to part with theirs. Mim knew of no one who did not support Hull House.

Addams was a frequent public speaker at the prominent clubs around town. Within the space of a month both Mim and Chauncey had heard her deliver impassioned speeches, which some called sermons.

In retrospect Mim admitted to Chauncey that it had been a mistake to take Italia, always impressionable, to hear Miss Addams. But she had justified inviting her daughter to accompany her because she wanted to expose her to more variety in her life than could be found in the fashion magazines and makeup mirrors Italia currently favored. After hearing Miss Addams speak, Italia had begun a relentless campaign to become a resident of Hull House.

"But Mother, you are the person who took me to hear Miss Addams. You are the one who told me, 'It will expand your horizons. It will help you to better understand that the world is a great deal more complicated than what you see here on Drexel Boulevard.' And that is precisely what I want to do. I would think you would be pleased."

"Italia, you are fourteen years old," Mim countered.

"Over my dead body," Chauncey said, glaring at Mim when she told him of Italia's idea.

"Chauncey, there is no reason to reprimand me. I completely agree with you. I have told her 'no', 'no,' and once again 'no.'

"But," continued Mim emphatically, "I do want to see if her interest in being of service is something more than just a ploy to get out of our house for a few weeks. After all, I don't want to discourage any authentic altruistic impulses she has. I am going to inquire about the possibility of her volunteering in the Child Care Center for a few hours a week. It will be good for her."

"As I have said to you many times, the girls are your responsibility. But any hint I get that Italia might become infected with that radical feminist virus passed from one suffragette to another at Hull House, I take over."

As it turned out, the only virus that infected Italia during her short and largely unsuccessful time at Hull House was smallpox. She had been recruited to help in the Child Care Center and, though she dressed as if she were going to the opera, she was at least another pair of hands for the Center that was overflowing with the children of the aspiring artists.

As Martin and Mim were making their final prize deliberations, Martin heard energetic knocking on the door and called, "Yes, who is it?"

Without waiting to provide the answer, Jane Addams opened the door, came into the room and said, peremptorily, "Have you two made a selection yet?"

Jane Addams was five years Mim's junior but with her martial manner, she could have been mistaken for a much older sister, or perhaps her mother. She had heavy dark eyebrows that drew attention to quite lovely grey eyes. She had a prominent nose and wispy grey hair that tonight was partially under the control of a large black hat adorned with three enormous red chrysanthemums.

Martin looked at Mim and said, "Mary, have we made a selection?"

"We have narrowed the field to three, but, Jane, we have only deliberated for a few minutes. Is there any hurry? I thought the announcement was to be at six o'clock. We still have half an hour," said Mim.

"That was indeed the plan. But," she said, addressing Mim, "you had better come and have a look at your daughter. Isn't she in the Children's Center helping with the babies tonight?"

"Yes, she is," answered Mim. Fearing that Italia had been negligent in some way, she continued, "Has something happened to her? Has there been a problem with any of the children? She may have been too young to be given responsibility for them."

"Nonsense," was Jane Addams' retort. "Most of the girls who are residents here have been taking care of babies since they were babies themselves. However, you best have a look at her. I think she may be unwell."

Turning to Martin, Mim said, "I am going to see what is going on. If Italia is ailing and I must leave, I give you my permission to select win, place and show. As you know, I completely trust you!"

As Mim made her way to Italia, she ran through a list of illnesses from the common to the life-threatening that Ity might have been exposed to. Ever magical in her thinking, she also tried to enumerate any moral lapses she herself might have made for which a sick child might be just punishment.

Mim found a very ill daughter slumped in a chair in a corner. She had the glassy, vacant look of someone whose body is spent with fatigue. Using the tried and true maternal method of assessing a fever, Mim leaned over and kissed her daughter's forehead, which left little doubt that her temperature was very high.

For two weeks, Mim devoted herself to nursing Italia and making sure that no one else in the household fell ill. Dr. Stephens placed Italia in isolation, allowing only a private duty nurse and Mim herself to come in direct contact with her ailing daughter.

"I forbid any of you to go near Hull House again," fumed Chauncey.

No amount of logical rebuttal from Mim or Dr. Stephens could convince him that Italia had most certainly carried the virus days before she had shown symptoms at the art show reception.

"She was perfectly healthy when she left here and she comes home with smallpox," Chauncey grumbled.

Fortunately, Italia's disease was called "ordinary smallpox" by everyone except those who had it, and it ran its course in the standard two-week cycle. Her rash gave way to oozing pustules that later dried up nicely. Also fortunate was Italia's ignorance of the fact that smallpox often left its victim scarred. She had several pustules on her forehead, which was typical of the disease, but they were hidden in her hairline. There were residual scars on her arms and legs, but none was a threat to her vanity.

At the end of the two weeks, Mim was more exhausted than Italia. But the virus had been successfully contained. Each night she fell into her bed relying on her ritual reading of her Book of Hours to calm her nerves. But her superstitious mind was beginning to wonder—Chauncey's heart attack, minor though it had been, the robbery, and now smallpox—calamities that coincided with the arrival of "Tres Riches Heures." Was there a message for her embedded in this compilation of unhappy events?

Middle Children

Spring 1898

"WHO IS IT, ROBERT?" SHE asked when he announced that she had a phone call.

"I don't know, Mrs. Blair. I asked, but the gentleman would not say."

Thinking it a tradesman of some kind, she said hello, prepared to tell him that all inquiries should be made to the cook, Mrs. Bertha Schmidt.

"Mrs. Blair? Is this Mrs. Blair?" asked the caller in an accented voice that sounded unfamiliar and unwelcome.

Foolishly, she said that yes, it was she, and then cautiously asked, "May I ask to whom I am speaking?"

"No, you may not. Suffice it to say that we did some business together in New York, several years ago which, I believe, left both of us more than satisfied. I have another piece, which I think would interest you. It is magnificent."

Fortunately there was a chair by the phone onto which she could

341

lower herself, since her legs had started to tremble. Unfortunately, Robert was still standing by her side.

Mim put her hand over the receiver and said, with as much equanimity as she could muster, "Thank you, Robert. That will be all."

Mim fought her impulse to ask the caller how this outrageous intrusion was possible. But that would only prolong the conversation so she simply said, "I am not interested in pursuing any further relationship with you," and hung up the phone.

The gentleman had apparently gotten the message, as she heard nothing more, but for months afterwards she gave a start whenever the phone or the doorbell rang.

Now that she had come to think of *"Tres Riches Heures"* as fully and eternally hers, she was able to move beyond mere adoration of it. Like her medieval predecessors, she made use of it. She gave up wrapping it in tissue and putting it away each night. She kept it by her bedside. She studied each plate and found new favorite tableaux; spent time categorizing secular and sacred scenes; spent a week comparing and contrasting all the shades of blue, another week all reds, another, green. She tried to identify recurring characters and found to her delight that the Limbourg brothers had a sense of humor. Every so often she could discern a surprising, almost shocking, resemblance to their patron, Le Duc de Berry, pushing a plow in one of the depictions of peasant life. *That was risky,* she thought.

Mildred was the only one of her children with whom she shared *Tres Riches Heures.* Her lovely daughter had come down with croup, and after two nights listening to that unceasing, rasping, barking cough, Nanny was spent, so Mim volunteered to keep Mildred in her sitting room so Nanny could regain her strength and, hopefully, her good humor.

None of the Blair children had ever been permitted to sleep that close to Mim. But one look at the wan, white face of their little sister and neither Italia nor CB dared to complain of the unfairness of their mother's decision. Once they heard the depth and sharpness of Mildred's cough, they were actually a little frightened of the child.

The divan was made up, an electric coil was hooked up, and a kitchen kettle boiled throughout the night to keep the room moist. It was refilled as needed by the night's attendant, in this case Mim herself. Every four hours Mim gave Mildred what she considered the most effective elixir for persistent cough—one quarter of a cup of honey, two tablespoons of bourbon and a spritz of lemon juice.

By ten o'clock, it was obvious that the treatments had not tamed her cough. When Mim went to check on her, she was somewhere between uncomfortable sleep and wakefulness. She was no longer pale but quite red in the face with a dainty trace of perspiration, like dewdrops, on her warm forehead.

Knowing he would get little sleep, Mim exiled Chauncey to a room down the hall, noting, "She has been barking for hours. It sets my nerves on edge. But if she is in my bed I won't have to get up and keep checking on her."

Mildred's relocation failed to subdue her coughing. It persisted. After one particularly prolonged siege, Mim decided that Mildred would do better sitting up. It certainly could not make things worse. She gathered all the extra pillows in the room, put them firmly behind Mildred's back and head, and then pulled Mildred, who was now coughing *and* crying, into a sitting position.

"Darling, you are all right. I think if you sit up, you will be much better."

"Mother, I want to stop coughing. It hurts."

"I know it does. Here," she said, pulling out the only book which was ever by her bedside.

"Let's take your mind off that nasty cough. I will show you my favorite book. Neither Ity nor CB has ever seen it. Just you. It is the most beautiful book in the world."

Mildred appeared not the least bit interested as Mim sidled closer to her.

"But I want a story," Mildred said, somewhat mollified now that her mother was as close as she could be.

"Oh, my darling, you will never have a better story than the one I will tell you now. Actually there are lots of stories on each of these pretty pages. I will stay with you and tell you as many as you want to hear. Maybe you can fall asleep better if you count angels."

And so Mim became the Scheherazade of the sick room. Mildred neither spoke nor coughed as Mim spun her stories of prophets and princes. As Mim's imagination took flight, and the stories spilled, Mildred settled, and then slept.

When Chauncey crept in in the morning, he saw one of the loveliest sights he had ever seen. His wife and his beautiful daughter were asleep with their heads so close that they might have been sharing secret dreams.

In another week Mildred was ever so much improved. Her cough had subsided, though Mim was convinced that she would occasionally feign a coughing fit and then ask for another story from "the beautiful book."

Mim used "*Tres Riches Heures*" to say her nightly prayers. She would read the words aloud and though she did not fully understand precisely the Latin she was reading, she was all but certain that somewhere in the words she intoned, she had both praised God and asked for his protection. Recently, the one prayer that Mim repeated nightly was that Chauncey would relent and not insist CB go to boarding school in the East.

"He will be a first former at Groton this fall and it will be the making of him," said Chauncey emphatically.

"But why Groton? Where is it, anyway?" asked Mim, hoping that maybe, if she found fault with the location, she could change the trajectory of this plan.

"It is thirty miles from Boston."

"Boston! He may as well be schooled in Europe. Is there no school in Ohio or even Pennsylvania that could serve him just as well? CB is a bright, studious boy. He will thrive wherever he goes. What is so special about Groton?"

Chauncey was ready for this question. "Because Groton was founded by a banking family."

"But Chauncey, he is not going to school to be a banker."

"Au contraire, that is exactly what he is going to school to learn. It is the people he meets from now on that will help him throughout his business life. They will pave the way. They are the young men who, like their fathers before them, will be doing the deals of the future.

"And to whom will they turn when they need financing?" asked

Chauncey, rhetorically. "I will tell you to whom they will turn, at least for any deal west of the Mississippi River—they will turn to their boyhood friend from Groton, CB Blair."

"I know how the system works, Chauncey. I am just not sure that boys need to leave home at twelve to master it."

"Remember, Mimsy, I have always said that while you had charge of the girls' education, I was to make the educational decisions for the boys. And Groton is my decision."

CB Blair had always been a miniature military man. His bedroom was more a battlefield than a room for rest. By now he had a collection of over one hundred toy soldiers and an imagination that, with little attention to historical accuracy, devised winning strategies for his favorite armies.

For years CB had read the sports pages of the *Tribune*, but now mornings brought him to the breakfast table with his appetite whetted for news of the war rather than for waffles. If there were family members at the table, he would insist on reading the dispatches from Cuba aloud.

February 16, 1898, Havana, Cuba— The U.S.S. Maine was sunk yesterday in Havana Harbor. First reports are insubstantial but the United States naval command estimates that losses will number well over two hundred sailors dead with many more wounded.

The explosions, which began yesterday evening, could be heard ricocheting well beyond the harbor, sending people throughout the city out of their homes and offices in a panic.

The American armored cruiser, built in 1895, had been sent to Havana to protect American business interests, primarily those of the sugar barons who have substantial holdings in Cuba. It is no secret that America has allied itself with the Cubans as they seek independence from Spanish hegemony.

While American officials said they will press for a full investigation of the circumstances surrounding the sinking of the U.S.S. Maine, there is little doubt in the minds of the general population that Spanish saboteurs are responsible for the devastation witnessed by thousands of Cubans.

CB, along with the rest of America, became a warmonger from the moment he read the dispatches about the sinking of the *Maine*. His war cry was taken from the headlines of the papers: 'REMEMBER THE *MAINE*! THE HELL WITH SPAIN.'

Anyone who asked him a question always got the same maddening response now, "Yes Mother, I will go upstairs and fetch your eyeglasses, but, 'Remember the *Maine*. The hell with Spain.'"

All through March and early April, CB grew increasingly frustrated with President McKinley who he thought was dilly-dallying in giving the Spanish their just deserts.

"Father, you know President McKinley. Didn't you give him a lot of money? Can't you make him do the right thing?"

"CB, declaring war is the most serious decision a President can make. And, if we do go to war, we will need many men to volunteer."

"Well, he could start with me. I would go tomorrow if I were old enough."

CB lost no time finding a map of Cuba, spreading it on his desk and deploying his lead soldiers in strategic configurations. As soon as the 1st United States Volunteer Cavalry was assembled and dubbed the "Rough Riders," the hearts of every literate boy in America were captured. This rough and tumble group was a mélange of cowboys, ranchers, civil war veterans, and police officers wanting more action. Though they were more an infantry outfit than a real cavalry, they were dashing in their slouch hats, blue flannel shirts, brown trousers and polished riding boots.

"Mother, which do you think would be more useful if you were shooting from a galloping horse—a Springfield Rifle, a Colt .45 or a Winchester Rifle? I mean the Rough Riders have all those guns, but which do you think they use most?"

Mim did her best not to scoff at these questions as they were so earnestly asked, as if he would be in need of the information as soon as possible.

"Well, CB, I should think a Colt .45 would be the best. I presume that because it is called a Colt, it should be shot from a horse," Mim answered.

If Mim made an effort not to dismiss CB's questions, he did *not* return the favor. "Mother, you do realize, don't you, that a Colt .45 is a pistol? It would be useless at distances. I think I would use either of the rifles, probably the Winchester as it is the newer model."

Oh, how I will miss this boy, Mim thought as she looked at his still freckled face. *I wonder if he will have freckles at all when I see him at Christmas? When will his hair be slicked back? I suppose he will wear long pants exclusively from now on. No more exposed bruised and knobby knees. No more socks drooping to his ankles. But at least he is going to Groton and not to Cuba,* she consoled herself.

"Robert, are you interested in the war with Spain?" CB asked the butler.

"Of course I am. Since I became an American citizen, I am interested in whatever happens to my country. I know all about the sinking of the American ship, the. You forget, Master Chauncey, that I was in the German Navy long before you were even born. So, yes, I have been following the war and the great Rough Rider, Theodore Roosevelt."

"Well, then," said CB, "you will want to hear this."

July 2, 1898 Santiago, Cuba—The Unites States Navy destroyed the Spanish Fleet as it tried and failed to escape from the port of Santiago, Cuba yesterday. So powerful was the American Navy, there was not a ship that remained afloat.

"Did you hear that, Robert? We crushed them. They are at the bottom of the sea!"

The Spanish government surrendered on August 12, 1898. When it was announced that the troops would return to America, landing at Montauk, New York, it was not long before CB had the atlas out again to see how far Montauk was from Groton School. As soon as he arrived, he would ask for permission to be part of the welcome home party for TR and the Rough Riders.

New Horizons

Fall 1898

ECAUSE FACTORIES COULD PRODUCE ONLY two auto-mobiles per week, it often took the better part of six months for a car to be delivered to a new owner, in this case, Mr. Chauncey Justus Blair of Chicago. Chauncey's car was built in Bridge-port, Connecticut, and he had just received word that it was now on a train heading west.

The only person Chauncey had consulted before placing his order with the Locomobile Company of America had been his butler, Robert Schmidt. Friends had recommended entrusting the most trusted man in his employ with the new car, no matter what holes that might leave in the remaining staff deployment.

A chauffeur was expected to be not only the driver of the automo-bile, but also its mechanic. A substantial toolbox came with the vehicle and the manufacturer suggested that all moving parts be cleaned and lu-bricated regularly, duties not usually in a gentleman owner's set of skills.

Robert had been pleased when Chauncey put the proposition to him.

"I very much appreciate your confidence, Mr. Blair," said Robert who was almost as enamored with the prospect of the new arrival as Chauncey was.

"Now that we are living in the age of the automobile," said Chauncey, "I see the job of chauffeur as being the most important position in the household. In addition you will receive a significant salary increase, and a new and, if I might say, quite dashing livery."

"Well, Mr. Blair, I don't care much about the livery, but the wage increase will be most welcome. Let me talk to Ber—"

"No!" blasted Chauncey, surprising both himself and Robert with the forcefulness of his outburst. "I am sorry, Robert. I did not mean to shout at you." Then lowering his voice to an almost inaudible whisper, he continued, "I thought you were going to say that you were going to talk it over with Bertha."

"You are right. I was going to say that. I normally do in matters such as this. Is there some reason that I should not?"

"Only that I have not yet informed Mrs. Blair that I am considering the purchase of an automobile. Well, that is not quite right. Actually, I have already ordered it. I wanted to present it to Mrs. Blair at the right moment. It should be here in about a month. Do you want to see a picture of it?"

With that invitation extended, master and servant made their way to the rear of the house where, in addition to an exchange of questions, answers and youthful enthusiasm, they made plans for the conversion of the carriage house into a garage. For those few moments, any class distinctions between gentleman and newly designated chauffeur were erased.

"What is it called again?" asked Mim.

"It is called a Locomobile," repeated Chauncey. The only thing missing from his suddenly boyish face was the freckles.

"You say it does not have room for our children and yet you tell me you see children as young as Mildred driving across the city?" asked Mim.

"That is correct," answered Chauncey, "I bought the model that has just enough room for one of us and Robert. It will be just the daisy for running around the city. Since I will not use it to go to the office, it will be yours most days. In a year or so we will order another one for family outings, after we both learn to be competent automobilists."

Astonished by the evident transformation in her normally parsimonious husband (the man who scrutinized the bills of every tradesman who did business with the household), Mim asked a question that she, at least not since her outlay for Tres Riches Heures, normally never asked, "How much did it cost?"

"Six hundred dollars. Well, maybe slightly more because I have ordered red leather instead of black leather seats. So much sportier, don't you think?"

"What I think," said Mim, "is that this Locomobile sounds like a dangerous toy for a man of a certain age.

"But I am willing to give it a try," said Mim, her spirit of adventure competing with her fear of one more reason for magical thinking.

When Edith Rockefeller McCormick asked to pay a call, there was always the potential of a dangerous outcome. She was the first woman in the city of Chicago to have her own automobile, far grander and more sumptuous than the one now residing in the Blairs' former carriage house. Edith had a chauffeur, of course, possibly several of them, but she preferred to drive herself, and often spun to a gravelly halt in the driveway, insistently honking her bulb horn until either Mim came out to join her or Robert arrived to escort her into the house.

Edith had asked to see Mim. She had something "of great excitement in mind." Thank God Chauncey had not heard those words.

She arrived sportily clothed in the au courant look of a "Gibson Girl," the iconic new American woman popularized by illustrator, Charles Dana Gibson. The original Gibson Girl, more athletic than fragile, was an intoxicating mix of sultry and self- confident. Hair softly piled *au bouffant* atop her head, the escaping tendrils were designed to look casually independent, just like the girls themselves.

When Robert opened the door for her, Edith, like most other ladies who came to call, stepped onto the driveway. Other callers smoothed their skirts, adjusted their hats and made their way up the steps to the front door. Edith did all of those things except for the move to the steps. Despite her wealth, Edith displayed a natural egalitarianism. She now engaged Robert in a conversation that appeared to be about the finer points of owning and operating an automobile.

It did not surprise Mim in the least that the conversation appeared to be rather one-sided. As Robert followed like a puppy in training, Edith talked as she circled the car— once, twice, and now three times—pointing to the special features she insisted Robert notice.

They spent a full five minutes inspecting the tires, Robert bending over a squatting Edith, who appeared to be counting each and every spoke on each tire. As much as she was enjoying the show that was Edith, Mim felt it was her duty to rescue Robert, so she moved from the window to the front door and called,

"Edith dear, it is time for Robert to go see about some errands, and it is time for us to chat."

"I know, I know. I simply wanted Robert's opinion on the new tire glue that I special ordered for the Stanhope. I think it superior and so does Robert."

"Excuse me, Mrs. McCormick," said Robert, "would you like me to move your car out of the sun?"

"No need, thank you, Robert. You can leave it where it is. I won't be long."

"I have never heard of Cora Scott," said Mim, Edith's face wincing slightly in disbelief.

"I will tell you more about her in a minute, but does the word 'paranormal' mean anything to you?"

Not wanting to disappoint her friend twice in such a short span of time, Mim scrambled to see if she could come close to an accurate definition. "I know it has something to do with those things that are beyond what most people would consider, well, normal."

"That is the conventional definition, though it begs the essential, universal question, 'What is normal?'" replied Edith, sitting on the edge of her chair as if she were a cat about to pounce. She had not even pretended to sip her tea, so intent was she to share her excitement with Mim.

"Have you never had an experience that seemed fully real at the time you were having it, but which defied scientific explanation?"

Yes, I have, thought Mim, *but I have never told anyone about it and if I did, it would not be you.*

"Mim, I want you to come to a séance with me. You do know what that is, don't you?"

"Yes, I know what a séance is, but I associate it with entertainment more than with instruction or insight. I am not saying I would not go to one, but it would be hard for me to take it seriously. Tables moving, ghosts talking, people levitating. It would be hard for me to sit there with a straight face."

"Could you keep an open mind?" asked Edith, by now almost crestfallen by her friend's discouraging reaction.

"Actually, I think I could. Maybe I will find out that I had another life in the Middle Ages, since that is where my artistic sensibilities lie. Yes," Mim concluded, "I think I could do that. It would depend on whether or not I thought the guru (is that what you call it?) seems like a charlatan or a—"

"Oh," interrupted Edith, who sensed the tide of approval turning in her direction. "That is where Cora Scott comes in. Here, look at this." Edith handed Mim a folded brochure that, when she opened it, announced itself as the *Religio-Philosophical Journal*. As Mim scanned the pamphlet, Edith began to talk, making concentration difficult.

"Edith," Mim said acerbically, "I cannot listen to you and read this at the same time." Unusually compliant, Edith got up and went to the tea service and refreshed her tea, as if only physical activity could restrain her from speaking.

Cora L.V. Scott, Pastor of the First Spiritual Society of Chicago, also known as the Church of the Soul, will lead a spiritual journey for interested parties on Sunday, April 30th from 7:30-9:30 p.m.

Mrs. Scott is the author of many books including Zulieka, which she wrote in an altered state. In 1893 she presented a paper entitled "Presentation of Spiritualism" at the Congress of Religions.

Interested parties will need to arrive at 7:15 p.m. Doors will close at precisely 7:30 p.m. and no persons will be allowed entrance or egress during the journey of souls.

When Mim had finished reading, she looked up at Edith, who had reseated herself and was intently staring at Mim, trying to assess her reaction. Mim obliged her curiosity quickly.

"It says here that we cannot leave," said Mim, giving voice to her instinctive fear of being trapped with a roomful of, at best, strange people and, at worst, menacing ghosts.

"You will not want to leave, I promise you," said Edith confidently, "Cora Scott is an authentic genius. She was a child prodigy in the world of the spirits. Please come, Mim. I cannot think of anyone else who will go with me."

"I will come. But I will go with a skeptical mind, albeit one I will try my best to keep open."

✒

"Chauncey," said Mim, filled with apprehension about telling him of her destination and companion. "I am afraid I will not be here on Sunday evening."

"Why ever not? You normally insist on making no special plans for Sunday nights. Mind you, I am not complaining. I am no enthusiast of Sunday socializing. But what takes you out? Will you need Robert or are you driving yourself?"

"That is too many questions to answer simultaneously. On the last two questions, I will neither need Robert, nor am I driving myself." But before she could complete her answers, Chauncey, as was his maddening habit, added to the list of interrogatories.

"Well then, how will you get where you are going? What time are you leaving and, more importantly, what time will you come home?"

"Chauncey, I am not on the witness stand. If you will give me the courtesy of listening all the way through until the end, I think all your questions will be answered," Mim scolded.

She began, "On Sunday, Edith is picking me up at seven o'clock and we are going to a séance." Without leaving even a second for his response, Mim continued, "It will last several hours and I will return no later than ten."

Quite to her surprise, Chauncey's reaction was neither derisive nor deflating.

"I did not know you were interested in the world of the spirits. I will be very curious to hear the details when you come home. Unlike Edith, you have an admirably level head on your shoulders so I will trust your report. I have often wondered if there are other worlds beyond our own. I guess you will find out."

"Actually, I have known for years there is another world available to us," Mim told her husband.

Over the course of the next hour, Mim recounted her still vivid recollections of the night that Billy was born—the light and how it had enveloped her, the purity of the love that she felt surrounding her, warming her chilled body and restoring her to life. She even told him that so magnificent was the transcendence that she would literally have given her life to be allowed to stay in the light.

Sensing the importance of this revelation, though seven years late, Chauncey never once interrupted her narrative. When she had finished, with one gesture he gave her the most intimate gift she had ever received. He brushed her damp cheek, and whispered, "Dearest girl. I am so glad you came back to me."

Chauncey's only other comment on the subject of the séance came on the appointed day as Mim left the library to freshen up before Edith's arrival.

"Mimsy, my deepest wish for you this evening is that it is everything you hope it will be. I hope that the light will reveal itself to you as before. But if it doesn't, just remember that does not mean it was never there."

Mim hoped her smile conveyed all the tenderness she felt towards Chauncey now that she had revealed her deepest, well, her second deepest secret to him. But in case a smile wasn't enough, she returned to face him and kissed, not his forehead, but his lips, fully and tenderly.

Edith arrived alone, but from the look of her outfit, she could have been taken for a chauffeur. It really was more of a costume than an outfit. She wore black leather knickerbockers with a matching auto jacket, custom-fitted to accentuate her slim waist. Her highly polished boots came up to her knees. Most incongruous of all was her hat, a girlish, wide-brimmed sun hat, anchored on her head by a gauzy, lavender chiffon scarf tied in an enormous bow.

After much hand wringing about the appropriate attire for a séance, Mim was dressed all in black, as if she were on her way to the funeral of all the spirits she was expecting to meet.

"Well?" said Edith.

Well, what?" asked Mim, hardly knowing where to begin as she watched Edith donning the enormous canvas and leather-cuffed driving gloves, more appropriately the attire of a Rough Rider cavalry officer. (Robert had told Mim the gloves were to protect the automobilist's hands from the detritus of the road.) Edith grabbed the tiller and spun out of the driveway.

Mim was pleased that the séance would take place at the Masonic Temple. At seven-thirty on a Sunday night, none of her friends was likely to be at the Temple, unless they too were going to the séance, in which case they would have little cause for censure.

Mim and Edith arrived at the fifteenth floor and were told to wait in an anteroom until they were escorted into Pastor Scott's "sanctuary of the spirits." They joined six other people—five women and a gentleman—who all looked respectable enough, though none among them could match Edith for eccentricity.

Mim would have been happy to sit in silence until they were summoned, but Edith had a more voluble approach to her new surroundings.

"Good evening to you all," Edith began. "My name is Edith—"

To Mim's relief, she was interrupted before she could do any more damage. "No names, please," said the attendant who was waiting with them (or guarding them, depending on one's level of suspicion).

"Pastor Scott is more interested in introducing you to the spirits than to one another. It will be only another few minutes. She is consecrating the space and sometimes it takes a little longer than usual. If you have any questions, please address them to me."

"Will each of us be able to talk to the dead person we want to reach?" asked Edith.

"Madam," said the attendant, "Pastor Scott prefers not to use the word 'dead' when referring to those whom we are trying to reach. The premise of the Spiritual Movement is that those with whom we wish to communicate are not dead at all, but simply in an alternative state."

Apparently satisfied with the answer to that particular question but undeterred in her curiosity, Edith made a little gesture indicating that she was not yet finished.

"I am told that often tables and chairs spontaneously leave the floor and float upwards. Should that happen, are we encouraged to pull them down?"

"I must warn you, Madam, that levitation, which is what we call the upward movement of quotidian objects of this world, does not occur on command. Months can go by without such an occurrence."

Mim was actually grateful for Edith's intrepidity.

"Am I correct in believing that the former First Lady, Mary Todd Lincoln, often hosted séances in the White House in order to speak with her dead son, Willie, and that the President attended?"

"Mrs. Lincoln drew great comfort from communication with her son," answered the attendant who gave the impression of having been there.

As the time grew near for the commencement of the séance, Mim tried to remind her unsettled nerves that she had come with no expectation of success. The very worst that could happen was that she would leave with no further evidence of a world beyond the reality of this one. She would have a good story to tell about an entertaining evening, nothing paranormal about it.

Before Edith could continue with another question, the soft ring of a bell sounded from the inner room. The attendant gestured for all of them to rise and enter through the door, which he now held open.

Cora Scott sat erect at a round table that almost filled the room. The space was dim but not dark, allowing Mim to notice that on the table were two small black slates on either side of Mrs. Scott, each with a piece of chalk nearby. In addition, a slender conical funnel, which aroused her curiosity.

Pastor Scott greeted entrants by wishing them "Good Evening," and then pointed to a specific seat for each person as if she were organizing an important dinner party.

Cora Scott was both very pretty and well turned out. Her brown hair was parted in the middle from which ringlets cascaded down to her shoulders. Her black *peau de soie* dress was almost provocative, cut low, baring her shoulders and some cleavage. Dangling into the décolleté was a large carved wooden cross, worn as if its size illuminated the depth of her love for Jesus, which in this setting seemed odd to Mim. Most Christians she knew would consider this event blasphemy.

When they were all seated, Pastor Scott looked slowly around the table, making prolonged eye contact with each participant, almost daring them to look away in discomfort.

"Welcome, ladies and gentlemen. I am Pastor Cora Scott. I have lived in Chicago for more than twenty years. I assure you that what we will experience here tonight is mundane. The spirits are around us all the time. My only gift is the power to summon them more easily than others do.

"Some may tell you that there is no reality to what you will see and hear tonight, that it is only entertainment, but you will see for yourselves that truth abounds in this room. You simply need to put yourself in a place of acceptance. If you cannot do that, the spirits will know, and you will be denied a glimpse into the world beyond ours.

"In a moment I will lead you through a meditation to prepare your mind for our journey. After that, I will put myself in a state that will allow me to be your guide.

I warn you that it is likely that my voice will be altered when I speak to you. Do not be afraid. I have no control over what our departed friends do when I am in that state.

"And now, if you will all place your hands, palms down on the table in front of you, we shall begin."

Fearing that Edith would use any pause to pose more questions, Mim was relieved that Pastor Scott allowed no time to elapse before she began.

"Ommmm…Ommmm . . .Ommmmm . . ." she hummed. "Now, please spread your fingers so that they are splayed on the surface of the table. Open them as wide as you can so our departed friends can see that our hands are as open as our minds and hearts.

"For the next few minutes I will lead you through some relaxing exercises to quiet the mind. Please close your eyes and picture yourself in a beautiful spring meadow filled with wild flowers and the music of the birds. There is peace in this world. Only peace. Breathe it in, deeply and slowly, and then exhale. "In…and out. In…and out. In…and out. In…and out.

"Keep your mind completely clear. When you have a thought, let is pass through your mind without judging it. Gently but firmly usher thoughts out of your mind. Feel each set of muscles as they succumb to total relaxation.

"Oh, spirits of our hearts, come to us, we pray. We invite you to join us tonight. We look for you in peace and love, only in peace and love."

Mim was fighting the temptation to open her eyes, fearing that Pastor Scott, or worse yet, an entering spirit might catch her. But Mim could not imagine that one quick peek through slit eyes would break any spell. When she capitulated to her curiosity, she squinted her eyes and saw Cora Scott sitting ramrod straight with the conical funnel protruding from her ear, presumably to amplify any voices that would come.

Mim now refocused on her breath, trying to recreate the rhythm Mrs. Scott had established. *In…and out. In…and out. In…and out,* she told herself.

"Someone is coming to me," intoned Mrs. Scott in the low guttural voice that she had predicted. "Henry, is it? Yes, Henry is here. Whom are you here to see, Henry?"

Mim scanned her mind for anyone she knew whose name was Henry. Relieved that this visitor was not for her, she listened as Mrs. Scott conducted a dialogue with the woman to her left who claimed Henry was her older brother who had been killed at the Battle of Gettysburg.

"But I came for Eddie. Can you ask him if Eddie is with him?" pleaded the woman, who had inched forward to the edge of her seat. Mrs. Scott posed the question to the spirit of Henry and then, readjusting the horn in her ear, nodded in apparent agreement with the voice of the departed Henry.

"Henry says that he often sees your son Eddie, though he is not with him at the moment."

"Does he have any details, so I know for certain it is he. Anything, please."

Once again Mrs. Scott inquired and a sweet smile came to her face as she listened and prepared to pass on new information.

"Henry wants you to know that Eddie is a charming boy and still has blonde hair and a face full of freckles. And—" Here she paused for a moment. "Henry wants you to know that Eddie no longer has to wear his glasses, which makes him very happy."

The woman took a deep inward breath, gave a little groan, and fell back into her chair.

"Henry is fading now. He bids you goodnight and tells you that all is well."

After several more contacts, all of which touched off astonished responses from their loved ones, Mim was all but certain that Pastor Scott was authentic. This sense both relieved and terrified her. So far neither she nor Edith had had a visitor, but Mim now believed that if she did, that spirit would come from the world she had once entered and from which she had since been exiled.

Having lost all track of time, Mim could only assume they were nearing the end of the two hours they had been promised. The last few minutes had been quiet and Mim was in a lovely, serene state, regulating her breathing whenever she felt her mind wandering away from her.

"Ah, we have another visitor making her way towards us," Mrs. Scott announced, as she reached to adjust her earpiece. "It is a woman and her voice tells me she is a very old soul. She has been departed for many years.

"She is looking for her granddaughter. Wait, I am trying to catch her name so she can be identified.

"Spirit, please be welcome into our midst. Who are you and whom is it you seek?"

There was a long pause. Pastor Scott lost her erectness and was slightly slumped over the table with her eyes firmly closed, as if concentrating on picking up a faint sound.

"'Mary'! I am hearing Mary. Is one of you Mary?"

Hearing no other candidate take ownership of such a common name, Mim volunteered, "My name is Mary."

"Mary, I am hearing something from—let me see if I can make out the name—" Another long pause, "The connection is beginning to fade. I am not hearing her name but it sounds to me like an old woman, maybe your grandmother? Wait. She is saying something. I hear it now, ever so slightly."

"I did have a grandmother to whom I was very close. Can you ask her another question so I can be sure?"

"She is definitely speaking to you, but I am sorry, she is fading. I can no longer hear her. Oh spirit, leave us not so soon."

Cora Scott paused, cocked her head so it almost lay on the table and squinted her eyes as if she were concentrating on a message that might be coming directly up from the table. Finally she lifted her head and said, "I am so sorry, but when the connection weakens, I cannot get it back simply by command. The spirits are in charge. But if your name is Mary and if you had a grandmother to whom you were very close, then I believe this message was for you. Perhaps another time."

How could it be over? This was the worst of all possible outcomes. Yes, there was a revelation for Mim, likely from Grandmother Mitchell, but then she disappeared. This charlatan, this rhapsodist, should have brought her back until Mim could ask Grandmother what she meant to say. It was her job to maintain the connection. What else was she being paid for? She was a fraud. All the equanimity Mim had breathed in that evening had evaporated. She was fuming mad. She was not a crier but when she did cry, she was either moved by something sad or something beautiful. Tonight, in the darkness of the room, she cried from pure undiluted fury.

The Sky Darkens

Spring 1899

*T*HE THREE OLDER BLAIR CHILDREN were members of the Chicago Young Players, a theater group for children between the ages of 10 and 18. The rules of the Young Players stipulated that all children over the age of 10 were eligible to be in the cast, but none could try out for a speaking part until he or she was twelve. Italia had been selected for every major romantic lead since she was eligible, not because of her natural dramatic flair, but because she was ravishing.

"Mother," said Mildred, "I have spent years being a fairy or a bird. I had to be the dog in *The Tempest* and a tree in *Love's Labour's Lost*. I am almost eleven and it is my turn to play a grown up."

"Well, dear, see if you can convince them to do *Romeo and Juliet*. You are exactly the right age for Juliet," answered Mim.

"You mean Juliet was eleven when she died? That is so sad. I certainly would not kill myself over a boy!"

"That is a very good decision, Mildred," replied her mother.

When the final selections for *A Midsummer's Night Dream* were announced, Mildred was astonished to learn that she had been cast as none of the heroines, but instead as the impish Puck, who was practically the most important character in the play. For weeks Mildred shuffled through the house, book in hand, spouting snippets of lines: "If we shadows have offended, think but this and all is mended—"

"You don't mind playing a boy?" asked Italia, giving a clear tonal indication of how she would feel about such a casting.

"*No*, I love Puck. He has much more to say than all the flouncy girls. He is the center of the play."

Attendance by her siblings was a command performance. The Blairs arrived at Parsons Parker Auditorium in their new Haynes touring car. Robert drove and afterwards was to pick them up at seven o'clock in front of the building. Then they would make a stop for ice cream and return to Drexel Boulevard.

A happy Blair family exited the auditorium after a strong performance by Mildred. She had stumbled over a few lines, once having to be prompted from offstage, but the audience sincerely applauded her spritely interpretation of Puck, though only her family rose to their feet during the curtain calls.

Billy was in the lead. He had been talking about ice cream flavors, toppings and candied fruit since the intermission.

"Where's Robert?" Billy asked, concerned about any delay in getting to his treat.

"Don't worry, Billy boy," CB said. "The line of cars goes all the way around the corner. It is a well-known fact that ice cream tastes all the sweeter the longer you have to wait for it."

"Rubbish," replied Billy.

But after twenty minutes, the Blair family still waited.

Mim was clearly concerned. "In twelve years of service, Robert has never once been derelict in his duties. Something is very wrong."

"Mimsy, don't fret. The Haynes is known for its pesky ignition. Maybe he had trouble getting it going. Five more minutes," Chauncey predicted. "Robert will be one of the next ten cars that passes by this corner. You'll see. Children, what number will Robert be? I say he will be number seven."

"Three."

"Eight."

"I am not playing," said Italia. "This is so annoying. If I were in charge, I would reduce Robert's pay this week. Really, we should not have been left waiting this long."

But Robert drove neither the third, nor the twentieth car. The next time Chauncey and Mim saw their loyal and much beloved servant he was lying waxen-faced in an open casket in the funeral parlor.

According to the Fire Marshall, the blaze was not the result of foul play, but had been caused by the faulty installation of electrical outlets in Bertha and Robert's small apartment on the second floor of the servants' quarters, which were in the rear of the mansion. Because he would be returning to pick the family up in only a couple of hours, Robert had left the car in the driveway and, most likely, as was his habit, spent a few minutes wiping away any filament of dust that had accumulated on the exterior. (Any time that Robert knew he was likely to be seen in a line of cars, he wanted to be sure that the Blair vehicle reflected well on the owners, and the chauffeur). Thus an immaculate Haynes touring car stood in the driveway when the clanging fire trucks arrived.

The servants had scattered for their Sunday of freedom. Given that spring had finally sprung, Bertha said she was going to take Roberta to the park but had told Robert she would have tea ready for him before he needed to fetch the Blairs.

Bertha believed that Robert must have smelled the smoke as he made his way through the formal rooms towards the kitchen, his tea and his family. There was a record of his call to the fire station, which came into the department at 4:26 p.m. The first truck had arrived at the mansion at 4:35. The firemen found the phone receiver off the hook in the hallway, indicating that this was the phone Robert had used to make the last call of his life.

In a written statement, the lieutenant who took the call swore that he had followed department policy and had made it clear to the man on the other end of the line that the fire engines were on the way, and he was to wait and take no action. However, everyone who knew Robert was convinced that even the slightest chance that Bertha and Roberta were trapped in their apartment would have led Robert to disregard those orders. His body was found on the second floor landing. Few burn marks appeared on his body, leading the medical examiner to conclude that he had died of smoke inhalation minutes before the fire truck arrived.

In addition to attending the funeral service, the Blair family sent an arrangement of flowers, Mim being careful that the bouquet was noteworthy but not ostentatious. Bertha had asked the Blair family to sit directly behind her and Roberta, which Mim originally thought meant that Bertha did not expect many others would attend the service, so when she looked behind her and saw that the church was almost filled, Mim was brought up short by her own presumptions and prejudices.

Where had Robert and Bertha met all of these people? How had they had time to cultivate so many friendships? She was struck by how little she knew about this family that she thought she knew so well. She watched in fascination as Bertha was hugged, patted and consoled by dozens and dozens of people who had no relationship to her life at 4830 Drexel Boulevard. Was Mim so insensitive an employer that she thought her cook and chauffeur were incapable of having a life beyond their service to her?

Chauncey had not mourned a death as deeply since the passing of his father. While neither Chauncey nor Robert would have been capable of putting class differences aside to become friends, they had understood and respected one another, especially as Robert assumed more responsibility for Chauncey's pride and joy, his growing fleet of automobiles. It was not uncommon on a Saturday morning to find both men's heads buried under the hood of one of the cars, with Robert explaining some new technicality to Chauncey.

Mim did her best to manage the grief within her home while trying to sort out her own feelings, the deepest of which was anger that God should punish such a wonderful family as the Schmidts.

This was the first intimate experience with death for the Blair children, who did their best to comfort Roberta. As it turned out, Billy, who had come into the world and the house shortly after Roberta, had the most success, spending hours showing her how to throw a baseball properly and using their shared love of the outdoors to divert her and occasionally make her laugh.

Despite urging her to take time off, even encouraging her to take the summer and go back to Germany to recuperate, Mim watched Bertha stoically return to her duties. It would have been easier for Mim to deal with a sobbing widow who took to her bed for weeks than to see such emotional courage.

Bertha drew on her Teutonic proclivity for work and therefore diced, stirred, beat, roasted and fried her way back to sanity or, at the very least, the appearance of it. When Mim went to Robert's grave with Bertha to see the newly installed gravestone and to help her plant some bulbs, she was astonished to see that Robert was only two years younger than Chauncey.

Chauncey was now fifty-four and she forty-four. She thought more and more about their mortality, imagining scenes of what life would be like should one of them die suddenly. Mim would look at Chauncey and wonder—how many more evenings would he kiss her good night on the cheek, pat her head in passing, and say, "Goodnight, sweets?" Who would go first? How would the survivor cope with loneliness? If she died first, which of her friends would wait only a minimal amount of time before seeing to the needs of a wealthy, grieving banker?

For the five years Mim had owned *Tres Riches Heures*, she had not missed a single day of its companionship. Ever since the scare of the burglary, it was rarely far from her sight. There was no diminution in her love for her treasured manuscript, nor in her absolute certainty that she had rescued it from a world that would never have appreciated it as she did.

When her life was running smoothly, she would simply enjoy the intricacies of color, design and sheer beauty. They never disappointed her.

When things were going badly, she looked to the book for more than beauty. She followed a ritual for guidance to break the cycle of bad fortune. Alone in her room, with *Tres Riches Heures* in her lap, she would close her eyes and let the book fall open randomly, assuming that the particular page had a lesson to teach her. More often than not, she interpreted the meaning quickly and did her best to let it guide her until her fortunes improved. She had become dependent on this process of understanding, delighting in the fact that the guidance she received from her book was clear and direct compared with the murky messages channeled by Mrs. Scott.

Really, *Tres Riches Heures* was all she needed to keep her behavior on the straight and narrow. However, recently she began to notice that her Book of Hours was developing a mind of its own. Over the last month, the book consistently fell open to the least uplifting illustrations under its cover. Was she just misreading the messages? It seemed to her that she was feeling castigation rather than consolation in its pages.

For three days in a row after Robert's death, *Tres Riches Heures* opened itself to the very same illustration! It was the one depicting the month of March. The central character, who looked uncannily like Robert, was painted in tattered peasant clothing, toiling to push two oxen across a rocky field to prepare it for planting. The other primary features in the painting were an enormous castle and manor house commanding the top of the hill.

There was no doubt to whom all the serfs in the painting were sub-servient. She could not get it out of her mind that the peasant was Robert, plowing his way through life in the service of the lords of the manor, namely the Blairs. Intellectually she knew that they were a long way from the fifteenth century and that she and Chauncey had treated Bertha and Robert with genuine affection, with more informality than most of her social set would have, but there it was, right before her eyes, the core of the relationship, master and servant. Was the message that she and Chauncey were somehow un-Christian?

"Mim, you are being ridiculous," she said out loud to herself. "This is a Book of Hours, not a Ouija Board."

Nonetheless, for the first time in years, Mim found herself a little frightened of her treasure. Occasionally she noticed that a few days would go by without looking at it.

In Extremis

Fall 1902

*T*HE BLAIR FAMILY STRUGGLED THROUGH the fall of 1902. All of them had been sick since school started. The house resounded with sniffles, sneezes, wheezes and coughs. No sooner would one of them be pronounced "cured" than the next one had a scratchy throat. The servants too had been sick. Mim calculated that it had been over a month since the staff had operated at full tilt.

In addition, a succession of chauffeurs had come, been found inadequate, and were gone, often in a matter of days. One drove too fast and the next too slow.

"You are like Goldilocks," Mim teased Chauncey. "I am afraid you must realize that there will not be another Robert. But we need to find the next best person. This house does not run smoothly without a chauffeur."

One diversion for the family was that the Chicago Young Players had been invited by the congregation at St. Matthew's Church to reprise their performance of *A Midsummer Night's Dream* for the needy children of the parish on Halloween night. Reverend James Farr, whose daughter

Anne was also a member of the cast, had found the performance "delight-ful." Perhaps the "scruffy ones" (as he referred to the poor children) might come off the streets trick-or-treat night (a wise strategy given the vandal-ism they had inflicted on the neighborhood the last two years).

"*Church*? I have to go to the play *and* to church?" whined Billy. That is completely unfair and I will probably fall asleep, I will be so bored."

"We are only going to the church to see the play, not to worship, though it would not hurt you in the least to thank God for all your good fortune more than once a week. And now that you have mentioned the danger of somnolence, I will be sure you take a short nap before we go."

"Thank you, Mother. I now feel worse than I did before."

"I am sorry, and by the way, Billy, be sure to look up the word 'som-nolence' and tell me what it means at supper."

Dear God, thought Mim. *I am turning into Grandmother Mitchell.*

Mildred was an even more persuasive Puck than she had been in the first performance. She forgot none of her lines and several of the children in the audience whistled their enthusiasm when she came out for her cur-tain call.

The reception afterwards began a little awkwardly. The idea was for the cast to mingle with the disadvantaged children while they shared apple cider and cookies.

"What will I say to them?" asked Mildred, when she was told what was expected of her. "I don't know any poor children."

"Just be yourself," said Mim. "All God's children are the same."

"Then why doesn't He give *them* more money?"

But the reception worked out beautifully. As children often do when left alone by hovering adults, they broke the ice in their own ways and on their own time. By the end of the reception, a few mingled groups ex-changed noticeable laughter.

Mildred, the young ingénue, was not blossoming at the moment. While the household in general was on the mend, Mildred still struggled to feel well enough to go out to play.

"Who is that coughing?" bellowed Chauncey from the smoking room near the foyer when he heard nocturnal footsteps descending the stairs. "Whoever it is, stop it and get back to bed!"

"I'm sorry, Father," said Mildred, "I can't help it. I need Mother."

"Come in, my girl," said Chauncey more softly. "Mother is right here."

Mim arose and gathered a red-faced, teary-eyed little girl into her arms.

"Mother, I can't sleep. Every time I lie down, all I do is cough. When I sit up, the cough goes away, but then I try to trick it by lying back down again very slowly so it doesn't know what I am doing, but it starts up all over again. I am so tired!"

"I am sorry, Mildred," a shame-faced Chauncey muttered. "I was just trying to scare the cough away."

"You almost scared *her* away," said Mim, none too pleased with Chauncey's gruffness. "Let's get you back to bed, and I will make up some of my foolproof cough syrup. It never fails."

"Can you stay with me until I fall asleep?" asked Mildred.

Mim walked Mildred to the bottom of the staircase, shooing her towards bed while she went to the kitchen to prepare the cough syrup. Normally she measured equal amounts of honey, whisky and lemon juice, but because Mildred had tried that the last few nights with only limited success, tonight Mim added an extra dose of whiskey in the hope that it would cause her daughter to sleep through the night and yet not awaken with a hangover!

When Mim entered Mildred's bedroom, her daughter was sitting up in bed, seized with coughing. Finally it stopped long enough for Mim to administer her potion.

"Mildred, slide all the way over and I will smooth your sheets and straighten your blankets. It looks like a small tornado touched down in this bed."

Mildred did so obediently and Mim began crisping the bottom sheet by moving her hands briskly over the wrinkles. It was then that she noticed how damp the sheets were, both top and bottom.

"Mildred, did you have an accident in bed?"

"What do you mean?"

"I mean your sheets are wet, did you go wee in your bed?"

Another bout of coughing delayed Mildred's answer, which, when it came, was emphatic.

"I did not wet the bed! The bed is wet because when I do fall asleep, I waken as soaked as if I had been swimming. Last night I had to change my nightgown three times. I get so cold and then it takes me a long time to warm up."

As if this last statement had taken from her body its last gasp of animation,

Mildred collapsed back onto her pillow.

Mim sat with Mildred while the whiskey did its work. She left her tossing in a light and restless sleep and went downstairs to report her concern to Chauncey.

Typically Mim was appreciative of Chauncey's soothing approach to illness. She realized that his more optimistic nature was a helpful antidote to her more easily troubled one. But tonight his "There, there Mimsy. she will be fine" struck her as a foolish illusion. She had a very sick child and tomorrow she would summon Dr. Stephens at daylight.

Mim spent that night fully awake, with the names of every life-threatening disease she had ever heard of bombarding her thoughts and dislocating her firm belief that Mildred always had been and would continue to be her "lucky" child. Every so often she would get up and walk into Mildred's room, check her forehead for a fever that thus far did not exist, listen to her breathing, which was only slightly shallow, and check the sheets which were once again drenched with perspiration.

Dr. Stephens arrived at nine o'clock the following morning and by eleven Mildred was admitted into Rush Hospital, where she would stay for the next six weeks. Mim had wanted her to go to Mercy Hospital, in which she had great faith, but she knew Chauncey would never be convinced that another family member in a Catholic hospital was an idea with an ounce of merit.

Mim was skilled at navigating and negotiating her way around the many roadblocks hospital personnel put in her way—words she did not understand like "sputum," "x-ray," and "mycobacterium." She was with Mildred each day, but visiting hours even for parents were tightly controlled. Nurses stalked the halls appearing to be in search of worried parents they could scold into leaving their children to rest.

"I did manage to corner, no, to accost, Dr. Barnett today," reported

Mim to Chauncey. "He has asked us to come in for a meeting on Tuesday of next week."

"Why must we wait until then?" challenged Chauncey. "It has been two weeks and we have not gotten a diagnosis, much less a prognosis. And remind me who Dr. Barnett is."

"He is Mildred's primary physician. He has explained to me that it has taken this amount of time to get back all the results of the tests they have done. Several of them are relatively new and it takes time for the 'team' to evaluate the results."

"Have you asked Dr. Stephens for his opinion?"

"No," Mim replied.

"Why in heavens not? He has been our doctor for years and you tell me he pops in to see Mildred every day. Surely he must have a hint as to what's going on. If after all his years in practice he doesn't have a clue, then perhaps we should find a new doctor!"

Despite her mother coming every day, her father coming when he could, piles of drawing pads, dolls, her favorite books and other treasures, Mildred was miserable. She hated the long hours before and after her parents' visits.

One day she made the mistake of asking one of the nurses when she could go home. "When we tell you, young lady."

Some days Mildred felt better than others, but the general trajectory of her illness continued downward. Her intermittent fever left her feeling achy and tired and even though militant nurses watched over her to see that she ate her meals, she lost weight week by week.

At the end of the first week, the meanest nurse of all taped a sign to Mildred's door.

"What does that say?" asked Mildred.

"Never you mind, Missy," was the unsatisfactory answer. What the staff did not reckon on was that their patient was a facile reader and, peering around the bed, quickly recognized the word ISOLATION. And if she had not known what the word meant, she would have understood the meaning because from that day on, no more visitors, including her parents. Mildred's mood deepened from miserable to despondent.

"Please be seated, Mrs. Blair," said Dr. Barnett. "I am sorry that Mr.

Blair could not join us. Let me introduce two of my colleagues, Dr. William Parsons, our infectious disease specialist, and Dr. Samuel Atkins, our resident pulmonologist. We are the team that is responsible for your daughter's care. May I offer you a cup of tea?"

"No, thank you, Dr. Barnett. I would prefer to hear what you have to say, words that I hope will end with your giving me permission to at least see my daughter. She has been in isolation for ten days and I have no way of knowing whether or not she is getting better or worse. My husband said I was to bring her home today, no matter what you said."

"I understand your frustration, Mrs. Blair, and I wish I had better news for you. Mildred is no better. She lost two pounds this week. On the other hand, she is no worse and, given her disease, that is something for which you can be grateful."

"First let me take you through some of the tests we have performed, the results of which have brought us to our conclusion and our suggestion of a plan for her future."

Mim, noticing that she was both literally and figuratively on the edge of her seat, allowed herself an infinitesimal easing of her nerves at the word, "future." Why would he use that word if there were nothing they could do for her?

"When Miss Blair first arrived here, the medical consensus was that she was suffering from a severe case of influenza. But we wanted to test our hypothesis and so, in addition to monitoring her presenting symptoms, we administered both a sputum test as well as an x-ray.

"Sputum is a mixture of saliva and mucus that is collected in the respiratory system. The patient coughs up whatever is in her lungs, we collect it and then analyze it for bacteria under a microscope.

"We also did an x-ray, a very important new weapon in our arsenal. It was invented only five or six years ago, but it is in use in the best hospitals all across the world. It is actually an interesting story..."

Dear God, spare me the digressions and tell me what is wrong with my daughter, thought Mim, smiling all the while at the pontificating doctor upon whom she and Mildred were so dependent.

"At any rate, we were able to take a picture of Mildred's lungs and, combined with the results of the sputum test, we have arrived at a diagnosis of tuberculosis."

Mim's stomach somersaulted violently while her mind scrambled to see if it could recall anything she knew about tuberculosis. But the first thing that came out of her mouth was actually the least relevant.

"I thought tuberculosis was a disease of the poor, of immigrants. That is certainly not us," she said as if this logic would make the doctors change their diagnosis.

Dr. Atkins fielded this comment. "You are correct, Mrs. Blair. Your family's status is one of the things that initially threw us off track. Despite some of the symptoms of TB that your daughter presented, we simply could not match its typical pattern of transmission with your family's style of living.

"Can you think of any place your daughter might have been where she would have been exposed to lower class people? Do any of your household servants present any of the same symptoms? TB is highly contagious, which is why, when we were almost certain of the diagnosis, we placed Miss Blair in isolation, where she will remain until she is substantially better."

Mim had regained her outward composure enough to pick up on another word that caught her full attention—"better."

"You mean she will get better?" asked Mim with all the courage she could muster.

"I mean, Mrs. Blair, that she *can* get better. She may never be fully cured but because she is young, it is possible that we can alter the category of the disease from active to latent."

"How would you do that?" asked Mim. "Are there cases of girls Mildred's age who can go on to lead a full life after they have contracted tuberculosis?"

Now Dr. Parsons spoke up. "I will be honest with you, Mrs. Blair—"

Oh, please don't, thought Mim.

"In most cases, ninety percent I would say, tuberculosis is fatal, but that is because, as we said, it is a disease that breeds in the slums. Because most patients do not have access to good care, it kills almost everyone it infects.

"But we also know that the disease feeds off those with what we call weakened immune systems. I would suspect that your daughter had been fighting some other virus when she was exposed to one of the five kinds of mycobacteria. Our job is to strengthen her immune system so her body can have a fighting chance."

"And just how do we do that?" asked Mim, ready to embark immediately on whatever suggestion he made.

The three doctors looked back and forth to see who would introduce the recommended protocol.

Dr. Barnett said, "You must take her from Chicago as soon as she is well enough to travel. Do you know what a sanitarium is, Mrs. Blair?"

Allowing her agitation to show for the first time, Mim snapped, "Of course I know what a sanitarium is. I just don't know of one to whom I would entrust my daughter."

Dr. Barnett continued unfazed, "The place we recommend, the one that has the best record of a cure, is in Davos. Do you know where that is?"

"I am not completely ignorant of the world. But why must we go all the way to Switzerland? Is there no place in America where we can receive the proper treatment to strengthen her immune system?"

Dr. Barnett said, "There is a sanitarium in Saranac Lake in the Adirondacks which is perfectly adequate…"

"I am not seeking 'perfectly adequate,' Dr. Barnett. I am seeking the best," Mim retorted.

"I am sure you are," said Dr. Parsons, to Mim the most compassionate of the three doctors. "Given that, I would recommend Davos. I know the medical director there and will wire him to expect you in about a month's time."

"Thank you, doctor. Can you tell me what is so special about Davos?"

"Most importantly, Davos is special because it is the highest city in Europe. At that elevation, Miss Blair will have the cleanest, coldest air she can breathe in contrast to Chicago, which is the dirtiest, most polluted environment in America.

"She will be made to sit in direct sunlight to absorb its gift of vitamin D, she will be fed the freshest of food, be given an exercise regimen to increase her lung capacity and be made to rest for extended periods each day."

"Will there be any children her age there? She would be so lonely. She already is lonely."

"There is a very good children's wing at Davos. After she has recovered sufficiently, she will be allowed to play with other children."

"But how will I get her there if she has to be isolated? No ship will accept a passenger with tuberculosis. For that matter, can I even bring her home? She so wants to be with her family."

It was at the mention of the word "family" that Mim lost her composure. In that instant, she felt the most intense love for all these wonderful, difficult, exuberant, imperious people in her family. All she wanted now was to be sure she did not lose one of them, the one they all adored.

"As to how you will travel, we will need her here for another two weeks and then she can go home for two weeks and then she should be ready to travel. If she has no fever for a week, I will write a letter to say that she is safe to travel, but she will have to be in semi-isolation en route. If she is no better by then, we will have to make another plan.

"I am so sorry, Mrs. Blair. This is not an enjoyable conversation for any of us. But you have resources that so few of our patients have. Just remember that as recently as fifty years ago, all TB patients were sequestered in caves."

❧

"In *church*? That is where she got it! Our daughter goes to church to perform for the downtrodden and she contracts a disease that may kill her. Tell me what kind of a God does that?" anguished Chauncey shouted, with tears coming down his cheeks.

Mim was so tired. Tired of being the organizer, the doer, but mostly she was tired of being the comforter. Her tender feelings for her stricken husband were tempered by a desire, assiduously repressed so far, to cry out, "Chauncey, take care of me. Please, for five minutes just take care of me."

She could not disagree with her husband's assessment of where Mildred had likely become infected with the tuberculosis bacteria. The doctors had been clear that TB was an airborne disease, almost exclusively attacking the poor, and transmitted only by inhalation. And where had Mildred come into contact with poor people lately?

Chauncey's answer was correct, at the theater production at church.

❧

Three weeks later, Mildred's fever was normal for three successive days and the doctors allowed her to return home. It proved to be harder for Mim to have her at home in isolation than it had been to have her in the hospital. Italia, CB, who was home for the Christmas holidays, and Billy had to be kept out of Mildred's room, which made Mildred sad and her siblings angry. Twice Mim apprehended CB as he planned a secret assault on his sister's sickroom.

After a week at home the doctors allowed Mildred's door to be open so people could at least talk to her standing in the doorway, but as much as the company delighted the thirteen-year-old, Mim had to sit on her bed and act as a traffic policeman.

"That is far enough, Italia."

"Back, Billy, take three steps back!"

Chauncey sweetly tried to engage his daughter by reading her *Treasure Island*, all the while standing at the door of her room. But Mildred, though she did her best to be polite and appreciative of her father's effort, was still not well enough to concentrate on the story. She would try to stay awake but, more often than not, she would fall asleep or be overtaken by a fit of coughing.

After two weeks at home and no fever for ten consecutive days, the doctors said it was time to begin preparations for the trip to Davos, a trip that Mim was dreading. She decided that Italia, along with a registered nurse, would accompany her and Mildred to Switzerland. CB was happier this year at Groton so Mim felt reasonably comfortable with leaving him in the United States. For the minor holidays he would go home to Chicago and during the summer he would come to Switzerland. It was what to do with Billy that was breaking her heart. Both he and his father had argued forcefully that he be allowed to stay in Chicago, Billy because he liked his school well enough and, though he never said so, he did not want to be dragged through Switzerland with his anxious mother and bossy oldest sister.

Chauncey would come when work allowed, and Mim would see both boys in the summer if Mildred were still in the sanitarium. If Mildred did not improve, or if Mildred did not survive all that was ahead of her, any solace would be a futile fantasy.

Epilogue

*W*HEN MIM'S THOUGHTS LAPSED INTO dark places and she was afraid, she found sanctuary with her most trusted friend, her counselor, her inspiration. Like an infallible talisman, *Tres Riches Heures* always rallied her spirits. But since Robert's death, she was becoming convinced that the manuscript had turned on her. It had been sending messages that Mim felt were censorious. Night after night she let the book fall open, looking for any sign that Mildred would get well. But instead of the illustrations of angels, feasts, and pastoral landscapes, Mim was confronted with horsemen of death, Good Friday and fallen angels.

"Stop!" she cried aloud. "No more death! Show me the light. I know it is in there. Show me your best."

Mim was well aware that her thinking was magical and irrational. She would be humiliated if anyone knew of her ritualized behavior. But so frightened that Mildred might die, so anguished that she did not have the

379

power to direct the outcome, she turned over the control of her daughter's fate to her book.

One night, exhausted by fatigue, and, oddly enough, after a particularly good day for Mildred, Mim felt certain things were turning, that the signs would be different tonight, that the sunshine of recovery was finally to shine. She just needed *Tres Riches Heures* to confirm it.

She was tempted to open to the many pages that were radiant with hope. She knew them by heart. But that would be cheating the book's power. The book had to speak to her, not she to the book. So she sat on her bed, uttered her prayer of thanks for bringing the book into her life, and let it fall where it would.

It opened to The Last Judgment. There was Jesus, arms outstretched, rising from the earth with the stigmata still visible on his hands and feet. Two supplicants, one of whom was his mother Mary, were on either side of him. Then Mim looked down and saw that on the earth below on Jesus' right hand were human beings on their knees in prayer, their androgynous naked bodies smooth and pure. They were the saved. On Jesus' left were the sinners, the damned with their cowering bodies engulfed in flames and half way down the throat of a saber-toothed Leviathan.

The minute she saw the word "Judgment," she knew. She knew why Mildred's illness was her fault. *Tres Riches Heures* was not hers. It never had been. All of her justification that only she could protect it was nothing but hubris. She had been wrong to pretend that she alone could protect beauty. Beauty did not need protection. She could no longer horde beauty. Beauty is strong. It can stand on its own to face the world.

January 11, 1903

Mr. Martin Gaylord

Prairie Avenue

Chicago, Illinois

Dear Martin:

As you may have heard, my daughters and I will be leaving Chicago at the end of the week. We are bound for Davos, Switzerland where my daughter Mildred will begin treatment at the sanitarium. The doctors say that because of her age and general good health, we may be hopeful for a full recovery. I will not be returning until she is fully cured.

Before I go, I must ask you to do for me an important favor, part of which is contained in the sealed package accompanying this letter. When you see it, I am confident you will understand what it is and why I send it.

My grandmother, you, and this beautiful Book of Hours have taught me everything I know about beauty. I thank you all. But I must now move on.

I trust you to see to it that Tres Riches Heures is placed where all the world may see it. Please do not attribute the gift to me. It was never mine, which I think you knew all along.

I will write from Geneva when I am settled.

Yours very truly,

Mary Mitchell Blair

Acknowledgments

I ALWAYS THOUGHT OF WRITING AS a solitary experience, so, I would look skeptically at acknowledgements, often page upon page, of people to thank. Can all these people really have helped the author complete the book? Now I know. The answer is, yes! So here is my list, along with my gratitude and love.

Dear friends Baba Parker, Bonnie Gardner, Betty Marsh, Liza Savory, Charles Rice, my sister, Maryah Wolszon, and my brother-in-law, Tom Vallely, read early drafts with enthusiasm and encouragement.

Gold star readers, and dear ones Cordelia Manning and my sister, Tory Vallely, read, reread and re-reread A Collection of Hours, artfully balancing gentle criticism and overly generous praise.

Wendy Griswold, who is Lady Gwendolyn in the chapter, Hunting Party, provided me with the details of an English shooting weekend as only she could have. She has been my friend for fifty three years.Thanks, Wens.

There are lots of good reasons to have many doctor friends, not the least of which is being able to ask about anesthesia, blood pressure, Cesarean sections and tuberculosis to be assured I was on solid ground. So for that and for years of literal tender loving care, thanks to Dr. Kenneth Adler, Dr. John Beirne, Dr. John Santoro, and of course, Dr. Stephen Leviss. When in doubt, call Steve.

Jay Meyer at Alphagraphics in Morristown printed and reprinted what she called "The Great American Novel." Though it is not, I loved hearing it.

Buck Rodgers, formerly of Scribner's and with whom I logged many running miles, talked me through the ins and outs of agents and publishing.

Additional thanks go to journalist David Hinckley, who gave the manuscript a final once over.

There are many delights to having a world-renowned pianist as your friend. Yossi Kalichstein has many charms, but having his music in my ears, as I wrote each afternoon, brought countless hours of pleasure and likely inspired many an improved turn of phrase.

Fran Wood is responsible for the delightful depictions of my story. She must be a mind reader. The scenes she has chosen and rendered are exactly as I saw them in my mind. Thank you, Fran, for the excellent editorial comments and for nailing the illustrations. Readers will treasure them as I do.

The "other" Daley clan of Chicago: Dan Daley, Joan Daley and Joan's husband Bob Butler graciously escorted me around and filled me with their considerable knowledge of and affection for a great American city.

There would be no book without my friend Kathleen Daley. In addition to extensive research of Chicago during the late 19th century, she has enhanced and polished whatever inherent merit there is in A Collection of Hours. Because I was writing about her beloved city of Chicago she kept me honest, and any factual or grammatical errors mean that I did not follow her directions. Kathleen's deserved reputation for brutal honesty made her compliments and encouragement all the sweeter.

Through many adventures Kathleen Daley has been my confidant and friend. I hope I have fixed a Chicago in her mind, which will always warm her heart. I cannot thank you enough, Kathleen.